W9-ACH-178

THE SALLEE ROVER.

THE ATTACK BY THE SALLEE ROVER

CHILDREN'S CLASSICS
EVERYMAN'S LIBRARY

CRUSOE DISCOVERS GOATS ON THE ISLAND

Daniel Defoe

Robinson Crusoe

With Illustrations
by W. J. Linton and others

EVERYMAN'S LIBRARY

CHILDREN'S CLASSICS

Alfred A. Knopf New York London Toronto

THIS IS A BORZOI BOOK
PUBLISHED BY ALFRED A. KNOPF

First published 1719
First included in Everyman's Library Children's Classics 1906
The text of this edition is reproduced by kind permission of
The Nonesuch Press Limited, London
Design and typography © 1993 by Everyman's Library
Book design by Barbara de Wilde, Carol Devine Carson
and Peter B. Willberg

Fifth printing (US)

Five of Ernest H. Shepard's illustrations from *Dream Days* by
Kenneth Grahame are reprinted on the endpapers by permission of
The Bodley Head, London. The sixth illustration is by S. C. Hulme Beaman.

www.randomhouse.com/everymans

ISBN 0-679-42819-4 (US)
1-85715-918-7 (UK)

A CIP catalogue record for this book is available from the British Library

Library of Congress Cataloging-in-Publication Data
Defoe, Daniel, 1661?–1731.
Robinson Crusoe/Daniel Defoe.
p. cm.—(Everyman's library children's classics)
Includes bibliographical references.
Summary: As the sole survivor of a shipwreck, an Englishman
lives for nearly thirty years on a deserted island.
ISBN 0-679-42819-4
[1. Shipwrecks—Fiction. 2. Survival—Fiction.] I. Title.
II. Series.
PZ7.D36Ro   1993   93-11263
[Fic]—dc20   CIP
                                                                      AC

Printed and bound in Germany by GGP Media, Pössneck

FOREWORD

EVER SINCE that day in April early in the eighteenth
century when Defoe's Robinson Crusoe was first
published, the book has been continuously in print. It is
to be found in many different languages and in a great
variety of editions, for besides being the first great
English novel it has always had a world-wide popularity.
The immediate success of the story of Crusoe's life on
the island gave rise to so many imitations that a new word
Robinsonades was used to describe them; and the influ-
ence of Defoe on later writers continued for well over a
hundred years. The chief part of the first book, *The Life
and Strange Surprising Adventures of Robinson Crusoe of York,
Mariner* (April 1719) — the account of Crusoe's shipwreck and of his resourcefulness and ingenuity during his
solitude and of his rescue of Man Friday — is what is best
known and most memorable, and is Defoe's greatest
creative work. In *The Farther Adventures of Robinson Crusoe:
being the Second and Last part of his Life* (August 1719), there
is remarkably vivid story-telling with detailed descrip-
tions of places and people. But perhaps the most remarkable feature of the book is the development in Crusoe's
character. No longer the lonely castaway, he is, despite
the ups and downs of fortune, a leader of men, a forceful
man of action and also an acute observer and commenta-

tor, during ten adventurous years, on land as well as at sea. A now little-known third book, *Serious Reflections during the Life and Surprising Adventures of Robinson Crusoe: with his Vision of the Angelick World* (August 1720), is in no sense a sequel. It is Defoe's attempt to restate in philosophic terms what he has already written, using Crusoe's experience as an allegory of his own life.

I planned in this edition to end where the 'castaway' story itself ends, and, in truth, the reader's interest, too — at the point of Crusoe's return to England; and I hoped to find a standard text divided into parts or chapters but in this I was not successful. (No edition with chapter divisions seems to have been issued before the nineteenth century — when many were published.) The text I have used is the complete one in the Oxford World's Classics. I have divided it into chapters and cut it slightly here and there, mainly to relieve the tedium of Crusoe's long meditations, which nearly always enlarge upon a point he has already clearly made (he, after all, had plenty of time to indulge his fondness to moralise); and this makes it possible to produce the book in a reasonable length for modern readers. The Epilogue, describing Crusoe's return visit to his island, and poor Friday's tragic and heroic death (we all want to know what happened to Friday), has been assembled from the last pages of the first book with relevant bits from *The Farther Adventures*. Apart from this rearrangement of

Defoe's words for the Epilogue nothing has been changed or added to the text of the story. The Glossary, which is to be found on page 405, is based on the one compiled by Charles Lee for the Everyman's Library edition (reprinted 1992).

In my young professional days as a librarian trying to pass on to children my own enthusiasm for Scott and explaining how to 'skip' so as to avoid the descriptive passages and keep hold of the story, I did think that one day it might be fun to abridge some of Scott's novels for young readers, but never did I aspire to or even consider the possibility of editing *Robinson Crusoe*. That is a task for which I have no qualifications. It is done now with humility. The one and only reconciling factor is that many others before me have 'mucked about' with the text, and most of them anonymously. Like, for example, one edition which gives both books (*Robinson Crusoe* and *The Farther Adventures*) in one, with no indication of this on the title-page, nor of where one begins and the other ends. It appears to be the genuine text, but in fact it has great chunks omitted (whole adventures in the second book) with here and there 'inserted' paragraphs summarising in a few lines the matter of several pages: and all this without editorial note or explanation of any kind.

Few books (probably none, excepting only the Bible) can have been treated with so little respect and so savagely mangled. Both books of the adventures of Robinson

Crusoe were abridged and 'pirated' in Defoe's own life-
time, and the first appeared very early in truncated
chapbook versions. Mrs Thwaite, in her *From Primer to
Pleasure*, gives the picture of one, the text reduced to
twenty-four pages, published about 1770. In more recent
times it has appeared as a strip cartoon and in countless
retold versions for children — for since the mid-
eighteenth century it has been included in lists of books
for children, along with *The Pilgrim's Progress* and *Gulliver's
Travels*, two other books quickly appropriated by the
young. (Mrs Trimmer, though, reviewing a then new edition in the *Guardian of Education* (1802–6), does not seem
to be entirely sure of its suitability. She wrote, 'It should
not be given to *all* boys without discrimination as it might
lead to an early taste for a rambling life and a desire for
adventure.') The story of Crusoe and Man Friday has frequently been adapted for the stage. In the early nineteenth century it was included in peepshows and in the
Juvenile Drama cut-out sheets; it has long been the subject of professional and amateur pantomime, often with
the addition of a comic 'Mrs Crusoe', and quite recently a
French film has been based on the book.

   This great variety of treatment shows no doubt how
tremendously permanent is the attraction of the book's
basic theme. But the quality of Defoe's treatment of the
theme has survived both parody and travesty. And
Robinson Crusoe himself survives as a person who can

still arouse our sympathy and interest. His story, written so convincingly and in such exactness of detail, still reads today like a true-to-life adventure.

Quite recently a traveller who had been to Crusoe's island, being interviewed by the B.B.C., said bad weather had rather spoilt his visit. It was during one of our bouts of unpleasant winter and the interviewer assumed that it had been cold. Not cold (the traveller explained), the climate was tropical, it was the torrential and continuous *rain*. Why, that's just what Crusoe said, was my involuntary thought. Desperately in need of a spade to dig out his cave and to prepare ground for cultivation, Crusoe sought out the 'iron tree' and with great labour, almost spoiling his axe, cut a chunk of wood and made an adequate implement for himself (though 'never was a shovel, I believe, made after that fashion, or so long a making'). This incident had meant little to me in previous readings, but now I remembered I too had handled this iron wood, and on a farm in Sussex where fence posts had been imported from the Argentine because of their long-lasting qualities. They looked like wood, but in weight and hardness they were like stone.

F. J. Harvey Darton (in *Children's Books in England*) suggests that it is the 'splendour of Defoe's matter-of-factness and the magic of the desert island idea' that accounts for the book's long popularity; Guy Pocock, in his Introduction to the 1975 Everyman edition, says, 'Its power and hold are extraordinary . . . the power of Defoe's writing lies in its *truth* — the piling up of innumerable apparently trivial details till the reader's mind is battered into acceptance. One feels unconsciously that this vast accumulative sequence is just what life is, and *must* be true.' This feeling of truth is underlined, increased, by the simple natural way Crusoe tells about his successes and his failures; his stupidity (the making of his first boat; the too big enclosure for the captured wild goats) and his foresight (in working non-stop to take what he could from the wreck; building his habitation away from the shore); and of his courage — always cautious, never foolhardy; and of his times of lonely terror. One feels that it *is* autobiography, whereas in fact Defoe (*c*.1660–1731) was born and died in London, and though before his marriage he had travelled in Italy, France, Spain and Germany, he was never a sailor and made no long sea trips.

Kathleen Lines

Note
This foreword and the text reproduced in this edition were prepared by Kathleen Lines in 1968 for Sir Francis Meynell's series of Nonesuch Cygnets.

ROBINSON CRUSOE

HIS LIFE AND STRANGE SURPRISING ADVENTURES

CHAPTER 1

Robinson Crusoe's birth and parentage. His disregard of his father's warning that distress and misery will follow if he persists in his desire to go to sea. He runs away from home when chance offers him a free passage. He is seasick and bitterly repents his hasty action, but fine weather removes his apprehension and he enjoys the life and company.

I WAS born in the year 1632, in the city of York, of a good family, though not of that country, my father being a foreigner of Bremen, who settled first at Hull. He got a good estate by merchandise, and leaving off his trade, lived afterward at York, from whence he had married my mother, whose relations were named Robinson, a very good family in that country, and from whom I was called Robinson Kreutznaer; but by the usual corruption of words in England we are now called, nay, we call ourselves, and write our name, Crusoe, and so my companions always called me.

I had two elder brothers, one of which was lieutenant-colonel to an English regiment of foot in Flanders, formerly commanded by the famous Colonel Lockhart, and was killed at the battle near Dunkirk against the Spaniards; what became of my second brother I never knew, any more than my father and mother did know what was become of me.

Being the third son of the family, and not bred to any

trade, my head began to be filled very early with rambling thoughts. My father, who was very ancient, had given me a competent share of learning, as far as house-education and a country free school generally goes, and designed me for the law; but I would be satisfied with nothing but going to sea; and my inclination to this led me so strongly against the will, nay, the commands, of my father, and against all the entreaties and persuasions of my mother and other friends, that there seemed to be something fatal in that propension of nature tending directly to the life of misery which was to befall me.

My father, a wise and grave man, gave me serious and excellent counsel against what he foresaw was my design. He called me one morning into his chamber, where he was confined by the gout, and expostulated very warmly with me upon this subject. He asked me what reasons more than a mere wandering inclination I had for leaving my father's house and my native country, where I might be well introduced, and had a prospect of raising my fortunes by application and industry, with a life of ease and pleasure. He told me it was for men of desperate fortunes on one hand, or of aspiring, superior fortunes on the other, who went abroad upon adventures, to rise by enterprise, and make themselves famous in undertakings of a nature out of the common road; that these things were all either too far above me, or too far below me; that mine was the middle state, or what might be called the upper

CRUSOE ADVISED BY HIS FATHER.

station of low life, which he had found by long experience was the best state in the world, the most suited to human happiness, not exposed to the miseries and hardships, the labour and sufferings, of the mechanic part of mankind, and not embarrassed with the pride, luxury, ambition, and envy of the upper part of mankind.

He bid me observe it, and I should always find, that the calamities of life were shared among the upper and lower part of mankind, but that the middle station had the fewest disasters, and was not exposed to so many vicissitudes as the higher or lower part of mankind. Nay, they were not subjected to so many distempers and uneasinesses either of body or mind as those were who, by vicious living, luxury, and extravagances on one hand, or by hard labour, want of necessaries, and mean or insufficient diet on the other hand, bring distempers upon themselves by the natural consequences of their way of living; that the middle station of life was calculated for all kind of virtues and all kind of enjoyments; that peace and plenty were the handmaids of a middle fortune; that temperance, moderation, quietness, health, society, all agreeable diversions, and all desirable pleasures, were the blessings attending the middle station of life; that this way men went silently and smoothly through the world, and comfortably out of it, not embarrassed with the labours of the hands or of the head, not sold to the life of slavery for daily bread, or harassed with perplexed circumstances, which rob the soul of peace, and the body of rest; not enraged with the passion of envy, or secret burning lust of ambition for great things; but in easy circumstances sliding gently through the world, and sensibly tasting the sweets of living, without the bitter, feeling that they are happy, and learning by every day's experience to know it more sensibly.

After this, he pressed me earnestly, and in the most affectionate manner, not to play the young man, not to precipitate myself into miseries which Nature and the station of life I was born in seemed to have provided against; that I was under no necessity of seeking my bread; that he would do well for me, and endeavour to enter me fairly into the station of life which he had been just recommending to me; and that if I was not very easy and happy in the world it must be my mere fate or fault that must hinder it, and that he should have nothing to answer for, having thus discharged his duty in warning me against measures which he knew would be to my hurt; in a word, that as he would do very kind things for me if I would stay and settle at home as he directed, so he would not have so much hand in my misfortunes, as to give me any encouragement to go away. And to close all, he told me I had my elder brother for an example, to whom he had used the same earnest persuasions to keep him from going into the Low Country wars, but could not prevail, his young desires prompting him to run into the army, where he was killed; and though he said he would not cease to pray for me, yet he would venture to say to me, that if I did take this foolish step, God would not bless me, and I would have leisure hereafter to reflect upon having neglected his counsel when there might be none to assist in my recovery.

I was sincerely affected with this discourse, as indeed who could be otherwise? and I resolved not to think of going abroad any more, but to settle at home according to my father's desire. But alas! a few days wore it all off; and, in short, to prevent any of my father's farther importunities, in a few weeks after I resolved to run quite away from him. However, I did not act so hastily neither as my first heat of resolution prompted, but I took my mother, at a time when I thought her a little pleasanter than ordinary, and told her, that my thoughts were so entirely bent upon seeing the world, that I should never settle to anything with resolution enough to go through with it, and my father had better give me his consent than force me to go without it; that I was now eighteen years old, which was too late to go apprentice to a trade, or clerk to an attorney, that I was sure if I did, I should never serve out my time, and I should certainly run away from my master before my time was out, and go to sea; and if she would speak to my father to let me go but one voyage abroad, if I came home again and did not like it, I would go no more, and I would promise by a double diligence to recover that time I had lost.

This put my mother into a great passion. She told me, she knew it would be to no purpose to speak to my father upon any such subject; that he knew too well what was my interest to give his consent to anything so much for my hurt, and that she wondered how I could think of any such thing after such a discourse as I had had with my father, and such kind and tender expressions as she knew my father had used to me; and that, in short, if I would ruin myself there was no help for me; but I might depend I should never have their consent to it; that for her part, she would not have so much hand in my destruction, and I should never have it to say, that my mother was willing when my father was not.

Though my mother refused to move it to my father, yet, as I have heard afterwards, she reported all the discourse to him, and that my father, after showing a great concern at it, said to her with a sigh, 'That boy might be happy if he would stay at home, but if he goes abroad he will be the miserablest wretch that was ever born: I can give no consent to it.'

It was not till almost a year after this that I broke loose, though in the meantime I continued obstinately deaf to all proposals of settling to business, and frequently expostulating with my father and mother about their being so positively determined against what they knew my inclinations prompted me to. But being one day at Hull, where I went casually, and without any purpose of making

an elopement that time; but I say, being there, and one of
my companions being going by sea to London, in his
father's ship, and prompting me to go with them, with
the common allurement of seafaring men, viz., that it
should cost me nothing for my passage, I consulted neither father or mother any more, nor so much as sent them
word of it; but leaving them to hear of it as they might,
without asking God's blessing, or my father's, without
any consideration of circumstances or consequences, and
in an ill hour, God knows, on the first of September, 1651,
I went on board a ship bound for London. Never any
young adventurer's misfortunes, I believe, began sooner,
or continued longer than mine. The ship was no sooner
gotten out of the Humber, but the wind began to blow,
and the waves to rise in a most frightful manner; and as I
had never been at sea before, I was most inexpressibly
sick in body, and terrified in my mind. I began now seriously to reflect upon what I had done, and how justly I
was overtaken by the judgment of heaven for my wicked
leaving my father's house, and abandoning my duty; all
the good counsel of my parents, my father's tears and my
mother's entreaties, came now fresh into my mind, and
my conscience, which was not yet come to the pitch of
hardness which it has been since, reproached me with the
contempt of advice, and the breach of my duty to God
and my father.

All this while the storm increased, and the sea, which I

had never been upon before, went very high, though nothing like what I have seen many times since; no, nor like what I saw a few days after. But it was enough to affect me then, who was but a young sailor, and had never known anything of the matter. I expected every wave would have swallowed us up, and that every time the ship fell down, as I thought, in the trough or hollow of the sea, we should never rise more; and in this agony of mind I made many vows and resolutions, that if it would please God here to spare my life this one voyage, if ever I got once my foot upon dry land again, I would go directly home to my father, and never set it into a ship again while I lived; that I would take his advice, and never run myself into such miseries as these any more. Now I saw plainly the goodness of his observations about the middle station of life, how easy, how comfortably he had lived all his days, and never had been exposed to tempests at sea, or troubles on shore; and I resolved that I would, like a true repenting prodigal, go home to my father.

These wise and sober thoughts continued all the while the storm continued, and indeed some time after; but the next day the wind was abated and the sea calmer, and I began to be a little inured to it. However, I was very grave for all that day, being also a little seasick still; but towards night the weather cleared up, the wind was quite over, and a charming fine evening followed; the sun went down perfectly clear, and rose so the next morning; and having little or no wind, and a smooth sea, the sun shining upon it, the sight was, as I thought, the most delightful that I ever saw.

I had slept well in the night, and was now no more seasick but very cheerful, looking with wonder upon the sea that was so rough and terrible the day before, and could be so calm and so pleasant in so little time after. And now lest my good resolutions should continue, my companion, who had indeed enticed me away, comes to me: 'Well, Bob,' says he, clapping me on the shoulder, 'how do you do after it? I warrant you were frighted, wa'n't you, last night, when it blew but a capful of wind?' 'A capful, d'you call it?' said I; ''twas a terrible storm.' 'A storm, you fool you,' replies he; 'do you call that a storm? Why, it was nothing at all; give us but a good ship and sea-room, and we think nothing of such a squall of wind as that; but you're but a fresh-water sailor, Bob. Come, let us make a bowl of punch, and we'll forget all that; d'ye see what charming weather 'tis now?' To make short this sad part of my story, we went the old way of all sailors; the punch was made, and I was made drunk with it, and in that one night's wickedness I drowned all my repentance, all my reflections upon my past conduct, and all my resolutions for my future. In a word, as the sea was returned to its smoothness of surface and settled calmness by the abatement of that storm, so the hurry of my thoughts being over, my fears and apprehensions of being swallowed up

by the sea being forgotten, and the current of my former
desires returned, I entirely forgot the vows and promises
that I made in my distress. I found indeed some intervals
of reflection, and the serious thoughts did, as it were,
endeavour to return again sometimes; but I shook them
off, and roused myself from them as it were from distemper, and applying myself to drink and company, soon mastered the return of those fits, for so I called them, and I
had in five or six days got as complete a victory over conscience as any young fellow that resolved not to be troubled with it could desire. But I was to have another trial
for it still; and Providence, as in such cases generally it
does, resolved to leave me entirely without excuse. For if
I would not take this for a deliverance, the next was to be
such a one as the worst and most hardened wretch among
us would confess both the danger and the mercy.

CHAPTER 2

Contrary winds in Yarmouth roads and a fearful storm. All hands to the pumps but in vain. The ship is abandoned and quickly founders. Townsmen succour the sailors, but Crusoe refusing to return to Hull proceeds to London.

THE SIXTH day of our being at sea we came into Yarmouth roads; the wind having been contrary and the weather calm, we had made but little way since the storm. Here we were obliged to come to an anchor, and here we lay, the wind continuing contrary, viz., at southwest, for seven or eight days, during which time a great many ships from Newcastle came into the same roads, as the common harbour where the ships might wait for a wind for the river.

We had not, however, rid here so long, but should have tided it up the river, but that the wind blew too fresh; and after we had lain four or five days, blew very hard. However, the roads being reckoned as good as a harbour, the anchorage good, and our ground-tackle very strong, our men were unconcerned, and not in the least apprehensive of danger, but spent the time in rest and mirth, after the manner of the sea; but the eighth day in the morning the wind increased, and we had all hands at work to strike our topmasts, and make everything snug and close, that the ship might ride as easy as possible. By noon the sea went very high indeed, and our ship rid forecastle in, shipped several seas, and we thought once or twice our anchor had come home; upon which our master ordered out the sheet-anchor, so that we rode with two anchors ahead, and the cables veered out to the better end.

By this time it blew a terrible storm indeed, and now I began to see terror and amazement in the faces even of the seamen themselves. The master, though vigilant to the business of preserving the ship, yet as he went in and out of his cabin by me, I could hear him softly to himself say several times, 'Lord be merciful to us, we shall be all lost, we shall be all undone'; and the like. During these first hurries I was stupid, lying still in my cabin, which was in the steerage, and cannot describe my temper; I could ill reassume the first penitence, which I had so apparently trampled upon, and hardened myself against; I thought the bitterness of death had been past, and that this would be nothing too, like the first. But when the master himself came by me, as I said just now, and said we should be all lost, I was dreadfully frighted; I got up out of my cabin, and looked out. But such a dismal sight I never saw; the sea went mountains high, and broke upon us every three or four minutes; when I could look about, I could see nothing but distress round us. Two ships that rid near us we found had cut their masts by the board, being deep loaden; and our men cried out, that a ship which rid about a mile ahead of us was foundered. Two more ships being driven from their anchors, were run out of the roads to sea at all adventures, and that with not a mast standing. The light ships fared the best, as not so much labouring in the sea; but two or three of them drove, and came close by us, running away with only their sprit-sail out before the wind.

Towards evening the mate and boatswain begged the master of our ship to let them cut away the foremast, which he was very unwilling to. But the boatswain protesting to him that if he did not the ship would founder, he consented; and when they had cut away the foremast, the mainmast stood so loose, and shook the ship so much, they were obliged to cut her away also, and make a clear deck.

Anyone may judge what a condition I must be in at all this, who was but a young sailor, and who had been in such a fright before at but a little. But if I can express at this distance the thoughts I had about me at that time, I was in tenfold more horror of mind upon account of my former convictions, and the having returned from them to the resolutions I had wickedly taken at first, than I was at death itself; and these, added to the terror of the storm, put me into such a condition, that I can by no words describe it. But the worst was not come yet; the storm continued with such fury, that the seamen themselves acknowledged they had never known a worse. We had a good ship, but she was deep loaden, and wallowed in the

sea, that the seamen every now and then cried out she
would founder. It was my advantage in one respect, that I
did not know what they meant by founder till I inquired.
However, the storm was so violent, that I saw what is not
often seen, the master, the boatswain, and some others
more sensible than the rest, at their prayers, and expecting every moment when the ship would go to the bottom.
In the middle of the night, and under all the rest of our
distresses, one of the men that had been down on purpose to see cried out we had sprung a leak, another said
there was four foot water in the hold. Then all hands were
called to the pump. At that very word my heart, as I
thought, died within me, and I fell backwards upon the
side of my bed where I sat, into the cabin. However, the
men roused me, and told me, that I, that was able to do
nothing before, was as well able to pump as another; at
which I stirred up and went to the pump and worked very
heartily. While this was doing, the master seeing some
light colliers, who, not able to ride out the storm, were
obliged to slip and run away to sea, and would come near
us, ordered to fire a gun as a signal of distress. I, who
knew nothing what that meant, was so surprised that I
thought the ship had broke, or some dreadful thing had
happened. In a word, I was so surprised that I fell down in
a swoon. As this was a time when everybody had his own
life to think of, nobody minded me, or what was become
of me; but another man stepped up to the pump, and

thrusting me aside with his foot, let me lie, thinking I had been dead; and it was a great while before I came to myself.

We worked on, but the water increasing in the hold, it was apparent that the ship would founder, and though the storm began to abate a little, yet it was not possible she could swim till we might run into a port, so the master continued firing guns for help; and a light ship, who had rid it out just ahead of us, ventured a boat out to help us. It was with the utmost hazard the boat came near us, but it was impossible for us to get on board, or for the boat to lie near the ship's side, till at last the men rowing very heartily, and venturing their lives to save ours, our men cast them a rope over the stern with a buoy to it, and then veered it out a great length, which they after great labour and hazard took hold of, and we hauled them close under our stern, and got all into their boat. It was to no purpose for them or us after we were in the boat to think of reaching to their own ship, so all agreed to let her drive, and only to pull her in towards shore as much as we could, and our master promised them that if the boat was staved upon the shore he would make it good to their master; so partly rowing and partly driving, our boat went away to the northward, sloping towards the shore almost as far as Winterton Ness.

We were not much more than a quarter of an hour out of our ship but we saw her sink, and then I understood for the first time what was meant by a ship foundering in the sea. I must acknowledge I had hardly eyes to look up when the seamen told me she was sinking; for from that moment they rather put me into the boat than that I might be said to go in; my heart was as it were dead within me, partly with fright, partly with horror of mind and the thoughts of what was yet before me.

While we were in this condition, the men yet labouring at the oar to bring the boat near the shore, we could see, when, our boat mounting the waves, we were able to see the shore, a great many people running along the shore to assist us when we should come near. But we made but slow way towards the shore, nor were we able to reach the shore, till being past the lighthouse at Winterton, the shore falls off to the westward towards Cromer, and so the land broke off a little the violence of the wind. Here we got in, and though not without much difficulty got all safe on shore, and walked afterwards on foot to Yarmouth, where, as unfortunate men, we were used with great humanity as well by the magistrates of the town, who assigned us good quarters, as by particular merchants and owners of ships, and had money given us sufficiently to carry us either to London or back to Hull, as we thought fit.

Had I now had the sense to have gone back to Hull, and have gone home, I had been happy, and my father, an emblem of our blessed Saviour's parable, had even killed

THE SHIPWRECK IN YARMOUTH ROADS.

the fatted calf for me; for hearing the ship I went away in was cast away in Yarmouth road, it was a great while before he had any assurance that I was not drowned.

But my ill fate pushed me on now with an obstinacy that nothing could resist; and though I had several times loud calls from my reason and my more composed judgment to go home, yet I had no power to do it. I know not what to call this, nor will I urge that it is a secret overruling decree that hurries us on to be the instruments of our own destruction, even though it be before us, and that we rush upon it with our eyes open. Certainly nothing but some such decreed unavoidable misery attending, and which it was impossible for me to escape, could have pushed me forward against the calm reasonings and persuasions of my most retired thoughts, and against two such visible instructions as I had met with in my first attempt.

My comrade, who had helped to harden me before, and who was the master's son, was now less forward than I. The first time he spoke to me after we were at Yarmouth, which was not till two or three days, for we were separated in the town to several quarters — I say, the first time he saw me, it appeared his tone was altered, and looking very melancholy and shaking his head, asked me how I did, and telling his father who I was, and how I had come this voyage only for a trial in order to go farther abroad, his father turning to me with a very grave and concerned tone, 'Young man,' says he, 'you ought never to go to sea any more, you ought to take this for a plain and visible token, that you are not to be a seafaring man.' 'Why, sir,' said I, 'will you go to sea no more?' 'That is another case,' said he; 'it is my calling, and therefore my duty; but as you made this voyage for a trial, you see what a taste Heaven has given you of what you are to expect if you persist.' He talked very gravely to me, exhorted me to go back to my father, and not tempt Providence to my ruin; told me I might see a visible hand of Heaven against me. 'And, young man,' said he, 'depend upon it, if you do not go back, wherever you go you will meet with nothing but disasters and disappointments, till your father's words are fulfilled upon you.'

We parted soon after; for I made him little answer, and I saw him no more; which way he went, I know not. As for me, having some money in my pocket, I travelled to London by land; and there, as well as on the road, had many struggles with myself what course of life I should take, and whether I should go home, or go to sea.

As to going home, shame opposed the best motions that offered to my thoughts; and it immediately occurred to me how I should be laughed at among the neighbours, and should be ashamed to see, not my father and mother only, but even everybody else; from whence I have since often observed how incongruous and irrational the common temper of mankind is, especially of youth, to that reason which ought to guide them in such cases, viz., that they are not ashamed to sin, and yet are ashamed to repent; not ashamed of the action for which they ought justly to be esteemed fools, but are ashamed of the returning, which only can make them be esteemed wise men.

In this state of life, however, I remained some time, uncertain what measures to take, and what course of life to lead. An irresistible reluctance continued to going home; and as I stayed a while, the remembrance of the distress I had been in wore off; and as that abated, the little motion I had in my desires to a return wore off with it, till at last I quite laid aside the thoughts of it, and looked out for a voyage.

CHAPTER 3

*Crusoe alone in London is befriended by an honest sea captain
and makes a successful trading trip. A second voyage, fight at sea
and capture. Crusoe is taken as slave by the pirates to Sallee in
Morocco. He escapes (after a few years) with the boy Xury. They
steer south along a wild inhospitable coast.*

I T WAS my great misfortune that in all these adventures
I did not ship myself as a sailor, whereby, though I
might indeed have worked a little harder than ordinary,
yet at the same time I had learned the duty and office of a
foremast man, and in time might have qualified myself
for a mate or lieutenant, if not for a master. But as it was
always my fate to choose for the worst, so I did here; for
having money in my pocket, and good clothes upon my
back, I would always go on board in the habit of a gentle-
man; and so I neither had any business in the ship, or
learned to do any.

It was my lot first of all to fall into pretty good company in London, which does not always happen to such
loose and misguided young fellows as I then was; the
devil generally not omitting to lay some snare for them
very early; but it was not so with me. I first fell
acquainted with the master of a ship who had been on the
coast of Guinea, and who, having had very good success
there, was resolved to go again; and who taking a fancy to

my conversation, which was not at all disagreeable at that time, hearing me say I had a mind to see the world, told me if I would go the voyage with him I should be at no expense; I should be his messmate and his companion; and if I could carry anything with me, I should have all the advantage of it that the trade would admit, and perhaps I might meet with some encouragement.

I embraced the offer; and, entering into a strict friendship with this captain, who was an honest and plain-dealing man, I went the voyage with him, and carried a small adventure with me, which, by the disinterested honesty of my friend the captain, I increased very considerably, for I carried about £40 in such toys and trifles as the captain directed me to buy. This £40 I had mustered together by the assistance of some of my relations whom I corresponded with, and who, I believe, got my father, or at least my mother, to contribute so much as that to my first adventure.

This was the only voyage which I may say was successful in all my adventures, and which I owe to the integrity and honesty of my friend the captain; under whom I also got a competent knowledge of the mathematics and the rules of navigation, learned how to keep an account of the ship's course, take an observation, and, in short, to understand some things that were needful to be understood by a sailor. For, as he took delight to introduce me, I took delight to learn; and, in a word, this voyage made me both

a sailor and a merchant; for I brought home five pounds
nine ounces of gold dust for my adventure, which yielded
me in London at my return almost £300, and this filled
me with those aspiring thoughts which have since so
completed my ruin.

Yet even in this voyage I had my misfortunes too; particularly, that I was continually sick, being thrown into a
violent calenture by the excessive heat of the climate; our
principal trading being upon the coast, from the latitude
of 15 degrees north even of the line itself.

I was now set up for a Guinea trader; and my friend, to
my great misfortune, dying soon after his arrival, I
resolved to go the same voyage again, and I embarked in
the same vessel with one who was his mate in the former
voyage, and had now got the command of the ship. This
was the unhappiest voyage that ever man made; for
though I did not carry quite £100 of my new-gained
wealth, so that I had £200 left, and which I lodged with
my friend's widow, who was very just to me, yet I fell into
terrible misfortunes in this voyage; and the first was this,
viz., our ship making her course towards the Canary
Islands, or rather between those islands and the African
shore, was surprised in the grey of the morning by a
Turkish rover of Sallee, who gave chase to us with all the
sail she could make. We crowded also as much canvas as
our yards would spread, or our masts carry, to have got
clear; but finding the pirate gained upon us, and would

certainly come up with us in a few hours, we prepared to
fight, our ship having twelve guns, and the rogue eighteen. About three in the afternoon he came up with us,
and bringing to, by mistake, just athwart our quarter,
instead of athwart our stern, as he intended, we brought
eight of our guns to bear on that side, and poured in a
broadside upon him, which made him sheer off again,
after returning our fire and pouring in also his small-shot
from near 200 men which he had on board. However, we
had not a man touched, all our men keeping close. He
prepared to attack us again, and we to defend ourselves;
but laying us on board the next time upon our other quarter, he entered sixty men upon our decks, who immediately fell to cutting and hacking the decks and rigging.
We plied them with small-shot, half-pikes, powder-
chests, and such like, and cleared our deck of them twice.
However, to cut short this melancholy part of our story,
our ship being disabled, and three of our men killed and
eight wounded, we were obliged to yield, and were carried all prisoners into Sallee, a port belonging to the
Moors.

The usage I had there was not so dreadful as at first I
apprehended, nor was I carried up the country to the
emperor's court, as the rest of our men were, but was kept
by the captain of the rover as his proper prize, and made
his slave, being young and nimble, and fit for his business.

At this surprising change of my circumstances from a

CRUSOE A SLAVE.

merchant to a miserable slave, I was perfectly
overwhelmed; and now as I looked back upon
my father's prophetic discourse to me, that I
should be miserable, and have none to relieve
me, which I thought was now so effectually
brought to pass, that it could not be worse;
that now the hand of Heaven had overtaken
me, and I was undone without redemption.
But alas! this was but a taste of the misery I
was to go through, as will appear in the sequel
of this story.

As my new patron, or master, had taken me home to his house, so I was in hopes that he would take me with him when he went to sea again, believing that it would some time or other be his fate to be taken by a Spanish or Portugal man-of-war; and that then I should be set at liberty. But this hope of mine was soon taken away; for when he went to sea, he left me on shore to look after his little garden, and do the common drudgery of slaves about his house; and when he came home again from his cruise, he ordered me to lie in the cabin to look after the ship.

Here I meditated nothing but my escape, and what method I might take to effect it, but found no way that had the least probability in it. Nothing presented to make the supposition of it rational; so that I never had the least encouraging prospect of putting it in practice.

After about two years an odd circumstance presented itself, which put the old thought of making some attempt for my liberty again in my head. My patron lying at home longer than usual without fitting out his ship, which, as I heard, was for want of money, he used constantly, once or twice a week, sometimes oftener, if the weather was fair, to take the ship's pinnace, and go out into the road a-fishing; and as he always took me and a young Maresco with him to row the boat, we made him very merry, and I proved very dexterous in catching fish; insomuch, that sometimes he would send me with a Moor, one of his kinsmen, and the youth the Maresco, as they called him, to catch a dish of fish for him.

It happened one time that, going a-fishing in a stark calm morning, a fog rose so thick, that though we were not half a league from the shore we lost sight of it; and rowing we knew not whither or which way, we laboured all day, and all the next night, and when the morning came we found we had pulled off to sea instead of pulling in for the shore; and that we were at least two leagues from the shore. However, we got well in again, though with a great deal of labour, and some danger, for the wind began to blow pretty fresh in the morning; but particularly we were all very hungry.

But our patron, warned by this disaster, resolved to take more care of himself for the future; and having lying by him the long-boat of our English ship which he had taken, he resolved he would not go a-fishing any more without a compass and some provision; so he ordered the carpenter of his ship, who also was an English slave, to build a little state-room, or cabin, in the middle of the long-boat, like that of a barge, with a place to stand behind it to steer and haul home the main-sheet, and room before for a hand or two to stand and work the sails. She sailed with what we call a shoulder-of-mutton sail; and the boom jibbed over the top of the cabin, which lay very snug and low, and had in it room for him to lie, with a slave or two, and a table to eat on, with some small lockers to put in some bottles of such liquor as he thought fit to drink; particularly his bread, rice, and coffee.

We went frequently out with this boat a-fishing, and as I was most dexterous to catch fish for him, he never went without me. It happened that he had appointed to go out in this boat, either for pleasure or for fish, with two or three Moors of some distinction in that place, and for whom he had provided extraordinarily; and had therefore sent on board the boat overnight a larger store of provisions than ordinary; and had ordered me to get ready three fuzees with powder and shot, which were on board his ship, for that they designed some sport of fowling as well as fishing.

I got all things ready as he had directed, and waited the next morning with the boat, washed clean, her ancient and pendants out, and everything to accommodate his guests; when by and by my patron came on board alone, and told me his guests had put off going, upon some business that fell out, and ordered me with the man and boy, as usual, to go out with the boat and catch them some fish, for that his friends were to sup at his house; and commanded that as soon as I had got some fish I should bring it home to his house; all which I prepared to do.

This moment my former notions of deliverance darted into my thoughts, for now I found I was like to have a little ship at my command; and my master being gone, I prepared to furnish myself, not for a fishing business, but for a voyage; though I knew not, neither did I so much as consider, whither I should steer; for anywhere, to get out of that place, was my way.

My first contrivance was to make a pretence to speak to this Moor, to get something for our subsistence on board; for I told him we must not presume to eat of our patron's bread. He said that was true; so he brought a large basket of rusk or biscuit of their kind, and three jars with fresh water, into the boat. I knew where my patron's case of bottles stood, which it was evident by the make were taken out of some English prize; and I conveyed them into the boat while the Moor was on shore, as if they had been there before for our master. I conveyed also a great lump of beeswax into the boat, which weighed above half a hundredweight, with a parcel of twine or thread, a hatchet, a saw, and a hammer, all which were great use to us afterwards, especially the wax to make candles. Another trick I tried upon him, which he innocently came into also. His name was Ismael, who they called Muly, or Moely; so I called to him, 'Moely,' said I, 'our patron's guns are on board the boat; can you not get a little powder and shot? it may be we may kill some alcamies (a fowl like our curlews) for ourselves, for I know he keeps the gunner's stores in the ship.' 'Yes,' says he, 'I'll bring some'; and accordingly he brought a great leather pouch which held about a pound and a half of powder, or rather more; and another with shot, that had five or six pounds, with some bullets, and put all into the boat. At the same time I had found some powder of my master's in the great cabin, with which I filled one of the large bottles in the case, which was almost empty, pouring what was in it into another; and thus furnished with everything needful, we sailed out of the port to fish. The castle, which is at the entrance of the port, knew who we were, and took no notice of us; and we were not above a mile out of the port before we hauled in our sail, and set us down to fish. The wind blew from the N.N.E., which was contrary to my desire; for had it blown southerly I had been sure to have made the coast of Spain, and at least reached to the bay of Cadiz; but my resolutions were, blow which way it would, I would be gone from the horrid place where I was, and leave the rest to Fate.

After we had fished some time and catched nothing, for when I had fish on my hook I would not pull them up, that he might not see them, I said to the Moor, 'This will not do; our master will not be thus served; we must stand farther off.' He, thinking no harm, agreed, and being in the head of the boat set the sails; and as I had the helm I run the boat near a league farther, and then brought her to as if I would fish; when giving the boy the helm, I stepped forward to where the Moor was, and making as if I stopped for something behind him, I took him by surprise with my arm under his twist, and tossed him clear overboard into the sea. He rose immediately, for he swam like a cork, and called to me, begged to be taken in, told me he would go all the world over with me. He swam so strong after the boat, that he would have reached me very quickly, there being but little wind; upon which I stepped into the cabin, and fetching one of the fowling-pieces, I presented it to him, and told him I had done him no hurt, and if he would be quiet I would do him none. 'But,' said I, 'you swim well enough to reach to the shore, and the sea is calm; make the best of your way to shore, and I will do you no harm; but if you come near the boat I'll shoot you through the head, for I am resolved to have my liberty.' So he turned himself about, and swam for the shore, and I make no doubt but he reached it with ease, for he was an excellent swimmer.

I could have been content to have taken this Moor with me, and have drowned the boy, but there was no venturing to trust him. When he was gone I turned to the boy, whom they called Xury, and said to him, 'Xury, if you will be faithful to me I'll make you a great man; but if you will not stroke your face to be true to me,' that is, swear by Mahomet and his father's beard, 'I must throw you into the sea too.' The boy smiled in my face, and spoke so innocently, that I could not mistrust him, and swore to be faithful to me, and go all over the world with me.

While I was in view of the Moor that was swimming, I stood out directly to sea with the boat, rather stretching to windward, that they might think me gone towards the straits' mouth (as indeed any one that had been in their wits must have been supposed to do); for who would have supposed we were sailed on to the southward to the truly barbarian coast, where we could ne'er once go on shore but we should be devoured by savage beasts, or more merciless savages of human kind?

But as soon as it grew dusk in the evening, I changed my course, and steered directly south and by east, bending my course a little toward the east, that I might keep in with the shore; and having a fair, fresh gale of wind, and a smooth, quiet sea, I made such sail that I believe by the next day, at three o'clock in the afternoon, when I first made the land, I could not be less than 150 miles south of Sallee; quite beyond the Emperor of Morocco's dominions, or indeed of any other king thereabouts, for we saw no people.

Yet such was the fright I had taken at the Moors, and the dreadful apprehensions I had of falling into their hands, that I would not stop, or go on shore, or come to anchor, the wind continuing fair, till I had sailed in that manner five days; and then the wind shifting to the southward, I concluded also that if any of our vessels were in chase of me, they also would now give over; so I ventured to make to the coast, and came to an anchor in the mouth of a little river, I knew not what, or where; neither what latitude, what country, what nations, or what river. I neither saw, or desired to see, any people; the principal thing I wanted was fresh water. We came into this creek in the evening, resolving to swim on shore as soon as it was dark, and discover the country; but as soon as it was quite dark we heard such dreadful noises of the barking, roaring, and howling of wild creatures, of we knew not what kinds, that the poor boy was ready to die with fear, and begged of me not to go on shore till day. 'Well, Xury,' said I, 'then I won't; but it may be we may see men by day, who will be as bad to us as those lions.' 'Then we give them the shoot gun,' says Xury, laughing; 'make them run away.' Such English Xury spoke by conversing among us slaves. However, I was glad to see the boy so cheerful, and I gave him a dram (out of our patron's case of bottles) to cheer him up. After all, Xury's advice was good, and I took it; we dropped our little anchor and lay still all night. I say still, for we slept none; for in two or three hours we saw vast great creatures (we knew not what to call them) of many sorts come down to the seashore and run into the water, wallowing and washing themselves for the pleasure of cooling themselves; and they made such hideous howlings and yellings, that I never indeed heard the like.

Xury was dreadfully frighted, and indeed so was I too; but we were both more frighted when we heard one of these mighty creatures come swimming towards our boat; we could not see him, but we might hear him by his blowing to be a monstrous huge and furious beast. Xury said it was a lion, and it might be so for aught I know; but poor

Xury cried to me to weigh the anchor and row away. 'No,' says I, 'Xury; we can slip our cable with the buoy to it, and go off to sea; they cannot follow us far.' I had no sooner said so, but I perceived the creature (whatever it was) within two oars' length, which something surprised me; however, I immediately stepped to the cabin door, and taking up my gun, fired at him, upon which he immediately turned about and swam towards the shore again.

But it is impossible to describe the horrible noises, and hideous cries and howlings, that were raised, as well upon the edge of the shore as higher within the country, upon the noise or report of the gun, a thing I have some reason to believe those creatures had never heard before. This convinced me that there was no going on shore for us in the night upon the coast; and how to venture on shore in the day was another question too; for to have fallen into the hands of any of the savages, had been as bad as to have fallen into the hands of lions and tigers; at least we were equally apprehensive of the danger of it.

Be that as it would, we were obliged to go on shore somewhere or other for water, for we had not a pint left in the boat; when or where to get to it, was the point. Xury said if I would let him go on shore with one of the jars, he would find if there was any water and bring some to me. I asked him why he would go? why I should not go and he stay in the boat? The boy answered with so much affection, that made me love him ever after. Says he, 'If wild mans come, they eat me, you go way.' 'Well, Xury,' said I, 'we will both go; and if the wild mans come, we will kill them, they shall eat neither of us.' So I gave Xury a piece of rusk bread to eat, and a dram out of our patron's case of bottles which I mentioned before; and we hauled in the boat as near the shore as we thought was proper, and so waded on shore, carrying nothing but our arms and two jars for water.

I did not care to go out of sight of the boat, fearing the coming of canoes with savages down the river; but the boy seeing a low place about a mile up the country, rambled to it; and by and by I saw him come running towards me. I thought he was pursued by some savage, or frighted with some wild beast, and I ran forward towards him to help him; but when I came nearer to him, I saw something hanging over his shoulders, which was a creature that he had shot, like a hare, but different in colour, and longer legs. However, we were very glad of it, and it was very good meat; but the great joy that poor Xury came with was to tell me he had found good water, and seen no wild mans.

But we found afterwards that we need not take such pains for water, for a little higher up the creek where we were we found the water fresh when the tide was out, which flowed but a little way up; so we filled our jars, and feasted on the hare we had killed, and prepared to go on our way, having seen no footsteps of any human creature in that part of the country.

As I had been one voyage to this coast before, I knew very well that the islands of the Canaries, and the Cape de Verde Islands also, lay not far off from the coast. But as I had no instruments to take an observation to know what latitude we were in, and did not exactly know, or at least remember, what latitude they were in, I knew not where to look for them, or when to stand off to sea towards them; otherwise I might now easily have found some of these islands. But my hope was, that if I stood along this coast till I came to that part where the English traded, I should find some of their vessels upon their usual design of trade, that would relieve and take us in.

CHAPTER 4

Crusoe shoots a lion. He and Xury take its skin. Cautious
dealings with savage natives to obtain food and water.
Crusoe kills a leopard to their astonishment and satisfaction.
Rescue at sea by a Portuguese trader. Crusoe sells Xury to the
kindly captain. He arrives at the Brazils.

BY THE best of my calculations, that place where I now
was must be that country which, lying between the
Emperor of Morocco's dominions and the negroes, lies
waste and uninhabited, except by wild beasts; the negroes
having abandoned it and gone farther south for fear of the
Moors, and the Moors not thinking it worth inhabiting, by
reason of its barrenness; and indeed both forsaking it
because of the prodigious numbers of tigers, lions, leopards,
and other furious creatures which harbour there. Indeed for
near an hundred miles together upon this coast we saw
nothing but a waste uninhabited country by day, and heard
nothing but howlings and roarings of wild beasts by night.

Once or twice in the daytime I thought I saw the Pico
of Teneriffe, being the high top of the Mountain
Teneriffe in the Canaries, and had a great mind to venture out, in hopes of reaching thither; but having tried
twice, I was forced in again by contrary winds, the sea also
going too high for my little vessel; so I resolved to pursue
my first design, and keep along the shore.

Several times I was obliged to land for fresh water after we had left this place; and once in particular, being early in the morning, we came to an anchor under a little point of land which was pretty high; and the tide beginning to flow, we lay still to go farther in. Xury, whose eyes were more about him than it seems mine were, calls softly to me, and tells me that we had best go farther off the shore; 'For,' says he, 'look, yonder lies a dreadful monster on the side of that hillock fast asleep.' I looked where he pointed, and saw a dreadful monster indeed, for it was a terrible great lion that lay on the side of the shore, under the shade of a piece of the hill that hung as it were a little over him. 'Xury', says I, 'you shall go on shore and kill him.' Xury looked frighted, and said, 'Me kill! he eat me at one mouth'; one mouthful he meant. However, I said no more to the boy, but bade him lie still, and I took our biggest gun, which was almost musket-bore, and loaded it with a good charge of powder, and with two slugs, and laid it down; then I loaded another gun with two bullets; and the third (for we had three pieces) I loaded with five smaller bullets. I took the best aim I could with the first piece to have shot him into the head, but he lay so with his leg raised a little above his nose, that the slugs hit his leg about the knee, and broke the bone. He started up growling at first, but finding his leg broke, fell down again, and then got up upon three legs and gave the most hideous roar that ever I heard. I was a little surprised that

I had not hit him on the head. However, I took up the second piece immediately, and, though he began to move off, fired again, and shot him into the head, and had the pleasure to see him drop, and make but little noise, but lay struggling for life. Then Xury took heart, and would have me let him go on shore. 'Well, go,' said I; so the boy jumped into the water, and taking a little gun in one hand, swam to shore with the other hand, and coming close to the creature, put the muzzle of the piece to his ear, and shot him into the head again, which despatched him quite.

This was game indeed to us, but this was no food; and I was very sorry to lose three charges of powder and shot upon a creature that was good for nothing to us. However, Xury said he would have some of him; so he comes on board, and asked me to give him the hatchet. 'For what, Xury?' said I. 'Me cut off his head,' said he. However, Xury could not cut off his head, but he cut off a foot, and brought it with him, and it was a monstrous great one.

I bethought myself, however, that perhaps the skin of him might one way or other be of some value to us; and I resolved to take off his skin if I could. So Xury and I went to work with him; but Xury was much the better workman at it, for I knew very ill how to do it. Indeed, it took us up both the whole day, but at last we got off the hide of him, and spreading it on the top of our cabin, the sun effectually dried it in two days' time, and it afterwards served me to lie upon.

After this stop we made on to the southward continually for ten or twelve days, living very sparing on our provisions, which began to abate very much, and going no oftener into the shore than we were obliged to for fresh water. My design in this was to make the river Gambia or Senegal — that is to say, anywhere about the Cape de Verde — where I was in hopes to meet with some European ship; and if I did not, I knew not what course I had to take, but to seek out for the islands, or perish there among the negroes. I knew that all the ships from Europe, which sailed either to the coast of Guinea or to Brazil, or to the East Indies, made this cape, or those islands; and in a word, I put the whole of my fortune upon this single point, either that I must meet with some ship, or must perish.

When I had pursued this resolution about ten days longer, as I have said, I began to see that the land was inhabited; and in two or three places, as we sailed by, we saw people stand upon the shore to look at us; we could also perceive they were quite black, and stark naked. I was once inclined to have gone on shore to them; but Xury was my better counsellor, and said to me, 'No go, no go.' However, I hauled in nearer the shore that I might talk to them, and I found they ran along the shore by me a good way. I observed they had no weapons in their hands, except one, who had a long slender stick, which Xury said was a lance, and that they would throw them a great way with good aim. So I kept at a distance, but talked with them by signs as well as I could, and particularly made signs for something to eat; they beckoned to me to stop my boat, and that they would fetch me some meat. Upon this I lowered the top of my sail, and lay by, and two of them ran up into the country, and in less than half an hour came back, and brought with them two pieces of dried flesh and some corn, such as is the produce of their country; but we neither knew what the one or the other was. However, we were willing to accept it, but how to come at it was our next dispute, for I was not for venturing on shore to them, and they were as much afraid of us; but they took a safe way for us all, for they brought it to the shore and laid it down, and went and stood a great way off till we fetched it on board, and then came close to us again.

We made signs of thanks to them, for we had nothing to make them amends. But an opportunity offered that very instant to oblige them wonderfully; for while we were lying by the shore came two mighty creatures, one pursuing the other (as we took it) with great fury from the mountains towards the sea; whether it was the male pursuing the female, or whether they were in sport or in rage, we could not tell, any more than we could tell whether it was usual or strange, but I believe it was the latter; because, in the first place, those ravenous creatures seldom appear but in the night; and in the second place, we found the people terribly frighted, especially the women. The man that had the lance or dart did not fly from them, but the rest did; however, as the two creatures ran directly into the water, they did not seem to offer to fall upon any of the negroes, but plunged themselves into the sea, and swam about, as if they had come for their diversion. At last, one of them began to come nearer our boat than at first I expected; but I lay ready for him, for I had loaded my gun with all possible expedition, and bade Xury load both the others. As soon as he came fairly within my reach, I fired, and shot him directly into the head; immediately he sunk down into the water, but rose instantly, and plunged up and down, as if he was struggling for life, and so indeed he was. He immediately made to the shore; but between the wound, which was his mortal hurt, and the strangling of the water, he died just before he reached the shore.

It is impossible to express the astonishment of these poor creatures, at the noise and the fire of my gun; some of them were even ready to die for fear, and fell down as dead with the very terror. But when they saw the creature dead, and sunk in the water, and that I made signs to them to come to the shore, they took heart and came to the shore, and began to search for the creature. I found him by his blood staining the water: and by the help of a rope, which I slung round him, and gave the negroes to haul, they dragged him on the shore, and found that it was a most curious leopard, spotted, and fine to an admirable degree; and the negroes held up their hands with admiration, to think what it was I had killed him with.

The other creature, frighted with the flash of fire and the noise of the gun, swam on shore, and ran up directly to the mountains from whence they came; nor could I, at that distance, know what it was. I found quickly the negroes were for eating the flesh of this creature, so I was willing to have them take it as a favour from me; which, when I made signs to them that they might take him, they were very thankful for. Immediately they fell to work with him; and though they had no knife, yet, with a sharpened piece of wood, they took off his skin as readily, and much more readily, than we could have done with a knife. They offered me some of the flesh, which I declined, making as if I would give it them, but made signs for the skin, which they gave me very freely, and brought me a great deal more of their provision, which, though I did not understand, yet I accepted. Then I made signs to them for some water, and held out one of my jars to them, turning it bottom upward, to show that it was empty, and that I wanted to have it filled. They called immediately to some of their friends, and there came two women, and brought a great vessel made of earth, and burnt, as I suppose, in the sun; this they set down for me, as before, and I sent Xury on shore with my jars, and filled them all three. The women were as stark naked as the men.

I was now furnished with roots and corn, such as it was, and water; and leaving my friendly negroes, I made forward for about eleven days more, without offering to go near the shore, till I saw the land run out a great length into the sea, at about the distance of four or five leagues before me; and the sea being very calm, I kept a large offing, to make this point. At length, doubling the point, at about two leagues from the land, I saw plainly land on the other side, to seaward; then I concluded, as it was most certain indeed, that this was the Cape de Verde, and those the islands, called from thence Cape de Verde Islands. However, they were at a great distance, and I could not tell well what I had best to do; for if I should be taken with a fresh of wind, I might neither reach one or other.

In this dilemma, as I was very pensive, I stepped into the cabin, and sat me down, Xury having the helm; when, on a sudden, the boy cried out, 'Master, master, a ship with a sail!' and the foolish boy was frighted out of his wits, thinking it must needs be some of his master's ships sent to pursue us, when I knew we were gotten far enough out of their reach. I jumped out of the cabin, and immediately saw, not only the ship, but what she was, viz., that it was a Portuguese ship, and, as I thought, was bound to the coast of Guinea, for negroes. But when I observed the course she steered, I was soon convinced they were bound some other way, and did not design to come any nearer to the shore; upon which I stretched out to sea as much as I could, resolving to speak with them, if possible.

With all the sail I could make, I found I should not be able to come in their way, but that they would be gone by before I could make any signal to them; but after I had crowded to the utmost, and began to despair, they, it seems, saw me by the help of their perspective glasses, and that it was some European boat, which, as they supposed, must belong to some ship that was lost, so they shortened sail to let me come up. I was encouraged with this; and as I had my patron's ancient on board, I made a waft of it to them for a signal of distress, and fired a gun, both which they saw; for they told me they saw the smoke, though they did not hear the gun. Upon these signals they very kindly brought to, and lay by for me; and in about three hours' time I came up with them.

They asked me what I was, in Portuguese, and in Spanish, and in French, but I understood none of them; but at last a Scots sailor, who was on board, called to me, and I answered him, and told him I was an Englishman, that I had made my escape out of slavery from the Moors, at Sallee. Then they bade me come on board, and very kindly took me in, and all my goods.

It was an inexpressible joy to me, that any one will believe, that I was thus delivered, as I esteemed it, from such a miserable, and almost hopeless, condition as I was

CRUSOE PICKED UP BY THE PORTUGUESE SHIP.

in; and I immediately offered all I had to the captain of the ship, as a return for my deliverance. But he generously told me he would take nothing from me, but that all I had should be delivered safe to me when I came to the Brazils. 'For,' says he, 'I have saved your life on no other terms than I would be glad to be saved myself; and it may, one time or other, be my lot to be taken up in the same condition. Besides,' says he, 'when I carry you to the Brazils, so great a way from your own country, if I should take from you what you have, you will be starved there, and then I only take away that life I have given. No, no, Seignior Inglese,' says he, 'Mr Englishman, I will carry you thither in charity, and those things will help you to buy your subsistence there, and your passage home again.'

As he was charitable in his proposal, so he was just in the performance to a tittle; for he ordered the seamen that none should offer to touch anything I had; then he took everything into his own possession, and gave me back an exact inventory of them, that I might have them, even so much as my three earthen jars.

As to my boat, it was a very good one, and that he saw, and told me he would buy it of me for the ship's use, and asked me what I would have for it? I told him he had been so generous to me in everything, that I could not offer to make any price of the boat, but left it entirely to him; upon which he told me he would give me a note of his

hand to pay me eighty pieces of eight for it at Brazil, and
when it came there, if any one offered to give more, he
would make it up. He offered me also sixty pieces of
eight more for my boy Xury, which I was loth to take; not
that I was not willing to let the captain have him, but I
was very loth to sell the poor boy's liberty, who had
assisted me so faithfully in procuring my own. However,
when I let him know my reasons, he owned it to be just,
and offered me this medium, that he would give the boy
an obligation to set him free in ten years if he turned
Christian. Upon this, and Xury saying he was willing to go
to him, I let the captain have him.

We had a very good voyage to the Brazils, and arrived in
the Bay de Todos los Santos, or All Saints' Bay, in about
twenty-two days after. And now I was once more delivered from the most miserable of all conditions of life; and
what to do next with myself, I was now to consider.

The generous treatment the captain gave me, I can
never enough remember. He would take nothing of me
for my passage, gave me twenty ducats for the leopard's
skin, and forty for the lion's skin, which I had in my boat,
and caused everything I had in the ship to be punctually
delivered me; and what I was willing to sell he bought,
such as the case of bottles, two of my guns, and a piece of
the lump of beeswax — for I had made candles of the
rest; in a word, I made about 220 pieces of eight of all my
cargo, and with this stock I went on shore in the Brazils.

CHAPTER 5

*Helped by the friendly Portuguese captain Crusoe buys land to
farm. Reflects that after much tribulation and many miles away
he is doing much as his parents wished him to do at home.
He abuses prosperity and in search of cheap labour boards a
slave-ship bound for Africa. Struck by a hurricane and driven
off course the ship is wrecked. All take to the boats and capsize.*

I HAD not long been here, but being recommended to
the house of a good honest man like himself, who had
an *ingenio* as they call it, that is, a plantation and a sugar-
house, I lived with him some time, and acquainted
myself by that means with the manner of their planting
and making of sugar; and seeing how well the planters
lived, and how they grew rich suddenly, I resolved, if I
could get licence to settle there, I would turn planter
among them, resolving in the meantime to find out some
way to get my money which I had left in London remit-
ted to me. To this purpose, getting a kind of a letter of
naturalisation, I purchased as much land that was
uncured as my money would reach, and formed a plan for
my plantation and settlement, and such a one as might be
suitable to the stock which I proposed to myself to
receive from England.

I had a neighbour, a Portuguese of Lisbon, but born of
English parents, whose name was Wells, and in much
such circumstances as I was. I called him my neighbour,

CRUSOE AND THE PLANTERS.

because his plantation lay next to mine, and we went on very sociably together. My stock was but low, as well as his; and we rather planted for food than anything else, for about two years. However, we began to increase, and our land began to come into order; so that the third year we planted some tobacco, and made each of us a large piece of ground ready for planting canes in the year to come. But we both wanted help; and now I found, more than before, I had done wrong in parting with my boy Xury.

But alas! for me to do wrong that never did right was no great wonder. I had no remedy but to go on. I was gotten into an employment quite remote to my genius, and directly contrary to the life I delighted in, and for which I forsook my father's house, and broke through all this good advice; nay, I was coming into the very middle station, or upper degree of low life, which my father advised me to before; and which, if I resolved to go on with, I might as well have stayed at home, and never have fatigued myself in the world as I had done. And I used often to say to myself, I could have done this as well in England among my friends, as have gone 5000 miles off to do it among strangers and savages, in a wilderness, and at such a distance as never to hear from any part of the world that had the least knowledge of me.

I was in some degree settled in my measures for carrying on the plantation before my kind friend, the captain of the ship that took me up at sea, went back; for the ship remained there in providing his loading, and preparing for his voyage, near three months; when, telling him what little stock I had left behind me in London, he gave me this friendly and sincere advice: 'Seignior Inglese,' says he, for so he always called me, 'if you will give me letters, and a procuration here in form to me, with orders to the person who has your money in London to send your effects to Lisbon, to such persons as I shall direct, and in such goods as are proper for this country, I will bring you the produce of them, God willing, at my return. But since human affairs are all subject to changes and disasters, I would have you give orders but for one hundred pound sterling, which, you say, is half your stock, and let the hazard be run for the first; so that if it come safe, you may order the rest the same way; and if it miscarry, you may have the other half to have recourse to for your supply.'

This was so wholesome advice, and looked so friendly, that I could not but be convinced it was the best course I could take; so I accordingly prepared letters to the gentlewoman with whom I had left my money, and a procuration to the Portuguese captain, as he desired.

I wrote the English Captain's widow a full account of all my adventures; my slavery, escape, and how I had met with the Portugal captain at sea, the humanity of his behaviour, and in what condition I was now in, with all other necessary directions for my supply. And when this honest captain came to Lisbon, he found means, by some of the English merchants there, to send over not the order only, but a full account of my story to a merchant at London, who represented it effectually to her; whereupon, she not only delivered the money, but out of her own pocket sent the Portugal captain a very handsome present for his humanity and charity to me.

The merchant in London vesting this hundred pounds in English goods, such as the captain had writ for, sent them directly to him at Lisbon, and he brought them all safe to me to the Brazils; among which, without my direction (for I was too young in my business to think of them), he had taken care to have all sorts of tools, ironwork, and utensils necessary for my plantation, and which were of great use to me.

When this cargo arrived, I thought my fortune made, for I was surprised with joy of it; and my good steward, the captain, had laid out the five pounds, which my friend had sent him for a present for himself, to purchase and bring me over a servant under bond for six years' service, and would not accept of any consideration, except a little tobacco, which I would have him accept, being of my own produce.

Neither was this all; but my goods being all English manufactures, such as cloth, stuffs, baize, and things particularly valuable and desirable in the country, I found means to sell them to a very great advantage; so that I may say I had more than four times the value of my first cargo, and was now infinitely beyond my poor neighbour, I mean in the advancement of my plantation; for the first thing I did, I bought me a negro slave, and an European servant also; I mean another besides that which the captain brought me from Lisbon.

But as abused prosperity is oftentimes made the very means of our greatest adversity, so was it with me. I went on the next year with great success in my plantation. I raised fifty great rolls of tobacco on my own ground, more than I had disposed of for necessaries among my neighbours; and these fifty rolls, being each of above a hundredweight, were well cured, and laid by against the return of the fleet from Lisbon. And now, increasing in business and in wealth, my head began to be full of projects and undertakings beyond my reach, such as are, indeed, often the ruin of the best heads in business.

You may suppose, that having now lived almost four years in the Brazils, and beginning to thrive and prosper very well upon my plantation, I had not only learned the language, but had contracted acquaintance and friendship among my fellow-planters, as well as among the merchants at St Salvador, which was our port, and that in my discourses among them I had frequently given them an account of my two voyages to the coast of Guinea, the manner of trading with the negroes there, and how easy it was to purchase upon the coast for trifles — such as beads, toys, knives, scissors, hatchets, bits of glass, and the like — not only gold-dust, Guinea grains, elephants' teeth, etc., but negroes, for the service of the Brazils, in great numbers.

They listened always very attentively to my discourses on these heads, but especially to that part which related to the buying negroes; which was a trade, at that time, not only not far entered into, but, as far as it was, had been carried on by the *assiento*, or permission, of the Kings of Spain and Portugal, and engrossed in the public, so that few negroes were brought, and those excessive dear.

It happened, being in company with some merchants and planters of my acquaintance, and talking of those things very earnestly, three of them came to me the next morning, and told me they had been musing very much upon what I had discoursed with them of, the last night, and they came to make a secret proposal to me. And after enjoining me secrecy, they told me that they had a mind to fit out a ship to go to Guinea; that they had all plantations as well as I, and were straitened for nothing so much as servants; that as it was a trade that could not be carried on because they could not publicly sell the negroes when they came home, so they desired to make but one voyage, to bring the negroes on shore privately, and divide them among their own plantations; and, in a word, the question was, whether I would go their supercargo in the ship, to manage the trading part upon the coast of Guinea; and they offered me that I should have my equal share of the negroes without providing any part of the stock.

This was a fair proposal, it must be confessed, had it been made to any one that had not a settlement and plantation of his own to look after, which was in a fair way of coming to be very considerable, and with a good stock upon it. But for me, that was thus entered and established, and had nothing to do but go on as I had begun, for three or four years more, and to have sent for the other hundred pounds from England; and who, in that time, and with that little addition, could scarce have failed of being worth three or four thousand pounds sterling, and that increasing too — for me to think of such a voyage, was the most preposterous thing that ever man, in such circumstances, could be guilty of.

But I, that was born to be my own destroyer, could no more resist the offer than I could restrain my first rambling designs, when my father's good counsel was lost upon me. In a word, I told them I would go with all my heart, if they would undertake to look after my plantation in my absence, and would dispose of it to such as I should direct if I miscarried. This they all engaged to do, and entered into writings or covenants to do so; and I made a formal will, disposing of my plantation and effects, in case of my death; making the captain of the ship that had saved my life, as before, my universal heir, but obliging him to dispose of my effects as I had directed in my will; one-half of the produce being to himself, and the other to be shipped to England.

In short, I took all possible caution to preserve my effects, and keep up my plantation. Had I used half as much prudence to have looked into my own interest, and have made a judgment of what I ought to have done and not to have done, I had certainly never gone away from so prosperous an undertaking, leaving all the probable views of a thriving circumstance, and gone upon a voyage to sea, attended with all its common hazards, to say nothing of the reasons I had to expect particular misfortunes to myself.

But I was hurried on, and obeyed blindly the dictates of my fancy rather than my reason. And accordingly, the ship being fitted out, and the cargo furnished, and all things done as by agreement by my partners in the voyage, I went on board in an evil hour, the [first] of [September 1659], being the same day eight year that I went from my father and mother at Hull, in order to act the rebel to their authority, and the fool to my own interest.

Our ship was about 120 tons burthen, carried six guns and fourteen men, besides the master, his boy, and myself. We had on board no large cargo of goods, except of such toys as were fit for our trade with the negroes — such as beads, bits of glass, shells, and odd trifles, especially little looking-glasses, knives, scissors, hatchets, and the like.

The same day I went on board we set sail, standing away to the northward upon our own coast, with design to stretch over for the African coast, when they came about 10 or 12 degrees of northern latitude, which, it seems, was the manner of their course in those days. We had very good weather, only excessive hot, all the way upon our own coast, till we came the height of Cape St Augustino, from whence, keeping farther off at sea, we lost sight of land, and steered as if we were bound for the Isle Fernando de Noronha, holding our course N.E. by N., and leaving those isles on the east. In this course we passed the line in about twelve days' time, and were, by our last observation, in 7 degrees 22 minutes northern latitude, when a violent tornado, or hurricane, took us quite out of our knowledge. It began from the south-east, came about to the north-west, and then settled into the north-east, from whence it blew in such a terrible manner, that for twelve days together we could do nothing but drive, and, scudding away before it, let it carry us wherever fate and the fury of the winds directed; and during these twelve days, I need not say that I expected every day to be swallowed up, nor, indeed, did any in the ship expect to save their lives.

In this distress we had, besides the terror of the storm, one of our men died of the calenture, and one man and the boy washed overboard. About the twelfth day, the weather abating a little, the master made an observation as well as he could, and found that he was in about 11 degrees north latitude, but that he was 22 degrees of longitude difference west from Cape St Augustino; so that he found he was gotten upon the coast of Guiana, or the north part of Brazil, beyond the river Amazon, toward that of the river Orinoco, commonly called the Great River, and began to consult with me what course he should take, for the ship was leaky and very much disabled, and he was going directly back to the coast of Brazil.

I was positively against that; and looking over the charts of the sea-coast of America with him, we concluded there was no inhabited country for us to have recourse to till we came within the circle of the Carribbee Islands, and therefore resolved to stand away for Barbadoes, which by keeping off at sea, to avoid the indraft of the Bay or Gulf of Mexico, we might easily perform, as we hoped, in about fifteen days' sail; whereas we could not possibly make our voyage to the coast of Africa without some assistance, both to our ship and to ourselves.

With this design we changed our course, and steered away N.W. by W. in order to reach some of our English islands, where I hoped for relief; but our voyage was otherwise determined; for being in the latitude of 12 degrees 18 minutes, a second storm came upon us, which carried us away with the same impetuosity westward, and drove us so out of the very way of all human commerce, that had all our lives been saved, as to the sea, we were rather in danger of being devoured by savages than ever returning to our own country.

In this distress, the wind still blowing very hard, one of our men early in the morning cried out, 'Land!' and we had no sooner ran out of the cabin to look out, in hopes of seeing whereabouts in the world we were, but the ship struck upon a sand, and in a moment, her motion being so stopped, the sea broke over her in a manner, that we expected we should all have perished immediately; and we were immediately driven into our close quarters, to shelter us from the very foam and spray of the sea.

It is not easy for any one, who has not been in the like condition, to describe or conceive the consternation of men in such circumstances. We knew nothing where we were, or upon what land it was we were driven, whether an island or the main, whether inhabited or not inhabited; and as the rage of the wind was still great, though rather less than at first, we could not so much as hope to have the ship hold many minutes without breaking in pieces, unless the winds by a kind of miracle, should turn immediately about. In a word, we sat looking one upon another, and expecting death every moment, and every man acting accordingly, as preparing for another world; for there was little or nothing more for us to do in this. That which was our present comfort, and all the comfort we had, was that, contrary to our expectation, the ship did not break yet, and that the master said the wind began to abate.

Now, though we thought that the wind did a little abate, yet the ship having thus struck upon the sand, and sticking too fast for us to expect her getting off, we were in a dreadful condition indeed, and had nothing to do but to think of saving our lives as well as we could. We had a boat at our stern just before the storm, but she was first staved by dashing against the ship's rudder, and in the next place, she broke away, and either sunk, or was driven

THE SHIPWRECK

off to sea, so there was no hope from her; we had another
boat on board, but how to get her off into the sea was a
doubtful thing. However, there was no room to debate,
for we fancied the ship would break in pieces every
minute, and some told us she was actually broken already.

In this distress, the mate of our vessel lays hold of the
boat, and with the help of the rest of the men they got
her slung over the ship's side; and getting all into her, let
go, and committed ourselves, being eleven in number, to
God's mercy, and the wild sea; for though the storm was
abated considerably, yet the sea went dreadful high upon
the shore, and might well be called *den wild zee*, as the
Dutch call the sea in a storm.

And now our case was very dismal indeed, for we all
saw plainly that the sea went so high, that the boat could
not live, and that we should be inevitably drowned. As to
making sail, we had none; nor, if we had, could we have
done anything with it; so we worked at the oar towards
the land, though with heavy hearts, like men going to
execution, for we all knew that when the boat came
nearer the shore, she would be dashed in a thousand
pieces by the breach of the sea. However, we committed
our souls to God in the most earnest manner; and the
wind driving us towards the shore, we hastened our
destruction with our own hands, pulling as well as we
could towards land.

What the shore was, whether rock or sand, whether

steep or shoal, we knew not; the only hope that could rationally give us the least shadow of expectation was, if we might happen into some bay or gulf, or the mouth of some river, where by great chance we might have run our boat in, or got under the lee of the land, and perhaps made smooth water. But there was nothing of this appeared; but as we made nearer and nearer the shore, the land looked more frightful than the sea.

After we had rowed, or rather driven, about a league and a half, as we reckoned it, a raging wave, mountainlike, came rolling astern of us, and plainly bade us expect the *coup de grâce*. In a word, it took us with such a fury, that it overset the boat at once; and separating us, as well from the boat as from one another, gave us not time hardly to say, 'O God!' for we were all swallowed up in a moment.

CHAPTER 6

Crusoe thrown by monstrous waves towards land, battles against undertow and climbs exhausted to safety. At nightfall seeks refuge in a tree. Next day he salvages clothes, provisions, tools and firearms from the wreck.

NOTHING CAN describe the confusion of thought which I felt when I sunk into the water; for though I swam very well, yet I could not deliver myself from the waves so as to draw breath, till that wave having driven me, or rather carried me, a vast way on towards the shore, and having spent itself, went back, and left me upon the land almost dry, but half dead with the water I took in. I had so much presence of mind, as well as breath left, that seeing myself nearer the mainland than I expected, I got upon my feet, and endeavoured to make on towards the land as fast as I could, before another wave should return and take me up again. But I soon found it was impossible to avoid it; for I saw the sea come after me as high as a great hill, and as furious as an enemy, which I had no means or strength to contend with. My business was to hold my breath, and raise myself upon the water, if I could; and so, by swimming, to preserve my breathing, and pilot myself towards the shore, if possible; my greatest concern now being, that the sea, as it would carry me a great way towards the shore when it came on, might not carry me back again with it when it gave back towards the sea.

The wave that came upon me again, buried me at once 20 or 30 feet deep in its own body, and I could feel myself carried with a mighty force and swiftness towards the shore a very great way; but I held my breath, and assisted myself to swim still forward with all my might. I was ready to burst with holding my breath, when, as I felt myself rising up, so, to my immediate relief, I found my head and hands shoot out above the surface of the water; and though it was not two seconds of time that I could keep myself so, yet it relieved me greatly, gave me breath and new courage. I was covered again with water a good while, but not so long but I held it out; and finding the water had spent itself, and began to return, I struck forward against the return of the waves, and felt ground again with my feet. I stood still a few moments to recover breath, and till the water went from me, and then took to my heels and ran with what strength I had farther towards the shore. But neither would this deliver me from the fury of the sea, which came pouring in after me again, and twice more I was lifted up by the waves and carried forwards as before, the shore being very flat.

The last time of these two had well near been fatal to me; for the sea, having hurried me along as before, landed me, or rather dashed me, against a piece of rock, and that with such force, as it left me senseless, and indeed helpless, as to my own deliverance; for the blow taking my side and breast, beat the breath as it were quite out of my body; and had it returned again immediately, I must have been strangled in the water. But I recovered a little before the return of the waves, and seeing I should be covered again with the water, I resolved to hold fast by a piece of the rock, and so to hold my breath, if possible, till the wave went back. Now as the waves were not so high as at first, being near land, I held my hold till the wave abated, and then fetched another run, which brought me so near the shore, that the next wave, though it went over me, yet did not so swallow me up as to carry me away, and the next run I took I got to the mainland, where, to my great comfort, I clambered up the cliffs of the shore, and sat me down upon the grass, free from danger, and quite out of the reach of the water.

I was now landed, and safe on shore, and began to look up and thank God that my life was saved in a case wherein there was some minutes before scarce any room to hope. I believe it is impossible to express to the life what the ecstasies and transports of the soul are when it is so saved, as I may say, out of the very grave.

For sudden joys, like griefs, confound at first.

I walked about on the shore, lifting up my hands, and my whole being, as I may say, wrapt up in the contemplation of my deliverance, making a thousand gestures and motions which I cannot describe, reflecting upon all my comrades that were drowned, and that there should not be one soul saved but myself; for, as for them, I never saw them afterwards, or any sign of them, except three of their hats, one cap, and two shoes that were not fellows.

I cast my eyes to the stranded vessel, when the breach and froth of the sea being so big, I could hardly see it, it lay so far off, and considered, Lord! how was it possible I could get on shore?

After I had solaced my mind with the comfortable part of my condition, I began to look round me to see what kind of place I was in, and what was next to be done, and I soon found my comforts abate, and that, in a word, I had a dreadful deliverance; for I was wet, had no clothes to shift me, nor anything either to eat or drink to comfort me, neither did I see any prospect before me but that of perishing with hunger, or being devoured by wild beasts; and that which was particularly afflicting to me was, that I had no weapon either to hunt and kill any creature for my sustenance, or to defend myself against any other creature that might desire to kill me for theirs. In a word, I had nothing about me but a knife, a tobacco-pipe, and a little tobacco in a box. This was all my provision; and this threw me into terrible agonies of mind, that for a while I ran about like a madman. Night coming upon me, I began, with a heavy heart, to consider what would be my lot if there were any ravenous beasts in that country, seeing at night they always come abroad for their prey.

All the remedy that offered to my thoughts at that time was, to get up into a thick bushy tree like a fir, but thorny, which grew near me, and where I resolved to sit all night, and consider the next day what death I should die, for as yet I saw no prospect of life. I walked about a furlong from the shore, to see if I could find any fresh water to drink, which I did, to my great joy; and having drank, and put a little tobacco in my mouth to prevent hunger, I went to the tree, and getting up into it, endeavoured to place myself so, as that if I should sleep I might not fall; and having cut me a short stick, like a truncheon, for my defence, I took up my lodging, and having been excessively fatigued, I fell fast asleep, and slept as comfortably as, I believe, few could have done in my condition, and found myself the most refreshed with it that I think I ever was on such an occasion.

When I waked it was broad day, the weather clear, and the storm abated, so that the sea did not rage and swell as before. But that which surprised me most was, that the ship was lifted off in the night from the sand where she lay, by the swelling of the tide, and was driven up almost as far as the rock which I first mentioned, where I had been so bruised by the dashing me against it. This being within about a mile from the shore where I was, and the ship seeming to stand upright still, I wished myself on board, that, at least, I might have some necessary things for my use.

When I came down from my apartment in the tree I looked about me again, and the first thing I found was the boat, which lay as the wind and the sea had tossed her up upon the land, about two miles on my right hand. I walked as far as I could upon the shore to have got to her, but found a neck or inlet of water between me and the boat, which was about half a mile broad; so I came back for the present, being more intent upon getting at the ship, where I hoped to find something for my present subsistence.

A little after noon I found the sea very calm, and the tide ebbed so far out, that I could come within a quarter of a mile of the ship; and here I found a fresh renewing of my grief, for I saw evidently, that if we had kept on board we had been all safe, that is to say, we had all got safe on shore, and I had not been so miserable as to be left entirely destitute of all comfort and company, as I now was. This forced tears from my eyes again; but as there was little relief in that, I resolved, if possible, to get to the ship; so I pulled off my clothes, for the weather was hot to extremity, and took the water. But when I came to the ship, my difficulty was still greater to know how to get on board; for as she lay aground, and high out of the water, there was nothing within my reach to lay hold of. I swam round her twice, and the second time I spied a small piece of a rope, which I wondered I did not see at first, hang down by the forechains so low, as that with

great difficulty I got hold of it, and by the help of that
rope got up into the forecastle of the ship. Here I found
that the ship was bulged, and had a great deal of water in
her hold, but that she lay so on the side of a bank of hard
sand, or rather earth, that her stern lay lifted up upon the
bank, and her head low almost to the water. By this means
all her quarter was free, and all that was in that part was
dry; for you may be sure my first work was to search and to
see what was spoiled and what was free. And first I found
that all the ship's provisions were dry and untouched by
the water; and being very well disposed to eat, I went to
the bread-room and filled my pockets with biscuit, and
eat it as I went about other things, for I had no time to
lose. I also found some rum in the great cabin, of which I
took a large dram, and which I had indeed need enough of
to spirit me for what was before me. Now I wanted nothing but a boat, to furnish myself with many things which I
foresaw would be very necessary to me.

It was in vain to sit still and wish for what was not to be
had, and this extremity roused my application. We had several spare yards, and two or three large spars of wood, and a
spare top-mast or two in the ship. I resolved to fall to work
with these, and flung as many of them overboard as I could
manage for their weight, tying every one with a rope, that
they might not drive away. When this was done I went
down the ship's side, and, pulling them to me, I tied four
of them fast together at both ends as well as I could, in the

form of a raft; and laying two or three short pieces of plank upon them cross-ways, I found I could walk upon it very well, but that it was not able to bear any great weight, the pieces being too light. So I went to work, and with the carpenter's saw I cut a spare top-mast into three lengths, and added them to my raft, with a great deal of labour and pains; but hope of furnishing myself with necessaries encouraged me to go beyond what I should have been able to have done upon another occasion.

My raft was now strong enough to bear any reasonable weight. My next care was what to load it with, and how to preserve what I laid upon it from the surf of the sea; but I was not long considering this. I first laid all the planks or boards upon it that I could get, and having considered well what I most wanted, I first got three of the seamen's chests, which I had broken open and emptied, and lowered them down upon my raft. The first of these I filled with provisions, viz., bread, rice, three Dutch cheeses, five pieces of dried goat's flesh, which we lived much upon, and a little remainder of European corn, which had been laid by for some fowls which we brought to sea with us, but the fowls were killed. There had been some barley and wheat together, but, to my great disappointment, I found afterwards that the rats had eaten or spoiled it all. As for liquors, I found several cases of bottles belonging to our skipper, in which were some cordial waters, and, in all, about five or six gallons of rack. These I stowed by

CRUSOE LOADING HIS RAFT.

themselves, there being no need to put them into the chest, nor no room for them. While I was doing this, I found the tide began to flow, though very calm, and I had the mortification to see my coat, shirt, and waistcoat, which I had left on shore upon the sand, swim away; as for my breeches, which were only linen, and open-kneed, I swam on board in them, and my stockings. However, this put me upon rummaging for clothes, of which I found enough, but took no more than I wanted for present use; for I had other things which my eye was more upon, as first tools to work with on shore; and it was after long searching that I found out the carpenter's chest, which was indeed a very useful prize to me, and much more valuable than a ship-loading of gold would have been at that time. I got it down to my raft, even whole as it was, without losing time to look into it, for I knew in general what it contained.

My next care was for some ammunition and arms; there were two very good fowling-pieces in the great cabin, and two pistols; these I secured first, with some powder-horns, and a small bag of shot, and two old rusty swords. I knew there were three barrels of powder in the ship, but knew not where our gunner had stowed them; but with much search I found them, two of them dry and good, the third had taken water; those two I got to my raft with the arms. And now I thought myself pretty well freighted, and began to think how I should get to shore with them, having neither sail, oar, or rudder; and the least capful of wind would have overset all my navigation.

I had three encouragements. 1. A smooth, calm sea. 2. The tide rising and setting in to the shore. 3. What little wind there was blew me towards the land. And thus, having found two or three broken oars belonging to the boat, and besides the tools which were in the chest, I found two saws, an axe, and a hammer, and with this cargo I put to sea. For a mile or thereabouts my raft went very well, only that I found it drive a little distant from the place where I had landed before, by which I perceived that there was some indraft of the water, and consequently I hoped to find some creek or river there, which I might make use of as a port to get to land with my cargo.

As I imagined, so it was; there appeared before me a little opening of the land, and I found a strong current of the tide set into it, so I guided my raft as well as I could to keep in the middle of the stream. But here I had like to have suffered a second shipwreck, which, if I had, I think verily would have broke my heart; for knowing nothing of the coast, my raft ran aground at one end of it upon a shoal, and not being aground at the other end, it wanted but a little that all my cargo had slipped off towards that end that was afloat, and so fallen into the water. I did my utmost by setting my back against the chests to keep them in their places, but could not thrust off the raft with all my strength, neither durst I stir from the posture I was in, but holding up the chests with all my might, stood in that manner near half an hour, in which time the rising of the water brought me a little more upon a level; and a little after, the water still rising, my raft floated again, and I thrust her off with the oar I had into the channel, and then driving up higher, I at length found myself in the mouth of a little river, with land on both sides, and a strong current or tide running up. I looked on both sides for a proper place to get to shore, for I was not willing to be driven too high up the river, hoping in time to see some ship at sea, and therefore resolved to place myself as near the coast as I could.

At length I spied a little cove on the right shore of the creek, to which, with great pain and difficulty, I guided my raft, and at last got so near, as that, reaching ground with my oar, I could thrust her directly in; but here I had like to have dipped all my cargo in the sea again; for that shore lying pretty steep, that is to say, sloping, there was no place to land but where one end of my float, if it run on shore, would lie so high and the other sink lower, as before, that it would endanger my cargo again. All that I could do was to wait till the tide was at the highest, keeping the raft with my oar like an anchor to hold the side of it fast to the shore, near a flat piece of ground, which I expected the water would flow over; and so it did. As soon as I found water enough, for my raft drew about a foot of water, I thrust her on upon that flat piece of ground, and there fastened or moored her by sticking my two broken oars into the ground; one on one side near one end, and one on the other side near the other end; and thus I lay till the water ebbed away, and left my raft and all my cargo safe on shore.

CHAPTER 7

*Crusoe surveys his surroundings from a hill-top. He is alone on
a desolate and uninhabited island. He contrives a tent for shelter,
and labours for many days to take from the wreck stores and
movable gear. A storm removes all traces of the ship. Crusoe
moves his tent to a flat green plain against a rising hill. He shoots
a wild goat.*

MY NEXT work was to view the country and seek a
proper place for my habitation, and where to stow
my goods to secure them from whatever might happen.
Where I was, I yet knew not; whether on the continent,
or on an island; whether inhabited, or not inhabited;
whether in danger of wild beasts, or not. There was a hill,
not above a mile from me, which rose up very steep and
high, and which seemed to overtop some other hills,
which lay as in a ridge from it, northward. I took out one
of the fowling-pieces and one of the pistols, and a horn of
powder; and thus armed, I travelled for discovery up to
the top of that hill, where, after I had with great labour
and difficulty got to the top, I saw my fate to my great
affliction, viz., that I was in an island environed every way
with the sea, no land to be seen, except some rocks which
lay a great way off, and two small islands less than this,
which lay about three leagues to the west.

I found also that the island I was in was barren, and, as

I saw good reason to believe, uninhabited, except by wild beasts, of whom, however, I saw none; yet I saw abundance of fowls, but knew not their kinds; neither when I killed them, could I tell what was fit for food, and what not. At my coming back, I shot at a great bird which I saw sitting upon a tree on the side of a great wood. I believe it was the first gun that had been fired there since the creation of the world. I had no sooner fired, but from all the parts of the wood there arose an innumerable number of fowls of many sorts, making a confused screaming, and crying every one according to his usual note; but not one of them of any kind that I knew. As for the creature I killed, I took it to be a kind of hawk, its colour and beak resembling it, but had no talons or claws more than common; its flesh was carrion, and fit for nothing.

Contented with this discovery, I came back to my raft, and fell to work to bring my cargo on shore, which took me up the rest of that day; and what to do with myself at night, I knew not, nor indeed where to rest; for I was afraid to lie down on the ground, not knowing but some wild beast might devour me, though, as I afterwards found, there was really no need for those fears. However, as well as I could, I barricaded myself round with the chests and boards that I had brought on shore, and made a kind of hut for that night's lodging; as for food, I yet saw not which way to supply myself, except that I had seen two or three creatures like hares run out of the wood where I shot the fowl.

I now began to consider, that I might yet get a great many things out of the ship, which would be useful to me, and particularly some of the rigging and sails, and such other things as might come to land; and I resolved to make another voyage on board the vessel, if possible. And as I knew that the first storm that blew must necessarily break her all in pieces, I resolved to set all other things apart till I got everything out of the ship that I could get. Then I called a council, that is to say, in my thoughts, whether I should take back the raft, but this appeared impracticable; so I resolved to go as before, when the tide was down; and I did so, only that I stripped before I went from my hut, having nothing on but a chequered shirt and a pair of linen drawers, and a pair of pumps on my feet.

I got on board the ship as before, and prepared a second raft, and having had experience of the first, I neither made this so unwieldy, nor loaded it so hard; but yet I brought away several things very useful to me; as, first, in the carpenter's stores I found two or three bags full of nails and spikes, a great screw-jack, a dozen or two of hatchets, and above all, that most useful thing called a grindstone. All these I secured, together with several things belonging to the gunner, particularly two or three iron crows, and two barrels of musket bullets, seven muskets, and another fowling-piece, with some small quantity of powder more; a large bag full of small-shot, and a great roll of sheet lead; but this last was so heavy, I could not hoist it up to get it over the ship's side. Besides these things, I took all the men's clothes that I could find, and a spare fore-top sail, a hammock, and some bedding; and with this I loaded my second raft, and brought them all safe on shore, to my very great comfort.

I was under some apprehensions during my absence from the land, that at least my provisions might be devoured on shore; but when I came back, I found no sign of any visitor, only there sat a creature like a wild cat upon one of the chests, which, when I came towards it, ran away a little distance, and then stood still. She sat very composed and unconcerned, and looked full in my face, as if she had a mind to be acquainted with me. I pre-sented my gun at her; but as she did not understand it, she was perfectly unconcerned at it, nor did she offer to stir away; upon which I tossed her a bit of biscuit, though, by the way, I was not very free of it, for my store was not great. However, I spared her a bit, I say, and she went to it, smelled of it, and ate it, and looked (as pleased) for more; but I thanked her, and could spare no more, so she marched off.

Having got my second cargo on shore, though I was fain to open the barrels of powder and bring them by parcels, for they were too heavy, being large casks, I went to work to make me a little tent with the sail and some poles which I cut for that purpose; and into this tent I brought everything that I knew would spoil either with rain or sun; and I piled all the empty chests and casks up in a circle round the tent, to fortify it from any sudden attempt, either from man or beast.

When I had done this I blocked up the door of the tent with some boards within, and an empty chest set up on end without; and spreading one of the beds upon the ground, laying my two pistols just at my head, and my gun at length by me, I went to bed for the first time, and slept very quietly all night, for I was very weary and heavy; for the night before I had slept little, and had laboured very hard all day, as well to fetch all those things from the ship, as to get them on shore.

I had the biggest magazine of all kinds now that ever was laid up, I believe, for one man; but I was not satisfied still, for while the ship sat upright in that posture, I thought I ought to get everything out of her that I could. So every day at low water I went on board, and brought away something or other; but, particularly the third time I went I brought away as much of the rigging as I could, as also all the small ropes and rope-twine I could get, with a piece of spare canvas, which was to mend the sails upon occasion, the barrel of wet gunpowder; in a word, I brought away all the sails first and last, only that I was fain to cut them in pieces, and bring as much at a time as I could; for they were no more useful to be sails, but as mere canvas only.

But that which comforted me more still was, that at

A LITTLE TENT

CRUSOE MAKES

WITH A SAIL

last of all, after I had made five or six such voyages as these, and thought I had nothing more to expect from the ship that was worth my meddling with; I say, after all this, I found a great hogshead of bread, and three large runlets of rum or spirits, and a box of sugar, and a barrel of fine flour; this was surprising to me, because I had given over expecting any more provisions, except what was spoilt by the water. I soon emptied the hogshead of that bread, and wrapped it up parcel by parcel in pieces of the sails, which I cut out; and, in a word, I got all this safe on shore also.

The next day I made another voyage. And now, having plundered the ship of what was portable and fit to hand out, I began with the cables; and cutting the great cable into pieces, such as I could move, I got two cables and a hawser on shore, with all the ironwork I could get; and having cut down the spirit-sail-yard, and the mizzen-yard, and everything I could to make a large raft, I loaded it with all those heavy goods, and came away. But my good luck began now to leave me; for this raft was so unwieldy, and so overladen, that after I was entered the little cove where I had landed the rest of my goods, not being able to guide it so handily as I did the other, it overset, and threw me and all my cargo into the water. As for myself, it was no great harm, for I was near the shore; but as to my cargo, it was great part of it lost, especially the iron, which I expected would have been of great use to me. However,

when the tide was out I got most of the pieces of cable
ashore, and some of the iron, though with infinite labour;
for I was fain to dip for it into the water, a work which
fatigued me very much. After this I went every day on
board, and brought away what I could get.

I had been now thirteen days on shore, and had been
eleven times on board the ship; in which time I had
brought away all that one pair of hands could well be supposed capable to bring, though I believe verily, had the
calm weather held, I should have brought away the whole
ship piece by piece. But preparing the twelfth time to go
on board, I found the wind begin to rise. However, at low
water I went on board, and though I thought I had rum-
maged the cabin so effectually as that nothing more could
be found, yet I discovered a locker with drawers in it, in
one of which I found two or three razors, and one pair of
large scissors, with some ten or a dozen of good knives
and forks; in another, I found about thirty-six pounds
value in money, some European coin, some Brazil, some
pieces of eight, some gold, some silver.

I smiled to myself at the sight of this money. 'O drug!'
said I aloud, 'what art thou good for? Thou art not worth
to me, no, not the taking off of the ground; one of those
knives is worth all this heap. I have no manner of use for
thee; even remain where thou art, and go to the bottom
as a creature whose life is not worth saving.' However,
upon second thoughts, I took it away; and wrapping all

this in a piece of canvas, I began to think of making another raft; but while I was preparing this, I found the sky overcast, and the wind began to rise, and in a quarter of an hour it blew a fresh gale from the shore. It presently occurred to me that it was in vain to pretend to make a raft with the wind off shore, and that it was my business to be gone before the tide of flood began, otherwise I might not be able to reach the shore at all. Accordingly I let myself down into the water, and swam across the channel, which lay between the ship and the sands, and even that with difficulty enough, partly with the weight of the things I had about me, and partly the roughness of the water; for the wind rose very hastily, and before it was quite high water it blew a storm.

But I was gotten home to my little tent, where I lay with all my wealth about me very secure. It blew very hard all that night, and in the morning, when I looked out, behold, no more ship was to be seen. I was a little surprised, but recovered myself with this satisfactory reflection, viz., that I had lost no time, nor abated no diligence, to get everything out of her that could be useful to me, and that indeed there was little left in her that I was able to bring away if I had had more time.

I now gave over any more thoughts of the ship, or of anything out of her, except what might drive on shore from her wreck, as indeed divers pieces of her afterwards did; but those things were of small use to me.

My thoughts were now wholly employed about securing myself against either savages, if any should appear, or wild beasts, if any were in the island; and I had many thoughts of the method how to do this, and what kind of dwelling to make, whether I should make me a cave in the earth, or a tent upon the earth; and, in short, I resolved upon both, the manner and description of which it may not be improper to give an account of.

I soon found the place I was in was not for my settlement, particularly because it was upon a low moorish ground near the sea, and I believed would not be wholesome; and more particularly because there was no fresh water near it. So I resolved to find a more healthy and more convenient spot of ground.

I consulted several things in my situation, which I found would be proper for me. First, health and fresh water, I just now mentioned. Secondly, shelter from the heat of the sun. Thirdly, security from ravenous creatures, whether men or beasts. Fourthly, a view to the sea, that if God sent any ship in sight I might not lose any advantage for my deliverance, of which I was not willing to banish all my expectation yet.

In search of a place proper for this, I found a little plain on the side of a rising hill, whose front towards this little plain was steep as a houseside, so that nothing could come down upon me from the top; on the side of this rock there was a hollow place, worn a little way in, like the entrance or door of a cave; but there was not really any cave, or way into the rock at all.

On the flat of the green, just before this hollow place, I resolved to pitch my tent. This plain was not above an hundred yards broad, and about twice as long, and lay like a green before my door, and at the end of it descended irregularly every way down into the low grounds by the seaside. It was on the N.N.W. side of the hill, so that I was sheltered from the heat every day, till it came to a W. and by S. sun, or thereabouts, which in those countries is near the setting.

Before I set up my tent, I drew a half-circle before the hollow place, which took in about ten yards in its semi-diameter from the rock, and twenty yards in its diameter from its beginning and ending. In this half-circle I pitched two rows of strong stakes, driving them into the ground till they stood very firm like piles, the biggest end being out of the ground about five feet and a half, and sharpened on the top. The two rows did not stand above six inches from one another.

Then I took the pieces of cable which I had cut in the ship, and laid them in rows one upon another, within the circle, between these two rows of stakes, up to the top, placing other stakes in the inside leaning against them, about two feet and a half high, like a spur to a post; and this fence was so strong, that neither man or beast could get into it, or over it. This cost me a great deal of time and labour, especially to cut the piles in the woods, bring them to the place, and drive them into the earth.

The entrance into this place I made to be not by a door, but by a short ladder to go over the top; which ladder, when I was in, I lifted over after me, and so I was completely fenced in, and fortified, as I thought, from all the world, and consequently slept secure in the night, which otherwise I could not have done; though as it appeared afterwards, there was no need of all this caution from the enemies that I apprehended danger from.

Into this fence or fortress, with infinite labour, I carried all my riches, all my provisions, ammunition, and stores, of which you have the account above; and I made me a large tent, which, to preserve me from the rains that in one part of the year are very violent there, I made double, viz., one smaller tent within, and one larger tent above it, and covered the uppermost with a large tarpaulin, which I had saved among the sails. And now I lay no more for a while in the bed which I had brought on shore, but in a hammock, which was indeed a very good one, and belonged to the mate of the ship.

Into this tent I brought all my provisions, and everything that would spoil by the wet; and having thus enclosed all my goods, I made up the entrance, which, till now, I had left open, and so passed and repassed, as I said, by a short ladder.

When I had done this, I began to work my way into the

rock; and bringing all the earth and stones that I dug down out through my tent, I laid them up within my fence in the nature of a terrace, so that it raised the ground within about a foot and a half; and thus I made me a cave just behind my tent, which served me like a cellar to my house.

It cost me much labour, and many days, before all these things were brought to perfection, and therefore I must go back to some other things which took up some of my thoughts. At the same time it happened, after I had laid my scheme for the setting up of my tent, and making the cave, that a storm of rain falling from a thick dark cloud, a sudden flash of lightning happened, and after that a great clap of thunder, as is naturally the effect of it. I was not so much surprised with the lightning, as I was with a thought which darted into my mind as swift as the lightning itself. O my powder! My very heart sunk within me when I thought, that at one blast all my powder might be destroyed, on which, not my defence only, but the providing me food, as I thought, entirely depended. I was nothing near so anxious about my own danger; though had the powder took fire, I had never known who had hurt me.

Such impression did this make upon me, that after the storm was over I laid aside all my works, my building, and fortifying, and applied myself to make bags and boxes to separate the powder, and keep it a little and a little in a parcel, in hope that whatever might come it might not all take fire at once, and to keep it so apart, that it should not be possible to make one part fire another. I finished this work in about a fortnight; and I think my powder, which in all was about 240 pounds weight, was divided in not less than a hundred parcels. As to the barrel that had been wet, I did not apprehend any danger from that, so I placed it in my new cave, which in my fancy I called my kitchen, and the rest I hid up and down in holes among the rocks, so that no wet might come to it, marking very carefully where I laid it.

In the interval of time while this was doing, I went out once, at least, every day with my gun, as well to divert myself, as to see if I could kill anything fit for food, and as near as I could to acquaint myself with what the island produced. The first time I went out, I presently discovered that there were goats in the island, which was a great satisfaction to me; but then it was attended with this misfortune to me, viz., that they were so shy, so subtle, and so swift of foot, that it was the difficultest thing in the world to come at them. But I was not discouraged at this, not doubting but I might now and then shoot one, as it soon happened; for after I had found their haunts a little, I laid wait in this manner for them. I observed if they saw me in the valleys, though they were upon the rocks, they would run away as in a terrible fright; but if they were feeding in the valleys, and I was upon the

rocks, they took no notice of me, from whence I concluded that, by the position of their optics, their sight
was so directed downward, that they did not readily see
objects that were above them. So afterward I took this
method; I always climbed the rocks first to get above
them, and then had frequently a fair mark. The first shot
I made among these creatures I killed a she-goat, which
had a little kid by her, which she gave suck to, which
grieved me heartily; but when the old one fell, the kid
stood stock still by her till I came and took her up; and
not only so, but when I carried the old one with me upon
my shoulders, the kid followed me quite to my enclosure;
upon which I laid down the dam, and took the kid in my
arms, and carried it over my pale, in hopes to have bred it
up tame; but it would not eat, so I was forced to kill it,
and eat it myself. These two supplied me with flesh a
great while, for I eat sparingly, and saved my provisions,
my bread especially, as much as possibly I could.

Having now fixed my habitation, I found it absolutely
necessary to provide a place to make a fire in, and fuel to
burn; and what I did for that, as also how I enlarged my
cave, and what conveniences I made, I shall give a full
account of in its place. But I must first give some little
account of myself, and of my thoughts about living, which
it may well be supposed were not a few.

CHAPTER 8

Crusoe makes plans for survival. He erects a wooden cross and carves upon it the date he was cast away. He intends by daily notches to keep track of time. In an effort to overcome despondency sets down the comforts he enjoys against the miseries he has endured. He decides to keep a journal.

I HAD a dismal prospect of my condition; for as I was not cast away upon that island without being driven, as is said, by a violent storm, quite out of the course of our intended voyage, and a great way, viz., some hundreds of leagues out of the ordinary course of the trade of mankind, I had great reason to consider it as a determination of Heaven, that in this desolate place, and in this desolate manner, I should end my life. One day, walking with my gun in my hand by the seaside, I was very pensive upon the subject of my present condition, when Reason, as it were, expostulated with me t'other way, thus: 'Well, you are in a desolate condition it is true, but pray remember, where are the rest of you? Did you not come eleven of you into the boat? Where are the ten? Why were not they saved, and you lost? Why were you singled out? Is it better to be here, or there?' And then I pointed to the sea. All evils are to be considered with the good that is in them, and with what worse attends them.

Then it occurred to me again, how well I was furnished

for my subsistence, and what would have been my case if it had not happened, which was an hundred thousand to one, that the ship floated from the place where she first struck and was driven so near to the shore that I had time to get all these things out of her; what would have been my case, if I had been to have lived in the condition in which I at first came on shore, without necessaries of life, or necessaries to supply and procure them? 'Particularly,' said I aloud (though to myself), 'what should I have done without a gun, without ammunition, without any tools to make anything or to work with, without clothes, bedding, a tent, or any manner of covering?' and that now I had all these to a sufficient quantity, and was in a fair way to provide myself in such a manner, as to live without my gun when my ammunition was spent; so that I had a tolerable view of subsisting without any want as long as I lived. For I considered from the beginning how I would provide for the accidents that might happen, and for the time that was to come, even not only after my ammunition should be spent, but even after my health or strength should decay.

And now being to enter into a melancholy relation of a scene of silent life, such, perhaps, as was never heard of in the world before, I shall take it from its beginning, and continue it in its order. It was, by my account, the 30th of September when, in the manner as above said, I first set foot upon this horrid island, when the sun being to us in its autumnal equinox, was almost just over my head, for I reckoned myself, by observation, to be in the latitude of 9 degrees 22 minutes north of the line.

After I had been there about ten or twelve days, it came into my thoughts that I should lose my reckoning of time for want of books and pen and ink, and should even forget the Sabbath days from the working days; but to prevent this, I cut it with my knife upon a large post, in capital letters; and making it into a great cross, I set it up on the shore where I first landed, viz., 'I came on shore here on the 30th September 1659.' Upon the sides of this square post I cut every day a notch with my knife, and every seventh notch was as long again as the rest, and every first day of the month as long again as that long one; and thus I kept my calendar, or weekly, monthly, and yearly reckoning of time.

In the next place we are to observe, that among the many things which I brought out of the ship in the several voyages, which, as above mentioned, I made to it, I got several things of less value, but not all less useful to me, which I omitted setting down before; as in particular, pens, ink, and paper, several parcels in the captain's, mate's, gunner's, and carpenter's keeping, three or four compasses, some mathematical instruments, dials, perspectives, charts, and books of navigation, all which I huddled together, whether I might want them or no. Also I found three very good Bibles, which came to me in my cargo from England, and which I had packed up among my things; some Portuguese books also, and among them two or three Popish prayer-books, and several other books, all which I carefully secured. And I must not forget, that we had in the ship a dog and two cats, of whose eminent history I may have occasion to say something in its place; for I carried both the cats with me, and as for the dog, he jumped out of the ship of himself, and swam on shore to me the day after I went on shore with my first cargo, and was a trusty servant to me many years. I wanted nothing that he could fetch me, nor any company that he could make up to me; I only wanted to have him talk to me, but that would not do. As I observed before, I found pen, ink, and paper, and I husbanded them to the utmost; and I shall show that while my ink lasted, I kept things very exact; but after that was gone, I could not, for I could not make any ink by any means that I could devise.

And this put me in mind that I wanted many things, notwithstanding all that I had amassed together; and of these, this of ink was one, as also spade, pick-axe, and shovel, to dig or remove the earth, needles, pins, and thread; as for linen, I soon learned to want that without much difficulty.

This want of tools made every work I did go on heavily; and it was near a whole year before I had entirely finished my little pale or surrounded habitation. The piles or stakes, which were as heavy as I could well lift, were a long time in cutting and preparing in the woods, and more by far in bringing home; so that I spent sometimes two days in cutting and bringing home one of those posts, and a third day in driving it into the ground; for which purpose I got a heavy piece of wood at first, but at last bethought myself of one of the iron crows, which, however, though I found it, yet it made driving those posts or piles very laborious and tedious work.

But what need I have been concerned at the tediousness of anything I had to do, seeing I had time enough to do it in? nor had I any other employment, if that had been over, at least, that I could foresee, except the ranging the island to seek for food, which I did more or less every day.

I now began to consider seriously my condition, and the circumstance I was reduced to; and I drew up the state of my affairs in writing; not so much to leave them to any that were to come after me, for I was like to have but few heirs, as to deliver my thoughts from daily poring upon them, and afflicting my mind. And as my reason began now to master my despondency, I began to comfort myself as well as I could, and to set the good against the evil, that I might have something to distinguish my case from worse; and I stated it very impartially, like debtor and creditor, the comforts I enjoyed against the miseries I suffered, thus:

Evil	*Good*
I am cast upon a horrible desolate island, void of all hope of recovery.	But I am alive, and not drowned, as all my ship's company was.
I am singled out and separated, as it were, from all the world to be miserable.	But I am singled out, too, from all the ship's crew to be spared from death; and He that miraculously saved me from death, can deliver me from this condition.
I am divided from mankind, a solitaire, one banished from human society.	But I am not starved and perishing on a barren place, affording no sustenance.
I have not clothes to cover me.	But I am in a hot climate, where if I had clothes I could hardly wear them.
I am without any defence or means to resist any violence of man or beast.	But I am cast on an island, where I see no wild beasts to hurt me, as I saw on the coast of Africa; and what if I had been shipwrecked there?
I have no soul to speak to, or relieve me.	But God wonderfully sent the ship in near enough to the shore, that I have gotten out so many necessary things as will either supply my wants, or enable me to supply myself even as long as I live.

Having now brought my mind a little to relish my condition, and given over looking out to sea, to see if I could
spy a ship; I say, giving over these things, I began to apply
myself to accommodate my way of living, and to make
things as easy to me as I could.

I have already described my habitation, which was a
tent under the side of a rock, surrounded with a strong
pale of posts and cables; but I might now rather call it a
wall, for I raised a kind of wall up against it of turfs, about
two feet thick on the outside, and after some time — I
think it was a year and a half — I raised rafters from it leading to the rock, and thatched or covered it with boughs of
trees and such things as I could get to keep out the rain,
which I found at some times of the year very violent.

I have already observed how I brought all my goods
into this pale, and into the cave which I had made behind
me. But I must observe, too, that at first this was a confused heap of goods, which as they lay in no order, so they
took up all my place; I had no room to turn myself. So I
set myself to enlarge my cave and works farther into the
earth; for it was a loose sandy rock, which yielded easily to
the labour I bestowed on it. And so, when I found I was
pretty safe as to beasts of prey, I worked sideways to the
right hand into the rock; and then, turning to the right
again, worked quite out, and made me a door to come out
on the outside of my pale or fortification. This gave me
not only egress and regress, as it were a back-way to my

tent and to my storehouse, but gave me room to stow my goods.

And now I began to apply myself to make such necessary things as I found I most wanted, as particularly a chair and a table; for without these I was not able to enjoy the few comforts I had in the world. I could not write or eat, or do several things with so much pleasure without a table.

So I went to work; and here I must needs observe, that as reason is the substance and original of the mathematics, so by stating and squaring everything by reason, and by making the most rational judgment of things, every man may be in time master of every mechanic art. I had never handled a tool in my life; and yet in time, by labour, application, and contrivance, I found at last that I wanted nothing but I could have made it, especially if I had had tools. However, I made abundance of things even without tools, and some with no more tools than an adze and a hatchet, which, perhaps, were never made that way before, and that with infinite labour. For example, if I wanted a board, I had no other way but to cut down a tree, set it on edge before me, and hew it flat on either side with my axe, till I had brought it to be thin as a plank, and then dub it smooth with my adze. It is true, by this method I could make but one board out of the whole tree; but this I had no remedy for but patience, any more than I had for the prodigious deal of time and labour which it took me up to make a plank or board. But my time or labour was little worth, and so it was as well employed one way as another.

However, I made me a table and a chair, as I observed above, in the first place, and this I did out of the short pieces of boards that I brought on my raft from the ship. But when I had wrought out some boards, as above, I made large shelves of the breadth of a foot and a half one over another, all along one side of my cave, to lay all my tools, nails, and iron-work; and, in a word, to separate everything at large in their places, that I might come easily at them. I knocked pieces into the wall of the rock to hang my guns and all things that would hang up; so that had my cave been to be seen, it looked like a general magazine of all necessary things; and I had everything so ready at my hand, that it was a great pleasure to me to see all my goods in such order, and especially to find my stock of necessaries so great.

And now it was when I began to keep a journal of every day's employment; for, indeed, at first, I was in too much hurry, and not only hurry as to labour, but in too much discomposure of mind; and my journal would have been full of many dull things.

But having gotten over these things in some measure, and having settled my household stuff and habitation, made me a table and a chair, and all as handsome about me as I could, I began to keep my journal, of which I shall here give you the copy (though in it will be told all these particulars over again) as long as it lasted; for, having no more ink, I was forced to leave it off.

THE JOURNAL

Crusoe describes his efforts to construct a safe dwelling place and to make essential furniture, tools and utensils.

SEPTEMBER *30, 1659.* — I, poor miserable Robinson Crusoe, being shipwrecked, during a dreadful storm, in the offing, came on shore on this dismal unfortunate island, which I called the Island of Despair, all the rest of the ship's company being drowned, and myself almost dead.

All the rest of that day I spent in afflicting myself at the dismal circumstances I was brought to, viz., I had neither food, house, clothes, weapon, or place to fly to; and in despair of any relief, saw nothing but death before me; either that I should be devoured by wild beasts, murdered by savages, or starved to death for want of food. At the approach of night, I slept in a tree for fear of wild creatures, but slept soundly, though it rained all night.

Oct. 1. — In the morning I saw, to my great surprise, the ship had floated with the high tide, and was driven on shore again much nearer the island; which, as it was some comfort on one hand, for seeing her sit upright, and not broken to pieces, I hoped, if the wind abated, I might get on board, and get some food and necessaries out of her for my relief; so, on the other hand, it renewed my grief at the loss of my comrades, who, I imagined, if we had all stayed on board, might have saved the ship, or at least that they would not have been all drowned as they were; and that had the men been saved, we might perhaps have built us a boat out of the ruins of the ship, to have carried us to some other part of the world. I spent great part of this day in perplexing myself on these things; but at length seeing the ship almost dry, I went upon the sand as near as I could, and then swam on board; this day also it continued raining, though with no wind at all.

From the *1st of October* to the *24th*. — All these days entirely spent in many several voyages to get all I could out of the ship, which I brought on shore, every tide of flood, upon rafts. Much rain also in these days, though with some intervals of fair weather; but, it seems, this was the rainy season.

Oct. 20. — I overset my raft, and all the goods I had got upon it; but being in shoal water, and the things being chiefly heavy, I recovered many of them when the tide was out.

Oct. 25. — It rained all night and all day, with some gusts of wind, during which time the ship broke in pieces, the wind blowing a little harder than before, and was no more to be seen, except the wreck of her, and that only at low water. I spent this day in covering and securing the goods which I had saved, that the rain might not spoil them.

Oct. 26. — I walked about the shore almost all day to

find out a place to fix my habitation, greatly concerned to secure myself from an attack in the night, either from wild beasts or men. Towards night I fixed upon a proper place under a rock, and marked out a semi-circle for my encampment, which I resolved to strengthen with a work, wall, or fortification made of double piles, lined within with cables, and without with turf.

From the 26th to the 30th I worked very hard in carrying all my goods to my new habitation, though some part of the time it rained exceeding hard.

The 31st, in the morning, I went out into the island with my gun to see for some food, and discover the country; when I killed a she-goat, and her kid followed me home, which I afterwards killed also, because it would not feed.

Nov. 1. — I set up my tent under a rock, and lay there for the first night, making it as large as I could, with stakes driven in to swing my hammock upon.

Nov. 2. — I set up all my chests and boards, and the pieces of timber which made my rafts, and with them formed a fence round me, a little within the place I had marked out for my fortification.

Nov. 3. — I went out with my gun, and killed two fowls like ducks, which were very good food. In the afternoon went to work to make me a table.

Nov. 4. — This morning I began to order my times of work, of going out with my gun, time of sleep, and time of diversion, viz., every morning I walked out with my gun for two or three hours, if it did not rain; then employed myself to work till about eleven o'clock; then eat what I had to live on; and from twelve to two I lay down to sleep, the weather being excessive hot; and then in the evening to work again. The working part of this day and of the next were wholly employed in making my table; for I was yet but a very sorry workman, though time and necessity made me a complete natural mechanic soon after, as I believe it would do any one else.

Nov. 5. — This day went abroad with my gun and my dog, and killed a wild cat; her skin pretty soft, but her flesh good for nothing. Every creature I killed, I took off the skins and preserved them. Coming back by the sea-shore, I saw many sorts of sea-fowls, which I did not understand; but was surprised, and almost frighted, with two or three seals, which, while I was gazing at, not well knowing what they were, got into the sea, and escaped me for that time.

Nov. 6. — After my morning walk I went to work with my table again, and finished it, though not to my liking; nor was it long before I learned to mend it.

Nov. 7. — Now it began to be settled fair weather. The 7th, 8th, 9th, 10th, and part of the 12th (for the 11th was Sunday) I took wholly up to make me a chair, and with much ado, brought it to a tolerable shape, but never to please me; and even in the making, I pulled it in pieces several times. Note, I soon neglected my keeping Sundays; for, omitting my mark for them on my post, I forgot which was which.

Nov. 13. — This day it rained, which refreshed me exceedingly, and cooled the earth; but it was accompanied with terrible thunder and lightning, which frighted me dreadfully, for fear of my powder. As soon as it was over, I resolved to separate my stock of powder into as many little parcels as possible, that it might not be in danger.

Nov. 14, 15, 16. — These three days I spent in making little square chests or boxes, which might hold about a pound, or two pound at most, of powder; and so putting the powder in, I stowed it in places as secure and remote from one another as possible. On one of these three days I killed a large bird that was good to eat, but I know not what to call it.

Nov. 17. — This day I began to dig behind my tent into the rock, to make room for my farther conveniency. Note, three things I wanted exceedingly for this work, viz., a pick-axe, a shovel, and a wheelbarrow or basket; so I desisted from my work, and began to consider how to supply that want, and make me some tools. As for a pick-axe, I made use of the iron crows, which were proper enough, though heavy; but the next thing was a shovel or spade. This was so absolutely necessary, that indeed I could do nothing effectually without it; but what kind of one to make, I knew not.

Nov. 18. — The next day, in searching the woods, I found a tree of that wood, or like it, which in the Brazils they call the iron tree, for its exceeding hardness; of this, with great labour, and almost spoiling my axe, I cut a piece, and brought it home too, with difficulty enough, for it was exceeding heavy.

The excessive hardness of the wood, and having no other way, made me a long while upon this machine, for I worked it effectually, by little and little, into the form of a shovel or spade, the handle exactly shaped like ours in England, only that the broad part having no iron shod upon it at bottom, it would not last me so long. However, it served me well enough for the uses which I had occasion to put it to; but never was a shovel, I believe, made after that fashion, or so long a-making.

I was still deficient, for I wanted a basket or a wheelbarrow. A basket I could not make by any means, having no such thing as twigs that would bend to make wicker ware, at least none yet found out. And as to a wheelbarrow, I fancied I could make all but the wheel, but that I had no notion of, neither did I know how to go about it; besides, I had no possible way to make the iron gudgeons for the spindle or axis of the wheel to run in; so I gave it over; and so for carrying away the earth which I dug out of the cave, I made me a thing like a hod which the labourers carry mortar in, when they serve the bricklayers.

This was not so difficult to me as the making the

shovel; and yet this, and the shovel, and the attempt which I made in vain to make a wheelbarrow, took me up no less than four days; I mean always, excepting my morning walk with my gun, which I seldom failed, and very seldom failed also bringing home something fit to eat.

Nov. 23. — My other work having now stood still because of my making these tools, when they were finished I went on, and working every day, as my strength and time allowed, I spent eighteen days entirely in widening and deepening my cave, that it might hold my goods commodiously.

Note. — During all this time I worked to make this room or cave spacious enough to accommodate me as a warehouse or magazine, a kitchen, a dining-room, and a cellar; as for my lodging, I kept to the tent, except that sometimes in the wet season of the year it rained so hard, that I could not keep myself dry, which caused me afterwards to cover all my place within my pale with long poles, in the form of rafters, leaning against the rock, and load them with flags and large leaves of trees, like a thatch.

Dec. 10. — I began now to think my cave or vault finished, when on a sudden (it seems I had made it too large) a great quantity of earth fell down from the top and one side, so much, that, in short, it frighted me, and not without reason too; for if I had been under it, I had never wanted a grave-digger. Upon this disaster I had a great deal of work to do over again; for I had the loose earth to carry out; and, which was of more importance, I had the ceiling to prop up, so that I might be sure no more would come down.

Dec. 11. — This day I went to work with it accordingly, and got two shores or posts pitched upright to the top, with two pieces of boards across over each post. This I finished the next day; and setting more posts up with boards, in about a week more I had the roof secured; and the posts standing in rows, served me for partitions to part of my house.

Dec. 17. — From this day to the twentieth I placed shelves, and knocked up nails on the posts to hang everything up that could be hung up; and now I began to be in some order within doors.

Dec. 20. — Now I carried everything into the cave, and began to furnish my house, and set up some pieces of boards, like a dresser, to order my victuals upon; but boards began to be very scarce with me; also I made me another table.

Dec. 24. — Much rain all night and all day; no stirring out.

Dec. 25. — Rain all day.

Dec. 26. — No rain, and the earth much cooler than before, and pleasanter.

Dec. 27. — Killed a young goat, and lamed another, so

that I catched it, and led it home in a string. When I had it home, I bound and splintered up its leg, which was broke. *N.B.* — I took such care of it, that it lived; and the leg grew well and as strong as ever; but by my nursing it so long it grew tame, and fed upon the little green at my door, and would not go away. This was the first time that I entertained a thought of breeding up some tame creatures, that I might have food when my powder and shot was all spent.

Dec. 28, 29, 30. — Great heats and no breeze, so that there was no stirring abroad, except in the evening, for food. This time I spent in putting all my things in order within doors.

Jan. 1. — Very hot still, but I went abroad early and late with my gun, and lay still in the middle of the day. This evening, going farther into the valleys which lay towards the centre of the island, I found there was plenty of goats, though exceeding shy, and hard to come at. However, I resolved to try if I could not bring my dog to hunt them down.

Jan. 2. — Accordingly, the next day, I went out with my dog, and set him upon the goats; but I was mistaken, for they all faced about upon the dog; and he knew his danger too well, for he would not come near them.

Jan. 3. — I began my fence or wall; which, being still jealous of my being attacked by somebody, I resolved to make very thick and strong.

N.B. — This wall being described before, I purposely omit what was said in the journal. It is sufficient to observe that I was no less time than from the 3rd of January to the 14th of April working, finishing, and perfecting this wall, though it was no more than about twenty-four yards in length, being a half-circle from one place in the rock to another place about eight yards from it, the door of the cave being in the centre behind it.

All this time I worked very hard, the rains hindering me many days, nay, sometimes weeks together; but I thought I should never be perfectly secure till this wall was finished. And it is scarce credible what inexpressible labour everything was done with, especially the bringing piles out of the woods, and driving them into the ground; for I made them much bigger than I need to have done.

When this wall was finished, and the outside double-fenced with a turf-wall raised up close to it, I persuaded myself that if any people were to come on shore there, they would not perceive anything like a habitation; and it was very well I did so, as may be observed hereafter upon a very remarkable occasion.

He makes a lamp from goat's tallow. Green shoots of barley cause him great surprise. Experiences a terrifying earthquake, hurricane and torrential rain.

During this time, I made my rounds in the woods for game every day, when the rain admitted me, and made frequent discoveries in these walks of something or other to my advantage; particularly I found a kind of wild pigeons, who built, not as wood pigeons in a tree, but rather as house pigeons, in the holes of the rocks. And taking some young ones, I endeavoured to breed them up tame, and did so; but when they grew older they flew all away, which, perhaps, was at first for want of feeding them, for I had nothing to give them. However, I frequently found their nests, and got their young ones, which were very good meat.

And now in the managing my household affairs I found myself wanting in many things, which I thought at first it was impossible for me to make, as indeed, as to some of them, it was. For instance, I could never make a cask to be hooped; I had a small runlet or two, as I observed before, but I could never arrive to the capacity of making one by them, though I spent many weeks about it. I could neither put in the heads, or joint the staves so true to one another, as to make them hold water; so I gave that also over.

In the next place, I was at a great loss for candle; so that as soon as ever it was dark, which was generally by seven o'clock, I was obliged to go to bed. I remembered the lump of beeswax with which I made candles in my African adventure, but I had none of that now. The only remedy I had was, that when I had killed a goat I saved the tallow, and with a little dish made of clay, which I baked in the sun, to which I added a wick of some oakum, I made me a lamp; and this gave me light, though not a clear steady light like a candle.

In the middle of all my labours it happened, that rummaging my things, I found a little bag, which, as I hinted before, had been filled with corn for the feeding of poultry, not for this voyage, but before, as I suppose, when the ship came from Lisbon. What little remainder of corn had been in the bag was all devoured with the rats, and I saw nothing in the bag but husks and dust; and being willing to have the bag for some other use, I think it was to put powder in, when I divided it for fear of the lightning, or some such use, I shook the husks of corn out of it on one side of my fortification, under the rock. It was a little before the great rains, just now mentioned, that I threw this stuff away, taking no notice of anything, and not so much as remembering that I had thrown anything there; when, about a month after, or thereabout, I saw some few stalks of something green shooting out of the ground, which I fancied might be some plant I had not seen; but I was surprised, and perfectly astonished, when, after a little longer time, I saw about ten or twelve ears come out, which were perfect green barley of the same kind as our European, nay, as our English barley.

I carefully saved the ears of this corn, you may be sure, in their season, which was about the end of June; and laying up every corn, I resolved to sow them all again, hoping

CRUSOE DISCOVERS THE BARLEY

in time to have some quantity sufficient to supply me with bread. But it was not till the fourth year that I could allow myself the least grain of this corn to eat, and even then but sparingly, as I shall say afterwards in its order; for I lost all that I sowed the first season, by not observing the proper time; for I sowed it just before the dry season, so that it never came up at all, at least not as it would have done; of which in its place.

Besides this barley, there was, as above, twenty or thirty stalks of rice, which I preserved with the same care, and whose use was of the same kind, or to the same purpose, viz., to make me bread, or rather food; for I found ways to cook it up without baking, though I did that also after some time. But to return to my journal.

I worked excessive hard these three or four months to get my wall done; and the 14th of April I closed it up, contriving to go into it, not by a door, but over the wall by a ladder, that there might be no sign in the outside of my habitation.

April 16. — I finished the ladder, so I went up with the ladder to the top, and then pulled it up after me, and let it down on the inside. This was a complete enclosure to me; for within I had room enough, and nothing could come at me from without, unless it could first mount my wall.

The very next day after this wall was finished, I had almost had all my labour overthrown at once, and myself killed. The case was thus: As I was busy in the inside of it, behind my tent, just in the entrance into my cave, I was terribly frighted with a most dreadful surprising thing indeed; for all on a sudden I found the earth come crumbling down from the roof of my cave, and from the edge of the hill over my head, and two of the posts I had set up in the cave cracked in a frightful manner. I was heartily scared, but thought nothing of what was really the cause, only thinking that the top of my cave was falling in, as some of it had done before; and for fear I should be buried in it, I ran forward to my ladder; and not thinking myself safe there neither, I got over my wall for fear of the pieces of the hill which I expected might roll down upon me. I was no sooner stepped down upon the firm ground, but I plainly saw it was a terrible earthquake; for the ground I stood on shook three times at about eight minutes' distance, with three such shocks, as would have overturned the strongest building that could be supposed to have stood on the earth; and a great piece of the top of a rock, which stood about half a mile from me next the sea, fell down with such a terrible noise, as I never heard in all my life. I perceived also the very sea was put into violent motion by it; and I believe the shocks were stronger under the water than on the island.

I was so amazed with the thing itself, having never felt the like, or discoursed with any one that had, that I was like one dead or stupefied; and the motion of the earth made my stomach sick, like one that was tossed at sea. But the noise of the falling of the rock awaked me, as it were, and rousing me from the stupefied condition I was in, filled me with horror, and I thought of nothing then but the hill falling upon my tent and all my household goods, and burying all at once; and this sunk my very soul within me a second time.

After the third shock was over, and I felt no more for some time, I began to take courage; and yet I had not heart enough to go over my wall again, for fear of being buried alive, but sat still upon the ground, greatly cast down and disconsolate, not knowing what to do. All this while I had not the least serious religious thought, nothing but the common, 'Lord, have mercy upon me!' and when it was over, that went away too.

While I sat thus, I found the air overcast, and grow cloudy, as if it would rain. Soon after that the wind rose by little and little, so that in less than half an hour it blew a most dreadful hurricane. The sea was all on a sudden covered over with foam and froth; the shore was covered with the breach of the water; the trees were torn up by the roots; and a terrible storm it was: and this held about three hours, and then began to abate; and in two hours more it was stark calm, and began to rain very hard.

All this while I sat upon the ground, very much terrified and dejected; when on a sudden it came into my thoughts, that these winds and rain being the consequences of the earthquake, the earthquake itself was spent and over, and I might venture into my cave again. With this thought my spirits began to revive; and the rain also helping to persuade me, I went in and sat down in my tent. But the rain was so violent, that my tent was ready to be beaten down with it and I was forced to go into my cave, though very much afraid and uneasy, for fear it should fall on my head.

This violent rain forced me to a new work, viz., to cut a hole through my new fortification, like a sink to let the water go out, which would else have drowned my cave.

After I had been in my cave some time, and found still no more shocks of the earthquake follow, I began to be more composed. And now to support my spirits, which indeed wanted it very much, I went to my little store, and took a small sup of rum, which, however, I did then, and always, very sparingly, knowing I could have no more when that was gone.

It continued raining all that night and great part of the next day, so that I could not stir abroad; but my mind being more composed, I began to think of what I had best do, concluding that if the island was subject to these earthquakes, there would be no living for me in a cave, but I must consider of building me some little hut in an open place, which I might surround with a wall, as I had done here, and so make myself secure from wild beasts or men; but concluded, if I stayed where I was, I should certainly, one time or other, be buried alive.

With these thoughts I resolved to remove my tent from the place where it stood, which was just under the hanging precipice of the hill, and which, if it should be shaken again, would certainly fall upon my tent; and I spent the two next days, being the 19th and 20th of April, in contriving where and how to remove my habitation.

The fear of being swallowed up alive made me that I never slept in quiet; and yet the apprehension of lying abroad without any fence was almost equal to it. But still, when I looked about and saw how everything was put in order, how pleasantly concealed I was, and how safe from danger, it made me very loth to remove.

In the meantime it occurred to me that it would require a vast deal of time for me to do this, and that I must be contented to run the venture where I was, till I had formed a camp for myself, and had secured it so as to remove to it. So with this resolution I composed myself for a time, and resolved that I would go to work with all speed to build me a wall with piles and cables, etc., in a circle as before, and set my tent up in it when it was finished, but that I would venture to stay where I was till it was finished, and fit to remove to. This was the 21st.

The hurricane has shifted the hulk of his old ship. He salvages timber and metal. He falls violently ill. Contemplating death he bemoans his past sinful life.

April 22. — The next morning I began to consider of means to put this resolve in execution; but I was at a great loss about my tools. I had three large axes, and abundance of hatchets (for we carried the hatchets for traffic with the Indians), but with much chopping and cutting knotty hard wood, they were all full of notches and dull; and though I had a grindstone, I could not turn it and grind my tools too. This cost me as much thought as a statesman would have bestowed upon a grand point of politics, or a judge upon the life and death of a man. At length I contrived a wheel with a string, to turn it with my foot, that I might have both my hands at liberty. Note, I had never seen any such thing in England, or at least not to take notice how it was done, though since I have observed it is very common there; besides that, my grindstone was very large and heavy. This machine cost me a full week's work to bring it to perfection.

April 28, 29. — These two whole days I took up in grinding my tools, my machine for turning my grindstone performing very well.

April 30. — Having perceived my bread had been low a great while, now I took a survey of it, and reduced myself to one biscuit-cake a day, which made my heart very heavy.

May 1. — In the morning, looking towards the seaside, the tide being low, I saw something lie on the shore bigger than ordinary, and it looked like a cask. When I came to it, I found a small barrel, and two or three pieces of the wreck of the ship, which were driven on shore by the late hurricane; and looking towards the wreck itself, I thought it seemed to lie higher out of the water than it use to do. I examined the barrel which was driven on shore, and soon found it was a barrel of gunpowder; but it had taken water, and the powder was caked as hard as a stone. However, I rolled it farther on shore for the present, and went on upon the sands as near as I could to the wreck of the ship to look for more.

When I came down to the ship I found it strangely

THE WRECK

removed. The forecastle, which lay before buried in sand, was heaved up at least six feet; and the stern, which was broken to pieces, and parted from the rest by the force of the sea soon after I had left rummaging her, was tossed, as it were, up, and cast on one side, and the sand was thrown so high on that side next her stern, that whereas there was a great place of water before, so that I could not come within a quarter of a mile of the wreck without swimming, I could now walk quite up to her when the tide was out. I was surprised with this at first, but soon concluded it must be done by the earthquake. And as by this violence the ship was more broken open than formerly, so many things came daily on shore, which the sea had loosened, and which the winds and water rolled by degrees to the land.

This wholly diverted my thoughts from the design of removing my habitation; and I busied myself mightily, that day especially, in searching whether I could make any way into the ship. But I found nothing was to be expected of that kind, for that all the inside of the ship was choked up with sand. However, as I had learned not to despair of anything, I resolved to pull everything to pieces that I could of the ship, concluding, that everything I could get from her would be of some use or other to me.

May 3. — I began with my saw, and cut a piece of a beam through, which I thought held some of the upper part or quarter-deck together; and when I had cut it through, I cleared away the sand as well as I could from the side which lay highest; but the tide coming in, I was obliged to give over for that time.

May 4. — I went a-fishing, but caught not one fish that I durst eat of, till I was weary of my sport; when, just going to leave off, I caught a young dolphin. I had made me a long line of some rope-yarn, but I had no hooks; yet I frequently caught fish enough, as much as I cared to eat; all which I dried in the sun, and eat them dry.

May 5. — Worked on the wreck, cut another beam asunder, and brought three great fir-planks off from the decks, which I tied together, and made swim on shore, when the tide of flood came on.

May 6. — Worked on the wreck, got several iron bolts out of her, and other pieces of ironwork; worked very hard, and came home very much tired, and had thoughts of giving it over.

May 7. — Went to the wreck again, but with an intent not to work, but found the weight of the wreck had broke itself down, the beams being cut; that several pieces of the ship seemed to lie loose, and the inside of the hold lay so open, that I could see into it, but almost full of water and sand.

May 8. — Went to the wreck, and carried an iron crow to wrench up the deck, which lay now quite clear of the water or sand. I wrenched open two planks, and brought them on shore also with the tide. I left the iron crow in the wreck for next day.

May 9. — Went to the wreck, and with the crow made way into the body of the wreck, and felt several casks, and loosened them with the crow, but could not break them up. I felt also the roll of English lead, and could stir it, but it was too heavy to remove.

May 10, 11, 12, 13, 14. — Went every day to the wreck, and got a great deal of pieces of timber, and boards, or plank, and two or three hundred-weight of iron.

May 15. — I carried two hatchets to try if I could not cut a piece off of the roll of lead, by placing the edge of one hatchet, and driving it with the other; but as it lay about a foot and a half in the water, I could not make any blow to drive the hatchet.

May 16. — It had blowed hard in the night, and the wreck appeared more broken by the force of the water; but I stayed so long in the woods to get pigeons for food, that the tide prevented me going to the wreck that day.

May 17. — I saw some pieces of the wreck blown on shore, at a great distance, near two miles off me, but resolved to see what they were, and found it was a piece of the head, but too heavy for me to bring away.

May 24. — Every day to this day I worked on the wreck, and with hard labour I loosened some things so much with the crow, that the first blowing tide several casks floated out, and two of the seamen's chests. But the wind blowing from the shore, nothing came to land that day but pieces of timber, and a hogshead, which had some Brazil pork in it, but the salt water and the sand had spoiled it.

I continued this work every day to the 15th of June, except the time necessary to get food, which I always appointed, during this part of my employment, to be when the tide was up, that I might be ready when it was ebbed out. And by this time I had gotten timber, and plank, and ironwork enough to have builded a good boat, if I had known how; and also, I got at several times, and in several pieces, near one hundredweight of the sheet lead.

June 16. — Going down to the seaside, I found a large tortoise, or turtle. This was the first I had seen, which it seems was only my misfortune, not any defect of the place, or scarcity; for had I happened to be on the other side of the island, I might have had hundreds of them every day, as I found afterwards; but perhaps, had paid dear enough for them.

June 17. — I spent in cooking the turtle. I found in her threescore eggs; and her flesh was to me, at that time, the most savoury and pleasant that ever I tasted in my life, having had no flesh, but of goats and fowls, since I landed in this horrid place.

June 18. — Rained all day, and I stayed within. I thought at this time the rain felt cold, and I was something chilly, which I knew was not usual in that latitude.

CRUSOE FINDS A TURTLE

June 19. — Very ill, and shivering, as if the weather had been cold.

June 20. — No rest all night; violent pains in my head, and feverish.

June 21. — Very ill, frighted almost to death with the apprehensions of my sad condition, to be sick, and no help. Prayed to God for the first time since the storm off of Hull, but scarce knew what I said, or why; my thoughts being all confused.

June 22. — A little better, but under dreadful apprehensions of sickness.

June 23. — Very bad again; cold and shivering, and then a violent headache.

June 24. — Much better.

June 25. — An ague very violent; the fit held me seven hours; cold fit, and hot, with faint sweats after it.

June 26. — Better; and having no victuals to eat, took my gun, but found myself very weak. However, I killed a she-goat, and with much difficulty got it home, and broiled some of it, and eat. I would fain have stewed it, and made some broth, but had no pot.

June 27. — The ague again so violent that I lay abed all day, and neither eat or drank. I was ready to perish for thirst; but so weak, I had not strength to stand up, or to get myself any water to drink. Prayed to God again, but was light-headed; and when I was not, I was so ignorant that I knew not what to say; only I lay and cried, 'Lord, look upon me! Lord, pity me! Lord, have mercy upon me!' I suppose I did nothing else for two or three hours, till the fit wearing off, I fell asleep, and did not wake till far in the night. When I waked, I found myself much refreshed, but weak, and exceeding thirsty. However, as I had no water in my whole habitation, I was forced to lie till morning, and went to sleep again. In this second sleep I had this terrible dream.

I thought that I was sitting on the ground, on the outside of my wall, where I sat when the storm blew after the earthquake, and that I saw a man descend from a great black cloud, in a bright flame of fire, and light upon the ground. He was all over as bright as a flame, so that I could but just bear to look towards him. His countenance was most inexpressibly dreadful, impossible for words to describe. When he stepped upon the ground with his feet, I thought the earth trembled, just as it had done before in the earthquake, and all the air looked, to my apprehension, as if it had been filled with flashes of fire.

He was no sooner landed upon the earth, but he moved forward towards me, with a long spear or weapon in his hand, to kill me; and when he came to a rising ground, at some distance, he spoke to me, or I heard a voice so terrible, that it is impossible to express the terror of it. All that I can say I understood was this: 'Seeing all these things have not brought thee repentance, now thou shalt die'; at which words I thought he lifted up the spear that was in his hand to kill me.

No one that shall ever read this account, will expect that I should be able to describe the horrors of my soul at this terrible vision; I mean, that even while it was a dream, I even dreamed of those horrors; nor is it any more possible to describe the impression that remained upon my mind when I awaked, and found it was but a dream.

I had, alas! no divine knowledge; what I had received by the good instruction of my father was then worn out, by an uninterrupted series, for eight years, of seafaring wickedness, and a constant conversation with nothing but such as were, like myself, wicked and profane to the last degree. I do not remember that I had, in all that time, one thought that so much as tended either to looking upwards toward God, or inwards towards a reflection upon my ways; I was all that the most hardened, unthinking, wicked creature among our common sailors can be supposed to be; not having the least sense, either of the fear of God, in danger, or of thankfulness to God, in deliverances.

It is true, when I got on shore first here, and found all my ship's crew drowned, and myself spared, I was surprised with a kind of ecstasy, and some transports of soul, which, had the grace of God assisted, might have come up to true thankfulness; but it ended where it begun, in a mere common flight of joy, or, as I may say, being glad I was alive, without the least reflection upon the distinguishing goodness of the hand which had preserved me, and had singled me out to be preserved, when all the rest were destroyed; or an inquiry why Providence had been thus merciful to me; even just the same common sort of joy which seamen generally have after they are got safe ashore from a shipwreck, which they drown all in the next bowl of punch, and forget almost as soon as it is over, and the rest of my life was like it.

Even when I was afterwards, on due consideration, made sensible of my condition, how I was cast on this dreadful place, out of the reach of human kind, out of all hope of relief, or prospect of redemption, as soon as I saw but a prospect of living, and that I should not starve and perish for hunger, all the sense of my affliction wore off, and I began to be very easy, applied myself to the works proper for my preservation and supply, and was far enough from being afflicted at my condition, as a judgment from heaven, or as the hand of God against me; these were thoughts which very seldom entered into my head.

Even the earthquake, though nothing could be more terrible in its nature, or more immediately directing to the invisible Power, which alone directs such things, yet no sooner was the first fright over, but the impression it had made went off also. I had no more sense of God or His judgments, much less of the present affliction of my circumstances being from His hand, than if I had been in the most prosperous condition of life.

But now, when I began to be sick, and a leisurely view of the miseries of death came to place itself before me; when my spirits began to sink under the burthen of a strong distemper, and Nature was exhausted with the violence of the fever; conscience, that had slept so long, began to awake, and I began to reproach myself with my past life, in which I had so evidently, by uncommon wickedness, provoked the justice of God to lay me under uncommon strokes, and to deal with me in so vindictive a manner.

'Now,' said I aloud, 'my dear father's words are come to pass; God's justice has overtaken me, and I have none to help or hear me. I rejected the voice of Providence, which had mercifully put me in a posture or station of life wherein I might have been happy and easy; but I would neither see it myself, or learn to know the blessing of it from my parents. I left them to mourn over my folly, and now I am left to mourn under the consequences of it. I refused their help and assistance, who would have lifted me into the world, and would have made everything easy for me; and now I have difficulties to struggle with, too great for even Nature itself to support, and no assistance, no help, no comfort, no advice.' Then I cried out, 'Lord, be my help, for I am in great distress.'

This was the first prayer, if I may call it so, that I had made for many years. I return to my journal.

> *Very wretched. Infusions of tobacco and rum prove a desperate cure for his sickness. Reads verses in the Bible most apt to his condition. Realises 'deliverance from sin a greater blessing than deliverance from affliction'.*

June 28. — Having been somewhat refreshed with the sleep I had had, and the fit being entirely off, I got up; and though the fright and terror of my dream was very great, yet I considered that the fit of ague would return again the next day, and now was my time to get something to refresh and support myself when I should be ill.

And the first thing I did I filled a large square case-bottle with water, and set it upon my table, in reach of my bed; and to take off the chill or aguish disposition of the water, I put about a quarter of a pint of rum into it, and mixed them together. Then I got me a piece of the goat's flesh, and broiled it on the coals, but could eat very little. I walked about, but was very weak, and withal very sad and heavy-hearted in the sense of my miserable condition, dreading the return of my distemper the next day. At night I made my supper of three of the turtle's eggs, which I roasted in the ashes, and eat, as we call it, in the shell; and this was the first bit of meat I had ever asked God's blessing to, even as I could remember, in my whole life.

After I had eaten, I tried to walk, but found myself so weak, that I could hardly carry the gun (for I never went out without that); so I went but a little way, and sat down upon the ground, looking out upon the sea, which was just before me, and very calm and smooth. As I sat there, some such thoughts as these occurred to me.

What is this earth and sea, of which I have seen so much? whence is it produced? And what am I, and all the other creatures, wild and tame, human and brutal, whence are we? Sure we are all made by some secret Power, who formed the earth and sea, the air and sky. And who is that?

Then it followed most naturally, It is God that has

made it all. Well, but then it came on strangely, if God has made all these things nothing can happen in the great circuit of His works, either without His knowledge or appointment. And if nothing happens without His knowledge, He knows that I am here, and am in this dreadful condition. And if nothing happens without His appointment, He has appointed all this to befall me.

Immediately it followed, Why has God done this to me? What have I done to be thus used?

My conscience presently checked me in that inquiry, as if I had blasphemed, and methought it spoke to me like a voice: 'Wretch! dost thou ask what thou hast done? Look back upon a dreadful misspent life, and ask thyself what thou hast not done? Ask, why is it that thou wert not long ago destroyed? Why wert thou not drowned in Yarmouth Roads; killed in the fight when the ship was taken by the Sallee man-of-war; devoured by the wild beasts on the coast of Africa; or drowned here, when all the crew perished but thyself? Dost thou ask, What have I done?'

I was struck dumb with these reflections, as one astonished, and had not a word to say, no, not to answer to myself, but rose up pensive and sad, walked back to my retreat, and went up over my wall, as if I had been going to bed. But my thoughts were sadly disturbed, and I had no inclination to sleep; so I sat down in my chair, and lighted my lamp, for it began to be dark. Now, as the apprehension of the return of my distemper terrified me

CRUSOE ILL READING THE BIBLE

very much, it occurred to my thought that the Brazilians take no physic but their tobacco for almost all distempers; and I had a piece of a roll of tobacco in one of the chests, which was quite cured, and some also that was green, and not quite cured.

I went, directed by Heaven no doubt; for in this chest I found a cure both for soul and body. I opened the chest, and found what I looked for, viz., the tobacco; and as the few books I had saved lay there too, I took out one of the Bibles which I mentioned before, and which to this time I had not found leisure, or so much as inclination, to look into. I say, I took it out, and brought both that and the tobacco with me to the table.

What use to make of the tobacco I knew not, as to my distemper, or whether it was good for it or no; but I tried several experiments with it, as if I was resolved it should hit one way or other. I first took a piece of a leaf, and chewed it in my mouth, which indeed at first almost stupefied my brain, the tobacco being green and strong, and that I had not been much used to it. Then I took some and steeped it an hour or two in some rum, and resolved to take a dose of it when I lay down. And lastly, I burnt some upon a pan of coals, and held my nose close over the smoke of it, as long as I could bear it, as well for the heat, as almost for suffocation.

In the interval of this operation, I took up the Bible, and began to read, but my head was too much disturbed with the tobacco to bear reading, at least that time; only having opened the book casually, the first words that occurred to me were these, 'Call on Me in the day of trouble, and I will deliver, and thou shalt glorify Me.'

The words were very apt to my case.

It grew now late, and the tobacco had, as I said, dozed my head so much, that I inclined to sleep; so I left my lamp burning in the cave, lest I should want anything in the night, and went to bed. But before I lay down, I did what I never had done in all my life; I kneeled down, and prayed to God to fulfil the promise to me, that if I called upon Him in the day of trouble, He would deliver me. After my broken and imperfect prayer was over, I drank the rum in which I had steeped the tobacco; which was so strong and rank of the tobacco, that indeed I could scarce get it down. Immediately upon this I went to bed. I found presently it flew up in my head violently; but I fell into a sound sleep, and waked no more till, by the sun, it must necessarily be near three o'clock in the afternoon the next day. Nay, to this hour I am partly of the opinion that I slept all the next day and night, and till almost three that day after; for otherwise I knew not how I should lose a day out of my reckoning in the days of the week, as it appeared some years after I had done. For if I had lost it by crossing and re-crossing the line, I should have lost more than one day. But certainly I lost a day in my account, and never knew which way.

Be that, however, one way or the other, when I awaked I found myself exceedingly refreshed, and my spirits lively and cheerful. When I got up, I was stronger than I was the day before, and my stomach better, for I was hungry; and, in short, I had no fit the next day, but continued much altered for the better. This was the 29th.

The 30th was my well day, of course, and I went abroad with my gun, but did not care to travel too far. I killed a sea-fowl or two, something like a brandgoose, and brought them home, but was not very forward to eat them; so I eat some more of the turtle's eggs, which were very good. This evening I renewed the medicine, which I had supposed did me good the day before, viz., the tobacco steeped in rum; only I did not take so much as before, nor did I chew any of the leaf, or hold my head over the smoke. However, I was not so well the next day, which was the first of July, as I hoped I should have been; for I had a little spice of the cold fit, but it was not much.

July 2. — I renewed the medicine all the three ways; and dozed myself with it as at first, and doubled the quantity which I drank.

July 3. — I missed the fit for good and all, though I did not recover my full strength for some weeks after. While I was thus gathering strength, my thoughts ran exceedingly upon this Scripture, 'I will deliver thee'; and the impossibility of my deliverance lay much upon my mind, in bar of my ever expecting it. But as I was discouraging myself

with such thoughts, it occurred to my mind that I pored
so much upon my deliverance from the main affliction,
that I disregarded the deliverance I had received; and I
was, as it were, made to ask myself such questions as
these, viz., Have I not been delivered, and wonderfully
too, from sickness? from the most distressing condition
that could be, and that was so frightful to me? and what
notice had I taken of it? Had I done my part? God had
delivered me, but I had not glorified Him; that is to say,
I had not owned and been thankful for that as a deliverance; and how could I expect greater deliverance?

This touched my heart very much; and immediately I
kneeled down, and gave God thanks aloud for my recovery from my sickness.

July 4. — In the morning I took the Bible; and beginning at the New Testament, I began seriously to read it,
and imposed upon myself to read awhile every morning
and every night, not tying myself to the number of chapters, but as long as my thoughts should engage me.

Now I began to construe the words mentioned above,
'Call on Me and I will deliver you,' in a different sense
from what I had ever done before; for then I had no
notion of anything being called deliverance but my being
delivered from the captivity I was in; for though I was
indeed at large in the place, yet the island was certainly a
prison for me, and that in the worst sense in the world.
But now I learned to take it in another sense; now I

looked back upon my past life with such horror, and my sins appeared so dreadful, that my soul sought nothing of God but deliverance from the load of guilt that bore down all my comfort. As for my solitary life, it was nothing; I did not so much as pray to be delivered from it, or think of it; it was all of no consideration, in comparison to this. And I add this part here, to hint to whoever shall read it, that whenever they come to a true sense of things, they will find deliverance from sin a much greater blessing than deliverance from affliction.

My condition began now to be, though not less miserable as to my way of living, yet much easier to my mind; and my thoughts being directed, by a constant reading the Scripture, and praying to God, to things of a higher nature, I had a great deal of comfort within, which, till now, I knew nothing of. Also, as my health and strength returned, I bestirred myself to furnish myself with everything that I wanted, and make my way of living as regular as I could.

From the 4th of July to the 14th, I was chiefly employed in walking about with my gun in my hand, a little and a little at a time, as a man that was gathering up his strength after a fit of sickness; for it is hardly to be imagined how low I was, and to what weakness I was reduced. The application which I made use of was perfectly new, and perhaps what had never cured an ague before; neither can I recommend it to any one to practise, by this experiment; and though it did carry off the fit, yet it rather contributed to weakening me; for I had frequent convulsions in my nerves and limbs for some time.

I had been now in this unhappy island above ten months; all possibility of deliverance from this condition seemed to be entirely taken from me; and I firmly believed that no human shape had ever set foot upon that place. Having now secured my habitation, as I thought, fully to my mind, I had a great desire to make a more perfect discovery of the island, and to see what other productions I might find, which I yet knew nothing of.

He explores and discovers pleasant meadows, and tobacco, citrus fruits, melons and grapes in abundance. Builds an inland 'country house'. Solemnly keeps his first anniversary. Shortage of ink compels him to discontinue diary.

It was the 15th July that I began to take a more particular survey of the island itself. I went up the creek first, where as I hinted, I brought my rafts on shore. I found, after I came about two miles up, that the tide did not flow any higher, and that it was no more than a little brook of running water, and very fresh and good; but this being the dry season, there was hardly any water in some parts of it, at least, not enough to run in any stream, so as it could be perceived.

On the bank of this brook I found many pleasant savannas or meadows, plain, smooth, and covered with grass; and on the rising parts of them, next to the higher grounds, where the water as might be supposed, never overflowed, I found a great deal of tobacco, green, and growing to a great and very strong stalk. There were divers other plants, which I had no notion of, or understanding about, and might perhaps have virtues of their own, which I could not find out.

I searched for the cassava root, which the Indians, in all that climate, make their bread of, but I could find none. I saw large plants of aloes, but did not then understand them. I saw several sugar-canes, but wild, and, for want of cultivation, imperfect. I contented myself with these discoveries for this time, and came back, musing with myself what course I might take to know the virtue and goodness of any of the fruits or plants which I should discover; but could bring it to no conclusion; for, in short, I had made so little observation while I was in the Brazils, that I knew little of the plants in the field, at least very little that might serve me to any purpose now in my distress.

The next day, the 16th, I went up the same way again; and after going something farther than I had gone the day before, I found the brook and the savannas began to cease, and the country became more woody than before. In this part I found different fruits, and particularly I found melons upon the ground in great abundance, and grapes upon the trees. The vines had spread indeed over the trees, and the clusters of grapes were just now in their prime, very ripe and rich. This was a surprising discovery, and I was exceeding glad of them; but I was warned by my experience to eat sparingly of them, remembering that when I was ashore in Barbary the eating of grapes killed several of our Englishmen, who were slaves there, by throwing them into fluxes and fevers. But I found an excellent use for these grapes; and that was, to cure or dry them in the sun, and keep them as dried grapes or raisins are kept, which I thought would be, as indeed they were, as wholesome as agreeable to eat, when no grapes might be to be had.

I spent all that evening there, and went not back to my habitation; which, by the way, was the first night, as I might say, I had lain from home. In the night, I took my first contrivance, and got up into a tree, where I slept well; and the next morning proceeded upon my discovery, travelling near four miles, as I might judge by the length of the valley, keeping still due north, with a ridge of hills on the south and north side of me.

At the end of this march I came to an opening, where the country seemed to descend to the west; and a little spring of fresh water, which issued out of the side of the hill by me, ran the other way, that is, due east; and the country appeared so fresh, so green, so flourishing, everything being in a constant verdure or flourish of spring, that it looked like a planted garden.

I descended a little on the side of that delicious vale, surveying it with a secret kind of pleasure, though mixed with my other afflicting thoughts, to think that this was all my own; that I was king and lord of all this country indefeasibly, and had a right of possession; and, if I could convey it, I might have it in inheritance as completely as any lord of a manor in England. I saw here abundance of cocoa trees, orange, and lemon, and citron trees; but all wild, and very few bearing any fruit, at least not then. However, the green limes that I gathered were not only pleasant to eat, but very wholesome; and I mixed their juice afterwards with water, which made it very wholesome, and very cool and refreshing.

I found now I had business enough to gather and carry home; and I resolved to lay up a store, as well of grapes as limes and lemons to furnish myself for the wet season, which I knew was approaching.

In order to this, I gathered a great heap of grapes in one place, and a lesser heap in another place, and great parcel of limes and lemons in another place; and, taking a few of each with me, I travelled homeward; and resolved to come again, and bring a bag or sack, or what I could make, to carry the rest home.

Accordingly, having spent three days in this journey, I came home (so I must now call my tent and my cave); but before I got thither, the grapes were spoiled; the richness of the fruits, and the weight of the juice, having broken them and bruised them, they were good for little or nothing: and to the limes, they were good, but I could bring but a few.

The next day, being the 19th, I went back, having made me two small bags to bring home my harvest; but I was surprised, when, coming to my heap of grapes, which were so rich and fine when I gathered them, I found them all spread about, trod to pieces, and dragged about, some here, some there, and abundance eaten and devoured. By this I concluded there were some wild creatures thereabouts, which had done this; but what they were, I knew not.

However, as I found that there was no laying them up on heaps, and no carrying them away in a sack, but that one way they would be destroyed, and the other way they would be crushed with their own weight, I took another course; for I gathered a large quantity of the grapes, and hung them up upon the out-branches of the trees, that they might cure and dry in the sun; and as for the limes and lemons, I carried as many back as I could well stand under.

When I came home from this journey, I contemplated with great pleasure the fruitfulness of that valley, and the pleasantness of the situation; the security from storms on that side the water and the wood; and concluded that I had pitched upon a place to fix my abode, which was by far the worst part of the country. Upon the whole, I began to consider of removing my habitation, and to look out for a place equally safe as where I now was situate, if possible, in that pleasant fruitful part of the island.

This thought ran long in my head, and I was exceeding

CRUSOE IN HIS BOWER

fond of it for some time, the pleasantness of the place tempting me; but when I came to a nearer view of it, and to consider that I was now by the seaside, where it was at least possible that something might happen to my advantage, and, by the same ill fate that brought me hither, might bring some other unhappy wretches to the same place; and though it was scarce probable that any such thing should ever happen, yet to enclose myself among the hills and woods in the centre of the island, was to anticipate my bondage, and to render such an affair not only improbable, but impossible; and that therefore I ought not by any means to remove.

However, I was so enamoured of this place, that I spent much of my time there for the whole remaining part of the month of July; and though, upon second thoughts, I resolved, as above, not to remove, yet I built me a little kind of a bower, and surrounded it at a distance with a strong fence, being a double hedge as high as I could reach, well staked, and filled between with brushwood. And here I lay very secure, sometimes two or three nights together, always going over it with a ladder, as before; so that I fancied now I had my country-house and my sea-coast house; and this work took me up to the beginning of August.

I had but newly finished my fence, and began to enjoy my labour, but the rains came on, and made me stick close to my first habitation; for though I had made me a tent like the other, with a piece of a sail, and spread it very well, yet I had not the shelter of a hill to keep me from storms, nor a cave behind me to retreat into when the rains were extraordinary.

About the beginning of August, as I said, I had finished my bower, and began to enjoy myself. The 3rd of August, I found the grapes I had hung up were perfectly dried, and indeed were excellent good raisins of the sun; so I began to take them down from the trees. And it was very happy that I did so, for the rains which followed would have spoiled them, and I had lost the best part of my winter food; for I had above two hundred large bunches of them. No sooner had I taken them all down, and carried most of them home to my cave, but it began to rain; and from hence, which was the 14th of August, it rained, more or less, every day till the middle of October, and sometimes so violently, that I could not stir out of my cave for several days.

In this season, I was much surprised with the increase of my family. I had been concerned for the loss of one of my cats, who run away from me, or, as I thought, had been dead, and I heard no more tale or tidings of her, till, to my astonishment, she came home about the end of August with three kittens. This was the more strange to me, because, though I had killed a wild cat, as I called it, with my gun, yet I thought it was a quite different kind from our European cats; yet the young cats were the same kind of house-breed like the old one; and both my cats being females, I thought it very strange. But from these three cats I afterwards came to be so pestered with cats, that I was forced to kill them like vermin, or wild beasts, and to drive them from my house as much as possible.

From the 14th of August to the 26th, incessant rain, so that I could not stir, and was now very careful not to be much wet. In this confinement, I began to be straitened for food; but venturing out twice, I one day killed a goat, and the last day, which was the 26th, found a very large tortoise, which was a treat to me, and my food was regulated thus: I eat a bunch of raisins for my breakfast, a piece of the goat's flesh, or of the turtle, for my dinner, broiled; for, to my great misfortune, I had no vessel to boil or stew anything; and two or three of the turtle's eggs for my supper.

During this confinement in my cover by the rain, I worked daily two or three hours at enlarging my cave, and by degrees worked it on towards one side, till I came to the outside of the hill, and made a door, or way out, which came beyond my fence or wall; and so I came in and out this way. But I was not perfectly easy at lying so open; for as I had managed myself before, I was in a perfect enclosure; whereas now, I thought I lay exposed, and open for anything to come in upon me; and yet I could not perceive that there was any living thing to fear, the biggest creature that I had yet seen upon the island being a goat.

Sept. 30. — I was now come to the unhappy anniversary of my landing. I cast up the notches on my post, and found I had been on shore three hundred and sixty-five days. I kept this day as a solemn fast, setting it apart to religious exercise, prostrating myself on the ground with the most serious humiliation, confessing my sins to God, acknowledging His righteous judgments upon me, and praying to Him to have mercy on me through Jesus Christ; and having not tasted the least refreshment for twelve hours, even till the going down of the sun, I then eat a biscuit-cake and a bunch of grapes, and went to bed, finishing the day as I began it.

I had all this time observed no Sabbath day, for as at first I had no sense of religion upon my mind, I had, after some time, omitted to distinguish the weeks, by making a longer notch than ordinary for the Sabbath day, and so did not really know what any of the days were. But now, having cast up the days, as above, I found I had been there a year, so I divided it into weeks, and set apart every seventh day for a Sabbath; though I found at the end of my account, I had lost a day or two in my reckoning.

A little after this my ink began to fail me, and so I contented myself to use it more sparingly, and to write down only the most remarkable events of my life, without continuing a daily memorandum of other things.

CHAPTER 9

Crusoe learns the pattern of weather from bitter experience in efforts at cultivation: wet and dry months replacing the European seasons. He sets out to walk the island, discovers unsuspected wild life and sees a distant shore. He catches a young parrot and rescues a kid. Rejoices in the comforts of 'home' on his return after more than four weeks' wandering.

THE RAINY season and the dry season began now to appear regular to me, and I learned to divide them so as to provide for them accordingly; but I bought all my experience before I had it, and this I am going to relate was one of the most discouraging experiments that I made at all. I have mentioned that I had saved the few ears of barley and rice, which I had so surprisingly found spring up, as I thought, of themselves, and believe there were about thirty stalks of rice, and about twenty of barley; and now I thought it a proper time to sow it after the rains, the sun being in its southern position, going from me.

Accordingly I dug up a piece of ground as well as I could with my wooden spade, and dividing it into two parts, I sowed my grain; but as I was sowing, it casually occurred to my thoughts that I would not sow it all at first, because I did not know when was the proper time for it, so I sowed about two-thirds of the seed, leaving about a handful of each.

It was a great comfort to me afterwards that I did so, for not one grain of that I sowed this time came to anything, for the dry months following, the earth having had no rain after the seed was sown, it had no moisture to assist its growth, and never came up at all till the wet season had come again, and then it grew as if it had been but newly sown.

Finding my first seed did not grow, which I easily imagined was by the drought, I sought for a moister piece of ground to make another trial in, and I dug up a piece of ground near my new bower, and sowed the rest of my seed in February, a little before the vernal equinox. And this having the rainy months of March and April to water it, sprung up very pleasantly, and yielded a very good crop; but having part of the seed left only, and not daring to sow all that I had, I had but a small quantity at last, my whole crop not amounting to above a half peck of each kind. But by this experiment I was made master of my business, and knew exactly when the proper season was to sow, and that I might expect two seed-times and two harvests every year.

While this corn was growing, I made a little discovery, which was of use to me afterwards. As soon as the rains were over, and the weather began to settle, which was about the month of November, I made a visit up the country to my bower, where, though I had not been some months, yet I found all things just as I left them. The

CRUSOE SOWING CORN

circle or double hedge that I had made was not only firm and entire, but the stakes which I had cut out of some trees that grew thereabouts were all shot out, and grown with long branches, as much as a willow-tree usually shoots the first year after lopping its head. I could not tell what tree to call it that these stakes were cut from. I was surprised, and yet very well pleased to see the young trees grow, and I pruned them, and led them up to grow as much alike as I could. And it is scarce credible how beautiful a figure they grew into in three years; so that though the hedge made a circle of about twenty-five yards in diameter, yet the trees, for such I might now call them, soon covered it, and it was a complete shade, sufficient to lodge under all the dry season.

This made me resolve to cut some more stakes, and make me a hedge like this, in a semicircle round my wall (I mean that of my first dwelling), which I did; and placing the trees or stakes in a double row, at about eight yards distance from my first fence, they grew presently, and were at first a fine cover to my habitation, and afterwards served for a defence also, as I shall observe in its order.

I found now that the seasons of the year might generally be divided, not into summer and winter, as in Europe, but into the rainy seasons and the dry seasons; which were generally thus:

Half *February* *March* Half *April*	} Rainy, the sun being then on, or near the equinox.

Half *April*
    May
    June
    July
Half *August*
	} Dry, the sun being then to the north of the line.

Half *August* *September* Half *October*	} Rainy, the sun being then come back.

Half *October*
    November
    December
    January
Half *February*
	} Dry, the sun being then to the south of the line.

The rainy season sometimes held longer or shorter as the winds happened to blow, but this was the general observation I made. After I had found by experience the ill consequence of being abroad in the rain, I took care to furnish myself with provisions beforehand, that I might not be obliged to go out; and I sat within doors as much as possible during the wet months.

In this I found much employment, and very suitable also to the time, for I found great occasion of many things which I had no way to furnish myself with but by hard

labour and constant application; particularly, I tried many
ways to make myself a basket; but all the twigs I could get
for the purpose proved so brittle, that they would do
nothing. It proved of excellent advantage to me now, that
when I was a boy I used to take great delight in standing
at a basket-maker's in the town where my father lived, to
see them make their wicker-ware; and being, as boys usually are, very officious to help, and a great observer of the
manner how they worked those things, and sometimes
lending a hand, I had by this means full knowledge of the
methods of it, that I wanted nothing but the materials;
when it came into my mind that the twigs of that tree
from whence I cut my stakes that grew might possibly be
as tough as the sallows, and willows, and osiers in
England, and I resolved to try.

Accordingly, the next day, I went to my country house,
as I called it; and cutting some of the smaller twigs, I
found them to my purpose as much as I could desire;
whereupon I came the next time prepared with a hatchet
to cut down a quantity, which I soon found, for there was
great plenty of them. These I set up to dry within my circle or hedge, and when they were fit for use, I carried
them to my cave; and here during the next season I
employed myself in making, as well as I could, a great
many baskets, both to carry earth, or to carry or lay up
anything as I had occasion. And though I did not finish
them very handsomely, yet I made them sufficiently

serviceable for my purpose. And thus, afterwards, I took
care never to be without them; and as my wicker-ware
decayed, I made more, especially I made strong deep
baskets to place my corn in, instead of sacks, when I
should come to have any quantity of it.

Having mastered this difficulty, and employed a world
of time about it, I bestirred myself to see, if possible, how
to supply two wants. I had no vessels to hold anything
that was liquid, except two runlets, which were almost
full of rum, and some glass bottles, some of the common
size, and others which were case-bottles square, for the
holding of waters, spirits, etc. I had not so much as a pot
to boil anything, except a great kettle, which I saved out
of the ship, and which was too big for such use as I
desired it, viz., to make broth, and stew a bit of meat by
itself. The second thing I would fain have had was a
tobacco-pipe; but it was impossible to me to make one.
However, I found a contrivance for that, too, at last.

I employed myself in planting my second rows of
stakes or piles and in this wicker-working all the summer
or dry season, when another business took me up more
time than it could be imagined I could spare.

I mentioned before that I had a great mind to see the
whole island, and that I had travelled up the brook, and so
on to where I built my bower, and where I had an opening
quite to the sea, on the other side of the island. I now
resolved to travel quite across to the seashore on that

side; so taking my gun, a hatchet, and my dog, and a larger quantity of powder and shot than usual, with two biscuit-cakes and a great bunch of raisins in my pouch for my store, I began my journey. When I had passed the vale where my bower stood, as above, I came within view of the sea to the west; and it being a very clear day, I fairly descried land, whether an island or a continent I could not tell; but it lay very high, extending from the west to the W.S.W. at a very great distance; by my guess, it could not be less than fifteen or twenty leagues off.

I found that side of the island, where I now was, much pleasanter than mine, the open or savanna fields sweet, adorned with flowers and grass, and full of very fine woods.

I saw abundance of parrots, and fain I would have caught one, if possible, to have kept it to be tame, and taught it to speak to me. I did, after some painstaking, catch a young parrot, for I knocked it down with a stick, and having recovered it, I brought it home; but it was some years before I could make him speak. However, at last I taught him to call me by my name very familiarly. But the accident that followed, though it be a trifle, will be very diverting in its place.

I was exceedingly diverted with this journey. I found on the low grounds hares, as I thought them to be, and foxes; but they differed greatly from all the other kinds I had met with, nor could I satisfy myself to eat them, though I killed several. But I had no need to be venturous, for I had no want of food, and of that which was very good too; especially these three sorts, viz., goats, pigeons, and turtle, or tortoise; which, added to my grapes, Leadenhall Market could not have furnished a table better than I, in proportion to the company. And though my case was deplorable enough, yet I had great cause for thankfulness, and that I was not driven to any extremities for food, but rather plenty, even to dainties.

I never travelled in this journey above two miles outright in a day, or thereabouts; but I took so many turns and returns, to see what discoveries I could make, that I came weary enough to the place where I resolved to sit down for all night; and then I either reposed myself in a tree, or surrounded myself with a row of stakes, set upright in the ground, either from one tree or another, or so as no wild creature could come at me without waking me.

As soon as I came to the seashore, I was surprised to see that I had taken up my lot on the worst side of the island, for here indeed the shore was covered with innumerable turtles; whereas, on the other side, I had found but three in a year and a half. Here was also an infinite number of fowls of many kinds, some of which I had seen, and some which I had not seen of before, and many of them very good meat, but such as I knew not the names of, except those called penguins.

I could have shot as many as I pleased, but was very sparing of my powder and shot, and therefore had more mind to kill a she-goat, if I could, which I could better feed on; and though there were many goats here, more than on my side of the island, yet it was with much more difficulty that I could come near them, the country being flat and even, and they saw me much sooner than when I was on the hill.

I confess this side of the country was much pleasanter than mine; but yet I had not the least inclination to remove, for as I was fixed in my habitation, it became natural to me, and I seemed all the while I was here to be as it were upon a journey, and from home. However, I travelled along the shore of the sea towards the east, I suppose about twelve miles, and then setting up a great pole upon the shore for a mark, I concluded I would go home again; and that the next journey I took should be on the other side of the island, east from my dwelling, and so round till I came to my post again; of which in its place.

I took another way to come back than that I went, thinking I could easily keep all the island so much in my view, that I could not miss finding my first dwelling by viewing the country. But I found myself mistaken; for being come about two or three miles, I found myself descended into a very large valley, but so surrounded with hills, and those hills covered with wood, that I could not see which was my way by any direction but that of the sun, nor even then, unless I knew very well the position of the sun at that time of the day.

It happened to my farther misfortune, that the weather proved hazy for three or four days while I was in this valley; and not being able to see the sun, I wandered about very uncomfortably, and at last was obliged to find out the seaside, look for my post, and come back the same way I went; and then by easy journeys I turned home-ward, the weather being exceeding hot, and my gun, ammunition, hatchet, and other things very heavy.

In this journey my dog surprised a young kid, and seized upon it, and I running in to take hold of it, caught it, and saved it alive from the dog. I had a great mind to bring it home if I could, for I had often been musing whether it might not be possible to get a kid or two, and so raise a breed of tame goats, which might supply me when my powder and shot should be all spent.

I made a collar to this little creature, and with a string, which I made of some rope-yarn, which I always carried about with me, I led him along, though with some diffi-culty, till I came to my bower, and there I enclosed him and left him, for I was very impatient to be at home, from whence I had been absent above a month.

I cannot express what a satisfaction it was to me to come into my old hutch, and lie down in my hammock-bed. This little wandering journey, without settled place of abode, had been so unpleasant to me, that my own house, as I called it to myself, was a perfect settlement to me compared to that; and it rendered everything about me so comfortable, that I resolved I would never go a great way from it again, while it should be my lot to stay on the island.

CHAPTER 10

Crusoe makes a cage for his parrot, Poll. Tames the kid. He now begins his third year of solitude. Dividing the day according to his several employments he is seldom idle. Is forced to take steps to prevent wild animals and birds destroying his crops. In primitive fashion reaps his harvest.

I REPOSED myself here a week, to rest and regale myself after my long journey; during which most of the time was taken up in the weighty affair of making a cage for my Poll, who began now to be a mere domestic, and to be mighty well acquainted with me. Then I began to think of the poor kid which I had penned in within my little circle, and resolved to go and fetch it home, or give it some food. Accordingly I went, and found it where I left it, for indeed it could not get out, but almost starved for want of food. I went and cut boughs of trees, and branches of such shrubs as I could find, and threw it over, and having fed it, I tied it as I did before, to lead it away; but it was so tame with being hungry, that I had no need to have tied it, for it followed me like a dog. And as I continually fed it, the creature became so loving, so gentle, and so fond, that it became from that time one of my domestics also, and would never leave me afterwards.

The rainy season of the autumnal equinox was now come, and I kept the 30th September in the same solemn

manner as before, being the anniversary of my landing on
the island, having now been there two years, and no more
prospect of being delivered than the first day I came
there. I spent the whole day in humble and thankful
acknowledgments of the many wonderful mercies which
my solitary condition was attended with, and without
which it might have been infinitely more miserable.

It was now that I began sensibly to feel how much
more happy this life I now led was, with all its miserable
circumstances, than the wicked, cursed, abominable life I
led all the past part of my days. And now I changed both
my sorrows and my joys; my very desires altered, my
affections changed their gusts, and my delights were perfectly new from what they were at my first coming, or
indeed for the two years past.

I sincerely gave thanks to God for opening my eyes, by
whatever afflicting providences, to see the former condition of my life, and to mourn for my wickedness, and
repent. I never opened the Bible, or shut it, but my very
soul within me blessed God for directing my friend in
England, without any order of mine, to pack it up among
my goods, and for assisting me afterwards to save it out of
the wreck of the ship.

Thus, and in this disposition of mind, I began my third
year; and though I have not given the reader the trouble
of so particular account of my works this year as the first,
yet in general it may be observed, that I was seldom idle,

but having regularly divided my time, according to the several daily employments that were before me, such as, first, my duty to God, and the reading the Scriptures, which I constantly set apart some time for, thrice every day; secondly, the going abroad with my gun for food, which generally took me up three hours in every morning, when it did not rain; thirdly, the ordering, curing, preserving, and cooking what I had killed or catched for my supply; these took up great part of the day; also, it is to be considered that the middle of the day, when the sun was in the zenith, the violence of the heat was too great to stir out; so that about four hours in the evening was all the time I could be supposed to work in, with this exception, that sometimes I changed my hours of hunting and working, and went to work in the morning, and abroad with my gun in the afternoon.

To this short time allowed for labour, I desire may be added the exceeding laboriousness of my work; the many hours which, for want of tools, want of help, and want of skill, everything I did took up out of my time. For example, I was full two and forty days making me a board for a long shelf, which I wanted in my cave; whereas two sawyers, with their tools and a saw-pit, would have cut six of them out of the same tree in half a day.

My case was this: it was to be a large tree which was to be cut down, because my board was to be a broad one. This tree I was three days a-cutting down, and two more cutting off the boughs, and reducing it to a log, or piece of timber. With inexpressible hacking and hewing, I reduced both sides of it into chips till it begun to be light enough to move; then I turned it, and made one side of it smooth and flat as a board from end to end; then turning that side downward, cut the other side, till I brought the plank to be about three inches thick, and smooth on both sides. Any one may judge the labour of my hands in such a piece of work; but labour and patience carried me through that, and many other things. I only observe this in particular, to show the reason why so much of my time went away with so little work, viz., that what might be a little to be done with help and tools, was a vast labour, and required a prodigious time to do alone, and by hand. But notwithstanding this, with patience and labour, I went through many things, and, indeed, everything that my circumstances made necessary to me to do, as will appear by what follows.

I was now, in the months of November and December, expecting my crop of barley and rice. The ground I had manured or dug up for them was not great; for as I observed, my seed of each was not above the quantity of half a peck; for I had lost one whole crop by sowing in the dry season. But now my crop promised very well, when on a sudden I found I was in danger of losing it all again by enemies of several sorts, which it was scarce possible to keep from it; as first the goats and wild creatures which I called hares, who, tasting the sweetness of the blade, lay in it night and day, as soon as it came up, and eat it so close, that it could get no time to shoot up into stalk.

This I saw no remedy for but by making an enclosure about it with a hedge, which I did with a great deal of toil, and the more, because it required speed. However, as my arable land was but small, suited to my crop, I got it totally well fenced in about three weeks' time, and shooting some of the creatures in the daytime, I set my dog to guard it in the night, tying him up to a stake in the gate, where he would stand and bark all night long; so in a little time the enemies forsook the place, and the corn grew very strong and well, and began to ripen apace.

But as the beasts ruined me before while my corn was in the blade, so the birds were as likely to ruin me now when it was in the ear; for going along by the place to see how it throve, I saw my little crop surrounded with fowls, of I know not how many sorts, who stood, as it were, watching till I should be gone. I immediately let fly among them, for I always had my gun with me. I had no sooner shot, but there rose up a little cloud of fowls, which I had not seen at all, from among the corn itself.

This touched me sensibly, for I foresaw that in a few days they would devour all my hopes, that I should be starved, and never be able to raise a crop at all, and what to do I could not tell. However, I resolved not to lose my corn, if possible, though I should watch it night and day.

In the first place, I went among it to see what damage was already done, and found they had spoiled a good deal of it, but that as it was yet too green for them, the loss was not so great but that the remainder was like to be a good crop if it could be saved.

I stayed by it to load my gun, and then coming away, I could easily see the thieves sitting upon all the trees about me, as if they only waited till I was gone away. And the event proved it to be so; for as I walked off, as if I was gone, I was no sooner out of their sight but they dropped down, one by one, into the corn again. I was so provoked, that I could not have patience to stay till more came on, knowing that every grain that they eat now was, as it might be said, a peck-loaf to me in the consequence; but coming up to the hedge, I fired again, and killed three of them. This was what I wished for; so I took them up, and served them as we serve notorious thieves in England, viz., hanged them in chains, for a terror to others. It is impossible to imagine almost that this should have such an effect as it had, for the fowls would not only not come at the corn, but, in short, they forsook all that part of the island, and I could never see a bird near the place as long as my scare-crows hung there.

This I was very glad of, you may be sure; and about the latter end of December, which was our second harvest of the year, I reaped my crop.

I was sadly put to it for a scythe or a sickle to cut it

down, and all I could do was to make one as well as I could out of one of the broadswords, or cutlasses, which I saved among the arms out of the ship. However, as my first crop was but small, I had no great difficulty to cut it down; in short, I reaped it my way, for I cut nothing off but the ears, and carried it away in a great basket which I had made, and so rubbed it out with my hands; and at the end of all my harvesting, I found that out of my half peck of seed I had near two bushels of rice, and above two bushels and a half of barley, that is to say, by my guess, for I had no measure at that time.

However, this was a great encouragement to me, and I foresaw that, in time, it would please God to supply me with bread. And yet here I was perplexed again, for I neither knew how to grind or make meal of my corn, or indeed how to clean it and pat it; nor, if made into meal, how to make bread of it, and if how to make it, yet I knew not how to bake it. These things being added to my desire of having a good quantity for store, and to secure a constant supply, I resolved not to taste any of this crop, but to preserve it all for seed against the next season, and, in the meantime, to employ all my study and hours of working to accomplish this great work of providing myself with corn and bread.

It might be truly said, that now I worked for my bread. 'Tis a little wonderful, and what I believe few people have thought much upon, viz., the strange multitude of little things necessary in the providing, producing, curing, dressing, making, and finishing this one article of bread.

I, that was reduced to a mere state of nature, found this to my daily discouragement, and was made more and more sensible of it every hour, even after I had got the first handful of seed-corn, which, as I have said, came up unexpectedly, and indeed to a surprise.

First, I had no plough to turn up the earth, no spade or shovel to dig it. Well, this I conquered by making a wooden spade, as I observed before, but this did my work in but a wooden manner; and though it cost me a great many days to make it, yet, for want of iron, it not only wore out the sooner, but made my work the harder, and made it be performed much worse.

However, this I bore with, and was content to work it out with patience, and bear with the badness of the performance. When the corn was sowed, I had no harrow, but was forced to go over it myself, and drag a great heavy bough of a tree over it, to scratch it, as it may be called, rather than rake or harrow it.

When it was growing and grown, I have observed already how many things I wanted to fence it, secure it, mow or reap it, cure and carry it home, thrash, part it from the chaff, and save it. Then I wanted a mill to grind it, sieves to dress it, yeast and salt to make it into bread, and an oven to bake it, and yet all these things I did without, as shall be observed; and yet the corn was an inestimable comfort and advantage to me too. All this, as I said, made everything laborious and tedious to me, but that there was no help for; neither was my time so much loss to me, because, as I had divided it, a certain part of it was every day appointed to these works, and as I resolved to use none of the corn for bread till I had a greater quantity by me, I had the next six months to apply myself wholly, by labour and invention, to furnish myself with utensils proper for the performing all the operations necessary for the making the corn, when I had it, fit for my use.

But first I was to prepare more land, for I had now seed enough to sow above an acre of ground. Before I did this, I had a week's work at least to make me a spade, which, when it was done, was but a sorry one indeed, and very heavy, and required double labour to work with it. However, I went through that, and sowed my seed in two large flat pieces of ground, as near my house as I could find them to my mind, and fenced them in with a good hedge, the stakes of which were all cut of that wood which I had set before, and knew it would grow; so that in one year's time I knew I should have a quick or living hedge, that would want but little repair. This work was not so little as to take me up less than three months, because great part of that time was of the wet season, when I could not go abroad.

CHAPTER 11

*During the wet season Crusoe succeeds in making cooking pots
and water jars. He enjoys his first stew. Contrives implements
and utensils to pound and sift his grain, and bakes his first loaves
of bread. Poll a diverting companion speaks the first word
Crusoe has heard in any voice save his own. In his fourth year
Crusoe's thoughts turn to escape.*

WITHIN DOORS, that is, when it rained, and I could not go out, I found employment on the following occasions; always observing, that all the while I was at work, I diverted myself with talking to my parrot, and teaching him to speak, and I quickly learned him to know his own name, and at last to speak it out pretty loud, 'Poll,' which was the first word I ever heard spoken in the island by any mouth but my own. This, therefore, was not my work, but an assistant to my work; for now, as I said, I had a great employment upon my hands, as follows, viz., I had long studied, by some means or other, to make myself some earthen vessels, which indeed I wanted sorely, but knew not where to come at them. However, considering the heat of the climate, I did not doubt but if I could find out any such clay, I might botch up some such pot as might, being dried in the sun, be hard enough and strong enough to bear handling, and to hold anything that was dry, and required to be kept so; and as this was necessary

CRUSOE TEACHES HIS PARROT TO TALK

in the preparing corn, meal, etc.,
which was the thing I was upon, I resolved to
make some as large as I could, and fit only to stand
like jars, to hold what should be put into them.

It would make the reader pity me, or rather laugh
at me, to tell how many awkward ways I took to
raise this paste; what odd, misshapen, ugly things I
made; how many of them fell in, and how many fell
out, the clay not being stiff enough to bear its own

weight; how many cracked by the over-violent heat of the sun, being set out too hastily; and how many fell in pieces with only removing, as well before as after they were dried; and, in a word, how, after having laboured hard to find clay, to dig it, to temper it, to bring it home, and work it, I could not make above two large earthen ugly things (I cannot call them jars) in about two months' labour.

However, as the sun baked these two very dry and hard, I lifted them very gently up, and set them down again in two great wicker baskets, which I had made on purpose for them, that they might not break; and as between the pot and the basket there was a little room to spare, I stuffed it full of the rice and barley straw, and these two pots being to stand always dry, I thought it would hold my dry corn, and perhaps the meal, when the corn was bruised.

Though I miscarried so much in my design for large pots, yet I made several smaller things with better success; such as little round pots, flat dishes, pitchers, and pipkins, and any things my hand turned to; and the heat of the sun baked them strangely hard. But all this would not answer my end, which was to get an earthen pot to hold what was liquid, and bear the fire, which none of these could do. I happened after some time, making a pretty large fire for cooking my meat, when I went to put it out after I had done with it, I found a broken piece of one of my earthenware vessels in the fire, burnt as hard as a stone, and red as a tile. I was agreeably surprised to see it, and said to myself, that certainly they might be made to burn whole, if they would burn broken.

This set me to studying how to order my fire, so as to make it burn me some pots. I had no notion of a kiln, such as the potters burn in, or of glazing them with lead, though I had some lead to do it with; but I placed three large pipkins, and two or three pots in a pile, one upon another, and placed my firewood all round it, with a great heap of embers under them. I plied the fire with fresh fuel round the outside, and upon the top, till I saw the pots in the inside red-hot quite through and observed that they did not crack at all. When I saw them clear red, I let them stand in that heat about five or six hours, till I found one of them, though it did not crack, did melt or run, for the sand which was mixed with the clay melted by the violence of the heat, and would have run into glass, if I had gone on; so I slacked my fire gradually till the pots began to abate of the red colour; and watching them all night, that I might not let the fire abate too fast, in the morning I had three very good, I will not say handsome, pipkins, and two other earthen pots, as hard burnt as could be desired, and one of them perfectly glazed with the running of the sand.

After this experiment, I need not say that I wanted no sort of earthenware for my use; but I must needs say, as to the shapes of them, they were very indifferent, as any one

may suppose, when I had no way of making them but as
the children make dirt pies, or as a woman would make
pies that never learned to raise paste.

No joy at a thing of so mean a nature was ever equal to
mine, when I had found I had made an earthen pot that
would bear the fire; and I had hardly patience to stay till
they were cold, before I set one upon the fire again, with
some water in it, to boil me some meat, which it did
admirably well; and with a piece of a kid I made some
very good broth, though I wanted oatmeal and several
other ingredients requisite to make it so good as I would
have had it been.

My next concern was to get me a stone mortar to
stamp or beat some corn in; for as to the mill, there was
no thought at arriving to that perfection of art with one
pair of hands. To supply this want I was at a great loss; for,
of all trades in the world, I was as perfectly unqualified
for a stone-cutter as for any whatever; neither had I any
tools to go about it with. I spent many a day to find out a
great stone big enough to cut hollow, and make fit for a
mortar, and could find none at all, except what was in the
solid rock, and which I had no way to dig or cut out; nor
indeed were the rocks in the island of hardness sufficient,
but were all of a sandy crumbling stone, which neither
would bear the weight of a heavy pestle, or would break
the corn without filling it with sand. So, after a great deal
of time lost in searching for a stone, I gave it over, and

resolved to look out for a great block of hard wood, which I found indeed much easier; and getting one as big as I had strength to stir, I rounded it, and formed it in the outside with my axe and hatchet, and then, with the help of fire, and infinite labour, made a hollow place in it, as the Indians in Brazil made their canoes. After this, I made a great heavy pestle, or beater, of the wood called the iron-wood; and this I prepared and laid by against I had my next crop of corn, when I proposed to myself to grind, or rather pound, my corn into meal, to make my bread.

My next difficulty was to make a sieve, or search, to dress my meal, and to part it from the bran and the husk, without which I did not see it possible I could have any bread. This was a most difficult thing, so much as but to think on, for to be sure I had nothing like the necessary thing to make it; I mean fine thin canvas or stuff, to search the meal through. And here I was at a full stop for many months, nor did I really know what to do; linen I had none left, but what was mere rags; I had goats'-hair, but neither knew I how to weave it or spin it; and had I known how, here was no tools to work it with. All the remedy that I found for this was, that at last I did remember I had, among the seamen's clothes which were saved out of the ship, some neckcloths of calico or muslin; and with some pieces of these I made three small sieves, but proper enough for the work; and thus I made shift for some years. How I did afterwards, I shall show in its place.

The baking part was the next thing to be considered, and how I should make bread when I came to have corn; for, first, I had no yeast. As to that part, as there was no supplying the want, so I did not concern myself much about it; but for an oven I was indeed in great pain. At length I found out an experiment for that also, which was this: I made some earthen vessels very broad, but not deep, that is to say, about two feet diameter, and not above nine inches deep; these I burned in the fire, as I had done the other, and laid them by; and when I wanted to bake, I made a great fire upon my hearth, which I had paved with some square tiles, of my own making, and burning also; but I should not call them square.

When the firewood was burned pretty much into embers, or live coals, I drew them forward upon this hearth, so as to cover it all over, and there I let them lie till the hearth was very hot; then sweeping away all the embers, I set down my loaf, or loaves, and whelming down the earthen pot upon them, drew the embers all round the outside of the pot, to keep in and add to the heat. And thus, as well as in the best oven in the world, I baked my barley-loaves, and became, in little time, a mere pastry-cook into the bargain; for I made myself several cakes of the rice, and puddings; indeed I made no pies, neither had I anything to put into them, supposing I had, except the flesh either of fowls or goats.

It need not be wondered at, if all these things took me

up most part of the third year of my abode here; for it is to be observed, that in the intervals of these things I had my new harvest and husbandry to manage; for I reaped my corn in its season, and carried it home as well as I could, and laid it up in the ear, in my large baskets, till I had time to rub it out, for I had no floor to thrash it on, or instrument to thrash it with.

And now, indeed, my stock of corn increasing, I really wanted to build my barns bigger. I wanted a place to lay it up in, for the increase of the corn now yielded me so much, that I had of the barley about twenty bushels, and of the rice as much, or more, insomuch that now I resolved to begin to use it freely; for my bread had been quite gone a great while; also, I resolved to see what quantity would be sufficient for me a whole year, and to sow but once a year.

Upon the whole, I found that the forty bushels of barley and rice was much more than I could consume in a year; so I resolved to sow just the same quantity every year that I sowed the last, in hopes that such a quantity would fully provide me with bread, etc.

All the while these things were doing, you may be sure my thoughts run many times upon the prospect of land which I had seen from the other side of the island, and I was not without secret wishes that I were on shore there, fancying the seeing the mainland, and in an inhabited country, I might find some way or other to convey myself farther, and perhaps at last find some means of escape.

But all this while I made no allowance for the dangers of such a condition, and how I might fall into the hands of savages, and perhaps such as I might have reason to think far worse than the lions and tigers of Africa; that if I once came into their power, I should run a hazard more than a thousand to one of being killed, and perhaps of being eaten; for I had heard that the people of the Caribbean coasts were cannibals, or man-eaters, and I knew by the latitude that I could not be far off from that shore. That suppose they were not cannibals, yet that they might kill me, as many Europeans who had fallen into their hands had been served, even when they had been ten or twenty together, much more I, that was but one, and could make little or no defence; all these things, I say, which I ought to have considered well of, and did cast up in my thoughts afterwards, yet took up none of my apprehensions at first, but my head ran mightily upon the thought of getting over to the shore.

Now I wished for my boy Xury, and the long-boat with the shoulder-of-mutton sail, with which I sailed above a thousand miles on the coast of Africa; but this was in vain. Then I thought I would go and look at our ship's boat, which, as I have said, was blown up upon the shore a great way, in the storm, when we were first cast away. She lay almost where she did at first, but not quite; and was turned, by the force of the waves and the winds, almost bottom upward, against a high ridge of beachy rough sand, but no water about her, as before.

If I had had hands to have refitted her, and to have launched her into the water, the boat would have done well enough, and I might have gone back into the Brazils with her easily enough; but I might have foreseen that I could no more turn her and set her upright upon her bottom, than I could remove the island. However, I went to the woods, and cut levers and rollers, and brought them to the boat, resolved to try what I could do; suggesting to myself that if I could but turn her down, I might easily repair the damage she had received, and she would be a very good boat, and I might go to sea in her very easily.

I spared no pains, indeed, in this piece of fruitless toil, and spent, I think, three or four weeks about it. At last finding it impossible to heave it up with my little strength, I fell to digging away the sand, to undermine it, and so to make it fall down, setting pieces of wood to thrust and guide it right in the fall. But when I had done this, I was unable to stir it up again, or to get under it, much less to move it forward towards the water; so I was forced to give it over. And yet, though I gave over the hopes of the boat, my desire to venture over for the main increased, rather than decreased, as the means for it seemed impossible.

CHAPTER 12

Crusoe decides to make a canoe, 'going to work the most like a fool'. After months of wasted labour he chides himself for his lack of foresight. To offset his discouragement he counts his blessings. Needing protection from heavy rain and scorching sun Crusoe makes himself an original outfit. After many attempts he achieves a fine umbrella.

THIS AT length put me upon thinking whether it was not possible to make myself a canoe, or *periagua*, such as the natives of those climates make, even without tools, or, as I might say, without hands, viz., of the trunk of a great tree. This I not only thought possible, but easy, and pleased myself extremely with the thoughts of making it, and with my having much more convenience for it than any of the negroes or Indians; but not at all considering the particular inconveniences which I lay under more than the Indians did, viz., want of hands to move it, when it was made, into the water, a difficulty much harder for me to surmount than all the consequences of want of tools could be to them. For what was it to me, that when I had chosen a vast tree in the woods, I might with much trouble cut it down, if, after I might be able with my tools to hew and dub the outside into the proper shape of a boat, and burn or cut out the inside to make it hollow, so to make a boat of it; if, after all this, I must leave it just there where I found it, and was not able to launch it into the water?

One would have thought I could not have had the least reflection upon my mind of my circumstance while I was making this boat, but I should have immediately thought how I should get it into the sea; but my thoughts were so intent upon my voyage over the sea in it, that I never once considered how I should get it off of the land; and it was really, in its own nature, more easy for me to guide it over forty-five miles of sea, than about forty-five fathoms of land, where it lay, to set it afloat in the water.

I went to work upon this boat the most like a fool that ever man did who had any of his senses awake. I pleased myself with the design, without determining whether I was ever able to undertake it. Not but that the difficulty of launching my boat came often into my head; but I put a stop to my own inquiries into it, by this foolish answer which I gave myself, 'Let's first make it; I'll warrant I'll find some way or other to get it along when 'tis done.'

This was a most preposterous method; but the eagerness of my fancy prevailed, and to work I went. I felled a cedar tree: I question much whether Solomon ever had such a one for the building of the Temple at Jerusalem. It was five feet ten inches diameter at the lower part next the stump, and four feet eleven inches diameter at the end of twenty-two feet, after which it lessened for awhile, and then parted into branches. It was not without infinite

CRUSOE MAKES A BOAT

W.L.THOMAS.Sc

labour that I felled this tree. I was twenty days hacking and hewing at it at the bottom; I was fourteen more getting the branches and limbs, and the vast spreading head of it cut off, which I hacked and hewed through with axe and hatchet, and inexpressible labour. After this, it cost me a month to shape it and dub it to a proportion, and to something like the bottom of a boat, that it might swim upright as it ought to do. It cost me near three months more to clear the inside, and work it so as to make an exact boat of it. This I did, indeed, without fire, by mere mallet and chisel, and by the dint of hard labour, till I had brought it to be a very handsome *periagua* and big enough to have carried six and twenty men, and consequently big enough to have carried me and all my cargo.

When I had gone through this work, I was extremely delighted with it. The boat was really much bigger than I ever saw a canoe or *periagua*, that was made of one tree, in my life. Many a weary stroke it had cost, you may be sure; and there remained nothing but to get it into the water; I make no question but I should have begun the maddest voyage, and the most unlikely to be performed, that ever was undertaken.

But all my devices to get it into the water failed me, though they cost me infinite labour too. It lay about one hundred yards from the water, and not more; but the first inconvenience was, it was uphill towards the creek. Well, to take away this discouragement, I resolved to dig into the surface of the earth, and so make a declivity. This I began, and it cost me a prodigious deal of pains; but who grudges pains, that have their deliverance in view? But when this was worked through, and this difficulty managed, it was still much at one, for I could no more stir the canoe than I could the other boat.

Then I measured the distance of ground, and resolved to cut a dock or canal, to bring the water up to the canoe, seeing I could not bring the canoe down to the water. Well, I began this work; and when I began to enter into it, and calculate how deep it was to be dug, how broad, how the stuff to be thrown out, I found that by the number of hands I had, being none but my own, it must have been ten or twelve years before I should have gone through with it; for the shore lay high, so that at the upper end it must have been at least twenty feet deep; so at length, though with great reluctancy, I gave this attempt over also.

This grieved me heartily; and now I saw, though too late, the folly of beginning a work before we count the cost, and before we judge rightly of our own strength to go through with it.

In the middle of this work I finished my fourth year in this place, and kept my anniversary with the same devotion, and with as much comfort as ever before; for, by a constant study and serious application of the Word of God, and by the assistance of His grace, I gained a different knowledge from what I had before. I entertained different notions of things. I looked now upon the world as a thing remote, which I had nothing to do with, no expectation from, and, indeed, no desires about. In a word, I had nothing indeed to do with it, nor was ever like to have; so I thought it looked, as we may perhaps look upon it hereafter, viz., as a place I had lived in, but was come out of it; and well might I say, as father Abraham to Dives, 'Between me and thee is a great gulf fixed.'

In the first place, I was removed from all the wickedness of the world here. I had neither the lust of the flesh, the lust of the eye, or the pride of life. I had nothing to covet, for I had all that I was now capable of enjoying. I was lord of the whole manor; or, if I pleased, I might call myself king or emperor over the whole country which I had possession of. There were no rivals; I had no competitor, none to dispute sovereignty or command with me. I might have raised ship-loadings of corn, but I had no use for it; so I let as little grow as I thought enough for my occasion. I had tortoise or turtles enough, but now and then one was as much as I could put to any use. I had timber enough to have built a fleet of ships. I had grapes enough to have made wine, or to have cured into raisins, to have loaded that fleet when they had been built.

But all I could make use of was all that was valuable. I had enough to eat and to supply my wants, and what was all the rest to me? If I killed more flesh than I could eat, the dog must eat it, or the vermin. If I sowed more corn than I could eat, it must be spoiled. The trees that I cut down were lying to rot on the ground; I could make no more use of them than for fuel, and that I had no occasion for but to dress my food.

In a word, the nature and experience of things dictated to me, upon just reflection, that all the good things of this world are no farther good to us than they are for our use; and that whatever we may heap up indeed to give others, we enjoy just as much as we can use, and no more. The most covetous, griping miser in the world would have been cured of the vice of covetousness, if he had been in my case; for I possessed infinitely more than I knew what to do with. I had no room for desire, except it was of things which I had not, and they were but trifles, though indeed of great use to me. I had, as I hinted before, a parcel of money, as well gold as silver, about thirty-six pounds sterling. Alas! there the nasty, sorry, useless stuff lay; I had no manner of business for it; and I often thought with myself, that I would have given a handful of it for a gross of tobacco-pipes, or for a hand-mill to grind my corn; nay, I would have given it all for sixpenny-worth of turnip and carrot seed out of England, or for a handful of peas and beans, and a bottle of ink. As it was, I had not the least advantage by it, or benefit from it; but there it lay in a drawer, and grew mouldy with the damp of the cave in the wet season; and if I had had the drawer full of diamonds, it had been the same case, and they had been of no manner of value to me because of no use.

CRUSOE AT DINNER

I had now brought my state of life to be much easier in itself than it was at first, and much easier to my mind, as well as to my body. I frequently sat down to my meat with thankfulness, and admired the hand of God's providence, which had thus spread my table in the wilderness. I learned to look more upon the bright side of my condition, and less upon the dark side, and to consider what I enjoyed, rather than what I wanted; and this gave me sometimes such secret comforts, that I cannot express them; and which I take notice of here, to put those discontented people in mind of it, who cannot enjoy comfortably what God has given them, because they see and covet something that He has not given them. All our discontents about what we want, appeared to me to spring from the want of thankfulness for what we have.

Another reflection was of great use to me, and doubtless would be so to any one that should fall into such distress as mine was; and this was, to compare my present condition with what I at first expected it should be; nay, with what it would certainly have been, if the good providence of God had not wonderfully ordered the ship to be cast up nearer to the shore, where I not only could come at her, but could bring what I got out of her to the shore, for my relief and comfort; without which I had wanted for tools to work, weapons for defence, or gunpowder and shot for getting my food.

I spent whole hours, I may say whole days, in representing to myself, in the most lively colours, how I must have acted if I had got nothing out of the ship. How I could not have so much as got any food, except fish and turtles; and that as it was long before I found any of them, I must have perished first; that I should have lived, if I had not perished, like a mere savage; that if I had killed a goat or a fowl, by any contrivance, I had no way to flay or open them, or part the flesh from the skin and the bowels, or to cut it up; but must gnaw it with my teeth, and pull it with my claws, like a beast.

These reflections made me very sensible of the goodness of Providence to me, and very thankful for my present condition, with all its hardships and misfortunes.

In a word, as my life was a life of sorrow one way, so it was a life of mercy another; and I wanted nothing to make it a life of comfort, but to be able to make my sense of God's goodness to me, and care over me in this condition, be my daily consolation; and after I did make a just improvement of these things, I went away, and was no more sad.

I had now been here so long, that many things which I brought on shore for my help were either quite gone, or very much wasted, and near spent. My ink, as I observed, had been gone for some time, all but a very little, which I eked out with water, a little and a little, till it was so pale it scarce left any appearance of black upon the paper. As long as it lasted, I made use of it to minute down the days of the month on which any remarkable thing happened to me. And, first, by casting up times past, I remember that there was a strange concurrence of days in the various providences which befell me, and which, if I had been superstitiously inclined to observe days as fatal or fortunate, I might have had reason to have looked upon with a great deal of curiosity.

First, I had observed that the same day that I broke away from my father and my friends, and run away to Hull, in order to go to sea, the same day afterwards I was taken by the Sallee man-of-war, and made a slave.

The same day of the year that I escaped out of the wreck of that ship in Yarmouth Roads, that same day-year afterwards I made my escape from Sallee in the boat.

The same day of the year I was born on, viz., the 30th of September, that same day I had my life so miraculously saved twenty-six years after, when I was cast on shore in this island; so that my wicked life and my solitary life began both on a day.

The next thing to my ink's being wasted, was that of my bread; I mean the biscuit, which I brought out of the ship. This I had husbanded to the last degree, allowing myself but one cake of bread a day for above a year; and yet I was quite without bread for near a year before I got any corn of my own; and great reason I had to be thankful that I had any at all, the getting it being, as has been already observed, next to miraculous.

My clothes began to decay, too, mightily. As to linen, I had none a good while, except some chequered shirts which I found in the chests of the other seamen, and which I carefully preserved, because many times I could bear no other clothes on but a shirt; and it was a very great help to me that I had, among all the men's clothes of the ship, almost three dozen of shirts. There were also several thick watch-coats of the seamen's which were left indeed, but they were too hot to wear; and though it is true that the weather was so violent hot that there was no need of clothes, yet I could not go quite naked, no, though I had been inclined to it, which I was not, nor could abide the thoughts of it, though I was all alone.

The reason why I could not go quite naked was, I could not bear the heat of the sun so well when quite naked as with some clothes on; nay, the very heat frequently blistered my skin; whereas, with a shirt on, the air itself made some motion, and whistling under the shirt, was twofold cooler than without it. No more could I ever bring myself to go out in the heat of the sun without a cap or a hat. The heat of the sun beating with such violence, as it does in that place, would give me the headache presently, by darting so directly on my head, without a cap or a hat on, so that I could not bear it; whereas, if I put on my hat, it would presently go away.

Upon these views, I began to consider about putting the few rags I had, which I called clothes, into some order.

CRUSOE MAKING A COAT.

I had worn out all the waistcoats I had, and my business was now to try if I could not make jackets out of the great watch-coats which I had by me, and with such other materials as I had; so I set to work a-tailoring, or rather, indeed, a-botching, for I made most piteous work of it. However, I made shift to make me two or three new waistcoats, which I hoped would serve me a great while. As for breeches or drawers, I made but a very sorry shift indeed till afterward.

I have mentioned that I saved the skins of all the creatures that I killed, I mean four-footed ones, and I had hung them up stretched out with sticks in the sun, by which means some of them were so dry and hard that they were fit for little, but others it seems were very useful. The first thing I made of these was a great cap for my head, with the hair on the outside, to shoot off the rain; and this I performed so well, that after this I made me a suit of clothes wholly of these skins, that is to say, a waistcoat, and breeches open at knees, and both loose, for they were rather wanting to keep me cool than to keep me warm. I must not omit to acknowledge that they were wretchedly made; for if I was a bad carpenter, I was a worse tailor. However, they were such as I made very good shift with; and when I was abroad, if it happened to rain, the hair of my waistcoat and cap being outermost, I was kept very dry.

After this I spent a great deal of time and pains to make me an umbrella. I was indeed in great want of one, and had a great mind to make one. I had seen them made in the Brazils, where they are very useful in the great heats which are there; and I felt the heats every jot as great here, and greater too, being nearer the equinox. Besides, as I was obliged to be much abroad, it was a most useful thing to me, as well for the rains as the heats. I took a world of pains at it, and was a great while before I could make anything likely to hold; nay, after I thought I had hit the way, I spoiled two or three before I made one to my mind; but at last I made one that answered indifferently well. The main difficulty I found was to make it to let down. I could make it to spread; but if it did not let down too, and draw in, it was not portable for me any way but just over my head, which would not do. However, at last, as I said, I made one to answer, and covered it with skins, the hair upwards, so that it cast off the rains like a penthouse, and kept off the sun so effectually, that I could walk out in the hottest of the weather with greater advantage than I could before in the coolest; and when I had no need of it, could close it, and carry it under my arm.

Thus I lived mighty comfortably, my mind being entirely composed by resigning to the will of God, and throwing myself wholly upon the disposal of His providence.

CHAPTER 13

*Crusoe makes a second boat. In an attempt to sail round the
island narrowly escapes disaster. After great exertion safely lands
at farthermost point from his habitation. Comes to his country
house at nightfall. Is startled from sleep by voice calling his name.
Greatly astonished to find Poll.*

ICANNOT say that after this, for five years, any extraordinary thing happened to me; but I lived on in the
same course, in the same posture and place, just as
before. The chief things I was employed in, besides my
yearly labour of planting my barley and rice, and curing
my raisins, of both which I always kept up just enough to
have sufficient stock of one year's provisions beforehand
— I say, besides this yearly labour, and my daily labour of
going out with my gun, I had one labour, to make me a
canoe, which at last I finished; so that by digging a canal
to it of six feet wide, and four feet deep, I brought it into
the creek, almost half a mile. As for the first, which was so
vastly big, as I made it without considering beforehand,
as I ought to do, how I should be able to launch it; so,
never being able to bring it to the water, or bring the
water to it, I was obliged to let it lie where it was, as a
memorandum to teach me to be wiser next time. Indeed,
the next time, though I could not get a tree proper for it,
and in a place where I could not get the water to it at any

less distance than, as I have said, near half a mile, yet as I saw it was practicable at last, I never gave it over; and though I was near two years about it, yet I never grudged my labour, in hopes of having a boat to go off to sea at last.

However, though my little *periagua* was finished, yet the size of it was not at all answerable to the design which I had in view when I made the first; I mean, of venturing over to the *terra firma*, where it was above forty miles broad. Accordingly, the smallness of my boat assisted to put an end to that design, and now I thought no more of it. But as I had a boat, my next design was to make a tour round the island; for as I had been on the other side in one place, crossing, as I have already described it, over the land, so the discoveries I made in that little journey made me very eager to see other parts of the coast; and now I had a boat, I thought of nothing but sailing round the island.

For this purpose, that I might do everything with discretion and consideration, I fitted up a little mast to my boat, and made a sail to it out of some pieces of the ship's sail, which lay in store, and of which I had a great stock by me.

Having fitted my mast and sail, and tried the boat, I found she would sail very well. Then I made little lockers, or boxes, at either end of my boat, to put provisions, necessaries, and ammunition, etc., into, to be kept dry, either from rain or the spray of the sea; and a little long hollow

CRUSOE SAILS OUT OF HIS CREEK.

place I cut in the inside of the boat, where I could lay my gun, making a flap to hang down over it to keep it dry.

I fixed my umbrella also in a step at the stern, like a mast, to stand over my head, and keep the heat of the sun off me, like an awning; and thus I now and then took a little voyage upon the sea, but never went far out, nor far from the little creek. But at last, being eager to view the circumference of my little kingdom, I resolved upon my tour; and accordingly I victualled my ship for the voyage, putting in two dozen of my loaves (cakes I should rather call them) of barley bread, an earthen pot full of parched rice, a food I eat a great deal of, a little bottle of rum, half a goat, and powder and shot for killing more, and two large watch-coats, of those which, as I mentioned before, I had saved out of the seamen's chests; these I took, one to lie upon, and the other to cover me in the night.

It was the 6th of November, in the sixth year of my reign, or my captivity, which you please, that I set out on this voyage, and I found it much longer than I expected; for though the island itself was not very large, yet when I came to the east side of it I found a great ledge of rocks lie out above two leagues into the sea, some above water, some under it, and beyond that a shoal of sand, lying dry half a league more; so that I was obliged to go a great way out to sea to double the point.

When I first discovered them, I was going to give over my enterprise, and come back again, not knowing how far it might oblige me to go out to sea, and, above all, doubting how I should get back again, so I came to an anchor; for I had made me a kind of an anchor with a piece of a broken grappling which I got out of the ship.

Having secured my boat, I took my gun and went on shore, climbing up upon a hill, which seemed to overlook that point, where I saw the full extent of it, and resolved to venture.

In viewing the sea from that hill, where I stood, I perceived a strong, and indeed a most furious current, which run to the east, and even came close to the point; and I took the more notice of it, because I saw there might be some danger that when I came into it I might be carried out to sea by the strength of it, and not be able to make the island again. And indeed, had I not gotten first up upon this hill, I believe it would have been so; for there was the same current on the other side the island, only that it set off at a farther distance; and I saw there was a strong eddy under the shore; so I had nothing to do but to get in out of the first current, and I should presently be in an eddy.

I lay here, however, two days; because the wind, blowing pretty fresh at E.S.E., and that being contrary to the said current, made a great breach of the sea upon the point; so that it was not safe for me to keep too close to the shore for the breach, nor to go too far off because of the stream.

The third day, in the morning, the wind having abated overnight, the sea was calm, and I ventured. But I am a warning piece again to all rash and ignorant pilots; for no sooner was I come to the point, when even I was not my boat's length from the shore, but I found myself in a great depth of water, and a current like the sluice of a mill. It carried my boat along with it with such violence, that all I could do could not keep her so much as on the edge of it, but I found it hurried me farther and farther out from the eddy, which was on my left hand. There was no wind stirring to help me, and all I could do with my paddlers signified nothing. And now I began to give myself over for lost; for, as the current was on both sides the island, I knew in a few leagues distance they must join again, and then I was irrecoverably gone. Nor did I see any possibility of avoiding it; so that I had no prospect before me but of perishing; not by the sea, for that was calm enough, but of starving for hunger. I had indeed found a tortoise on the shore, as big almost as I could lift, and had tossed it into the boat; and I had a great jar of fresh water, that is to say, one of my earthen pots; but what was all this to being driven into the vast ocean, where, to be sure, there was no shore, no mainland or island, for a thousand leagues at least.

And now I saw how easy it was for the providence of God to make the most miserable condition mankind could be in worse. Now I looked back upon my desolate solitary island as the most pleasant place in the world, and all the happiness my heart could wish for was to be but there again. I stretched out my hands to it, with eager wishes. 'O happy desert!' said I, 'I shall never see thee more. O miserable creature,' said I, 'whither am I going?' Then I reproached myself with my unthankful temper, and how I had repined at my solitary condition; and now what would I give to be on shore there again. However, I worked hard, till indeed my strength was almost exhausted, and kept my boat as much to the northward, that is, towards the side of the current which the eddy lay on, as possibly I could; when about noon, as the sun passed the meridian, I thought I felt a little breeze of wind in my face, springing up from the S.S.E. This cheered my heart a little, and especially when, in about half an hour more, it blew a pretty small gentle gale. By this time I was gotten at a frightful distance from the island; and had the least cloud or hazy weather intervened, I had been undone another way too; for I had no compass on board, and should never have known how to have steered towards the island if I had but once lost sight of it. But the weather continuing clear, I applied myself to get up my mast again, and spread my sail, standing away to the north as much as possible, to get out of the current.

Just as I had set my mast and sail, and the boat began to stretch away, I saw even by the clearness of the water some alteration of the current was near; for where the current was so strong, the water was foul. But perceiving the water clear, I found the current abate, and presently I found to the east, at about half a mile, a breach of the sea upon some rocks. These rocks I found caused the current to part again; and as the main stress of it ran away more southerly, leaving the rocks to the north-east, so the other returned by the repulse of the rocks, and made a strong eddy, which ran back again to the north-west with a very sharp stream.

They who know what it is to have a reprieve brought to them upon the ladder, or to be rescued from thieves just going to murder them, or who have been in such like extremities, may guess what my present surprise of joy was, and how gladly I put my boat into the stream of this eddy; and the wind also freshening, how gladly I spread my sail to it, running cheerfully before the wind, and with a strong tide or eddy under foot.

This eddy carried me about a league in my way back again, directly towards the island, but about two leagues more to the northward than the current which carried me away at first; so that when I came near the island, I found myself open to the northern shore of it, that is to say, the other end of the island, opposite to that which I went out from.

When I had made something more than a league of way by the help of this current or eddy, I found it was spent, and served me no farther. However, I found that being between the two great currents, viz., that on the south side, which had hurried me away, and that on the north, which lay about a league on the other side; I say, between these two, in the wake of the island, I found the water at least still, and running no way; and having still a breeze of wind fair for me, I kept on steering directly for the island, though not making such fresh way as I did before.

About four o'clock in the evening, being then within about a league of the island, I found the point of rocks which occasioned this disaster stretching out, as is described before, to the southward, and casting off the current more southwardly had, of course, made another eddy to the north, and this I found very strong, but not directly setting the way my course lay, which was due west, but almost full north. However, having a fresh gale, I stretched across this eddy, slanting north-west, and in about an hour came within about a mile of the shore, where, it being smooth water, I soon got to land.

When I was on shore, I fell on my knees, and gave God thanks for my deliverance, resolving to lay aside all thoughts of my deliverance by my boat; and refreshing myself with such things as I had, I brought my boat close to the shore, in a little cove that I had spied under some trees, and laid me down to sleep, being quite spent with the labour and fatigue of the voyage.

I was now at a great loss which way to get home with my boat. I had run so much hazard, and knew too much the case, to think of attempting it by the way I went out; and what might be at the other side (I mean the west side) I knew not, nor had I any mind to run any more ventures. So I only resolved in the morning to make my way westward along the shore, and to see if there was no creek where I might lay up my frigate in safety, so as to have her again if I wanted her. In about three miles, or thereabouts, casting the shore, I came to a very good inlet or bay, about a mile over, which narrowed till it came to a very little rivulet or brook, where I found a very convenient harbour for my boat, and where she lay as if she had been in a little dock made on purpose for her. Here I put in, and having stowed my boat very safe, I went on shore to look about me, and see where I was.

I soon found I had but a little passed by the place where I had been before, when I travelled on foot to that shore; so taking nothing out of my boat but my gun and my umbrella, for it was exceeding hot, I began my march. The way was comfortable enough after such a voyage as I had been upon, and I reached my old bower in the evening, where I found everything standing as I left it; for I always kept it in good order, being, as I said before, my country house.

I got over the fence, and laid me down in the shade to rest my limbs, for I was very weary, and fell asleep. But judge you, if you can, that read my story, what a surprise I must be in, when I was waked out of my sleep by a voice calling me by my name several times, 'Robin, Robin, Robin Crusoe, poor Robin Crusoe! Where are you, Robin Crusoe? Where are you? Where have you been?'

I was so dead asleep at first, being fatigued with rowing, or paddling, as it is called, the first part of the day, and with walking the latter part, that I did not wake thoroughly; but dozing between sleeping and waking, thought I dreamed that somebody spoke to me. But as the voice continued to repeat 'Robin Crusoe, Robin Crusoe,' at last I began to wake more perfectly, and was at first dreadfully frighted, and started up in the utmost consternation. But no sooner were my eyes open, but I saw my Poll sitting on the top of the hedge, and immediately knew that it was he that spoke to me; for just in such bemoaning language I had used to talk to him, and teach him; and he had learned it so perfectly, that he would sit upon my finger, and lay his bill close to my face, and cry, 'Poor Robin Crusoe! Where are you? Where have you been? How come you here?' and such things as I had taught him.

However, even though I knew it was the parrot, and that indeed it could be nobody else, it was a good while before I could compose myself. First, I was amazed how the creature got thither, and then, how he should just keep about the place, and nowhere else. But as I was well satisfied it could be nobody but honest Poll, I got it over; and holding out my hand, and calling him by his name, Poll, the sociable creature came to me, and sat upon my thumb, as he used to do, and continued talking to me, 'Poor Robin Crusoe! and how did I come here? and where had I been?' just as if he had been overjoyed to see me again; and so I carried him home along with me.

CHAPTER 14

Crusoe thankful to live a sedate retired life after this frightening experience of travel. He improves in carpentry, pot-making and basketry, but is never more vain of his performance than for making a tobacco pipe. In the eleventh year, disturbed by diminishing powder and shot, decides to domesticate wild goats. In two years he has a sizeable flock providing meat and long-wanted milk. Crusoe lives now in plentiful style lacking nothing save society. He sets out to retrieve his boat.

I HAD now had enough of rambling to sea for some time, and had enough to do for many days to sit still, and reflect upon the danger I had been in. I would have been very glad to have had my boat again on my side of the island; but I knew not how it was practicable to get it about. As to the east side of the island, which I had gone round, I knew well enough there was no venturing that way; my very heart would shrink, and my very blood run chill, but to think of it. And as to the other side of the island, I did not know how it might be there; but supposing the current ran with the same force against the shore at the east as it passed by it on the other, I might run the same risk of being driven down the stream, and carried by the island, as I had been before of being carried away from it. So, with these thoughts, I contented myself to be without any boat, though it had been the product of so many months' labour to make it, and of so many more to get it unto the sea.

In this government of my temper I remained near a year, living a very sedate, retired life, as you may well suppose; and my thoughts being very much composed as to my condition, and fully comforted in resigning myself to the dispositions of Providence, I thought I lived really very happily in all things, except that of society.

I improved myself in this time in all the mechanic exercises which my necessities put me upon applying myself to, and I believe could, upon occasion, make a very good carpenter, especially considering how few tools I had. Besides this, I arrived at an unexpected perfection in my earthenware, and contrived well enough to make them with a wheel, which I found infinitely easier and better, because I made things round and shapable which before were filthy things indeed to look on. But I think I was never more vain of my own performance, or more joyful for anything I found out, than for my being able to make a tobacco-pipe. And though it was a very ugly, clumsy thing when it was done, and only burnt red, like other earthen ware, yet as it was hard and firm, and would draw the smoke, I was exceedingly comforted with it; for I had been always used to smoke, and there were pipes in the ship, but I forgot them at first, not knowing there was tobacco in the island; and afterwards, when I searched the ship again, I could not come at any pipes at all.

In my wicker-ware also I improved much, and made

abundance of necessary baskets, as well as my invention showed me; though not very handsome, yet they were such as were very handy and convenient for my laying things up in, or fetching things home in. For example, if I killed a goat abroad, I could hang it up in a tree, flay it, and dress it, and cut it in pieces, and bring it home in a basket; and the like by a turtle; I could cut it up, take out the eggs, and a piece or two of the flesh, which was enough for me, and bring them home in a basket, and leave the rest behind me. Also large deep baskets were my receivers for my corn, which I always rubbed out as soon as it was dry, and cured, and kept it in great baskets.

I began now to perceive my powder abated considerably, and this was a want which it was impossible for me to supply, and I began seriously to consider what I must do when I should have no more powder; that is to say, how I should do to kill any goats. I had, as is observed, in the third year of my being here kept a young kid, and bred her up tame, and I was in hope of getting a he-goat. But I could not by any means bring it to pass, till my kid grew an old goat; and I could never find in my heart to kill her, till she died at last of mere age.

But being now in the eleventh year of my residence, and, as I have said, my ammunition growing low, I set myself to study some art to trap and snare the goats, to see whether I could not catch some of them alive; and particularly, I wanted a she-goat great with young.

To this purpose, I made snares to hamper them, and I do believe they were more than once taken in them; but my tackle was not good, for I had no wire, and I always found them broken, and my bait devoured. At length I resolved to try a pitfall; so I dug several large pits in the earth, in places where I had observed the goats used to feed, and over these pits I placed hurdles, of my own making too, with a great weight upon them; and several times I put ears of barley and dry rice, without setting the trap, and I could easily perceive that the goats had gone in and eaten up the corn, for I could see the mark of their feet. At length I set three traps in one night, and going the next morning, I found them all standing, and yet the bait eaten and gone; this was very discouraging. However, I altered my trap; and, not to trouble you with particulars, going one morning to see my trap, I found in one of them a large old he-goat, and in one of the other three kids, a male and two females.

As to the old one, I knew not what to do with him, he was so fierce I durst not go into the pit to him; that is to say, to go about to bring him away alive, which was what I wanted. I could have killed him, but that was not my business, nor would it answer my end; so I even let him out, and he ran away, as if he had been frighted out of his wits. But I had forgot then what I learned afterwards, that hunger will tame a lion. If I had let him stay there three or four days without food, and then have carried him some water to drink, and then a little corn, he would have been as tame as one of the kids, for they are mighty sagacious, tractable creatures where they are well used.

However, for the present I let him go, knowing no better at that time. Then I went to the three kids, and taking them one by one, I tied them with strings together, and with some difficulty brought them all home.

It was a good while before they would feed, but throwing them some sweet corn, it tempted them, and they began to be tame. And now I found that if I expected to supply myself with goat-flesh when I had no powder or shot left, breeding some up tame was my only way, when perhaps I might have them about my house like a flock of sheep.

But then it presently occurred to me that I must keep the tame from the wild, or else they would always run wild when they grew up; and the only way for this was to have some enclosed piece of ground, well fenced either with hedge or pale, to keep them in so effectually, that those within might not break out, or those without break in.

This was a great undertaking for one pair of hands; yet as I saw there was an absolute necessity of doing it, my first piece of work was to find out a proper piece of ground, viz., where there was likely to be herbage for them to eat, water for them to drink, and cover to keep them from the sun.

Those who understand such enclosures will think I

had very little contrivance when I pitched upon a place
very proper for all these, being a plain open piece of
meadow land, or savanna (as our people call it in the
western colonies), which had two or three little drills of
fresh water in it, and at one end was very woody; I say,
they will smile at my forecast, when I shall tell them I
began my enclosing of this piece of ground in such a manner, that my hedge or pale must have been at least two
miles about. Nor was the madness of it so great as to the
compass, for if it was ten miles about, I was like to have
time enough to do it in. But I did not consider that my
goats would be as wild in so much compass as if they had
had the whole island, and I should have so much room to
chase them in, that I should never catch them.

My hedge was begun and carried on, I believe, about
fifty yards, when this thought occurred to me, so I
presently stopped short, and, for the first beginning, I
resolved to enclose a piece of about 150 yards in length,
and 100 yards in breadth; which, as it would maintain as
many as I should have in any reasonable time, so, as my
flock increased, I could add more ground to my enclosure.

This was acting with some prudence, and I went to
work with courage. I was about three months hedging in
the first piece, and, till I had done it, I tethered the three
kids in the best part of it, and used them to feed as near
me as possible, to make them familiar; and very often I
would go and carry them some ears of barley, or a handful

of rice, and feed them out of my hand; so that after my enclosure was finished, and I let them loose, they would follow me up and down, bleating after me for a handful of corn.

This answered my end, and in about a year and half I had a flock of about twelve goats, kids and all; and in two years more I had three and forty, besides several that I took and killed for my food. And after that I enclosed five several pieces of ground to feed them in, with little pens to drive them into, to take them as I wanted, and gates out of one piece of ground into another.

But this was not all, for now I not only had goat's flesh to feed on when I pleased, but milk too, a thing, which, indeed, in my beginning, I did not so much think of, and which, when it came into my thoughts, was really an agreeable surprise. For now I set up my dairy, and had sometimes a gallon or two of milk in a day; and as Nature, who gives supplies of food to every creature, dictates even naturally how to make use of it, so I, that had never milked a cow, much less a goat, or seen butter or cheese made, very readily and handily, though after a great many essays and miscarriages, made me both butter and cheese at last, and never wanted it afterwards.

It would have made a stoic smile, to have seen me and my little family sit down to dinner. There was my majesty, the prince and lord of the whole island; I had the lives of all my subjects at my absolute command. I could hang, draw, give liberty, and take it away; and no rebels among all my subjects.

Then to see how like a king I dined, too, all alone, attended by my servants. Poll, as if he had been my favourite, was the only person permitted to talk to me. My dog, who was now grown very old and crazy, and had found no species to multiply his kind upon, sat always at my right hand, and two cats, one on one side the table, and one on the other, expecting now and then a bit from my hand, as a mark of special favour.

But these were not the two cats which I brought on shore at first, for they were both of them dead, and had been interred near my habitation, by my own hand. But one of them having multiplied by I know not what kind of creature, these were two which I had preserved tame, whereas the rest run wild in the woods, and became indeed troublesome to me till at last I was obliged to shoot them. With this attendance, and in this plentiful manner, I lived; neither could I be said to want anything but society; and of that in some time after this, I was like to have too much.

I was something impatient, as I have observed, to have the use of my boat, though very loth to run any more hazards; and therefore sometimes I sat contriving ways to get her about the island, and at other times I sat myself down contented enough without her. But I had a strange uneasiness in my mind to go down to the point of the

island, where, as I have said, in my last ramble, I went up
the hill to see how the shore lay, and how the current set,
that I might see what I had to do. This inclination
increased upon me every day, and at length I resolved to
travel thither by land, following the edge of the shore. I
did so; but had any one in England been to meet such a
man as I was, it must either have frighted them, or raised
a great deal of laughter; and as I frequently stood still to
look at myself, I could not but smile at the notion of my
travelling through Yorkshire, with such an equipage, and
in such a dress. Be pleased to take a sketch of my figure,
as follows.

I had a great high shapeless cap, made of a goat's skin,
with a flap hanging down behind, as well to keep the sun
from me, as to shoot the rain off from running into my
neck; nothing being so hurtful in these climates as the
rain upon flesh, under the clothes.

I had a short jacket of goat-skin, the skirts coming down
to about the middle of my thighs; and a pair of open-kneed
breeches of the same. The breeches were made of the skin
of an old he-goat, whose hair hung down such a length on
either side, that, like pantaloons, it reached to the middle
of my legs. Stockings and shoes I had none, but had made
me a pair of somethings, I scarce know what to call them,
like buskins, to flap over my legs, and lace on either side
like spatterdashes; but of a most barbarous shape, as
indeed were all the rest of my clothes.

I had on a broad belt of goat's skin dried, which I drew together with two thongs of the same, instead of buckles; and in a kind of a frog on either side of this, instead of a sword and a dagger, hung a little saw and a hatchet, one on one side, one on the other. I had another belt, not so broad, and fastened in the same manner, which hung over my shoulder; and at the end of it, under my left arm, hung two pouches, both made of goat's skin too; in one of which I hung my powder, in the other my shot. At my back I carried my basket, on my shoulder my gun, and over my head a great clumsy ugly goat-skin umbrella, but which, after all, was the most necessary thing I had about me, next to my gun. As for my face, the colour of it was really not so mulatto-like as one might expect from a man not at all careful of it, and living within nineteen degrees of the equinox. My beard I had once suffered to grow till it was about a quarter of a yard long; but as I had both scissors and razors sufficient, I had cut it pretty short, except what grew on my upper lip, which I had trimmed into a large pair of Mahometan whiskers, such as I had seen worn by some Turks whom I saw at Sallee; for the Moors did not wear such, though the Turks did. Of these mustachios or whiskers, I will not say they were long enough to hang my hat upon them, but they were of a length and shape monstrous enough, and such as, in England, would have passed for frightful.

But all this is by the bye; for, as to my figure, I had so

few to observe me, that it was of no manner of consequence; so I say no more to that part. In this kind of figure I went my new journey, and was out five or six days. I
travelled first along the sea-shore, directly to the place
where I first brought my boat to an anchor, to get up upon
the rocks. And having no boat now to take care of, I went
over the land, a nearer way, to the same height that I was
upon before; when, looking forward to the point of the
rocks which lay out, and which I was obliged to double
with my boat, as is said above, I was surprised to see the
sea all smooth and quiet, no rippling, no motion, no current, any more there than in other places.

I was at a strange loss to understand this, and resolved
to spend some time in the observing it, to see if nothing
from the sets of the tide had occasioned it. But I was
presently convinced how it was, viz., that the tide of ebb
setting from the west, and joining with the current of
waters from some great river on the shore, must be the
occasion of this current; and that according as the wind
blew more forcibly from the west, or from the north, this
current came near, or went farther from the shore; for wait-
ing thereabouts till evening, I went up to the rock again,
and then the tide of ebb being made, I plainly saw the current again as before, only that it run farther off, being near
half a league from the shore; whereas in my case it set close
upon the shore, and hurried me and my canoe along with
it, which, at another time, it would not have done.

This observation convinced me that I had nothing to do but to observe the ebbing and the flowing of the tide, and I might very easily bring my boat about the island again. But when I began to think of putting it in practice, I had such terror upon my spirits at the remembrance of the danger I had been in, that I could not think of it again with any patience; but, on the contrary, I took up another resolution, which was more safe, though more laborious; and this was, that I would build, or rather make me another *periagua* or canoe; and so have one for one side of the island, and one for the other.

You are to understand that now I had, as I may call it, two plantations in the island; one, my little fortification or tent, with the wall about it, under the rock, with the cave behind me, which, by this time, I had enlarged into several apartments or caves, one within another. One of these, which was the driest and largest, and had a door out beyond my wall or fortification, that is to say, beyond where my wall joined to the rock, was all filled up with the large earthen pots, of which I have given an account, and with fourteen or fifteen great baskets, which would hold five or six bushels each, where I laid up my stores of provision, especially my corn, some in the ear, cut off short from the straw, and the other rubbed out with my hand.

As for my wall, made, as before, with long stakes or piles, those piles grew all like trees, and were by this time grown so big, and spread so very much, that there was not the least appearance, to any one's view, of any habitation behind them.

Near this dwelling of mine, but a little farther within the land, and upon lower ground, lay my two pieces of corn ground, which I kept duly cultivated and sowed, and which duly yielded me their harvest in its season; and whenever I had occasion for more corn, I had more land adjoining as fit as that.

Besides this, I had my country seat, and I had now a tolerable plantation there also; for, first, I had my little bower, as I called it, which I kept in repair; that is to say, I kept the hedge which circled it in constantly fitted up to its usual height, the ladder standing always in the inside. I kept the trees, which at first were no more than my stakes, but were now grown very firm and tall, I kept them always so cut, that they might spread and grow thick and wild, and make the more agreeable shade, which they did effectually to my mind. In the middle of this, I had my tent always standing, being a piece of a sail spread over poles, set up for that purpose, and which never wanted any repair or renewing; and under this I had made me a squab or couch, with the skins of the creatures I had killed, and with other soft things, and a blanket laid on them, such as belonged to our sea-bedding, which I had saved, and a great watch-coat to cover me; and here, whenever I had occasion to be absent from my chief seat, I took up my country habitation.

Adjoining to this I had my enclosures for my cattle, that is to say, my goats. And as I had taken an inconceivable deal of pains to fence and enclose this ground, so I was so uneasy to see it kept entire, lest the goats should break through, that I never left off till, with infinite labour, I had stuck the outside of the hedge so full of small stakes, and so near to one another, that it was rather a pale than a hedge, and there was scarce room to put a hand through between them; which afterwards, when those stakes grew, as they all did in the next rainy season, made the enclosure strong like a wall, indeed, stronger than any wall.

This will testify for me that I was not idle, and that I spared no pains to bring to pass whatever appeared necessary for my comfortable support; for I considered the keeping up a breed of tame creatures thus at my hand would be a living magazine of flesh, milk, butter and cheese for me as long as I lived in the place, if it were to be forty years; and that keeping them in my reach depended entirely upon my perfecting my enclosures to such a degree, that I might be sure of keeping them together; which, by this method, indeed, I so effectually secured, that when these little stakes began to grow, I had planted them so very thick, I was forced to pull some of them up again.

In this place also I had my grapes growing, which I principally depended on for my winter store of raisins, and which I never failed to preserve very carefully, as the best and most agreeable dainty of my whole diet. And indeed they were not agreeable only, but physical, whole-some, nourishing and refreshing to the last degree.

As this was also about half-way between my other habi-tation and the place where I had laid up my boat, I gener-ally stayed and lay here in my way thither; for I used frequently to visit my boat, and I kept all things about, or belonging to her, in good order. Sometimes I went out in her to divert myself, but no more hazardous voyages would I go, nor scarce ever above a stone's cast or two from the shore, I was so apprehensive of being hurried out of my knowledge again by the currents or winds, or any other accident. But now I come to a new scene of my life.

CHAPTER 15

After resting at his country house Crusoe proceeds towards the
shore. Near his hidden boat is the single imprint of a naked
human foot. 'Never frighted hare fled to cover or fox to earth
with more terror of mind' than Crusoe to his retreat. He
strengthens his fortifications against expected attack and keeps
constant watch. Two uneasy years pass without sign of visitors,
then Crusoe discovers on S.W. coast ghastly remains of cannibal
feasts. He realises his presence is not known and that they do not
come for plunder. Resolves to keep his existence secret.

IT HAPPENED one day, about noon, going towards my
boat, I was exceedingly surprised with the print of a
man's naked foot on the shore, which was very plain to be
seen in the sand. I stood like one thunder-struck, or as if I
had seen an apparition. I listened, I looked around me, I
could hear nothing, nor see anything. I went up to a rising
ground, to look farther. I went up the shore, and down the
shore, but it was all one; I could see no other impression
but that one. I went to it again to see if there were any
more, and to observe if it might not be my fancy; but
there was no room for that, for there was exactly the very
print of a foot — toes, heel, and every part of a foot. How
it came thither I knew not, nor could in the least imagine.
But after innumerable fluttering thoughts, like a man
perfectly confused and out of myself, I came home to my
fortification, not feeling, as we say, the ground I went on,

CRUSOE SEES

· A FOOT-PRINT IN THE SAND ·

but terrified to the last degree, looking behind me at every two or three steps, mistaking every bush and tree, and fancying every stump at a distance to be a man; nor is it possible to describe how many various shapes affrighted imagination represented things to me in, how many wild ideas were found every moment in my fancy, and what strange, unaccountable whimsies came into my thoughts by the way.

When I came to my castle, for so I think I called it ever after this, I fled into it like one pursued. Whether I went over by the ladder, as first contrived, or went in at the hole in the rock, which I called a door, I cannot remember; no, nor could I remember the next morning, for never frighted hare fled to cover, or fox to earth, with more terror of mind than I to this retreat.

I slept none that night. The farther I was from the occasion of my fright, the greater my apprehensions were; which is something contrary to the nature of such things, and especially to the usual practice of all creatures in fear. But I was so embarrassed with my own frightful ideas of the thing, that I formed nothing but dismal imaginations to myself, even though I was now a great way off it. Sometimes I fancied it must be the devil, and reason joined in with me upon this supposition; for how should any other thing in human shape come into the place? Where was the vessel that brought them? What marks was there of any other footsteps? And how was it possible a man should come there? But then to think that Satan should take human shape upon him in such a place, where there could be no manner of occasion for it, but to leave the print of his foot behind him, and that even for no purpose too, for he could not be sure I should see it; this was an amusement the other way. I considered that the devil might have found out abundance of other ways to have terrified me than this of the single print of a foot; that as I lived quite on the other side of the island, he would never have been so simple to leave a mark in a place where it was ten thousand to one whether I should ever see it or not, and in the sand too, which the first surge of the sea, upon a high wind, would have defaced entirely. All this seemed inconsistent with the thing itself, and with all the notions we usually entertain of the subtilty of the devil.

Abundance of such things as these assisted to argue me out of all apprehensions of its being the devil; and I presently concluded then, that it must be some more dangerous creature, viz., that it must be some of the savages of the mainland over against me, who had wandered out to sea in their canoes, and, either driven by the currents or by contrary winds, had made the island, and had been on shore, but were gone away again to sea, being as loth, perhaps, to have stayed in this desolate island as I would have been to have had them.

While these reflections were rolling upon my mind, I

was very thankful in my thoughts that I was so happy as not to be thereabouts at that time, or that they did not see my boat, by which they would have concluded that some inhabitants had been in the place, and perhaps have searched farther for me. Then terrible thoughts racked my imagination about their having found my boat, and that there were people here; and that if so, I should certainly have them come again in greater numbers, and devour me; and if it should happen so that they should not find me, yet they would find my enclosure, destroy all my corn, carry away all my flock of tame goats, and I should perish at last for mere want.

Thus my fear banished all my religious hope. All that former confidence in God, which was founded upon such wonderful experience as I had had of His goodness, now vanished, as if He that had fed me by miracle hitherto could not preserve, by His power, the provision which He had made for me by His goodness. I reproached myself with my easiness, that would not sow any more corn one year than would just serve me till the next season, as if no accident could intervene to prevent my enjoying the crop that was upon the ground. And this I thought so just a reproof, that I resolved for the future to have two or three years' corn beforehand, so that, whatever might come, I might not perish for want of bread.

I then reflected that God, who was not only righteous, but omnipotent, as He had thought fit thus to punish and afflict me, so He was able to deliver me; that if He did not think fit to do it, 'twas my unquestioned duty to resign myself absolutely and entirely to His will; and, on the other hand, it was my duty also to hope in Him, pray to Him, and quietly to attend the dictates and directions of His daily providence.

These thoughts took me up many hours, days, nay, I may say, weeks and months; and one particular effect of my cogitations on this occasion I cannot omit, viz., one morning early, lying in my bed, and filled with thought about my danger from the appearance of savages, I found it discomposed me very much; upon which those words of the Scripture came into my thoughts, 'Call upon Me in the day of trouble, and I will deliver, and thou shalt glorify Me.'

Upon this, rising cheerfully out of my bed, my heart was not only comforted, but I was guided and encouraged to pray earnestly to God for deliverance. When I had done praying, I took up my Bible, and opening it to read, the first words that presented to me were, 'Wait on the Lord, and be of good cheer, and He shall strengthen thy heart; wait, I say, on the Lord.' It is impossible to express the comfort this gave me. In answer, I thankfully laid down the book, and was no more sad, at least, not on that occasion.

In the middle of these cogitations, apprehensions, and reflections, it came into my thought one day, that all this might be a mere chimera of my own; and that this foot might be the print of my own foot, when I came on shore from my boat. This cheered me up a little too, and I began to persuade myself it was all a delusion, that it was nothing else but my own foot; and why might not I come that way from the boat, as well as I was going that way to the boat? Again, I considered also, that I could by no means tell for certain, where I had trod, and where I had not; and that if, at last, this was only the print of my own foot, I had played the part of those fools who strive to make stories of spectres and apparitions, and then are frighted at them more than anybody.

Now I began to take courage, and to peep abroad again, for I had not stirred out of my castle for three days and nights, so that I began to starve for provision; for I had little or nothing within doors but some barley cakes and water. Then I knew that my goats wanted to be milked too, which usually was my evening diversion; and the poor creatures were in great pain and inconvenience for want of it; and, indeed, it almost spoiled some of them, and almost dried up their milk.

Heartening myself, therefore, with the belief that this was nothing but the print of one of my own feet, and so I might be truly said to start at my own shadow, I began to go abroad again, and went to my country house to milk my flock. But to see with what fear I went forward, how often I looked behind me, how I was ready, every now and then, to lay down my basket, and run for my life, it would have made any one have thought I was haunted with an evil conscience, or that I had been lately most terribly frighted; and so, indeed, I had.

However, as I went down thus two or three days, and having seen nothing, I began to be a little bolder, and to think there was really nothing in it but my own imagination. But I could not persuade myself fully of this till I should go down to the shore again, and see this print of a foot, and measure it by my own, and see if there was any similitude or fitness, that I might be assured it was my own foot. But when I came to the place, first, it appeared evidently to me, that when I laid up my boat, I could not possibly be on shore anywhere thereabout; secondly, when I came to measure the mark with my own foot, I found my foot not so large by a great deal. Both these things filled my head with new imaginations, and gave me the vapours again to the highest degree; so that I shook with cold, like one in an ague; and I went home again, filled with the belief that some man or men had been on shore there; or, in short, that the island was inhabited, and I might be surprised before I was aware. And what course to take for my security, I knew not.

Oh, what ridiculous resolution men take when possessed with fear! It deprives them of the use of those means which reason offers for their relief. The first thing I proposed to myself was to throw down my enclosures, and turn all my tame cattle wild into the woods, that the enemy might not find them, and then frequent the island in prospect of the same or the little booty; then to the simple thing of digging up my two corn-fields, that they might not find such a grain there, and still be prompted to frequent the island; then to demolish my bower and tent, that they might not see any vestiges of habitation, and be prompted to look farther, in order to find out the persons inhabiting.

This confusion of my thoughts kept me waking all night, but in the morning I fell asleep; and having, by the amusement of my mind, been, as it were, tired, and my spirits exhausted, I slept very soundly, and waked much better composed than I had ever been before. And now I began to think sedately; and upon the utmost debate with myself, I concluded that this island, which was so exceeding pleasant, fruitful, and no farther from the mainland than as I had seen, was not so entirely abandoned as I might imagine; that although there were no stated inhabitants who lived on the spot, yet that there might sometimes come boats off from the shore, who, either with design, or perhaps never but when they were driven by cross winds, might come to this place; that I had lived here fifteen years now, and had not met with the least shadow or figure of any people yet; and that if at any time they should be driven here, it was probable they went away again as soon as ever they could, seeing they had never thought fit to fix there upon any occasion to this time; that the most I could suggest any danger from, was from any such casual accidental landing of straggling people from the main, who, as it was likely, if they were driven hither, were here against their wills; so they made no stay here, but went off again with all possible speed, seldom staying one night on shore, lest they should not have the help of the tides and daylight back again; and that, therefore, I had nothing to do but to consider of some safe retreat, in case I should see any savages land upon the spot.

Now I began sorely to repent that I had dug my cave so large as to bring a door through again, which door, as I said, came out beyond where my fortification joined to the rock. Upon maturely considering this, therefore, I resolved to draw me a second fortification, in the same manner of a semi-circle, at a distance from my wall, just where I had planted a double row of trees about twelve years before, of which I made mention. These trees having been planted so thick before, they wanted but a few piles to be driven between them, that they should be thicker and stronger, and my wall would be soon finished.

So that I had now a double wall; and my outer wall was thickened with pieces of timber, old cables, and everything I could think of, to make it strong, having in it seven little holes, about as big as I might put my arm out at. In the inside of this I thickened my wall to above ten feet thick, with continual bringing earth out of my cave, and laying it at the foot of the wall, and walking upon it; and through the seven holes I contrived to plant the muskets, of which I took notice that I got seven on shore out of the ship. These, I say, I planted like my cannon, and fitted them into frames, that held them like a carriage, that so I could fire all the seven guns in two minutes' time. This wall I was many a weary month a-finishing, and yet never thought myself safe till it was done.

When this was done, I stuck all the ground without my wall, for a great way every way, as full with stakes, or sticks, of the osier-like wood, which I found so apt to grow, as they could well stand; insomuch, that I believe I might set in near twenty thousand of them, leaving a pretty large space between them and my wall, that I might have room to see an enemy, and they might have no shelter from the young trees, if they attempted to approach my outer wall.

Thus in two years' time I had a thick grove; and in five or six years' time I had a wood before my dwelling, growing so monstrous thick and strong, that it was indeed perfectly impassable; and no men, of what kind soever, would ever imagine that there was anything beyond it, much less a habitation. As for the way which I proposed to myself to go in and out, for I left no avenue, it was by setting two ladders, one to a part of the rock which was low, and then broke in, and left room to place another ladder upon that; so when the two ladders were taken down, no man living could come down to me without mischieving himself; and if they had come down, they were still on the outside of my outer wall.

Thus I took all the measures human prudence could suggest for my own preservation; and it will be seen, at length, that they were not altogether without just reason; though I foresaw nothing at that time more than my mere fear suggested to me.

While this was doing, I was not altogether careless of my other affairs; for I had a great concern upon me for my little herd of goats. They were not only a present supply to me upon every occasion, and began to be sufficient to me, without the expense of powder and shot, but also without the fatigue of hunting after the wild ones; and I was loth to lose the advantage of them, and to have them all to nurse up over again.

To this purpose, after long consideration, I could think of but two ways to preserve them. One was, to find another convenient place to dig a cave under ground, and to drive them into it every night; and the other was, to enclose two or three little bits of land, remote from one another, and as much concealed as I could, where I might keep about half a dozen young goats in each place; so that if any disaster happened to the flock in general, I might be able to raise them again with little trouble and time. And this, though it would require a great deal of time and labour, I thought was the most rational design.

Accordingly I spent some time to find out the most retired parts of the island; and I pitched upon one which was as private indeed as my heart could wish for. It was a little damp piece of ground, in the middle of the hollow and thick woods, where, as is observed, I almost lost myself once before, endeavouring to come back that way from the eastern part of the island. Here I found a clear piece of land, near three acres, so surrounded with woods, that it was almost an enclosure by Nature; at least, it did not want near so much labour to make it so as the other pieces of ground I had worked so hard at.

I immediately went to work with this piece of ground, and in less than a month's time I had so fenced it round, that my flock, or herd, call it which you please, who were not so wild now as at first they might be supposed to be, were well enough secured in it. So, without any farther delay, I removed ten young she-goats and two he-goats to this piece. And when they were there, I continued to perfect the fence, till I had made it as secure as the other, which, however, I did at more leisure, and it took me up more time by a great deal.

All this labour I was at the expense of, purely from my apprehensions on the account of the print of a man's foot which I had seen; for, as yet, I never saw any human creature come near the island. And I had now lived two years under these uneasinesses, which, indeed, made my life much less comfortable than it was before, as may well be

imagined by any who know what it is to live in the constant snare of the fear of man. And this I must observe,
with grief, too, that the discomposure of my mind had too
great impressions also upon the religious part of my
thoughts; for the dread and terror of falling into the hands
of savages and cannibals lay so upon my spirits, that I seldom found myself in a due temper for application to my
Maker, at least not with the sedate calmness and resigna-
tion of soul which I was wont to do. I rather prayed to
God as under great affliction and pressure of mind, surrounded with danger, and in expectation every night of
being murdered and devoured before morning.

But to go on. After I had thus secured one part of my
little living stock, I went about the whole island, searching for another private place to make such another
deposit; when, wandering more to the west point of the
island than I had ever done yet, and looking out to sea, I
thought I saw a boat upon the sea, at a great distance. I
had found a prospective glass or two in one of the seamen's chests, which I saved out of our ship, but I had it
not about me; and this was so remote, that I could not tell
what to make of it, though I looked at it till my eyes were
not able to hold to look any longer. Whether it was a boat
or not, I do not know; but as I descended from the hill, I
could see no more of it, so I gave it over; only I resolved to
go no more out without a prospective glass in my pocket.

When I was come down the hill to the end of the

CRUSOE ON THE LOOK OUT ON THE HILL

island, where, indeed, I had never been
before, I was presently convinced that the seeing the print of a man's foot was not such a strange
thing in the island as I imagined. And, but that it was
a special providence that I was cast upon the side of
the island where the savages never came, I should
easily have known that nothing was more frequent

than for the canoes from the main, when they happened
to be a little too far out at sea, to shoot over to that side of
the island for harbour; likewise, as they often met and
fought in their canoes, the victors having taken any prisoners would bring them over to this shore, where, according to their dreadful customs, being all cannibals, they
would kill and eat them; of which hereafter.

When I was come down the hill to the shore, as I said
above, being the S.W. point of the island, I was perfectly
confounded and amazed; nor is it possible for me to
express the horror of my mind at seeing the shore spread
with skulls, hands, feet, and other bones of human bodies; and particularly, I observed a place where there had
been a fire made, and a circle dug in the earth, like a cock-
pit, where it is supposed the savage wretches had sat
down to their inhuman feastings upon the bodies of their
fellow-creatures.

I was so astonished with the sight of these things, that
I entertained no notion of any danger to myself from it for
a long while. All my apprehensions were buried in the
thoughts of such a pitch of inhuman, hellish brutality, and
the horror of the degeneracy of human nature, which,
though I had heard of often, yet I never had so near a view
of before. In short, I turned away my face from the horrid
spectacle. My stomach grew sick, and I was just at the
point of fainting, when Nature discharged the disorder
from my stomach. And having vomited with an uncom-

mon violence, I was a little relieved, but could not bear to stay in the place a moment; so I got me up the hill again with all the speed I could, and walked on towards my own habitation.

When I came a little out of that part of the island, I stood still a while, as amazed; and then recovering myself, I looked up with the utmost affection of my soul, and with a flood of tears in my eyes, gave God thanks, that had cast my first lot in a part of the world where I was distinguished from such dreadful creatures as these; and that, though I had esteemed my present condition very miserable, had yet given me so many comforts in it, that I had still more to give thanks for than to complain of; and this above all, that I had, even in this miserable condition, been comforted with the knowledge of Himself, and the hope of His blessing; which was a felicity more sufficiently equivalent to all the misery which I had suffered, or could suffer.

In this frame of thankfulness I went home to my castle, and began to be much easier now, as to the safety of my circumstances, than ever I was before; for I observed that these wretches never came to this island in search of what they could get; perhaps not seeking, not wanting, or not expecting, anything here; and having often, no doubt, been up in the covered, woody part of it, without finding anything to their purpose. I knew I had been here now almost eighteen years, and never saw the least footsteps of human creature there before; and I might be here eighteen more as entirely concealed as I was now, if I did not discover myself to them, which I had no manner of occasion to do; it being my only business to keep myself entirely concealed where I was, unless I found a better sort of creatures than cannibals to make myself known to.

Yet I entertained such an abhorrence of the savage wretches that I have been speaking of, and of the wretched inhuman custom of their devouring and eating one another up, that I continued pensive and sad, and kept close within my own circle for almost two years after this. When I say my own circle, I mean by it my three plantations, viz., my castle, my country seat, which I called my bower, and my enclosure in the woods. Nor did I look after this for any other use than as an enclosure for my goats; for the aversion which Nature gave me to these hellish wretches was such, that I was fearful of seeing them as of seeing the devil himself. Nor did I so much as go to look after my boat in all this time, but began rather to think of making me another; for I could not think of ever making any more attempts to bring the other boat round the island to me, lest I should meet with some of these creatures at sea, in which, if I had happened to have fallen into their hands, I knew what would have been my lot.

Time, however, and the satisfaction I had that I was in no danger of being discovered by these people, began to wear off my uneasiness about them; and I began to live just in the same composed manner as before; only with this difference, that I used more caution, and kept my eyes more about me, than I did before, lest I should happen to be seen by any of them; and particularly, I was more cautious of firing my gun, lest any of them being on the island, should happen to hear of it. And it was, therefore, a very good providence to me that I had furnished myself with a tame breed of goats, that I needed not hunt any more about the woods, or shoot at them. And if I did catch any of them after this, it was by traps and snares, as I had done before; so that for two years after this I believe I never fired my gun once off, though I never went out without it; and, which was more, as I had saved three pistols out of the ship, I always carried them out with me, or at least two of them, sticking them in my goat-skin belt. Also I furbished up one of the great cutlasses that I had out of the ship, and made me a belt to put it on also; so that I was now a most formidable fellow to look at when I went abroad, if you add to the former description of myself the particular of two pistols and a great broadsword hanging at my side in a belt, but without a scabbard.

Things going on thus, as I have said, for some time, I seemed, excepting these cautions, to be reduced to my former calm, sedate way of living. All these things tended to showing me, more and more, how far my condition was from being miserable, compared to some others; nay, to many other particulars of life, which it might have pleased God to have made my lot. It put me upon reflecting how little repining there would be among mankind at any condition of life, if people would rather compare their condition with those that are worse, in order to be thankful, than be always comparing them with those which are better, to assist their murmurings and complainings.

As in my present condition there were not really many things which I wanted, so indeed I thought that the frights I had been in about these savage wretches, and the concern I had been in for my own preservation, had taken off the edge of my invention for my own conveniences. And I had dropped a good design, which I had once bent my thoughts too much upon; and that was, to try if I could not make some of my barley into malt, and then try to brew myself some beer. This was really a whimsical thought, and I reproved myself often for the simplicity of it; for I presently saw there would be the want of several things necessary to the making of my beer, that it would be impossible for me to supply. As, first, casks to preserve it in, which was a thing that, as I have observed already, I could never compass; no, though I spent not many days, but weeks, nay, months, in attempting it, but to no purpose. In the next place, I had no hops to make it keep, no yeast to make it work, no copper or kettle to make it boil; and yet all these things notwithstanding, I verily believe, had not these things intervened, I mean the frights and terrors I was in about the savages, I had undertaken it, and perhaps brought it to pass too; for I seldom gave anything over without accomplishing it when I once had it in my head enough to begin it.

But my invention now ran quite another way; for, night and day, I could think of nothing but how I might destroy some of these monsters in their cruel, bloody entertainment, and, if possible, save the victim they should bring hither to destroy. It would take up a larger volume than this whole work is intended to be, to set down all the contrivances I hatched, or rather brooded upon, in my thought, for the destroying these creatures, or at least frighting them so as to prevent their coming hither any more. But all was abortive; nothing could be possible to take effect, unless I was to be there to do it myself. And what could one man do among them, when perhaps there might be twenty or thirty of them together, with their darts, or their bows and arrows, with which they could shoot as true to a mark as I could with my gun?

Sometimes I contrived to dig a hole under the place where they made their fire, and put in five or six pound of gunpowder, which, when they kindled their fire, would consequently take fire, and blow up all that was near it. But as, in the first place, I should be very loth to waste so much powder upon them, my store being now within the quantity of one barrel, so neither could I be sure of its going off at any certain time, when it might surprise them; and, at best, that it would do little more than just blow the fire about their ears, and fright them, but not sufficient to make them forsake the place. So I laid it aside, and then proposed that I would place myself in ambush in some convenient place, with my three guns all double-loaded, and, in the middle of their bloody ceremony, let fly at them, when I should be sure to kill or wound perhaps two or three at every shot; and then falling in upon them with my three pistols and my sword, I made no doubt but that if there was twenty I should kill them all. This fancy pleased my thoughts for some weeks; and I was so full of it, that I often dreamed of it, and sometimes that I was just going to let fly at them in my sleep.

I went so far with it in my imagination, that I employed myself several days to find out proper places to put myself in ambuscade, as I said, to watch for them; and I went frequently to the place itself, which was now grown more familiar to me; and especially while my mind was thus filled with thoughts of revenge, and of a bloody putting twenty or thirty of them to the sword, as I may call it, the horror I had at the place, and at the signals of the barbarous wretches devouring one another, abated my malice.

Well, at length I found a place in the side of the hill, where I was satisfied I might securely wait till I saw any of their boats coming; and might then, even before they would be ready to come on shore, convey myself, unseen, into thickets of trees, in one of which there was a hollow large enough to conceal me entirely; and where I might sit and observe all their bloody doings, and take my full aim at their heads, when they were so close together, as that it would be next to impossible that I should miss my shot, or that I could fail wounding three or four of them at the first shot.

In this place, then, I resolved to fix my design; and, accordingly, I prepared two muskets and my ordinary fowling-piece. The two muskets I loaded with a brace of slugs each, and four or five smaller bullets, about the size of pistol-bullets; and the fowling-piece I loaded with near a handful of swan-shot, of the largest size. I also loaded my pistols with about four bullets each; and in this posture, well provided with ammunition for a second and third charge, I prepared myself for my expedition.

After I had thus laid the scheme of my design, and in my imagination put it into practice, I continually made my tour every morning up to the top of the hill, which was from my castle, as I called it, about three miles, or more, to see if I could observe any boats upon the sea coming near the island, or standing over towards it. But I began to tire of this hard duty, after I had, for two or three months, constantly kept my watch, but came always back without any discovery; there having not, in all that time, been the least appearance, not only on or near the shore, but not on

the whole ocean, so far as my eyes or glasses could reach
every way.

As long as I kept up my daily tour to the hill to look
out, so long also I kept up the vigour of my design, and my
spirits seemed to be all the while in a suitable form for so
outrageous an execution as the killing twenty or thirty
naked savages for an offence which I had not at all
entered into a discussion of in my thoughts, any farther
than my passions were at first fired by the horror I con-
ceived at the unnatural custom of that people of the
country. But now when, as I have said, I began to be weary
of the fruitless excursion which I had made so long and so
far every morning in vain, so my opinion of the action
itself began to alter; and I began, with cooler and calmer
thoughts, to consider what it was I was going to engage
in. What authority or call I had to pretend to be judge and
executioner upon these men as criminals, whom Heaven
had thought fit, for so many ages, to suffer, unpunished,
to go on, and to be, as it were, the executioners of His
judgments one upon another. It is certain these people
either do not commit this as a crime; it is not against their
own consciences' reproving, or their light reproaching
them. They do not know it to be an offence, and then
commit it in defiance of Divine justice, as we do in almost
all the sins we commit. They think it no more a crime to
kill a captive taken in war, than we do to kill an ox; nor to
eat human flesh, than we do to eat mutton.

When I had considered this a little, it followed necessarily that I was certainly in the wrong in it; that these people were not murderers in the sense that I had before condemned them in my thoughts, any more than those Christians were murderers who often put to death the prisoners taken in battle; or more frequently, upon many occasions, put whole troops of men to the sword, without giving quarter, though they threw down their arms and submitted.

In the next place it occurred to me, that albeit the usage they thus gave one another was thus brutish and inhuman, yet it was really nothing to me; these people had done me no injury. That if they attempted me, or I saw it necessary for my immediate preservation to fall upon them, something might be said for it; but that as I was yet out of their power, and they had really no knowledge of me, and consequently no design upon me, and therefore it could not be just for me to fall upon them.

These considerations really put me to a pause, and to a kind of a full stop; and I began, by little and little, to be off of my design, and to conclude I had taken wrong measures in my resolutions to attack the savages; that it was not my business to meddle with them, unless they first attacked me; and this was my business, if possible, to prevent; but that if I were discovered and attacked, then I knew my duty.

On the other hand, I argued with myself that this

really was the way not to deliver myself, but entirely to ruin and destroy myself; for unless I was sure to kill every one that not only should be on shore at that time, but that should ever come on shore afterwards, if but one of them escaped to tell their country people what had happened, they would come over again by thousands to revenge the death of their fellows, and I should only bring upon myself a certain destruction, which, at present, I had no manner of occasion for.

Upon the whole, I concluded that neither in principles nor in policy I ought, one way or other, to concern myself in this affair. That my business was, by all possible means, to conceal myself from them, and not to leave the least signal to them to guess by that there were any living creatures upon the island; I mean of human shape.

Religion joined in with this prudential, and I was convinced now, many ways, that I was perfectly out of my duty when I was laying all my bloody schemes for the destruction of innocent creatures; I mean innocent as to me. As to the crimes they were guilty of towards one another, I had nothing to do with them. They were national, and I ought to leave them to the justice of God, who is the Governor of nations, and knows how, by national punishments, to make a just retribution for national offences, and to bring public judgments upon those who offend in a public manner by such ways as best pleases Him.

CHAPTER 16

Crusoe at length fetches back his boat. He lives cautiously. Makes charcoal so that he can have fire without smoke. Discovers inland natural stronghold to which he takes stores and weapons. During December harvest in the twenty-third year observes savages dancing and feasting but two miles from his habitation. He watches from his outlook hill their departure by canoe. Crusoe now endures fifteen months of anxiety and perplexity of mind.

IN THIS disposition I continued for near a year after this; and so far was I from desiring an occasion for falling upon these wretches, that in all that time I never once went up the hill to see whether there were any of them in sight, or to know whether any of them had been on shore there or not, that I might not be tempted to renew any of my contrivances against them, or be provoked, by any advantage which might present itself, to fall upon them. Only this I did, I went and removed my boat, which I had on the other side of the island, and carried it down to the east end of the whole island, where I ran it into a little cove, which I found under some high rocks, and where I knew, by reason of the currents, the savages durst not, at least would not come, with their boats, upon any account whatsoever.

With my boat I carried away everything that I had left there belonging to her, though not necessary for the bare going thither, viz., a mast and sail which I had made for her, and a thing like an anchor, but indeed which could not be called either anchor or grappling; however, it was the best I could make of its kind. All these I removed, that there might not be the least shadow of any discovery, or any appearance of any boat, or of any human habitation, upon the island.

Besides this, I kept myself, as I said, more retired than ever, and seldom went from my cell, other than upon my constant employment, viz., to milk my she-goats, and manage my little flock in the wood, which, as it was quite on the other part of the island, was quite out of danger; for certain it is, that these savage people, who sometimes haunted this island, never came with any thoughts of finding anything here, and consequently never wandered off from the coast; and I doubt not but they might have been several times on shore after my apprehensions of them had made me cautious, as well as before; and indeed, I looked back with some horror upon the thoughts of what my condition would have been if I had chopped upon them and been discovered before that, when, naked and unarmed, except with one gun, and that loaded often only with small shot, I walked everywhere, peeping and peeping about the island to see what I could get. What a surprise should I have been in if, when I discovered the print of a man's foot, I had, instead of that, seen fifteen or twenty savages, and found them pursuing me, and by the swiftness of their running, no possibility of my escaping them!

The thoughts of this sometimes sunk my very soul within me, and distressed my mind so much, that I could not soon recover it, to think what I should have done, and how I not only should not have been able to resist them, but even should not have had presence of mind enough to do what I might have done, much less what now, after so much consideration and preparation, I might be able to do. Indeed, after serious thinking of these things, I should be very melancholy, and sometimes it would last a great while; but I resolved it, at last, all into thankfulness to that Providence which had delivered me from so many unseen dangers, and had kept me from those mischiefs which I could no way have been the agent in delivering myself from, because I had not the least notion of any such thing depending, or the least supposition of it being possible.

I believe the reader of this will not think strange if I confess that these anxieties, these constant dangers I lived in, and the concern that was now upon me, put an end to all invention, and to all the contrivances that I had laid for my future accommodations and conveniences. I had the care of my safety more now upon my hands than that of my food. I cared not to drive a nail, or chop a stick of wood now, for fear the noise I should make should be heard; much less would I fire a gun, for the same reason;

and, above all, I was intolerably uneasy at making any fire, lest the smoke, which is visible at a great distance in the day, should betray me; and for this reason I removed that part of my business which required fire, such as burning of pots and pipes, etc., into my new apartment in the woods; where, after I had been some time, I found, to my unspeakable consolation, a mere natural cave in the earth, which went in a vast way, and where, I dare say, no savage, had he been at the mouth of it, would be so hardy as to venture in; nor, indeed, would any man else, but one who, like me, wanted nothing so much as a safe retreat.

The mouth of this hollow was at the bottom of a great rock, where, by mere accident I would say (if I did not see abundant reason to ascribe all such things now to Providence), I was cutting down some thick branches of trees to make charcoal; and before I go on, I must observe the reason of my making this charcoal, which was thus.

I was afraid of making a smoke about my habitation, as I said before; and yet I could not live there without baking my bread, cooking my meat, etc. So I contrived to burn some wood here, as I had seen done in England, under turf, till it became chark, or dry coal; and then putting the fire out, I preserved the coal to carry home, and perform the other services which fire was wanting for at home, without danger of smoke.

But this is by the bye. While I was cutting down some wood here, I perceived that behind a very thick branch of low brushwood, or underwood, there was a kind of hollow place. I was curious to look into it; and getting with difficulty into the mouth of it, I found it was pretty large; that is to say, sufficient for me to stand upright in it, and perhaps another with me. But I must confess to you I made more haste out than I did in when, looking farther into the place, and which was perfectly dark, I saw two broad shining eyes of some creature, whether devil or man I knew not, which twinkled like two stars, the dim light from the cave's mouth shining directly in, and making the reflection.

However, after some pause I recovered myself, and began to call myself a thousand fools, and tell myself that he that was afraid to see the devil was not fit to live twenty years in an island all alone, and that I durst to believe there was nothing in this cave that was more frightful than myself. Upon this, plucking up my courage, I took up a great firebrand, and in I rushed again, with the stick flaming in my hand. I had not gone three steps in, but I was almost as much frighted as I was before; for I heard a very loud sigh, like that of a man in some pain, and it was followed by a broken noise, as if of words half expressed, and then a deep sigh again. I stepped back, and was indeed struck with such a surprise, that it put me into a cold sweat; and if I had had a hat on my head, I will not answer for it, that my hair might not have lifted it off. But still plucking up my spirits as well as I could, and encouraging myself a little with considering that the power and presence of God was everywhere, and was able to protect me, upon this I stepped forward again, and by the light of the firebrand, holding it up a little over my head, I saw lying on the ground a most monstrous frightful old he-goat, just making his will, as we say, and gasping for life; and dying, indeed, of mere old age.

I stirred him a little to see if I could get him out, and he essayed to get up, but was not able to raise himself; and I thought with myself he might even lie there; for if he had frighted me so, he would certainly fright any of the savages, if any of them should be so hardy as to come in there while he had any life in him.

I was now recovered from my surprise, and began to look round me, when I found the cave was but very small; that is to say, it might be about twelve feet over, but in no manner of shape, either round or square, no hands having ever been employed in making it but those of mere Nature. I observed also that there was a place at the farther side of it that went in farther, but was so low, that it required me to creep upon my hands and knees to go into it, and whither I went I knew not; so having no candle, I gave it over for some time, but resolved to come again the next day, provided with candles and a tinder-box, which I had made of the lock of one of the muskets, with some wild-fire in the pan.

Accordingly, the next day I came provided with six

CRUSOE FINDS A DYING GOAT.

large candles of my own making, for I made very good candles now of goat's tallow; and going into this low place, I was obliged to creep upon all fours, as I have said, almost ten yards; which, by the way, I thought was a venture bold enough, considering that I knew not how far it might go, nor what was beyond it. When I was got through the strait, I found the roof rose higher up, I believe near twenty feet. But never was such a glorious sight seen in the island, I dare say, as it was, to look round the sides and roof of this vault or cave; the walls reflected a hundred thousand lights to me from my two candles. What it was in the rock, whether diamonds, or any other precious stones, or gold, which I rather supposed it to be, I knew not.

The place I was in was a most delightful cavity or grotto of its kind, as could be expected, though perfectly dark. The floor was dry and level, and had a sort of small loose gravel upon it, so that there was no nauseous or venomous creature to be seen; neither was there any damp or wet on the sides or roof. The only difficulty in it was the entrance, which, however, as it was a place of security, and such a retreat as I wanted, I thought that was a convenience; so that I was really rejoiced at the discovery, and resolved, without any delay, to bring some of those things which I was most anxious about to this place; particularly I resolved to bring hither my magazine of powder, and all my spare arms, viz., two fowling-pieces, for I

CRUSOE IN HIS FORT

had three in all, and three muskets, for of them I had
eight in all. So I kept at my castle only five, which
stood ready-mounted, like pieces of cannon, on my
outmost fence; and were ready also to take out upon
any expedition.

Upon this occasion of removing my ammunition, I took occasion to open the barrel of powder, which I took up out of the sea, and which had been wet; and I found that the water had penetrated about three or four inches into the powder on every side, which caking, and growing hard, had preserved the inside like a kernel in a shell; so that I had near sixty pounds of very good powder in the centre of the cask. And this was an agreeable discovery to me at that time; so I carried all away thither, never keeping above two or three pounds of powder with me in my castle, for fear of a surprise of any kind. I also carried thither all the lead I had left for bullets.

I fancied myself now like one of the ancient giants, which were said to live in caves and holes in the rocks, where none could come at them; for I persuaded myself, while I was here, if five hundred savages were to hunt me, they could never find me out; or, if they did, they would not venture to attack me here.

The old goat, whom I found expiring, died in the mouth of the cave the next day after I made this discovery; and I found it much easier to dig a great hole there, and throw him in and cover him with earth, than to drag him out; so I interred him there, to prevent the offence to my nose.

I was now in my twenty-third year of residence in this island; and was so naturalised to the place, and to the manner of living, that could I have but enjoyed the

certainty that no savages would come to the place to dis-
turb me, I could have been content to have capitulated
for spending the rest of my time there, even to the last
moment, till I had laid me down and died, like the old
goat in the cave. I had also arrived to some little diversions and amusements, which made the time pass more
pleasantly with me a great deal than it did before. As,
first, I had taught my Poll, as I noted before, to speak; and
he did it so familiarly, and talked so articulately and plain,
that it was very pleasant to me; and he lived with me no
less than six and twenty years. How long he might live
afterwards I know not, though I know they have a notion
in the Brazils that they live a hundred years. Perhaps poor
Poll may be alive there still, calling after poor Robin
Crusoe to this day. I wish no Englishman the ill luck to
come there and hear him; but if he did, he would certainly believe it was the devil. My dog was a very pleasant
and loving companion to me for no less than sixteen years
of my time, and then died of mere old age. As for my cats,
they multiplied, as I have observed, to that degree, that I
was obliged to shoot several of them at first to keep them
from devouring me and all I had; but at length, when the
two old ones I brought with me were gone, and after
some time continually driving them from me, and letting
them have no provision with me, they all ran wild into the
woods, except two or three favourites, which I kept tame,
and whose young, when they had any, I always drowned;

and these were part of my family. Besides these, I always kept two or three household kids about me, whom I taught to feed out of my hand. And I had two more parrots, which talked pretty well, and would all call 'Robin Crusoe,' but none like my first; nor, indeed, did I take the pains with any of them that I had done with him. I had also several tame sea-fowls, whose names I know not, whom I caught upon the shore, and cut their wings; and the little stakes which I planted before my castle wall being now grown up to a good thick grove, these fowls all lived among these low trees, and bred there, which was very agreeable to me; so that, as I said above, I began to be very well contented with the life I led, if it might but have been secured from the dread of the savages.

But it was otherwise directed; and it may not be amiss for all people who shall meet with my story, to make this just observation from it, viz., how frequently, in the course of our lives, the evil which in itself we seek most to shun, and which, when we are fallen into it, is the most dreadful to us, is oftentimes the very means or door of our deliverance, by which alone we can be raised again from the affliction we are fallen into. I could give many examples of this in the course of my unaccountable life; but in nothing was it more particularly remarkable, than in the circumstances of my last years of solitary residence in this island.

It was now the month of December, as I said above, in

my twenty-third year; and this, being the southern sol-
stice (for winter I cannot call it), was the particular time
of my harvest, and required my being pretty much abroad
in the fields; when, going out pretty early in the morning,
even before it was thorough daylight, I was surprised with
seeing a light of some fire upon the shore, at a distance
from me of about two miles, towards the end of the
island, where I had observed some savages had been, as
before. But not on the other side; but, to my great affliction, it was on my side of the island.

I was indeed terribly surprised at the sight, and
stopped short within my grove, not daring to go out, lest I
might be surprised; and yet I had no more peace within,
from the apprehensions I had that if these savages, in
rambling over the island, should find my corn standing or
cut, or any of my works and improvements, they would
immediately conclude that there were people in the
place, and would then never give over till they had found
me out. In this extremity I went back directly to my
castle, pulled up the ladder after me, and made all things
without look as wild and natural as I could.

Then I prepared myself within, putting myself in a
posture of defence. I loaded all my cannon, as I called
them, that is to say, my muskets, which were mounted
upon my new fortification, and all my pistols, and
resolved to defend myself to the last gasp; not forgetting
seriously to commend myself to the Divine protection,

and earnestly to pray to God to deliver me out of the hands of the barbarians. And in this posture I continued about two hours; but began to be mighty impatient for intelligence abroad, for I had no spies to send out.

After sitting a while longer, and musing what I should do in this case, I was not able to bear sitting in ignorance any longer; so setting up my ladder to the side of the hill where there was a flat place, as I observed before, and then pulling the ladder up after me, I set it up again, and mounted to the top of the hill; and pulling out my perspective-glass, which I had taken on purpose, I laid me down flat on my belly on the ground, and began to look for the place. I presently found there was no less than nine naked savages sitting round a small fire they had made, not to warm them, for they had no need of that, the weather being extreme hot, but, as I supposed, to dress some of their barbarous diet of human flesh which they had brought with them, whether alive or dead, I could not know.

They had two canoes with them, which they had hauled up upon the shore; and as it was then tide of ebb, they seemed to me to wait for the return of the flood to go away again. It is not easy to imagine what confusion this sight put me into, especially seeing them come on my side of the island, and so near me too. But when I observed their coming must be always with the current of

the ebb, I began afterwards to be more sedate in my
mind, being satisfied that I might go abroad with safety
all the time of the tide of flood, if they were not on shore
before; and having made this observation, I went abroad
about my harvest-work with the more composure.

As I expected, so it proved; for as soon as the tide made
to the westward, I saw them all take boat, and row (or
paddle, as we call it) all away. I should have observed, that
for an hour and more before they went off, they went to
dancing; and I could easily discern their postures and gestures by my glasses. I could not perceive, by my nicest
observation, but that they were stark naked, and had not
the least covering upon them; but whether they were
men or women that I could not distinguish.

As soon as I saw them shipped and gone, I took my two
guns upon my shoulders, and two pistols at my girdle, and
my great sword by my side, without a scabbard, and with
all the speed I was able to make I went away to the hill
where I had discovered the first appearance of all. And as
soon as I gat thither, which was not less than two hours
(for I could not go apace, being so loaden with arms as I
was), I perceived there had been three canoes more of
savages on that place; and looking out farther, I saw they
were all at sea together, making over the main.

This was a dreadful sight to me, especially when going
down to the shore, I could see the marks of horror which
the dismal work they had been about had left behind it,

viz., the blood, the bones, and part of the flesh of human bodies, eaten and devoured by those wretches with merriment and sport. I was so filled with indignation at the sight that I began now to premeditate the destruction of the next that I saw there, let them be who or how many soever.

It seemed evident to me that the visits which they thus made to this island are not very frequent, for it was above fifteen months before any more of them came on shore there again; that is to say, I neither saw them, or any footsteps or signals of them, in all that time; for, as to the rainy seasons, then they are sure not to come abroad, at least not so far. Yet all the while I lived uncomfortably, by reason of the constant apprehensions I was in of their coming upon me by surprise; from whence I observe, that the expectation of evil is more bitter than the suffering, especially if there is no room to shake off that expectation, or those apprehensions.

During all this time I was in a murdering humour, and took up most of my hours, which should have been better employed, in contriving how to circumvent and fall upon them the very next time I should see them; especially if they should be divided, as they were the last time, into two parties. Nor did I consider at all that if I killed one party, suppose ten or a dozen, I was still the next day, or week, or month, to kill another, and so another, even *ad infinitum*, till I should be at length no less a murderer than they were in being man-eaters, and perhaps much more so.

I spent my days now in great perplexity and anxiety of mind, expecting that I should, one day or other, fall into the hands of these merciless creatures; and if I did at any time venture abroad, it was not without looking round me with the greatest care and caution imaginable. And now I found, to my great comfort, how happy it was that I provided for a tame flock or herd of goats; for I durst not, upon any account, fire my gun, especially near that side of the island where they usually came, lest I should alarm the savages. And if they had fled from me now, I was sure to have them come back again, with perhaps two or three hundred canoes with them, in a few days, and then I knew what to expect.

However, I wore out a year and three months more before I ever saw any more of the savages, and then I found them again, as I shall soon observe. It is true they might have been there once or twice, but either they made no stay, or at least I did not hear them; but in the month of May, as near as I could calculate, and in my four and twentieth year, I had a very strange encounter with them; of which in its place.

CHAPTER 17

A day of storm and a foul night. Crusoe hears sound of gunshot
from sea and lights a signal fire. Daylight reveals a wreck on
distant rocks. Crusoe makes his way out when weather permits.
Is grieved to find no living creature but a hungry dog.
He removes useful articles, and bags of money which are as but
'dirt under his feet'.

THE PERTURBATION of my mind, during this fifteen
or sixteen months' interval, was very great. I slept
unquiet, dreamed always frightful dreams, and often
started out of my sleep in the night. In the day great troubles overwhelmed my mind, and in the night I dreamed
often of killing the savages, and of the reasons why I
might justify the doing of it. But, to waive all this for a
while, it was in the middle of May, on the sixteenth day, I
think, as well as my poor wooden calendar would reckon,
for I marked all upon the post still; I say, it was the sixteenth of May that it blew a very great storm of wind all
day, with a great deal of lightning and thunder, and a very
foul night it was after it. I know not what was the particular occasion of it, but as I was reading in the Bible, and
taken up with very serious thoughts about my present
condition, I was surprised with a noise of a gun, as I
thought, fired at sea.

This was, to be sure, a surprise of a quite different

nature from any I had met with before; for the notions
this put into my thoughts were quite of another kind. I
started up in the greatest haste imaginable, and, in a
trice, clapped my ladder to the middle place of the rock,
and pulled it after me, and mounting it the second time,
got to the top of the hill the very moment that a flash of
fire bid me listen for a second gun, which accordingly, in
about half a minute, I heard; and, by the sound, knew
that it was from that part of the sea where I was driven
down the current in my boat.

I immediately considered that this must be some ship
in distress, and that they had some comrade, or some
other ship in company, and fired these guns for signals of
distress, and to obtain help. I had this presence of mind,
at that minute, as to think that though I could not help
them, it may be they might help me; so I brought
together all the dry wood I could get at hand, and, making
a good handsome pile, I set it on fire upon the hill. The
wood was dry, and blazed freely; and though the wind
blew very hard, yet it burnt fairly out; so that I was certain, if there was any such thing as a ship, they must
needs see it, and no doubt they did; for as soon as ever my
fire blazed up I heard another gun, and after that several
others, all from the same quarter. I plied my fire all night
long till day broke; and when it was broad day, and the
air cleared up, I saw something at a great distance at sea,
full east of the island, whether a sail or a hull I could not

distinguish, no, not with my glasses, the distance was so great, and the weather still something hazy also; at least it was so out at sea.

I looked frequently at it all that day, and soon perceived that it did not move; so I presently concluded that it was a ship at an anchor. And being eager, you may be sure, to be satisfied, I took my gun in my hand and ran toward the south side of the island, to the rocks where I had formerly been carried away with the current; and getting up there, the weather by this time being perfectly clear, I could plainly see, to my great sorrow, the wreck of a ship, cast away in the night upon those concealed rocks which I found when I was out in my boat; and which rocks, as they checked the violence of the stream, and made a kind of counter-stream or eddy, were the occasion of my recovering from the most desperate hopeless condition that ever I had been in in all my life.

Thus, what is one man's safety is another man's destruction; for it seems these men, whoever they were, being out of their knowledge, and the rocks being wholly under water, had been driven upon them in the night, the wind blowing hard at E. and E.N.E. Had they seen the island, as I must necessarily suppose they did not, they must, as I thought, have endeavoured to have saved themselves on shore by the help of their boat; but their firing of guns for help, especially when they saw, as I imagined, my fire, filled me with many thoughts. First, I imagined that upon seeing my light, they might have put themselves into their boat, and have endeavoured to make the shore; but that the sea going very high, they might have been cast away. Other times I imagined that they might have lost their boat before, as might be the case many ways; as, particularly, by the breaking of the sea upon their ship, which many times obliges men to stave, or take in pieces their boat, and sometimes to throw it overboard with their own hands. Other times I imagined they had some other ship or ships in company, who, upon the signals of distress they had made had taken them up and carried them off. Other whiles I fancied they were all gone off to sea in their boat, and being hurried away by the current that I had been formerly in, were carried out into the great ocean, where there was nothing but misery and perishing; and that, perhaps, they might by this time think of starving, and of being in a condition to eat one another.

As all these were but conjectures at best, so, in the condition I was in, I could do no more than look on upon the misery of the poor men, and pity them; which had still this good effect on my side, that it gave me more and more cause to give thanks to God, who had so happily and comfortably provided for me in my desolate condition; and that of two ships' companies who were now cast away upon this part of the world, not one life should be spared but mine. I learned here again to observe, that it is very rare that the providence of God casts us into any condition of life so low, or any misery so great, but we may see something or other to be thankful for, and may see others in worse circumstances than our own.

I cannot explain, by any possible energy of words, what a strange longing or hankering of desires I felt in my soul upon this sight, breaking out sometimes thus: 'Oh, that there had been but one or two, nay, or but one soul, saved out of this ship, to have escaped to me, that I might but have had one companion, one fellow-creature, to have spoken to me, and to have conversed with!' In all the time of my solitary life, I never felt so earnest, so strong a desire after the society of my fellow-creatures, or so deep a regret at the want of it.

Such were these earnest wishings that but one man had been saved! 'Oh that it had been but one!' I believe I repeated the words, 'Oh that it had been one!' a thousand times; and the desires were so moved by it, that when I spoke the words my hands would clinch together, and my fingers press the palms of my hands, that if I had had any soft thing in my hand, it would have crushed it involuntarily; and my teeth in my head would strike together, and set against one another so strong, that for some time I could not part them again.

It was doubtless the effect of ardent wishes, and of strong ideas formed in my mind, realising the comfort

which the conversation of one of my fellow-Christians
would have been to me.

But it was not to be. Either their fate or mine, or both,
forbid it; for, till the last year of my being on this island, I
never knew whether any were saved out of that ship or
no; and had only the affliction, some days after, to see the
corpse of a drowned boy come on shore at the end of the
island which was next the shipwreck. He had on no
clothes but a seaman's waistcoat, a pair of open-kneed
linen drawers, and a blue linen shirt; but nothing to
direct me so much as to guess what nation he was of. He
had nothing in his pocket but two pieces of eight and a
tobacco-pipe. The last was to me of ten times more value
than the first.

It was now calm, and I had a great mind to venture out
in my boat to this wreck, not doubting but that I might
find something on board that might be useful to me. But
that did not altogether press me so much as the possibility
that there might be yet some living creature on board,
whose life I might not only save, but might, by saving that
life, comfort my own to the last degree. And this thought
clung so to my heart, that I could not be quiet night or day,
but I must venture out in my boat on board this wreck; and
committing the rest to God's providence, I thought, the
impression was so strong upon my mind that it could not
be resisted, that it must come from some invisible direction, and that I should be wanting to myself if I did not go.

Under the power of this impression, I hastened back to my castle, prepared everything for my voyage, took a quantity of bread, a great pot for fresh water, a compass to steer by, a bottle of rum (for I had still a great deal of that left), a basket full of raisins. And thus, loading myself with everything necessary, I went down to my boat, got the water out of her, and got her afloat, loaded all my cargo in her, and then went home again for more. My second cargo was a great bag full of rice, the umbrella, to set up over my head for shade, another large pot full of fresh water, and about two dozen of my small loaves, or barley-cakes, more than before, with a bottle of goat's milk and a cheese; all which, with great labour and sweat, I brought to my boat. And praying to God to direct my voyage, I put out; and rowing, or paddling, the canoe along the shore, I came at last to the utmost point of the island on that side, viz., N.E. And now I was to launch out into the ocean, and either to venture or not to venture. I looked on the rapid currents which ran constantly on both sides of the island at a distance, and which were very terrible to me, from the remembrance of the hazard I had been in before, and my heart began to fail me; for I foresaw that if I was driven into either of those currents, I should be carried a vast way out to sea, and perhaps out of my reach, or sight of the island again; and that then, as my boat was but small, if any little gale of wind should rise, I should be inevitably lost.

These thoughts so oppressed my mind, that I began to give over my enterprise; and having hauled my boat into a little creek on the shore, I stepped out, and sate me down upon a little rising bit of ground, very pensive and anxious, between fear and desire, about my voyage; when, as I was musing, I could perceive that the tide was turned, and the flood come on; upon which my going was for many hours impracticable. Upon this, presently it occurred to me that I should go up to the highest piece of ground I could find and observe, if I could, how the sets of the tide, or currents, lay when the flood came in, that I might judge whether, if I was driven one way out, I might not expect to be driven another way home, with the same rapidness of the currents. This thought was no sooner in my head but I cast my eye upon a little hill, which sufficiently overlooked the sea both ways, and from whence I had a clear view of the currents, or sets of the tide, and which way I was to guide myself in my return. Here I found, that as the current of the ebb set out close by the south point of the island, so the current of the flood set in close by the shore of the north side; and that I had nothing to do but to keep to the north of the island in my return, and I should do well enough.

Encouraged with this observation, I resolved the next morning to set out with the first of the tide, and reposing myself for the night in the canoe, under the great watch-coat I mentioned, I launched out. I made first a little out

CRUSOE VISITS THE SPANISH SHIP

W.J. LINTON SC.

to sea, full north, till I began to feel the benefit of the
current which set eastward, and which carried me at a
great rate; and yet did not so hurry me as the southern
side current had done before, and so as to take from me
all government of the boat; but having a strong steerage
with my paddle, I went at a great rate directly for the
wreck, and in less than two hours I came up to it.

It was a dismal sight to look at. The ship, which, by its
building, was Spanish, stuck fast, jammed in between
two rocks. All the stern and quarter of her was beaten to
pieces with the sea; and as her forecastle, which stuck in
the rocks, had run on with great violence, her mainmast
and foremast were brought by the board; that is to say,
broken short off; but her bowsprit was sound, and the
head and bow appeared firm. When I came close to her a
dog appeared upon her, who, seeing me coming, yelped
and cried; and as soon as I called him, jumped into the sea
to come to me, and I took him into the boat, but found
him almost dead for hunger and thirst. I gave him a cake
of my bread, and he eat it like a ravenous wolf that had
been starving a fortnight in the snow. I then gave the poor
creature some fresh water, with which, if I would have let
him, he would have burst himself.

After this I went on board; but the first sight I met
with was two men drowned in the cook-room, or forecastle of the ship, with their arms fast about one another.
I concluded, as is indeed probable, that when the ship

struck, it being in a storm, the sea broke so high, and so
continually over her, that the men were not able to bear
it, and were strangled with the constant rushing in of the
water, as much as if they had been under water. Besides
the dog, there was nothing left in the ship that had life;
nor any goods that I could see, but what were spoiled by
the water. There were some casks of liquor, whether wine
or brandy I knew not, which lay lower in the hold, and
which, the water being ebbed out, I could see; but they
were too big to meddle with. I saw several chests, which I
believed belonged to some of the seamen; and I got two
of them into the boat, without examining what was in
them.

Had the stern of the ship been fixed, and the forepart
broken off, I am persuaded I might have made a good voyage; for by what I found in these two chests, I had room to
suppose the ship had a great deal of wealth on board; and
if I may guess by the course she steered, she must have
been bound from the Buenos Ayres, or the Rio de la Plata,
in the south part of America, beyond the Brazils, to the
Havana, in the Gulf of Mexico, and so perhaps to Spain.
She had, no doubt, a great treasure in her, but of no use,
at that time, to anybody; and what became of the rest of
her people, I then knew not.

I found, besides these chests, a little cask full of liquor,
of about twenty gallons, which I got into my boat with
much difficulty. There were several muskets in a cabin,

CRUSOE SLEEPING IN HIS BOAT

and a great powder-horn, with about four
pounds of powder in it. As for the muskets, I had no
occasion for them, so I left them, but took the powder-horn. I took a fire-shovel and tongs, which I

wanted extremely; as also two little brass kettles, a copper pot to make chocolate, and a gridiron. And with this cargo, and the dog, I came away, the tide beginning to make home again; and the same evening, about an hour within night, I reached the island again, weary and fatigued to the last degree.

I reposed that night in the boat; and in the morning I resolved to harbour what I had gotten in my new cave, not carry it home to my castle. After refreshing myself, I got all my cargo on shore, and began to examine the particulars. The cask of liquor I found to be a kind of rum, but not such as we had at the Brazils, and, in a word, not at all good. But when I came to open the chests, I found several things of great use to me. For example, I found in one a fine case of bottles, of an extraordinary kind, and filled with cordial waters, fine, and very good; the bottles held about three pints each, and were tipped with silver. I found two pots of very good succades, or sweetmeats, so fastened also on top, that the salt water had not hurt them; and two more of the same, which the water had spoiled. I found some very good shirts, which were very welcome to me; and about a dozen and a half of linen white handkerchiefs and coloured neck-cloths. The former were also very welcome, being exceedingly refreshing to wipe my face in a hot day. Besides this, when I came to the till in the chest, I found there three great bags of pieces of eight, which held out about eleven hundred pieces in all; and in one of them, wrapped up in a paper, six doubloons of gold, and some small bars or wedges of gold. I suppose they might all weigh near a pound.

The other chest I found had some clothes in it, but of little value; but by the circumstances, it must have belonged to the gunner's mate; though there was no powder in it, but about two pounds of fine glazed powder, in three small flasks, kept, I suppose, for charging their fowling-pieces on occasion. Upon the whole, I got very little by this voyage that was of any use to me; for as to the money, I had no manner of occasion for it: 'twas to me as the dirt under my feet; and I would have given it all for three or four pairs of English shoes and stockings, which were things I greatly wanted, but had not had on my feet now for many years. I had indeed gotten two pairs of shoes now, which I took off of the feet of the two drowned men whom I saw in the wreck, and I found two pair more in one of the chests, which were very welcome to me; but they were not like our English shoes, either for ease or service, being rather what we call pumps than shoes. I found in this seaman's chest about fifty pieces of eight in royals, but no gold. I suppose this belonged to a poorer man than the other, which seemed to belong to some officer.

Well, however, I lugged this money home to my cave, and laid it up, as I had done that before which I brought from our own ship; but it was great pity, as I said, that the other part of this ship had not come to my share, for I am satisfied I might have loaded my canoe several times over with money, which, if I had ever escaped to England, would have lain here safe enough till I might have come again and fetched it.

Having now brought all my things on shore, and secured them, I went back to my boat, and rowed or paddled her along the shore to her old harbour, where I laid her up, and made the best of my way to my old habitation, where I found everything safe and quiet. So I began to repose myself, live after my old fashion, and take care of my family affairs; and, for a while, I lived easy enough, only that I was more vigilant than I used to be, looked out oftener, and did not go abroad so much; and if at any time I did stir with any freedom, it was always to the east part of the island, where I was pretty well satisfied the savages never came, and where I could go without so many precautions, and such a load of arms and ammunition as I always carried with me if I went the other way.

I lived in this condition near two years more; but my unlucky head, that was always to let me know it was born to make my body miserable, was all this two years filled with projects and designs, how, if it were possible, I might get away from this island; for sometimes I was for making another voyage to the wreck, though my reason told me that there was nothing left there worth the haz-ard of my voyage; sometimes for a ramble one way, sometimes another; and I believe verily, if I had had the boat that I went from Sallee in, I should have ventured to sea, bound anywhere, I knew not whither.

I have been, in all my circumstances, a memento to those who are touched with the general plague of mankind, whence, for aught I know, one-half of their miseries flow; I mean, that of not being satisfied with the station wherein God and Nature has placed them; for not to look back upon my primitive condition, and the excellent advice of my father, the opposition to which was, as I may call it, my *original sin*, my subsequent mistakes of the same kind had been the means of my coming into this miserable condition; for had that Providence, which so happily had seated me at the Brazils as a planter, blessed me with confined desires, and I could have been contented to have gone on gradually, I might have been, by this time, I mean in the time of my being in this island, one of the most considerable planters in the Brazils; nay, I am persuaded that by the improvements I had made in that little time I lived there, and the increase I should probably have made if I had stayed, I might have been worth an hundred thousand moidores. And what business had I to leave a settled fortune, a well-stocked plantation, improving and increasing, to turn supercargo to Guinea to fetch negroes, when patience and time would have so increased our stock at home, that we could have bought them at our own door from those whose business it was to fetch them; and though it had cost us something more, yet the difference of that price was by no means worth saving at so great a hazard.

But as this is ordinarily the fate of young heads, so reflection upon the folly of it is as ordinarily the exercise of more years, or of the dear-bought experience of time; and so it was with me now. And yet, so deep had the mistake taken root in my temper, that I could not satisfy myself in my station, but was continually poring upon the means and possibility of my escape from this place. And that I may, with the greater pleasure to the reader, bring on the remaining part of my story, it may not be improper to give some account of my first conceptions on the subject of this foolish scheme for my escape, and how, and upon what foundation, I acted.

I am now supposed to be retired into my castle, after my late voyage to the wreck, my frigate laid up and secured under water, as usual, and my condition restored to what it was before. I had more wealth, indeed, than I had before, but was not at all the richer; for I had no more use for it than the Indians of Peru had before the Spaniards came there.

CHAPTER 18

Crusoe reflects miserably upon his solitary state. He dreams a strange dream. Cannibals come again in numbers with captives. Crusoe hastens to the aid of fleeing victim, felling two pursuers. Fugitive falls in supplication at his feet and Crusoe takes him to safety.

I T WAS one of the nights in the rainy season in March, the four and twentieth year of my first setting foot in this island of solitariness. I was lying in my bed, or hammock, awake, very well in health, had no pain, no distemper, no uneasiness of body, no, nor any uneasiness of mind, more than ordinary, but could by no means close my eyes, that is, so as to sleep; no, not to wink all night long, otherwise than as follows.

It is as impossible, as needless, to set down the innumerable crowd of thoughts that whirled through that great thoroughfare of the brain, the memory, in this night's time. I ran over the whole history of my life in miniature, or by abridgment, as I may call it, to my coming to this island, and also of the part of my life since I came to this island. In my reflections upon the state of my case since I came on shore on this island, I was comparing the happy posture of my affairs in the first years of my habitation here compared to the life of anxiety, fear, and care which I had lived ever since I had seen the print

of a foot in the sand; not that I did not believe the savages
had frequented the island even all the while, and might
have been several hundreds of them at times on shore
there; but I had never known it, and was incapable of any
apprehensions about it.

When these thoughts were over, my head was for some
time taken up in considering the nature of these
wretched creatures, I mean the savages, and how it came
to pass in the world that the wise Governor of all things
should give up any of His creatures to such inhumanity;
nay, to something so much below even brutality itself, as
to devour its own kind. But as this ended in some (at that
time fruitless) speculations, it occurred to me to inquire
what part of the world these wretches lived in? how far off
the coast was from whence they came? what they ventured over so far from home for? what kind of boats they
had? and why I might not order myself and my business
so, that I might be as able to go over thither, as they were
to come to me.

I never so much as troubled myself to consider what I
should do with myself when I came thither; what would
become of me, if I fell into the hands of the savages; or
how I should escape from them, if they attempted me;
no, nor so much as how it was possible for me to reach the
coast, and not be attempted by some or other of them,
without any possibility of delivering myself; and if I
should not fall into their hands, what I should do for

CRUSOE AND FRIDAY.

provision, or whither I should bend my course. None of these thoughts, I say, so much as came in my way; but my mind was wholly bent upon the notion of my passing over in my boat to the mainland. I looked back upon my present condition as the most miserable that could possibly be; that I was not able to throw myself into anything, but death, that could be called worse; that if I reached the shore of the main, I might perhaps meet with relief, or I might coast along, as I did on the shore of Africa, till I came to some inhabited country, and where I might find some relief; and after all, perhaps I might fall in with some Christian ship that might take me in; and if the worse came to the worst, I could but die, which would put an end to all these miseries at once.

When this had agitated my thoughts for two hours, or more, with such violence that it set my very blood into a ferment, and my pulse beat as high as if I had been in a fever, merely with the extraordinary fervour of my mind about it, Nature, as if I had been fatigued and exhausted with the very thought of it, threw me into a sound sleep. One would have thought I should have dreamed of it, but I did not, nor of anything relating to it; but I dreamed that as I was going out in the morning, as usual, from my castle, I saw upon the shore two canoes and eleven savages coming to land, and that they brought with them another savage, whom they were going to kill in order to eat him; when, on a sudden, the savage that they were

going to kill jumped away, and ran for his life. And I
thought, in my sleep, that he came running into my little
thick grove before my fortification to hide himself; and
that I, seeing him alone, and not perceiving that the
other sought him that way, showed myself to him, and
smiling upon him, encouraged him; that he kneeled
down to me, seeming to pray me to assist him; upon
which I showed my ladder, made him go up, and carried
him into my cave, and he became my servant; and that as
soon as I had gotten this man, I said to myself, 'Now I
may certainly venture to the mainland; for this fellow will
serve me as a pilot, and will tell me what to do, and
whither to go for provisions, and whither not to go for fear
of being devoured; what places to venture into, and what
to escape.' I waked with this thought, and was under such
inexpressible impressions of joy at the prospect of my
escape in my dream, that the disappointments which I
felt upon coming to myself and finding it was no more
than a dream were equally extravagant the other way, and
threw me into a very great dejection of spirit.

Upon this, however, I made this conclusion; that my
only way to go about an attempt for an escape was, if possible, to get a savage into my possession; and, if possible,
it should be one of their prisoners whom they had condemned to be eaten, and should bring thither to kill. But
these thoughts still were attended with this difficulty,
that it was impossible to effect this without attacking a

whole caravan of them, and killing them all; and this was not only a very desperate attempt, and might miscarry, but, on the other hand, I had greatly scrupled the lawfulness of it to me; and my heart trembled at the thoughts of shedding so much blood, though it was for my deliverance. I need not repeat the arguments which occurred to me against this, they being the same mentioned before. But though I had other reasons to offer now, viz., that those men were enemies to my life, and would devour me if they could; that it was self-preservation, in the highest degree, to deliver myself from this death of a life, and was acting in my own defence as much as if they were actually assaulting me, and the like; I say, though these things argued for it, yet the thoughts of shedding human blood for my deliverance were very terrible to me, and such as I could by no means reconcile myself to a great while.

However, at last, after many secret disputes with myself, and after great perplexities about it, for all these arguments, one way and another, struggled in my head a long time, the eager prevailing desire of deliverance at length mastered all the rest, and I resolved, if possible, to get one of those savages into my hands, cost what it would. My next thing then was to contrive how to do it, and this indeed was very difficult to resolve on. But as I could pitch upon no probable means for it, so I resolved to put myself upon the watch, to see them when they came on shore, and leave the rest to the event, taking such measures as the opportunity should present, let be what would be.

With these resolutions in my thoughts, I set myself upon the scout as often as possible, and indeed so often, till I was heartily tired of it; for it was above a year and half that I waited; and for great part of that time went out to the west end, and to the south-west corner of the island, almost every day, to see for canoes, but none appeared. This was very discouraging, and began to trouble me much; though I cannot say that it did in this case, as it had done some time before that, viz., wear off the edge of my desire to the thing. But the longer it seemed to be delayed, the more eager I was for it. In a word, I was not at first so careful to shun the sight of these savages, and avoid being seen by them, as I was now eager to be upon them.

Besides, I fancied myself able to manage one, nay, two or three savages, if I had them, so as to make them entirely slaves to me, to do whatever I should direct them, and to prevent their being able at any time to do me any hurt. It was a great while that I pleased myself with this affair; but nothing still presented. All my fancies and schemes came to nothing, for no savages came near me for a great while.

About a year and half after I had entertained these notions, and by long musing had, as it were, resolved them all into nothing, for want of an occasion to put them

in execution, I was surprised, one morning early, with seeing no less than five canoes all on shore together on my
side of the island, and the people who belonged to them
all landed, and out of my sight. The number of them
broke all my measures; for seeing so many, and knowing
that they always came four, or six, or sometimes more, in a
boat, I could not tell what to think of it, or how to take my
measures to attack twenty or thirty men single-handed;
so I lay still in my castle, perplexed and discomforted.
However, I put myself into all the same postures for an
attack that I had formerly provided, and was just ready for
action if anything had presented. Having waited a good
while, listening to hear if they made any noise, at length,
being very impatient, I set my guns at the foot of my ladder, and clambered up to the top of the hill, by my two
stages as usual; standing so, however, that my head did
not appear above the hill, so that they could not perceive
me by any means. Here I observed, by the help of my perspective-glass, that they were no less than thirty in number, that they had a fire kindled, that they had had meat
dressed. How they had cooked it, that I knew not, or
what it was; but they were all dancing, in I know not how
many barbarous gestures and figures, their own way,
round the fire.

While I was thus looking on them, I perceived by my
perspective two miserable wretches dragged from the
boats, where, it seems, they were laid by, and were now

brought out for the slaughter. I perceived one of them immediately fell, being knocked down, I suppose, with a club or wooden sword, for that was their way, and two or three others were at work immediately, cutting him open for their cookery, while the other victim was left standing by himself, till they should be ready for him. In that very moment this poor wretch seeing himself a little at liberty, Nature inspired him with hopes of life, and he started away from them, and ran with incredible swiftness along the sands directly towards me, I mean towards that part of the coast where my habitation was.

I was dreadfully frighted (that I must acknowledge) when I perceived him to run my way, and especially when, as I thought, I saw him pursued by the whole body; and now I expected that part of my dream was coming to pass, and that he would certainly take shelter in my grove; but I could not depend, by any means, upon my dream for the rest of it, viz., that the other savages would not pursue him thither, and find him there. However, I kept my station, and my spirits began to recover when I found that there was not above three men that followed him; and still more was I encouraged when I found that he outstripped them exceedingly in running, and gained ground of them; so that if he could but hold it for half an hour, I saw easily he would fairly get away from them all.

There was between them and my castle the creek, which I mentioned often at the first part of my story, when I landed my cargoes out of the ship; and this I saw plainly he must necessarily swim over, or the poor wretch would be taken there. But when the savage escaping came thither he made nothing of it, though the tide was then up; but plunging in, swam through in about thirty strokes or thereabouts, landed, and ran on with exceeding strength and swiftness. When the three persons came to the creek, I found that two of them could swim, but the third could not, and that, standing on the other side, he looked at the other, but went no further, and soon after went softly back, which, as it happened, was very well for him in the main.

I observed, that the two who swam were yet more than twice as long swimming over the creek as the fellow was that fled from them. It came now very warmly upon my thoughts, and indeed irresistibly, that now was my time to get me a servant, and perhaps a companion or assistant, and that I was called plainly by Providence to save this poor creature's life. I immediately run down the ladders with all possible expedition, fetched my two guns, for they were both but at the foot of the ladders, as I observed above, and getting up again, with some haste, to the top of the hill, I crossed toward the sea, and having a very short cut, and all down hill, clapped myself in the way between the pursuers and the pursued, hallooing aloud to him that fled, who, looking back, was at first perhaps as much frighted at me as at them; but I beckoned with my hand to him to come back; and, in the mean-time, I slowly advanced toward the two that followed; then rushing at once upon the foremost, I knocked him down with the stock of my piece. I was loth to fire, because I would not have the rest hear; though, at that distance, it would not have been easily heard, and being out of sight of the smoke too, they would not have easily known what to make of it. Having knocked this fellow down, the other who pursued with him stopped, as if he had been frighted, and I advanced apace towards him; but as I came nearer, I perceived presently he had a bow and arrow, and was fitting it to shoot at me; so I was then necessitated to shoot at him first, which I did, and killed him at the first shot.

The poor savage who fled, but had stopped, though he saw both his enemies fallen and killed, as he thought, yet was so frighted with the fire and noise of my piece, that he stood stock-still, and neither came forward or went backward, though he seemed rather inclined to fly still, than to come on. I hallooed again to him, and made signs to come forward, which he easily understood, and came a little way, then stopped again, and then a little further, and stopped again; and I could then perceive that he stood trembling, as if he had been taken prisoner, and had just been to be killed, as his two enemies were. I beck-oned him again to come to me, and gave him all the signs of encouragement that I could think of; and he came nearer and nearer, kneeling down every ten or twelve steps, in token of acknowledgment for my saving his life. I smiled at him, and looked pleasantly, and beckoned to him to come still nearer. At length he came close to me, and then he kneeled down again, kissed the ground, and laid his head upon the ground, and taking me by the foot, set my foot upon his head. This, it seems, was in token of swearing to be my slave for ever. I took him up, and made much of him, and encouraged him all I could. But there was more work to do yet; for I perceived the savage whom I knocked down was not killed, but stunned with the blow, and began to come to himself; so I pointed to him, and showing him the savage, that he was not dead, upon this he spoke some words to me; and though I could not understand them, yet I thought they were pleasant to hear; for they were the first sound of a man's voice that I had heard, my own excepted, for above twenty-five years. But there was no time for such reflections now. The savage who was knocked down recovered himself so far as to sit up upon the ground, and I perceived that my savage began to be afraid; but when I saw that, I presented my other piece at the man, as if I would shoot him. Upon this my savage, for so I call him now, made a motion to me to lend him my sword, which hung naked in a belt by my side; so I did. He no sooner had it but he runs to his enemy, and, at one blow, cut off his head as cleverly, no executioner in Germany could have done it sooner or better; which I thought very strange for one who, I had reason to believe, never saw a sword in his life before, except their own wooden swords. However, it seems, as I learned afterwards, they make their wooden swords so sharp, so heavy, and the wood is so hard, that they will cut off heads even with them, ay, and arms, and that at one blow too. When he had done this, he comes laughing to me in sign of triumph, and brought me the sword again, and with abundance of gestures, which I did not understand, laid it down, with the head of the savage that he had killed, just before me.

But that which astonished him most, was to know how I had killed the other Indian so far off; so pointing to him, he made signs to me to let him go to him; so I bade him go, as well as I could. When he came to him, he stood like one amazed, looking at him, turned him first on one side, then on t'other, looked at the wound the bullet had made, which, it seems, was just in his breast, where it had made a hole, and no great quantity of blood had followed; but he had bled inwardly, for he was quite dead. He took up his bow and arrows, and came back; so I turned to go away, and beckoned to him to follow me, making signs to him that more might come after them.

Upon this he signed to me that he should bury them with sand, that they might not be seen by the rest if they followed; and so I made signs again to him to do so. He fell to work, and in an instant he had scraped a hole in the sand with his hands big enough to bury the first in, and then dragged him into it, and covered him, and did so also by the other. I believe he had buried them both in a quarter of an hour. Then calling him away, I carried him, not to my castle, but quite away to my cave, on the farther part of the island; so I did not let my dream come to pass in that part, viz., that he came into my grove for shelter.

Here I gave him bread and a bunch of raisins to eat, and a draught of water, which I found he was indeed in great distress for, by his running; and having refreshed him, I made signs for him to go lie down and sleep, pointing to a place where I had laid a great parcel of rice-straw, and a blanket upon it, which I used to sleep upon myself sometimes; so the poor creature laid down, and went to sleep.

CHAPTER 19

Crusoe and Man Friday go to the scene of the horrid feast. They cremate all grisly remains. Crusoe makes clothes for Friday, who though wearing them awkwardly at first is greatly pleased. Friday is an apt pupil and a faithful loving servant.

HE WAS a comely, handsome fellow, perfectly well made, with straight strong limbs, not too large, tall, and well-shaped, and, as I reckon, about twenty-six years of age. He had a very good countenance, not a fierce and surly aspect, but seemed to have something very manly in his face; and yet he had all the sweetness and softness of an European in his countenance too, especially when he smiled. His hair was long and black, not curled like wool; his forehead very high and large; and a great vivacity and sparkling sharpness in his eyes. The colour of his skin was not quite black, but very tawny; and yet not of an ugly, yellow, nauseous tawny, as the Brazilians and Virginians, and other natives of America are, but of a bright kind of a dun olive colour, that had in it something very agreeable, though not very easy to describe. His face was round and plump; his nose small, not flat like the negroes; a very good mouth, thin lips, and his fine teeth well set, and white as ivory.

After he had slumbered, rather than slept, about half an hour, he waked again, and comes out of the cave to me,

for I had been milking my goats, which I had in the enclosure just by. When he espied me, he came running to me,
laying himself down again upon the ground, with all the
possible signs of an humble, thankful disposition, making
a many antic gestures to show it. At last he lays his head
flat upon the ground, close to my foot, and sets my other
foot upon his head, as he had done before, and after this
made all the signs to me of subjection, servitude, and
submission imaginable, to let me know how he would
serve me as long as he lived. I understood him in many
things, and let him know I was very well pleased with
him. In a little time I began to speak to him, and teach
him to speak to me; and, first, I made him know his name
should be Friday, which was the day I saved his life. I
called him so for the memory of the time. I likewise
taught him to say master, and then let him know that was
to be my name. I likewise taught him to say Yes and No,
and to know the meaning of them. I gave him some milk
in an earthen pot, and let him see me drink it before him,
and sop my bread in it; and I gave him a cake of bread to
do the like, which he quickly complied with, and made
signs that it was very good for him.

I kept there with him all that night; but as soon as it
was day, I beckoned to him to come with me, and let him
know I would give him some clothes; at which he seemed
very glad, for he was stark naked. As we went by the place
where he had buried the two men, he pointed exactly to

the place, and showed me the marks that he had made to find them again, making signs to me that we should dig them up again, and eat them. At this I appeared very angry, expressed my abhorrence of it, made as if I would vomit at the thoughts of it, and beckoned with my hand to him to come away; which he did immediately, with great submission. I then led him up to the top of the hill, to see if his enemies were gone; and pulling out my glass, I looked, and saw plainly the place where they had been, but no appearance of them or of their canoes; so that it was plain that they were gone, and had left their two comrades behind them, without any search after them.

But I was not content with this discovery; but having now more courage, and consequently more curiosity, I takes my man Friday with me, giving him the sword in his hand, with the bow and arrows at his back, which I found he could use very dexterously, making him carry one gun for me, and I two for myself, and away we marched to the place where these creatures had been; for I had a mind now to get some fuller intelligence of them. When I came to the place, my very blood ran chill in my veins, and my heart sunk within me, at the horror of the spectacle. Indeed, it was a dreadful sight, at least it was so to me, though Friday made nothing of it. The place was covered with human bones, the ground dyed with their blood, great pieces of flesh left here and there, half-eaten, mangled and scorched; and, in short, all the tokens of the triumphant feast they had been making there, after a victory over their enemies. I saw three skulls, five hands, and the bones of three or four legs and feet, and abundance of other parts of the bodies; and Friday, by his signs, made me understand that they brought over four prisoners to feast upon; that three of them were eaten up, and that he, pointing to himself, was the fourth; that there had been a great battle between them and their next king, whose subjects it seems he had been one of, and that they had taken a great number prisoners; all which were carried to several places by those that had taken them in the fight, in order to feast upon them, as was done here by these wretches upon those they brought hither.

I caused Friday to gather all the skulls, bones, flesh, and whatever remained, and lay them together on a heap, and make a great fire upon it, and burn them all to ashes. I found Friday had still a hankering stomach after some of the flesh, and was still a cannibal in his nature; but I discovered so much abhorrence at the very thoughts of it, and at the least appearance of it, that he durst not discover it; for I had, by some means, let him know that I would kill him if he offered it.

When we had done this we came back to our castle, and there I fell to work for my man Friday; and, first of all, I gave him a pair of linen drawers, which I had out of the poor gunner's chest I mentioned, and which I found in the wreck; and which, with a little alteration, fitted him very well. Then I made him a jerkin of goat's-skin, as well as my skill would allow, and I was now grown a tolerable good tailor; and I gave him a cap, which I had made of hare-skin, very convenient and fashionable enough; and thus he was clothed for the present tolerably well, and was mighty well pleased to see himself almost as well clothed as his master. It is true he went awkwardly in these things at first; wearing the drawers was very awkward to him, and the sleeves of the waistcoat galled his shoulders, and the inside of his arms; but a little easing them where he complained they hurt him, and using himself to them, at length he took to them very well.

The next day after I came home to my hutch with him, I began to consider where I should lodge him. And that I might do well for him, and yet be perfectly easy myself, I made a little tent for him in the vacant place between my two fortifications, in the inside of the last and in the outside of the first; and as there was a door or entrance there into my cave, I made a formal framed door-case, and a door to it of boards, and set it up in the passage, a little within the entrance; and causing the door to open on the inside, I barred it up in the night, taking in my ladders too; so that Friday could no way come at me in the inside of my innermost wall without making so much noise in getting over, that it must needs waken me; for my first wall had now a complete roof over it of long poles, covering all my tent, and leaning up to the side of the hill, which was again laid cross with smaller sticks instead of laths, and then thatched over a great thickness with the rice-straw, which was strong like reeds; and at the hole or place which was left to go in or out by the ladder, I had placed a kind of trap-door, which, if it had been attempted on the outside, would not have opened at all, but would have fallen down, and made a great noise; and as to weapons, I took them all into my side every night.

But I needed none of all this precaution; for never man had a more faithful, loving, sincere servant than Friday was to me; without passions, sullenness, or designs, per-fectly obliged and engaged; his very affections were tied to me, like those of a child to a father; and I dare say he would have sacrificed his life for the saving mine, upon any occasion whatsoever. The many testimonies he gave me of this put it out of doubt, and soon convinced me that I needed to use no precautions as to my safety on his account.

This frequently gave me occasion to observe, and that with wonder, that however it had pleased God, in His providence, and in the government of the works of His hands, to take from so great a part of the world of His creatures the best uses to which their faculties and the powers of their souls are adapted, yet that He has bestowed upon them the same powers, the same reason, the same affections, the same sentiments of kindness and obligation, the same passions and resentments of wrongs, the same sense of gratitude, sincerity, fidelity, and all the capacities of doing good, and receiving good, that He has given to us; and that when He pleases to offer to them occasions of exerting these, they are as ready, nay, more ready, to apply them to the right uses for which they were bestowed than we are.

But to return to my new companion. I was greatly delighted with him, and made it my business to teach him everything that was proper to make him useful, handy, and helpful; but especially to make him speak, and understand me when I spake. And he was the aptest scholar that ever was; and particularly was so merry, so constantly diligent, and so pleased when he could but understand me, or make me understand him, that it was very pleasant to me to talk to him. And now my life began to be so easy, that I began to say to myself, that could I but have been safe from more savages, I cared not if I was never to remove from the place while I lived.

After I had been two or three days returned to my castle, I thought that, in order to bring Friday off from his horrid way of feeding, and from the relish of a cannibal's stomach, I ought to let him taste other flesh; so I took him out with me one morning to the woods. I went, indeed, intending to kill a kid out of my own flock, and bring him home and dress it; but as I was going, I saw a she-goat lying down in the shade, and two young kids sitting by her. I catched hold of Friday. 'Hold,' says I, 'stand still,' and made signs to him not to stir. Immediately I presented my piece, shot and killed one of the kids. The poor creature, who had, at a distance indeed, seen me kill the savage, his enemy, but did not know, or could imagine, how it was done, was sensibly surprised, trembled and shook, and looked so amazed, that I thought he would have sunk down. He did not see the kid I had shot at, or perceive I had killed it, but ripped up his waistcoat to feel if he was not wounded; and, as I found presently, thought I was resolved to kill him; for he came and kneeled down to me, and embracing my knees, said a great many things I did not understand; but I could easily see that the meaning was to pray me not to kill him.

I soon found a way to convince him that I would do him no harm; and taking him up by the hand, laughed at him, and pointing to the kid which I had killed, beckoned to him to run and fetch it, which he did; and while he was wondering, and looking to see how the creature was killed, I loaded my gun again; and by and by I saw a great fowl, like a hawk, sit upon a tree, within shot; so, to let Friday understand a little what I would do, I called him to me again, pointing at the fowl, which was indeed a parrot, though I thought it had been a hawk; I say, pointing to the parrot, and to my gun, and to the ground under the parrot, to let him see I would make it fall, I made him understand that I would shoot and kill that bird. Accordingly I fired, and bade him look, and immediately he saw the parrot fall. He stood like one frighted again, notwithstanding all I had said to him; and I found he was the more amazed, because he did not see me put anything into the gun, but thought that there must be some wonderful fund of death and destruction in that thing, able to kill man, beast, bird, or anything near or far off; and the astonishment this created in him was such as could not wear off for a long time; and I believe, if I would have let him, he would have worshipped me and my gun. As for the gun itself, he would not so much as touch it for several days after; but would speak to it, and talk to it, as if it had answered him, when he was by himself; which, as I afterwards learned of him, was to desire it not to kill him.

Well, after his astonishment was a little over at this, I pointed to him to run and fetch the bird I had shot, which he did, but stayed some time; for the parrot, not being quite dead, was fluttered a good way off from the place where she fell. However, he found her, took her up, and brought her to me; and as I had perceived his ignorance about the gun before, I took this advantage to charge the gun again, and not let him see me do it, that I might be ready for any other mark that might present. But nothing more offered at that time; so I brought home the kid, and the same evening I took the skin off, and cut it out as well

CRUSOE AND FRIDAY OUT SHOOTING

as I could; and having a pot for that purpose, I boiled or stewed some of the flesh, and made some very good broth; and after I had begun to eat some, I gave some to my man, who seemed very glad of it, and liked it very well; but that which was strangest to him, was to see me eat salt with it. He made a sign to me that the salt was not good to eat, and putting a little into his own mouth, he seemed to nauseate it, and would spit and sputter at it, washing his mouth with fresh water after it. On the other hand, I took some meat in my mouth without salt, and I pretended to spit and sputter for want of salt, as fast as he had done at the salt. But it would not do; he would never care for salt with his meat or in his broth; at least, not a great while, and then but a very little.

Having thus fed him with boiled meat and broth, I was resolved to feast him the next day with roasting a piece of the kid. This I did by hanging it before the fire in a string, as I had seen many people do in England, setting two poles up, one on each side of the fire, and one cross on the top, and tying the string to the cross stick, letting the meat turn continually. This Friday admired very much. But when he came to taste the flesh he took so many ways to tell me how well he liked it, that I could not but understand him; and at last he told me he would never eat man's flesh any more, which I was very glad to hear.

The next day I set him to work to beating some corn

out, and sifting it in the manner I used to do, as I observed before; and he soon understood how to do it as well as I, especially after he had seen what the meaning of it was, and that it was to make bread of; for after that I let him see me make my bread, and bake it too; and in a little time Friday was able to do all the work for me, as well as I could do it myself.

I began now to consider that, having two mouths to feed instead of one, I must provide more ground for my harvest, and plant a larger quantity of corn than I used to do; so I marked out a larger piece of land, and began the fence in the same manner as before, in which Friday not only worked very willingly and very hard, but did it very cheerfully; and I told him what it was for; that it was for corn to make more bread, because he was now with me, and that I might have enough for him and myself too. He appeared very sensible of that part, and let me know that he thought I had much more labour upon me on his account, than I had for myself; and that he would work the harder for me, if I would tell him what to do.

This was the pleasantest year of all the life I led in this place. Friday began to talk pretty well, and understand the names of almost everything I had occasion to call for, and of every place I had to send him to, and talk a great deal to me; so that, in short, I began now to have some use for my tongue again, which, indeed, I had very little occasion for before, that is to say, about speech. Besides the pleasure of talking to him, I had a singular satisfaction in the fellow himself. His simple, unfeigned honesty appeared to me more and more every day, and I began really to love the creature; and, on his side, I believe he loved me more than it was possible for him ever to love anything before.

I had a mind once to try if he had any hankering inclination to his own country again; and having learned him English so well that he could answer almost any questions, I asked him whether the nation that he belonged to never conquered in battle? At which he smiled, and said, 'Yes, yes, we always fight the better'; that is, he meant, always get the better in fight; and so we began the following discourse: 'You always fight the better,' said I. 'How came you to be taken prisoner then, Friday?'

Friday. My nation beat much for all that.

Master. How beat? If your nation beat them, how came you to be taken?

Friday. They more many than my nation in the place where me was; they take one, two, three, and me. My nation overbeat them in the yonder place, where me no was; there my nation take one, two, great thousand.

Master. But why did not your side recover you from the hands of your enemies then?

Friday. They run one, two, three, and me, and make go in the canoe; my nation have no canoe that time.

Master. Well, Friday, and what does your nation do with

the men they take? Do they carry them away and eat them, as these did?

Friday. Yes, my nation eat mans too; eat all up.

Master. Where do they carry them?

Friday. Go to other place, where they think.

Master. Do they come hither?

Friday. Yes, yes, they come hither; come other else place.

Master. Have you been here with them?

Friday. Yes, I been here. (*Points to the N.W. side of the island, which, it seems, was their side.*)

By this I understood that my man Friday had formerly been among the savages who used to come on shore on the farther part of the island, on the same man-eating occasions that he was now brought for; and, some time after, when I took the courage to carry him to that side, being the same I formerly mentioned, he presently knew the place, and told me he was there once when they eat up twenty men, two women, and one child. He could not tell twenty in English, but he numbered them by laying so many stones on a row, and pointing to me to tell them over.

I have told this passage, because it introduces what follows; that after I had had this discourse with him, I asked him how far it was from our island to the shore, and whether the canoes were not often lost. He told me there was no danger, no canoes ever lost; but that, after a little way out to the sea, there was a current and a wind, always one way in the morning, the other in the afternoon.

This I understood to be no more than the sets of the tide, as going out or coming in; but I afterwards understood it was occasioned by the great draught and reflux of the mighty river Oroonoko, in the mouth or the gulf of which river, as I found afterwards, our island lay; and this land which I perceived to the W. and N.W. was the great island Trinidad, on the north point of the mouth of the river. I asked Friday a thousand questions about the country, the inhabitants, the sea, the coast, and what nation were near. He told me all he knew, with the greatest openness imaginable. I asked him the names of the several nations of his sort of people, but could get no other name than Caribs; from whence I easily understood that these were the Caribbees, which our maps place on the part of America which reaches from the mouth of the river Oroonoko to Guiana, and onwards to St Martha. He told me that up a great way beyond the moon, that was, beyond the setting of the moon, which must be W. from their country, there dwelt white-bearded men, like me, and pointed to my great whiskers, which I mentioned before; and that they had killed much mans, that was his word; by all which I understood he meant the Spaniards, whose cruelties in America had been spread over the whole countries, and was remembered by all the nations from father to son.

I inquired if he could tell me how I might come from this island and get among those white men. He told me, 'Yes, yes, I might go in two canoe.' I could not understand what he meant, or make him describe to me what he meant by two canoe; till at last, with great difficulty, I found he meant it must be in a large great boat, as big as two canoes.

This part of Friday's discourse began to relish with me very well; and from this time I entertained some hopes that, one time or other, I might find an opportunity to make my escape from this place, and that this poor savage might be a means to help me to do it.

CHAPTER 20

Crusoe instructs Friday in the Christian faith, learning much himself in the process. Three years pass. Friday tells Crusoe about bearded white men living near his people and on a clear day points out the mainland where is his home. Crusoe offers him freedom but Friday declares his absolute devotion. They build a big periagua *in which to visit the white men. Crusoe teaches Friday to navigate.*

DURING THE long time that Friday had now been with me, and that he began to speak to me, and understand me, I was not wanting to lay a foundation of religious knowledge in his mind; particularly I asked him one time, Who made him? The poor creature did not understand me at all, but thought I had asked who was his father. But I took it by another handle, and asked him who made the sea, the ground we walked on, and the hills and woods? He told me it was one old Benamuckee, that lived beyond all. He could describe nothing of this great person, but that he was very old, much older, he said, than the sea or the land, than the moon or the stars. I asked him then, if this old person had made all things, why did not all things worship him? He looked very grave, and with a perfect look of innocence said, 'All things do say O to him.' I asked him if the people who die in his country went away anywhere? He said, 'Yes, they all went to Benamuckee.' Then I asked him whether these they eat up went thither too? He said 'Yes.'

From these things I began to instruct him in the knowledge of the true God. I told him that the great Maker of all things lived up there, pointing up towards heaven; that He governs the world by the same power and providence by which He had made it; that He was omnipotent, could do everything for us, give everything to us, take everything from us; and thus, by degrees, I opened his eyes. He listened with great attention, and received with pleasure the notion of Jesus Christ being sent to redeem us, and of the manner of making our prayers to God, and His being able to hear us, even into heaven. He told me one day that if our God could hear us up beyond the sun, He must needs be a greater God than their Benamuckee, who lived but a little way off, and yet could not hear till they went up to the great mountains where he dwelt to speak to him. I asked him if he ever went thither to speak to him? He said, No; they never went that were young men; none went thither but the old men, whom he called their Oowokakee, that is, as I made him explain it to me, their religious, or clergy; and that they went to say O (so he called saying prayers), and then came back, and told them what Benamuckee said.

I endeavoured to clear up this fraud to my man Friday, and told him that the pretence of their old men going up to the mountains to say O to their god Benamuckee was a cheat, and their bringing word from thence what he said was much more so; that if they met with any answer, or spoke with any one there, it must be with an evil spirit; and then I entered into a long discourse with him about the devil, the original of him, his rebellion against God, his enmity to man, the reason of it, his setting himself up in the dark parts of the world to be worshipped instead of God, and as God, and the many strategems he made use of to delude mankind to their ruin; how he had a secret access to our passions and to our affections, to adapt his snares so to our inclinations, as to cause us even to be our own tempters, and to run upon our destruction by our own choice.

I found it was not so easy to imprint right notions in his mind about the devil, as it was about the being of a God. Nature assisted all my arguments to evidence to him even the necessity of a great First Cause and overruling, governing Power, a secret directing Providence, and of the equity and justice of paying homage to Him that made us, and the like. But there appeared nothing of all this in the notion of an evil spirit; of his original, his being, his nature, and above all, of his inclination to do evil, and to draw us in to do so too; and the poor creature puzzled me once in such a manner by a question merely natural and innocent, that I scarce knew what to say to him.

After this I had been telling him how the devil was

God's enemy in the hearts of men, and used all his malice and skill to defeat the good designs of Providence, and to ruin the kingdom of Christ in the world, and the like. 'Well,' says Friday, 'but you say God is so strong, so great; is He not much strong, much might as the devil?' 'Yes, yes,' says I, 'Friday, God is stronger than the devil; God is above the devil, and therefore we pray to God to tread him down under our feet, and enable us to resist his temptation, and quench his fiery darts.' 'But,' says he again, 'if God much strong, much might as the devil, why God no kill the devil, so make him no more do wicked?'

I was strangely surprised at his question; and after all, though I was now an old man, yet I was but a young doctor, and ill enough qualified for a casuist, or a solver of difficulties; and at first I could not tell what to say; so I pretended not to hear him, and asked him what he said? But he was too earnest for an answer to forget his question, so that he repeated it in the very same broken words as above. By this time I had recovered myself a little, and I said, 'God will at last punish him severely; he is reserved for the judgment, and is to be cast into the bottomless pit, to dwell with everlasting fire.' This did not satisfy Friday; but he returns upon me, repeating my words, 'Reserve at last! me no understand; but why not kill the devil now? not kill great ago?' 'You may as well ask me,' said I, 'why God does not kill you and I, when we do wicked things here that offend Him; we are preserved to repent and be pardoned.' He muses awhile at this. 'Well, well,' says he, mighty affectionately, 'that well; so you, I, devil, all wicked, all preserve, repent, God pardon all.'

Here I was run down again by him to the last degree. I therefore diverted the present discourse between me and my man, rising up hastily, as upon some sudden occasion of going out; then sending him for something a good way off, I seriously prayed to God that He would enable me to instruct savingly this poor savage, assisting, by His Spirit, the heart of the poor ignorant creature to receive the light of the knowledge of God in Christ, reconciling him to Himself, and would guide me to speak so to him from the Word of God as his conscience might be convinced, his eyes opened, and his soul saved. When he came again to me, I entered into a long discourse with him upon the subject of the redemption of man by the Saviour of the world, and of the doctrine of the Gospel preached from heaven, viz., of repentance towards God, and faith in our blessed Lord Jesus. I then explained to him as well as I could why our blessed Redeemer took not on Him the nature of angels, but the seed of Abraham; and how, for that reason, the fallen angels had no share in the redemption; that He came only to the lost sheep of the house of Israel, and the like.

I had, God knows, more sincerity than knowledge in all the methods I took for this poor creature's instruction, and must acknowledge, what I believe all that act upon the same principle will find, that in laying things open to him, I really informed and instructed myself in many things that either I did not know, or had not fully considered before, but which occurred naturally to my mind upon my searching into them for the information of this poor savage. And I had more affection in my inquiry after things upon this occasion than ever I felt before; so that whether this poor wild wretch was the better for me or no, I had great reason to be thankful that ever he came to me. When I reflected upon all these things, a secret joy ran through every part of my soul, and I frequently rejoiced that ever I was brought to this place, which I had so often thought the most dreadful of all afflictions that could possibly have befallen me.

In this thankful frame I continued all the remainder of my time, and the conversation which employed the hours between Friday and I was such, as made the three years which we lived there together perfectly and completely happy, if any such thing as complete happiness can be formed in a sublunary state. The savage was now a good Christian, a much better than I; though I have reason to hope, and bless God for it, that we were equally penitent, and comforted, restored penitents. We had here the Word of God to read, and no farther off from His Spirit to instruct than if we had been in England.

I always applied myself to reading the Scriptures, to let him know, as well as I could, the meaning of what I read;

and he again, by his serious inquiries and questions, made me, as I said before, a much better scholar in the Scripture-knowledge than I should ever have been by my own private mere reading. Another thing I cannot refrain from observing here also, from experience in this retired part of my life, viz., how infinite and inexpressible a blessing it is that the knowledge of God, and of the doctrine of salvation by Christ Jesus, is so plainly laid down in the Word of God, so easy to be received and understood; that as the bare reading the Scripture made me capable of understanding enough of my duty to carry me directly on to the great work of sincere repentance for my sins, and laying hold of a Saviour for life and salvation, to a stated reformation in practice, and obedience to all God's commands, and this without any teacher or instructor (I mean human); so the same plain instruction sufficiently served to the enlightening this savage creature, and bringing him to be such a Christian, as I have known few equal to him in my life.

After Friday and I became more intimately acquainted, and that he could understand almost all I said to him, and speak fluently, though in broken English, to me, I acquainted him with my own story, or at least so much of it as related to my coming into the place; how I had lived there, and how long. I let him into the mystery, for such it was to him, of gunpowder and bullet, and taught him how to shoot; I gave him a knife, which he was wonderfully delighted with, and I made him a belt, with a frog hanging to it, such as in England we wear hangers in; and in the frog, instead of a hanger, I gave him a hatchet, which was not only as good a weapon, in some cases, but much more useful upon other occasions.

I described to him the country of Europe, and particularly England, which I came from; how we lived, how we worshipped God, how we behaved to one another, and how we traded in ships to all parts of the world. I gave him an account of the wreck which I had been on board of, and showed him, as near as I could, the place where she lay; but she was all beaten in pieces before, and gone.

I showed him the ruins of our boat, which we lost when we escaped, and which I could not stir with all my whole strength then, but was now fallen almost all to pieces. Upon seeing this boat, Friday stood musing a great while, and said nothing. I asked him what it was he studied upon. At last says he, 'Me see such boat like come to place at my nation.'

I did not understand him a good while; but at last, when I had examined further into it, I understood by him that a boat such as that had been, came on shore upon the country where he lived; that is, as he explained it, was driven thither by stress of weather. I presently imagined that some European ship must have been cast away upon their coast, and the boat might get loose and drive ashore; but was so dull, that I never once thought of men making

escape from a wreck thither, much less whence they might
come; so I only inquired after a description of the boat.

Friday described the boat to me well enough; but
brought me better to understand him when he added
with some warmth, 'We save the white mans from drown.'
Then I presently asked him if there was any white mans,
as he called them, in the boat. 'Yes,' he said, 'the boat full
of white mans.' I asked him how many. He told upon his
fingers seventeen. I asked him then what became of
them. He told me, 'They live, they dwell at my nation.'

This put new thoughts into my head; for I presently
imagined that these might be the men belonging to the
ship that was cast away in sight of my island, as I now call
it; and who, after the ship was struck on the rock, and
they saw her inevitably lost, had saved themselves in
their boat, and were landed upon that wild shore among
the savages.

Upon this I inquired of him more critically what was
become of them. He assured me they lived still there;
that they had been there about four years; that the savages let him alone, and gave them victuals to live. I asked
him how it came to pass they did not kill them, and eat
them. He said, 'No, they make brother with them'; that
is, as I understood him, a truce; and then he added, 'They
no eat mans but when make the war fight'; that is to say,
they never eat any men but such as come to fight with
them and are taken in battle.

It was after this some considerable time, that being on top of the hill, at the east side of the island (from whence, as I have said, I had in a clear day discovered the main or continent of America), Friday, the weather being very serene, looks very earnestly towards the mainland, and, in a kind of surprise, falls a-jumping and dancing, and calls out to me, for I was at some distance from him. I asked him what was the matter? 'O joy!' says he, 'O glad! there see my country, there my nation!'

I observed an extraordinary sense of pleasure appeared in his face, and his eyes sparkled, and his countenance discovered a strange eagerness, as if he had a mind to be in his own country again; and this observation of mine put a great many thoughts into me, which made me at first not so easy about my new man Friday as I was before; and I made no doubt but that if Friday could get back to his own nation again, he would not only forget all his religion, but all his obligation to me; and would be forward enough to give his countrymen an account of me, and come back perhaps with a hundred or two of them, and make a feast upon me, at which he might be as merry as he used to be with those of his enemies, when they were taken in war.

But I wronged the poor honest creature very much, for which I was very sorry afterwards. However, as my jealousy increased, and held me some weeks, I was a little more circumspect, and not so familiar and kind to him as before; in which I was certainly in the wrong too, the

honest, grateful creature having no thought about it but
what consisted with the best principles, both as a religious Christian and as a grateful friend, as appeared afterwards to my full satisfaction.

While my jealousy of him lasted, you may be sure I was
every day pumping him, to see if he would discover any of
the new thoughts which I suspected were in him; but I
found everything he said was so honest and so innocent,
that I could find nothing to nourish my suspicion; and, in
spite of all my uneasiness, he made me at last entirely his
own again, nor did he in the least perceive that I was
uneasy, and therefore I could not suspect him of deceit.

One day, walking up the same hill, but the weather
being hazy at sea, so that we could not see the continent,
I called to him, and said, 'Friday, do not you wish yourself
in your own country, your own nation?' 'Yes,' he said, 'I be
much O glad to be at my own nation.' 'What would you do
there?' said I. 'Would you turn wild again, eat men's flesh
again, and be a savage as you were before?' He looked full
of concern, and shaking his head said, 'No, no; Friday tell
them to live good; tell them to pray to God; tell them to
eat corn-bread, cattle-flesh, milk, no eat man again.' 'Why
then,' said I to him, 'they will kill you.' He looked grave at
that, and then said, 'No, they no kill me, they willing love
learn.' He meant by this they would be willing to learn.
He added, they learned much of the bearded mans that
come in the boat. Then I asked him if he would go back

to them? He smiled at that, and told me he could not swim so far. I told him I would make a canoe for him. He told me he would go, if I would go with him. 'I go!' says I; 'why, they will eat me if I come there.' 'No, no,' says he, 'me make they no eat you; me make they much love you.' He meant, he would tell them how I had killed his ene-mies, and saved his life, and so he would make them love me. Then he told me, as well as he could, how kind they were to seventeen white men, or bearded men, as he called them, who came on shore there in distress.

From this time I confess I had a mind to venture over, and see if I could possibly join with these bearded men, who, I made no doubt, were Spaniards or Portuguese; not doubting but, if I could, we might find some method to escape from thence, being upon the continent, and a good company together, better than I could from an island forty miles off the shore, and alone, without help. So, after some days, I took Friday to work again, by way of discourse, and told him I would give him a boat to go back to his own nation; and accordingly I carried him to my frigate, which lay on the other side of the island, and hav-ing cleared it of water, for I always kept it sunk in the water, I brought it out, showed it him, and we both went into it.

I found he was a most dexterous fellow at managing it, would make it go almost as swift and fast again as I could. So when he was in I said to him, 'Well now, Friday, shall

we go to your nation?' He looked very dull at my saying
so, which, it seems, was because he thought the boat too
small to go so far. I told him then I had a bigger; so the
next day I went to the place where the first boat lay
which I had made, but which I could not get into the
water. He said that was big enough; but then, as I had
taken no care of it, and it had lain two or three and twenty
years there, the sun had split and dried it, that it was in a
manner rotten. Friday told me such a boat would do very
well, and would carry 'much enough victual, drink,
bread'; that was his way of talking.

Upon the whole, I was by this time so fixed upon my
design of going over with him to the continent, that I told
him we would go and make one as big as that, and he
should go home in it. He answered not one word, but
looked very grave and sad. I asked him what was the matter with him? He asked me again thus, 'Why you angry
mad with Friday? what me done?' I asked him what he
meant. I told him I was not angry with him at all. 'No
angry! no angry!' says he, repeating the words several
times. 'Why send Friday home away to my nation?' 'Why,'
said I, 'Friday, did you not say you wished you were
there?' 'Yes, yes,' says he, 'wish be both there, no wish
Friday there, no master there.' In a word, he would not
think of going there without me. 'I go there, Friday!' says
I; 'what shall I do there?' He turned very quick upon me
at this: 'You do great deal much good,' says he, 'you teach

wild mans to be good, sober, tame mans; you tell them know God, pray God, and live new life.' 'Alas! Friday,' says I, 'thou knowest not what thou sayest. I am but an ignorant man myself.' 'Yes, yes,' says he, 'you teachee me good, you teachee them good.' 'No, no, Friday,' says I, 'you shall go without me; leave me here to live by myself, as I did before.' He looked confused again at that word, and running to one of the hatchets which he used to wear, he takes it up hastily, comes and gives it me. 'What must I do with this?' says I to him. 'You take kill Friday,' says he. 'What must I kill you for?' said I again. He returns very quickly, 'What you send Friday away for? Take kill Friday, no send Friday away.' This he spoke so earnestly, that I saw tears stand in his eyes. In a word, I so plainly discovered the utmost affection in him to me, and a firm resolution in him, that I told him then, and often after, that I would never send him away from me if he was willing to stay with me.

Upon the whole, as I found by all his discourse a settled affection to me, and that nothing should part him from me, so I found all the foundation of his desire to go to his own country was laid in his ardent affection to the people, and his hopes of my doing them good; a thing which, as I had no notion of myself, so I had not the least thought or intention or desire of undertaking it. But still I found a strong inclination to my attempting an escape, as above, founded on the supposition gathered from the discourse, viz., that there were seventeen bearded men there; and, therefore, without any more delay I went to work with Friday to find out a great tree proper to fell, and make a large *periagua*, or canoe, to undertake the voyage. There were trees enough in the island to have built a little fleet, not of *periaguas* and canoes, but even of good large vessels. But the main thing I looked at was, to get one so near the water that we might launch it when it was made, to avoid the mistake I committed at first.

At last Friday pitched upon a tree, for I found he knew much better than I what kind of wood was fittest for it; nor can I tell, to this day, what wood to call the tree we cut down, except that it was very like the tree we call fustic, or between that and the Nicaragua wood, for it was much of the same colour and smell. Friday was for burning the hollow or cavity of this tree out, to make it for a boat, but I showed him how rather to cut it out with tools; which, after I had showed him how to use, he did very handily; and in about a month's hard labour we finished it, and made it very handsome; especially when, with our axes, which I showed him how to handle, we cut and hewed the outside into the true shape of a boat. After this, however, it cost us near a fortnight's time to get her along, as it were inch by inch, upon great rollers into the water; but when she was in, she would have carried twenty men with great ease.

When she was in the water, and though she was so big,

it amazed me to see with what dexterity, and how swift
my man Friday would manage her, turn her, and paddle
her along. So I asked him if he would, and if we might
venture over in her. 'Yes,' he said, 'he venture over in her
very well, though great blow wind.' However, I had a farther design that he knew nothing of, and that was to
make a mast and sail, and to fit her with an anchor and
cable. As to a mast, that was easy enough to get; so I
pitched upon a straight young cedar tree, which I found
near the place, and which there was great plenty of in the
island; and I set Friday to work to cut it down, and gave
him directions how to shape and order it. But as to the
sail, that was my particular care. I knew I had old sails, or
rather pieces of old sails enough; but as I had had them
now twenty-six years by me, and had not been very careful to preserve them, not imagining that I should ever
have this kind of use for them, I did not doubt but they
were all rotten, and, indeed, most of them were so.
However, I found two pieces which appeared pretty good,
and with these I went to work, and with a great deal of
pains, and awkward tedious stitching (you may be sure)
for want of needles, I, at length, made a three-cornered
ugly thing, like what we call in England a shoulder-of-
mutton sail, to go with a boom at bottom, and a little
short-sprit at the top, such as usually our ships' longboats
sail with, and such as I best knew how to manage;
because it was such a one as I had to the boat in which I

CRUSOE AND FRIDAY, FELLING WOOD.

ROBINSON CRUSOE   325

made my escape from Barbary, as related in the first part of my story.

I was near two months performing this last work, viz., rigging and fitting my mast and sails; for I finished them very complete, making a small stay, and a sail, or foresail, to it, to assist, if we should turn to windward; and, which was more than all, I fixed a rudder to the stern of her to steer with; and though I was but a bungling shipwright, yet as I knew the usefulness, and even necessity, of such a thing, I applied myself with so much pains to do it, that at last I brought it to pass; though, considering the many dull contrivances I had for it that failed, I think it cost me almost as much labour as making the boat.

After all this was done too, I had my man Friday to teach as to what belonged to the navigation of my boat; for though he knew very well how to paddle a canoe, he knew nothing what belonged to a sail and a rudder; and was the most amazed when he saw me work the boat to and again in the sea by the rudder, and how the sail jibbed, and filled this way, or that way, as the course we sailed changed; I say, when he saw this, he stood like one astonished and amazed. However, with a little use I made all these things familiar to him, and he became an expert sailor, except that as to the compass I could make him understand very little of that. On the other hand, as there was very little cloudy weather, and seldom or never any fogs in those parts, there was the less occasion for a compass, seeing the stars were always to be seen by night, and the shore by day, except in the rainy seasons, and then nobody cared to stir abroad, either by land or sea.

I was now entered on the seven and twentieth year of my captivity in this place; though the three last years that I had this creature with me ought rather to be left out of the account, my habitation being quite of another kind than in all the rest of the time. I kept the anniversary of my landing here with the same thankfulness to God for His mercies as at first; and if I had such cause of acknowledgment at first, I had much more so now, having such additional testimonies of the care of Providence over me, and the great hopes I had of being effectually and speedily delivered; for I had an invincible impression upon my thoughts that my deliverance was at hand, and that I should not be another year in this place. However, I went on with my husbandry, digging, planting, fencing, as usual. I gathered and cured my grapes, and did every necessary thing as before.

CHAPTER 21

The boat is laid up during rains. Provisions collected and plans made for voyage. Savages in great numbers land on near beach with captives. Crusoe and Friday shoot twenty-one and rescue a white victim and Friday's father.

THE RAINY season was, in the meantime, upon me, when I kept more within doors than at other times; so I had stowed our new vessel as secure as we could, bringing her up into the creek, where, as I said in the beginning, I landed my rafts from the ship; and hauling her up to the shore at high-water mark, I made my man Friday dig a little dock, just big enough to hold her, and just deep enough to give her water enough to float in; and then when the tide was out, we made a strong dam cross the end of it, to keep the water out; and so she lay dry, as to the tide, from the sea; and to keep the rain off, we laid a great many boughs of trees, so thick, that she was as well thatched as a house; and thus we waited for the month of November and December, in which I designed to make my adventure.

When the settled season began to come in, as the thought of my design returned with the fair weather, I was preparing daily for the voyage; and the first thing I did was to lay by a certain quantity of provisions, being the stores for our voyage; and intended, in a week or a fortnight's time, to open the dock, and launch out our boat. I was busy one morning upon something of this kind, when I called to Friday, and bid him go to the sea-shore and see if he could find a turtle, or tortoise, a thing which we generally got once a week, for the sake of the eggs as well as the flesh.

Friday had not been long gone when he came running back, and flew over my outer wall, or fence, like one that felt not the ground, or the steps he set his feet on; and before I had time to speak to him, he cries out to me, 'O master! O master! O sorrow! O bad!' 'What's the matter, Friday?' says I. 'O yonder, there,' says he, 'one, two, three canoe! one, two, three!' By his way of speaking, I concluded there were six; but, on inquiry, I found it was but three. 'Well, Friday,' says I, 'do not be frighted.' So I heartened him up as well as I could. However, I saw the poor fellow was most terribly scared; for nothing ran in his head but that they were come to look for him, and would cut him in pieces, and eat him; and the poor fellow trembled so, that I scarce knew what to do with him. I comforted him as well as I could, and told him I was in as much danger as he, and that they would eat me as well as him. 'But,' says I, 'Friday, we must resolve to fight them. Can you fight, Friday?' 'Me shoot,' says he; 'but there come many great number.' 'No matter for that,' said I again; 'our guns will fright them that we do not kill.' So I asked him whether, if I resolved to defend him, he would defend me, and stand by me, and do just as I bid him. He said, 'Me die when you bid die, master.' So I went and fetched a good dram of rum, and gave him; for I had been so good a husband of my rum, that I had a great deal left. When he had drank it, I made him take the two fowling-pieces, which we always carried, and load them with large swan-shot, as big as small pistol-bullets. Then I took four muskets, and loaded them with two slugs and five small bullets each; and my two pistols I loaded with a brace of bullets each. I hung my great sword, as usual, naked by my side, and gave Friday his hatchet.

When I had thus prepared myself, I took my perspective-glass, and went up to the side of the hill to see what I could discover; and I found quickly, by my glass, that there were one and twenty savages, three prisoners, and three canoes, and that their whole business seemed to be the triumphant banquet upon these three human bodies; a barbarous feast indeed, but nothing more than, as I had observed, was usual with them.

I observed also that they were landed, not where they had done when Friday made his escape, but nearer to my creek, where the shore was low, and where a thick wood came close almost down to the sea. This, with the abhorrence of the inhuman errand these wretches came about, filled me with such indignation, that I came down again to Friday, and told him I was resolved to go down to them, and kill them all, and asked him if he would stand by me. He was now gotten over his fright, and his spirits being a little raised with the dram I had given him, he was very cheerful, and told me, as before, he would die when I bid die.

In this fit of fury, I took first and divided the arms which I had charged, as before, between us. I gave Friday one pistol to stick in his girdle, and three guns upon his shoulder; and I took one pistol, and the other three myself, and in this posture we marched out. I took a small bottle of rum in my pocket, and gave Friday a large bag with more powder and bullet; and as to orders, I charged him to keep close behind me, and not to stir, or shoot, or do anything, till I bid him, and in the meantime not to speak a word. In this posture I fetched a compass to my right hand of near a mile, as well to get over the creek as to get into the wood, so that I might come within shot of them before I should be discovered, which I had seen, by my glass, it was easy to do.

While I was making this march, my former thoughts returning, I began to abate my resolution. I do not mean that I entertained any fear of their number; for as they were naked, unarmed wretches, 'tis certain I was superior to them; nay, though I had been alone. But it occurred to my thoughts what call, what occasion, much less what necessity, I was in to go and dip my hands in blood, to attack people who had neither done or intended me any wrong; who, as to me, were innocent, and whose

barbarous customs were their own disaster; being in them
a token indeed of God's having left them, with the other
nations of that part of the world, to such stupidity, and to
such inhuman courses; but did not call me to take upon
me to be a judge of their actions, much less an executioner of His justice; that whenever He thought fit, He
would take the cause into His own hands, and by national
vengeance, punish them, as a people, for national crimes;
but that, in the meantime, it was none of my business;
that, it was true, Friday might justify it, because he was a
declared enemy, and in a state of war with those very particular people, and it was lawful for him to attack them;
but I could not say the same with respect to me. These
things were so warmly pressed upon my thoughts all the
way as I went, that I resolved I would only go and place
myself near them, that I might observe their barbarous
feast, and that I would act then as God should direct; but
that, unless something offered that was more a call to me
than yet I knew of, I would not meddle with them.

With this resolution I entered the wood, and with all
possible wariness and silence, Friday following close at
my heels, I marched till I came to the skirt of the wood,
on the side which was next to them; only that one corner
of the wood lay between me and them. Here I called
softly to Friday, and showing him a great tree, which was
just at the corner of the wood, I bade him go to the tree
and bring me word if he could see there plainly what they

were doing. He did so, and came immediately back to me, and told me they might be plainly viewed there; that they were all about their fire, eating the flesh of one of their prisoners, and that another lay bound upon the sand, a little from them, which, he said, they would kill next; and, which fired all the very soul within me, he told me it was not one of their nation, but one of the bearded men, whom he had told me of, that came to their country in the boat. I was filled with horror at the very naming the white, bearded man; and going to the tree, I saw plainly, by my glass, a white man, who lay upon the beach of the sea, with his hands and his feet tied with flags, or things like rushes, and that he was an European, and had clothes on.

There was another tree, and a little thicket beyond it, about fifty yards nearer to them than the place where I was, which by going a little way about, I saw I might come at undiscovered, and that then I should be within half shot of them; so I withheld my passion, though I was indeed enraged to the highest degree; and going back about twenty paces, I got behind some bushes, which held all the way till I came to the other tree; and then I came to a little rising ground, which gave me a full view of them, at the distance of about eighty yards.

I had now not a moment to lose, for nineteen of the dreadful wretches sat upon the ground, all close huddled together, and had just sent the other two to butcher the poor Christian, and bring him, perhaps limb by limb, to their fire; and they were stooped down to untie the bands at his feet. I turned to Friday: 'Now, Friday,' said I, 'do as I bid thee.' Friday said he would. 'Then, Friday,' says I, 'do exactly as you see me do; fail in nothing.' So I set down one of the muskets and the fowling-piece upon the ground, and Friday did the like by his; and with the other musket I took my aim at the savages, bidding him do the like. Then asking him if he was ready, he said, 'Yes.' 'Then fire at them,' said I; and the same moment I fired also.

Friday took his aim so much better than I, that on the side that he shot he killed two of them, and wounded three more; and on my side I killed one, and wounded two. They were, you may be sure, in a dreadful consternation; and all of them who were not hurt jumped up upon their feet, but did not immediately know which way to run, or which way to look, for they knew not from whence their destruction came. Friday kept his eyes close upon me, that, as I had bid him, he might observe what I did; so as soon as the first shot was made I threw down the piece, and took up the fowling-piece, and Friday did the like. He sees me cock and present; he did the same again. 'Are you ready, Friday?' said I. 'Yes,' says he. 'Let fly, then,' says I, 'in the name of God!' and with that I fired again among the amazed wretches, and so did Friday; and as our pieces were now loaded with what I called swan-shot, or small pistol-bullets, we found only two drop, but so many were wounded, that they ran about yelling and screaming like mad creatures, all bloody, and miserably wounded most of them; whereof three more fell quickly after, though not quite dead.

'Now, Friday,' says I, laying down the discharged pieces, and taking up the musket which was yet loaded, 'follow me,' says I, which he did with a great deal of courage; upon which I rushed out of the wood, and showed myself, and Friday close at my foot. As soon as I perceived they saw me, I shouted as loud as I could, and bade Friday do so too; and running as fast as I could, which, by the way, was not very fast, being loaden with arms as I was, I made directly towards the poor victim, who was, as I said, lying upon the beach, or shore, between the place where they sat and the sea. The two butchers, who were just going to work with him, had left him at the surprise of our first fire, and fled in a terrible fright to the seaside, and had jumped into a canoe, and three more of the rest made the same way. I turned to Friday, and bid him step forwards and fire at them. He understood me immediately, and running about forty yards, to be near them, he shot at them, and I thought he had killed them all, for I saw them all fall of a heap into the boat; though I saw two of them up again quickly. However, he killed two of them, and wounded the third, so that he lay down in the bottom of the boat as if he had been dead.

While my man Friday fired at them, I pulled out my knife and cut the flags that bound the poor victim; and loosing his hands and feet, I lifted him up, and asked him in the Portuguese tongue what he was. He answered in Latin, Christianus; but was so weak and faint, that he could scarce stand or speak. I took my bottle out of my pocket and gave it him, making signs that he should drink, which he did; and I gave him a piece of bread, which he eat. Then I asked him what countryman he was; and he said, Espagniole; and being a little recovered, let me know, by all the signs he could possibly make, how much he was in my debt for his deliverance. 'Seignior,' said I, with as much Spanish as I could make up, 'we will talk afterwards, but we must fight now. If you have any strength left, take this pistol and sword, and lay about you.' He took them very thankfully, and no sooner had he the arms in his hands but, as if they had put new vigour into him, he flew upon his murderers like a fury, and had cut two of them in pieces in an instant; for the truth is, as the whole was a surprise to them, so the poor creatures were so much frighted with the noise of our pieces, that they fell down for mere amazement and fear, and had no more power to attempt their own escape, than their flesh had to resist our shot; and that was the case of those five that Friday shot at in the boat; for as three of them fell with the hurt they received, so the other two fell with the fright.

I kept my piece in my hand still without firing, being willing to kept my charge ready, because I had given the Spaniard my pistol and sword. So I called to Friday, and bade him run up to the tree from whence we first fired, and fetch the arms which lay there that had been discharged, which he did with great swiftness; and then giving him my musket, I sat down myself to load all the rest again, and bade them come to me when they wanted. While I was loading these pieces, there happened a fierce engagement between the Spaniard and one of the savages, who made at him with one of their great wooden swords, the same weapon that was to have killed him before if I had not prevented it. The Spaniard, who was as bold and as brave as could be imagined, though weak, had fought this Indian a good while, and had cut him two great wounds on his head; but the savage being a stout, lusty fellow, closing in with him, had thrown him down, being faint, and was wringing my sword out of his hand, when the Spaniard, though undermost, wisely quitting the sword, drew the pistol from his girdle, shot the savage through the body, and killed him upon the spot, before I, who was running to help him, could come near him.

Friday being now left to his liberty, pursued the flying wretches with no weapon in his hand but his hatchet; and with that he despatched those three who, as I said before, were wounded at first, and fallen, and all the rest he could come up with; and the Spaniard coming to me for a

CRUSOE RESCUES THE SPANIARD

gun, I gave him one of the fowling-pieces, with which he pursued two of the savages, and wounded them both; but as he was not able to run, they both got from him into the wood, where Friday pursued them, and killed one of them; but the other was too nimble for him, and though he was wounded, yet had plunged himself into the sea, and swam with all his might off to those two who were left in the canoe; which three in the canoe, with one wounded, who we know not whether he died or no, were all that escaped our hands of one and twenty. The account of the rest is as follows:—

3 killed at our first shot from the tree.

2 killed at the next shot.

2 killed by Friday in the boat.

2 killed by ditto, of those at first wounded.

1 killed by ditto in the wood.

3 killed by the Spaniard.

4 killed, being found dropped here and there of their wounds, or killed by Friday in his chase of them.

4 escaped in the boat, whereof one wounded, if not dead.

—

21 in all.

Those that were in the canoe worked hard to get out of gun-shot; and though Friday made two or three shots at them, I did not find that he hit any of them. Friday would fain have had me take one of their canoes, and pursue them; and, indeed, I was very anxious about their escape, lest carrying the news home to their people they should come back perhaps with two or three hundred of their canoes, and devour us by mere multitude. So I consented to pursue them by sea, and running to one of their canoes I jumped in, and bade Friday follow me. But when I was in the canoe, I was surprised to find another poor creature lie there alive, bound hand and foot, as the Spaniard was, for the slaughter, and almost dead with fear, not knowing what the matter was; for he had not been able to look up over the side of the boat, he was tied so hard, neck and heels, and had been tied so long, that he had really but little life in him.

I immediately cut the twisted flags or rushes, which they had bound him with, and would have helped him up; but he could not stand or speak, but groaned most piteously, believing, it seems, still that he was only unbound in order to be killed.

When Friday came to him, I bade him speak to him, and tell him of his deliverance; and pulling out my bottle, made him give the poor wretch a dram; which, with the news of his being delivered, revived him, and he sat up in the boat. But when Friday came to hear him speak, and look in his face, it would have moved any one to tears to have seen how Friday kissed him, embraced him, hugged him, cried, laughed, halloed, jumped about, danced,

sung; then cried again, wrung his hands, beat his own face
and head, and then sung and jumped about again, like a
distracted creature. It was a good while before I could
make him speak to me, or tell me what was the matter;
but when he came a little to himself, he told me that it
was his father.

It is not easy for me to express how it moved me to see
what ecstasy and filial affection had worked in this poor
savage at the sight of his father, and of his being delivered
from death; nor, indeed, can I describe half the extravagances of his affection after this; for he went into the boat,
and out of the boat, a great many times. When he went in
to him, he would sit down by him, open his breast, and
hold his father's head close to his bosom, half an hour
together, to nourish it; then he took his arms and ankles,
which were numbed and stiff with the binding, and
chafed and rubbed them with his hands; and I, perceiving
what the case was, gave him some rum out of my bottle to
rub them with, which did them a great deal of good.

This action put an end to our pursuit of the canoe with
the other savages, who were now gotten almost out of
sight; and it was happy for us that we did not, for it blew
so hard within two hours after, and before they could have
gotten a quarter of their way, and continued blowing so
hard all night, and that from the north-west, which was
against them, that I could not suppose their boat could
live, or that they ever reached to their own coast.

But to return to Friday. He was so busy about his father, that I could not find in my heart to take him off for some time; but after I thought he could leave him a little, I called him to me, and he came jumping and laughing, and pleased to the highest extreme. Then I asked him if he had given his father any bread. He shook his head, and said, 'None; ugly dog eat all up self.' So I gave him a cake of bread out of the little pouch I carried on purpose. I also gave him a dram for himself, but he would not taste it, but carried it to his father. I had in my pocket also two or three bunches of my raisins, so I gave him a handful of them for his father. He had no sooner given his father these raisins, but I saw him come out of the boat and run away, as if he had been bewitched, he ran at such a rate; for he was the swiftest fellow of his foot that ever I saw. I say, he run at such a rate, that he was out of sight, as it were, in an instant; and though I called, and hallooed too, after him, it was all one, away he went; and in a quarter of an hour I saw him come back again, though not so fast as he went; and as he came nearer I found his pace was slacker, because he had something in his hand.

When he came up to me, I found he had been quite home for an earthen jug, or pot, to bring his father some fresh water, and that he had got two more cakes or loaves of bread. The bread he gave me, but the water he carried to his father. However, as I was very thirsty too, I took a little sup of it. This water revived his father more than all the rum or spirits I had given him, for he was just fainting with thirst.

When his father had drank, I called to him to know if there was any water left. He said 'Yes'; and I bade him give it to the poor Spaniard, who was in as much want of it as his father; and I sent one of the cakes, that Friday brought, to the Spaniard too, who was indeed very weak, and was reposing himself upon a green place under the shade of a tree; and whose limbs were also very stiff, and very much swelled with the rude bandage he had been tied with. When I saw that upon Friday's coming to him with the water he sat up and drank, and took the bread, and began to eat, I went to him, and gave him a handful of raisins. He looked up in my face with all the tokens of gratitude and thankfulness that could appear in any countenance; but was so weak, notwithstanding he had so exerted himself in the fight, that he could not stand up upon his feet. He tried to do it two or three times, but was really not able, his ankles were so swelled and so painful to him; so I bade him sit still, and caused Friday to rub his ankles, and bathe them with rum, as he had done his father's.

I observed the poor affectionate creature, every two minutes, or perhaps less, all the while he was here, turned his head about to see if his father was in the same place, and posture as he left him sitting; and at last he found he was not to be seen; at which he started up, and without speaking a word, flew with that swiftness to him, that one could scarce perceive his feet to touch the ground as he went. But when he came, he only found he had laid himself down to ease his limbs; so Friday came back to me presently, and I then spoke to the Spaniard to let Friday help him up, if he could, and lead him to the boat, and then he should carry him to our dwelling, where I would take care of him. But Friday, a lusty, strong fellow, took the Spaniard quite up upon his back, and carried him away to the boat, and set him down softly upon the side or gunnel of the canoe, with his feet in the inside of it, and then lifted him quite in, and set him close to his father; and presently stepping out again, launched the boat off, and paddled it along the shore faster than I could walk, though the wind blew pretty hard too. So he brought them both safe into our creek, and leaving them in the boat, runs away to fetch the other canoe. As he passed me, I spoke to him, and asked him whither he went. He told me, 'Go fetch more boat.' So away he went like the wind, for sure never man or horse ran like him; and he had the other canoe in the creek almost as soon as I got to it by land; so he wafted me over, and then went to help our new guests out of the boat, which he did; but they were neither of them able to walk, so that poor Friday knew not what to do.

To remedy this I went to work in my thought, and calling to Friday to bid them sit down on the bank while he came to me, I soon made a kind of hand-barrow to lay them on, and Friday and I carried them up both together upon it between us. But when we got them to the outside of our wall, or fortification, we were at a worse loss than before, for it was impossible to get them over, and I was resolved not to break it down. So I set to work again; and Friday and I, in about two hours' time, made a very handsome tent, covered with old sails, and above that with boughs of trees, being in the space without our outward fence, and between that and the grove of young wood which I had planted; and here we made them two beds of such things as I had, viz., of good rice-straw, with blankets laid upon it to lie on, and another to cover them, on each bed.

CHAPTER 22

Crusoe hears the Spaniard's story and plans to rescue his sixteen companions, survivors of shipwreck, when there is sufficient food. Great activity produces splendid harvest. Spaniard and Friday's father set out to fetch the sailors. After eight days Friday awakens Crusoe: 'Master, Master, they are come!' But English sailors land in a boat from a ship anchored out at sea. Crusoe apprehensive seeing three men are prisoners. Friday assumes he is to witness white cannibal feast.

MY ISLAND was now peopled, and I thought myself very rich in subjects; and it was a merry reflection, which I frequently made, how like a king I looked. First of all, the whole country was my own mere property, so that I had undoubted right of dominion. Secondly, my people were perfectly subjected. I was absolute lord and lawgiver; they all owed their lives to me, and were ready to lay down their lives, if there had been occasion of it, for me. It was remarkable too, we had but three subjects, and they were of three different religions. My man Friday was a Protestant, his father was a Pagan and a cannibal, and the Spaniard was a Papist. However, I allowed liberty of conscience throughout my dominions. But this is by the way.

As soon as I had secured my two weak rescued prisoners, and given them shelter, and a place to rest them upon, I began to think of making some provision for them; and the first thing I did, I ordered Friday to take a yearling goat, betwixt a kid and a goat, out of my particular flock, to be killed; when I cut off the hinder-quarter, and chopping it into small pieces, I set Friday to work to boiling and stewing, and made them a very good dish, I assure you, of flesh and broth, having put some barley and rice also into the broth; and as I cooked it without doors, for I made no fire within my inner wall, so I carried it all into the new tent, and having set a table there for them, I sat down and ate my own dinner also with them, and as well as I could cheered them, and encouraged them; Friday being my interpreter, especially to his father, and, indeed, to the Spaniard too; for the Spaniard spoke the language of the savages pretty well.

After we had dined, or rather supped, I ordered Friday to take one of the canoes and go and fetch our muskets and other firearms, which, for want of time, we had left upon the place of battle; and the next day I ordered him to go and bury the dead bodies of the savages, which lay open to the sun, and would presently be offensive; and I also ordered him to bury the horrid remains of their barbarous feast, which I knew were pretty much, and which I could not think of doing myself; nay, I could not bear to see them, if I went that way. All of which he punctually performed, and defaced the very appearance of the savages being there; so that when I went again I could scarce know where it was, otherwise than by the corner of the wood pointing to the place.

I then began to enter into a little conversation with my two new subjects; and first, I set Friday to inquire of his father what he thought of the escape of the savages in that canoe, and whether we might expect a return of them, with a power too great for us to resist. His first opinion was, that the savages in the boat never could live out the storm which blew that night they went off, but must, of necessity, be drowned, or drive south to those other shores, where they were as sure to be devoured as they were to be drowned if they were cast away. But as to what they would do if they came safe on shore, he said he knew not; but it was his opinion that they were so dreadfully frighted with the manner of their being attacked, the noise, and the fire, that he believed they would tell their people they were all killed by thunder and lightning, not by the hand of man; and that the two which appeared, viz., Friday and me, were two heavenly spirits, or furies, come down to destroy them, and not men with weapons. This, he said, he knew, because he heard them all cry out so in their language to one another; for it was impossible to them to conceive that a man could dart fire, and speak thunder, and kill at a distance without lifting up the hand, as was done now. And this old savage was in the right; for, as I understood since by other hands, the savages never attempted to go over to the island afterwards. They were so terrified with the accounts given by those four men (for, it seems, they did escape the sea), that they believed whoever went to that enchanted island would be destroyed with fire from the gods.

This, however, I knew not, and therefore was under continual apprehensions for a good while, and kept always upon my guard, me and all my army; for as we were now four of us, I would have ventured upon a hundred of them, fairly in the open field, at any time.

In a little time, however, no more canoes appearing, the fear of their coming wore off, and I began to take my former thoughts of a voyage to the main into consideration; being likewise assured, by Friday's father, that I might depend upon good usage from their nation, on his account, if I would go.

But my thoughts were a little suspended when I had a serious discourse with the Spaniard, and when I understood that there were sixteen more of his countrymen and Portuguese, who, having been cast away, and made their escape to that side, lived there at peace, indeed, with the savages, but were very sore put to it for necessaries, and indeed for life. I asked him all the particulars of their voyage, and found they were a Spanish ship bound from the Rio de la Plata to the Havana, being directed to leave their loading there, which was chiefly hides and silver, and to bring back what European goods they could meet with there; that they had five Portuguese seamen on board, whom they took out of another wreck; that five of their own men were drowned when the first ship was lost, and that these escaped, through infinite dangers and hazards, and arrived, almost starved, on the cannibal coast, where they expected to have been devoured every moment.

He told me they had some arms with them, but they were perfectly useless, for that they had neither powder or ball, the washing of the sea having spoiled all their powder but a little, which they used, at their first landing, to provide themselves some food.

I asked him what he thought would become of them there, and if they had formed no design of making any escape? He said they had many consultations about it; but that having neither vessel, or tools to build one, or provisions of any kind, their councils always ended in tears and despair.

I asked him how he thought they would receive a proposal from me, which might tend towards an escape; and whether, if they were all here, it might not be done? I told him with freedom, I feared mostly their treachery and ill usage of me if I put my life in their hands; for that gratitude was no inherent virtue in the nature of man, nor did men always square their dealings by the obligations they had received, so much as they did by the advantages they expected. I told him it would be very hard that I should be the instrument of their deliverance, and that they should afterwards make me their prisoner in New Spain, where an Englishman was certain to be made a sacrifice, what necessity or what accident soever brought him thither; and that I had rather be delivered up to the savages, and be devoured alive, than fall into the merciless claws of the priests, and be carried into the Inquisition. I added, that otherwise I was persuaded, if they were all here, we might, with so many hands, build a bark large enough to carry us all away, either to the Brazils, southward, or to the islands, or Spanish coast, northward; but that if, in requital, they should, when I had put weapons into their hands, carry me by force among their own people, I might be ill used for my kindness to them, and make my case worse than it was before.

He answered, with a great deal of candour and ingenuity, that their condition was so miserable, and they were so sensible of it, that he believed they would abhor the thought of using any man unkindly that should contribute to their deliverance; and that, if I pleased, he would go to them with the old man, and discourse with them about it, and return again, and bring me their answer; that he would make conditions with them upon their solemn oath that they should be absolutely under my leading, as their commander and captain; and that they should swear upon the holy sacraments and the gospel to be true to me, and to go to such Christian country as that I should agree to, and no other, and to be directed wholly and absolutely by my orders till they were landed safely in such country as I intended; and that he should bring a contract from them, under their hands, for that purpose.

Then he told me he would first swear to me himself, that he would never stir from me as long as he lived till I gave him orders; and that he would take my side to the last drop of his blood, if there should happen the least breach of faith among his countrymen.

He told me they were all of them very civil, honest men, and they were under the greatest distress imaginable, having neither weapons or clothes, or any food, but at the mercy and discretion of the savages; out of all hopes of ever returning to their own country; and that he was sure, if I would undertake their relief, they would live and die by me.

Upon these assurances, I resolved to venture to relieve them, if possible, and to send the old savage and this Spaniard over to them to treat. But when we had gotten all things in a readiness to go, the Spaniard himself started an objection, which had so much prudence in it on one hand, and so much sincerity on the other hand, that I could not but be very well satisfied in it, and by his advice put off the deliverance of his comrades for at least half a year. The case was thus.

He had been with us now about a month, during which time I had let him see in what manner I had provided, with the assistance of Providence, for my support; and he saw evidently what stock of corn and rice I had laid up;

which, as it was more than sufficient for myself, so it was not sufficient, at least without good husbandry, for my family, now it was increased to number four; but much less would it be sufficient if his countrymen, who were, as he said, fourteen, still alive, should come over; and least of all would it be sufficient to victual our vessel, if we should build one, for a voyage to any of the Christian colonies of America. So he told me he thought it would be more advisable to let him and the two others dig and cultivate some more land, as much as I could spare seed to sow; and that we should wait another harvest, that we might have a supply of corn for his countrymen when they should come; for want might be a temptation to them to disagree, or not to think themselves delivered, otherwise than out of one difficulty into another. 'You know,' says he, 'the children of Israel, though they rejoiced at first for their being delivered out of Egypt, yet rebelled even against God Himself, that delivered them, when they came to want bread in the wilderness.'

His caution was so seasonable, and his advice so good, that I could not but be very well pleased with his proposal, as well as I was satisfied with his fidelity. So we fell to digging all four of us, as well as the wooden tools we were furnished with permitted; and in about a month's time, by the end of which it was seed-time, we had gotten as much land cured and trimmed up as we sowed twenty-two bushels of barley on, and sixteen jars of rice;

which was, in short, all the seed we had to spare; nor, indeed, did we leave ourselves barley sufficient for our own food for the six months that we had to expect our crop; that is to say, reckoning from the time we set our seed aside for sowing; for it is not to be supposed it is six months in the ground in that country.

Having now society enough, and our number being sufficient to put us out of fear of the savages, if they had come, unless their number had been very great, we went freely all over the island, wherever we found occasion; and as here we had our escape or deliverance upon our thoughts, it was impossible, at least for me, to have the means of it out of mine. To this purpose I marked out several trees which I thought fit for our work, and I set Friday and his father to cutting them down; and then I caused the Spaniard, to whom I imparted my thought on that affair, to oversee and direct their work. I showed them with what indefatigable pains I had hewed a large tree into single planks, and I caused them to do the like, till they had made about a dozen large planks of good oak, near two feet broad, thirty-five feet long, and from two inches to four inches thick. What prodigious labour it took up, any one may imagine.

At the same time, I contrived to increase my little flock of tame goats as much as I could; and to this purpose I made Friday and the Spaniard go out one day, and myself with Friday the next day, for we took our turns, and by this means we got above twenty young kids to breed up with the rest; for whenever we shot the dam, we saved the kids, and added them to our flock. But above all, the season for curing the grapes coming on, I caused such a prodigious quantity to be hung up in the sun, that I believe, had we been at Alicant, where the raisins of the sun are cured, we could have filled sixty or eighty barrels; and these, with our bread, was a great part of our food, and very good living too, I assure you; for it is an exceeding nourishing food.

It was now harvest, and our crop in good order. It was not the most plentiful increase I had seen in the island, but, however, it was enough to answer our end; for from our twenty-two bushels of barley we brought in and thrashed out above two hundred and twenty bushels, and the like in proportion of the rice; which was store enough for our food to the next harvest, though all the sixteen Spaniards had been on shore with me; or if we had been ready for a voyage, it would very plentifully have victualled our ship to have carried us to any part of the world, that is to say, of America.

When we had thus housed and secured our magazine of corn, we fell to work to make more wicker-work, viz., great baskets, in which we kept it; and the Spaniard was very handy and dexterous at this part, and often blamed me that I did not make some things for the defence of this kind of work; but I saw no need of it.

And now having a full supply of food for all the guests I expected, I gave the Spaniard leave to go over to the main, to see what he could do with those he had left behind him there. I gave him strict charge in writing not to bring any man with him who would not first swear, in the presence of himself and of the old savage, that he would in no way injure, fight with, or attack the person he should find in the island, who was so kind to send for them in order to their deliverance; but that they would stand by and defend him against all such attempts, and wherever they went would be entirely under and subjected to his commands; and that this should be put in writing, and signed with their hands. How we were to have this done, when I knew they had neither pen or ink, that indeed was a question which we never asked.

Under these instructions, the Spaniard with the old savage, the father of Friday, went away in one of the canoes which they might be said to come in, or rather were brought in, when they came as prisoners to be devoured by the savages.

I gave each of them a musket, with a firelock on it, and about eight charges of powder and ball, charging them to be very good husbands of both, and not to use either of them but upon urgent occasion.

This was a cheerful work, being the first measures used by me, in view of my deliverance, for now twenty-seven years and some days. I gave them provisions of

CRUSOE · SEES · AN · ENGLISH · SHIP.

bread and of dried grapes sufficient for themselves for many days, and sufficient for all their countrymen for about eight days' time; and wishing them a good voyage, I see them go, agreeing with them about a signal they should hang out at their return, by which I should know them again, when they came back, at a distance, before they came on shore.

They went away with a fair gale on the day that the moon was at full, by my account in the month of October; but as for an exact reckoning of days, after I had once lost it, I could never recover it again; nor had I kept even the number of years so punctually as to be sure that I was right, though as it proved, when I afterwards examined my account, I found I had kept a true reckoning of years.

It was no less than eight days I had waited for them, when a strange and unforeseen accident intervened, of which the like has not perhaps been heard of in history. I was fast asleep in my hutch one morning, when my man Friday came running in to me, and called aloud, 'Master, master, they are come, they are come!'

I jumped up, and, regardless of danger, I went out as soon as I could get my clothes on, through my little grove, which, by the way, was by this time grown to be a very thick wood; I say, regardless of danger, I went without my arms, which was not my custom to do; but I was surprised when, turning my eyes to the sea, I presently saw a boat at about a league and a half's distance standing in for the shore, with a shoulder-of-mutton sail, as they call it, and the wind blowing pretty fair to bring them in; also I observed presently that they did not come from that side which the shore lay on, but from the southernmost end of the island. Upon this I called Friday in, and bid him lie close, for these were not the people we looked for, and that we might not know yet whether they were friends or enemies.

In the next place, I went in to fetch my perspective-glass, to see what I could make of them; and having taken the ladder out, I climbed up to the top of the hill, as I used to do when I was apprehensive of anything, and to take my view the plainer, without being discovered.

I had scarce set my foot on the hill, when my eye plainly discovered a ship lying at an anchor at about two leagues and a half's distance from me, south-south-east, but not above a league and a half from the shore. By my observation, it appeared plainly to be an English ship, and the boat appeared to be an English longboat.

I cannot express the confusion I was in; though the joy of seeing a ship, and one who I had reason to believe was manned by my own countrymen, and consequently friends, was such as I cannot describe. But yet I had some secret doubts hung about me, I cannot tell from whence they came, bidding me keep upon my guard. In the first place, it occurred to me to consider what business an English ship could have in that part of the world, since it was not the way to or from any part of the world where the English had any traffic; and I knew there had been no storms to drive them in there as in distress; and that if they were English really, it was most probable that they were here upon no good design; and that I had better continue as I was, than fall into the hands of thieves and murderers.

Let no man despise the secret hints and notices of danger which sometimes are given him when he may think there is no possibility of its being real. That such hints and notices are given us, I believe few that have made observations of things can deny; that they are certain discoveries of an invisible world, and a converse of spirits, we cannot doubt; and if the tendency of them seems to be to warn us of danger, why should we not suppose they are from some friendly agent, whether supreme, or inferior and subordinate, is not the question, and that they are given for our good?

The present question abundantly confirms me in the justice of this reasoning; for had I not been made cautious by this secret admonition, come it from whence it will, I had been undone inevitably, and in a far worse condition than before, as you will see presently.

I had not kept myself long in this posture, but I saw the boat draw near the shore, as if they looked for a creek to thrust in at, for the convenience of landing. However, as they did not come quite far enough, they did not see the little inlet where I formerly landed my rafts; but run their boat on shore upon the beach, at about half a mile from me, which was very happy for me; for otherwise they would have landed just, as I may say, at my door, and would soon have beaten me out of my castle, and perhaps have plundered me of all I had.

When they were on shore, I was fully satisfied that they were Englishmen, at least most of them; one or two I thought were Dutch, but it did not prove so. There were in all eleven men, whereof three of them I found were unarmed, and, as I thought, bound; and when the first four or five of them were jumped on shore, they took those three out of the boat, as prisoners. One of the three I could perceive using the most passionate gestures of entreaty, affliction, and despair, even to a kind of extravagance; the other two, I could perceive, lifted up their hands sometimes, and appeared concerned indeed, but not to such a degree as the first.

I was perfectly confounded at the sight, and knew not what the meaning of it should be. Friday called out to me in English as well as he could, 'O master! you see English mans eat prisoner as well as savage mans.' 'Why,' says I, 'Friday, do you think they are agoing to eat them then?' 'Yes,' says Friday, 'they will eat them.' 'No, no,' says I, 'Friday, I am afraid they will murder them indeed, but you may be sure they will not eat them.'

All this while I had no thought of what the matter

really was, but stood trembling with the horror of the sight, expecting every moment when the three prisoners should be killed; nay, once I saw one of the villains lift up his arm with a great cutlass, as the seamen call it, or sword, to strike one of the poor men; and I expected to see him fall every moment, at which all the blood in my body seemed to run chill in my veins.

CHAPTER 23

Crusoe notices the ship's boat hard aground after fall of tide and sailors dispersed. Cautiously investigates with Friday and discovers Captain and Mate with a passenger are to be abandoned by mutineers. Crusoe plans action. Shoots ringleaders and so compels the rest to submit. Sailors from the ship come to seek their companions. Crusoe watches their mystification.

I WISHED heartily now for my Spaniard, and the savage that was gone with him; or that I had any way to have come undiscovered within shot of them, that I might have rescued the three men, for I saw no firearms they had among them; but it fell out to my mind another way.

After I had observed the outrageous usage of the three men by the insolent seamen, I observed the fellows run scattering about the land, as if they wanted to see the country. I observed that the three other men had liberty to go also where they pleased; but they sat down all three upon the ground, very pensive, and looked like men in despair.

This put me in mind of the first time when I came on shore, and began to look about me; how I gave myself over for lost; how wildly I looked around me; what dreadful apprehensions I had; and how I lodged in the tree all night, for fear of being devoured by wild beasts.

As I knew nothing that night of the supply I was to

receive by the providential driving of the ship nearer the land by the storms and tide, by which I have since been so long nourished and supported; so these three poor desolate men knew nothing how certain of deliverance and supply they were, how near it was to them, and how effectually and really they were in a condition of safety, at the same time that they thought themselves lost, and their case desperate.

It was just at the top of high-water when these people came on shore; and while partly they stood parleying with the prisoners they brought, and partly while they rambled about to see what kind of a place they were in, they had carelessly stayed till the tide was spent, and the water ebbed considerably away, leaving their boat aground.

They had left two men in the boat, who, as I found afterwards, having drank a little too much brandy, fell asleep. However, one of them waking sooner than the other, and finding the boat too fast aground for him to stir it, hallooed for the rest, who were straggling about, upon which they all soon came to the boat; but it was past all their strength to launch her, the boat being very heavy, and the shore on that side being a soft oozy sand, almost like a quicksand.

In this condition, like true seamen, who are perhaps the least of all mankind given to forethought, they gave it over, and away they strolled about the country again; and I heard one of them say aloud to another, calling them off from the boat, 'Why, let her alone, Jack, can't ye? she will float next tide'; by which I was fully confirmed in the main inquiry of what countrymen they were.

All this while I kept myself very close, not once daring to stir out of my castle, any farther than to my place of observation near the top of the hill; and very glad I was to think how well it was fortified. I knew it was no less than ten hours before the boat could be on float again, and by that time it would be dark, and I might be at more liberty to see their motions, and to hear their discourse, if they had any.

In the meantime, I fitted myself up for a battle, as before, though with more caution, knowing I had to do with another kind of enemy than I had at first. I ordered Friday also, whom I had made an excellent marksman with his gun, to load himself with arms. I took myself two fowling-pieces, and I gave him three muskets. My figure, indeed, was very fierce. I had my formidable goat-skin coat on, with the great cap I have mentioned, a naked sword by my side, two pistols in my belt, and a gun upon each shoulder.

It was my design, as I said above, not to have made any attempt till it was dark; but about two o'clock, being the heat of the day, I found that, in short, they were all gone straggling into the woods, and, as I thought, were laid down to sleep. The three poor distressed men, too anxious for their condition to get any sleep, were, however, set down under the shelter of a great tree, at about a quarter of a mile from me, and, as I thought, out of sight of any of the rest.

Upon this I resolved to discover myself to them, and learn something of their condition. Immediately I marched in the figure as above, my man Friday at a good distance behind me, as formidable for his arms as I, but not making quite so staring a spectre-like figure as I did.

I came as near them undiscovered as I could, and then, before any of them saw me, I called aloud to them in Spanish, 'What are ye, gentlemen?'

They started up at the noise, but were ten times more confounded when they saw me, and the uncouth figure that I made. They made no answer at all, but I thought I perceived them just going to fly from me, when I spoke to them in English. 'Gentlemen,' said I, 'do not be surprised at me; perhaps you may have a friend near you, when you did not expect it.' 'He must be sent directly from heaven then,' said one of them very gravely to me, and pulling off his hat at the same time to me, 'for our condition is past the help of man.' 'All help is from heaven, sir,' said I. 'But can you put a stranger in the way how to help you, for you seem to me to be in some great distress? I saw you when you landed; and when you seemed to make applications to the brutes that came with you, I saw one of them lift up his sword to kill you.'

The poor man, with tears running down his face, and

trembling, looking like one astonished, returned, 'Am I talking to God, or man? Is it a real man, or an angel?' 'Be in no fear about that, sir,' said I. 'If God had sent an angel to relieve you, he would have come better clothed, and armed after another manner than you see me in. Pray lay aside your fears; I am a man, an Englishman, and disposed to assist you, you see. I have one servant only; we have arms and ammunition; tell us freely, can we serve you? What is your case?'

'Our case,' said he, 'sir, is too long to tell you while our murderers are so near; but in short, sir, I was commander of that ship; my men have mutinied against me, they have been hardly prevailed on not to murder me; and at last have set me on shore in this desolate place, with these two men with me, one my mate, the other a passenger, where we expected to perish, believing the place to be uninhabited, and know not yet what to think of it.'

'Where are those brutes, your enemies?' said I. 'Do you know where they are gone?' 'There they lie sir,' said he, pointing to a thicket of trees. 'My heart trembles for fear they have seen us, and heard you speak. If they have, they will certainly murder us all.'

'Have they any firearms?' said I. He answered, they had only two pieces, and one which they left in the boat. 'Well then,' said I, 'leave the rest to me, I see they are all asleep; it is an easy thing to kill them all; but shall we rather take them prisoners?' He told me there were two

CRUSOE DISCOVERS HIMSELF TO THE ENGLISH CAPTAIN.

desperate villains among them that it was scarce safe to show any mercy to; but if they were secured, he believed all the rest would return to their duty. I asked him which they were? He told me he could not at that distance describe them, but he would obey my orders in anything I would direct. 'Well,' says I, 'let us retreat out of their view or hearing, lest they awake, and we will resolve further.' So they willingly went back with me, till the woods covered us from them.

'Look you, sir,' said I, 'if I venture upon your deliverance, are you willing to make two conditions with me?' He anticipated my proposals, by telling me that both he and the ship, if recovered, should be wholly directed and commanded by me in everything; and if the ship was not recovered, he would live and die with me in what part of the world soever I would send him; and the two other men said the same.

'Well,' says I, 'my conditions are but two. 1. That while you stay on this island with me, you will not pretend to any authority here; and if I put arms into your hands, you will, upon all occasions, give them up to me, and do no prejudice to me or mine upon this island; and in the meantime, be governed by my orders. 2. That if the ship is, or may be, recovered, you will carry me and my man to England, passage free.'

He gave me all the assurances that the invention and faith of man could devise that he would comply with these most reasonable demands; and, besides, would owe his life to me, and acknowledge it upon all occasions, as long as he lived.

'Well then,' said I, 'here are three muskets for you, with powder and ball; tell me next what you think is proper to be done.' He showed all the testimony of his gratitude that he was able, but offered to be wholly guided by me. I told him I thought it was hard venturing anything; but the best method I could think of was to fire upon them at once, as they lay; and if any was not killed at the first volley, and offered to submit, we might save them, and so put it wholly upon God's providence to direct the shot.

He said very modestly that he was loth to kill them, if he could help it; but that those two were incorrigible villains, and had been the authors of all the mutiny in the ship, and if they escaped, we should be undone still; for they would go on board and bring the whole ship's company, and destroy us all. 'Well then,' says I, 'necessity legitimates my advice, for it is the only way to save our lives.' However, seeing him still cautious of shedding blood, I told him they should go themselves, and manage as they found convenient.

In the middle of this discourse we heard some of them awake, and soon after we saw two of them on their feet. I asked him if either of them were of the men who he had said were the heads of the mutiny? He said, 'No.' 'Well then,' said I, 'you may let them escape; and Providence seems to have awakened them on purpose to save themselves. Now,' says I, 'if the rest escape you, it is your fault.'

Animated with this, he took the musket I had given him in his hand, and a pistol in his belt, and his two comrades with him, with each man a piece in his hand. The two men who were with him going first made some noise, at which one of the seamen who was awake turned about, and seeing them coming cried out to the rest; but it was too late then, for the moment he cried out they fired; I mean the two men, the captain wisely reserving his own piece. They had so well aimed their shot at the men they knew, that one of them was killed on the spot, and the other very much wounded; but not being dead, he started up upon his feet, and called eagerly for help to the other. But the captain stepping to him, told him 'twas too late to cry for help, he should call upon God to forgive his villainy; and with that word knocked him down with the stock of his musket, so that he never spoke more. There were three more in the company, and one of them was also slightly wounded. By this time I was come; and when they saw their danger, and that it was in vain to resist, they begged for mercy. The captain told them he would spare their lives if they would give him any assurance of their abhorrence of the treachery they had been guilty of, and would swear to be faithful to him in recovering the ship, and afterwards in carrying her back to Jamaica, from whence they came. They gave him all the protestations of their sincerity that could be desired, and he was willing to believe them, and spare their lives, which I was not against, only I obliged him to keep them bound hand and foot while they were upon the island.

While this was doing, I sent Friday with the captain's mate to the boat, with orders to secure her, and bring away the oars and sail, which they did; and by and by three straggling men, that were (happily for them) parted from the rest, came back upon hearing the guns fired; and seeing their captain, who before was their prisoner, now their conqueror, they submitted to be bound also, and so our victory was complete.

It now remained that the captain and I should inquire into one another's circumstances. I began first, and told him my whole history, which he heard with an attention even to amazement; and particularly at the wonderful manner of my being furnished with provisions and ammunition; and, indeed, as my story is a whole collection of wonders, it affected him deeply. But when he reflected from thence upon himself, and how I seemed to have been preserved there on purpose to save his life, the tears ran down his face, and he could not speak a word more.

After this communication was at an end, I carried him and his two men into my apartment, leading them in just where I came out, viz., at the top of the house, where I

THE MUTINEERS OVERPOWERED.

refreshed them with such provisions as I had, and showed them all the contrivances I had made during my long, long inhabiting that place.

All I showed them, all I said to them, was perfectly amazing; but above all, the captain admired my fortification, and how perfectly I had concealed my retreat with a grove of trees, which, having now been planted near twenty years, and the trees growing much faster than in England, was become a little wood, and so thick, that it was unpassable in any part of it but at that one side where I had reserved my little winding passage into it. I told him this was my castle and my residence, but that I had a seat in the country, as most princes have, whither I could retreat upon occasion, and I would show him that too another time; but at present, our business was to consider how to recover the ship. He agreed with me as to that, but told me he was perfectly at a loss what measures to take, for that there were still six and twenty hands on board, who having entered into a cursed conspiracy, by which they had all forfeited their lives to the law, would be hardened in it now by desperation, and would carry it on, knowing that if they were reduced, they should be brought to the gallows as soon as they came to England, or to any of the English colonies; and that therefore there would be no attacking them with so small a number as we were.

I mused for some time upon what he said, and found it

was a very rational conclusion, and that therefore something was to be resolved on very speedily, as well to draw the men on board into some snare for their surprise, as to prevent their landing upon us, and destroying us. Upon this it presently occurred to me that in a little while the ship's crew, wondering what was become of their comrades, and of the boat, would certainly come on shore in their other boat to see for them; and that then, perhaps, they might come armed, and be too strong for us. This he allowed was rational.

Upon this, I told him the first thing we had to do was to stave the boat, which lay upon the beach, so that they might not carry her off; and taking everything out of her, leave her so far useless as not to be fit to swim. Accordingly we went on board, took the arms which were left on board out of her, and whatever else we found there, which was a bottle of brandy, and another of rum, a few biscuit-cakes, a horn of powder, and a great lump of sugar in a piece of canvas — the sugar was five or six pounds; all which was very welcome to me, especially the brandy and sugar, of which I had had none left for many years.

When we had carried all these things on shore (the oars, mast, sail, and rudder of the boat were carried away before, as above), we knocked a great hole in her bottom, that if they had come strong enough to master us, yet they could not carry off the boat.

Indeed, it was not much in my thoughts that we could be able to recover the ship; but my view was, that if they went away without the boat, I did not much question to make her fit again to carry us away to the Leeward Islands, and call upon our friends the Spaniards in my way; for I had them still in my thoughts.

While we were thus preparing our designs, and had first, by main strength, heaved the boat up upon the beach so high that the tide would not fleet her off at high-water mark; and besides, had broke a hole in her bottom too big to be quickly stopped, and were sat down musing what we should do, we heard the ship fire a gun, and saw her make a waft with her ancient as a signal for the boat to come on board. But no boat stirred; and they fired several times, making other signals for the boat.

At last, when all their signals and firings proved fruit-less, and they found the boat did not stir, we saw them, by the help of my glasses, hoist another boat out, and row towards the shore; and we found, as they approached, that there was no less than ten men in her, and that they had firearms with them.

As the ship lay almost two leagues from the shore, we had a full view of them as they came, and a plain sight of the men, even of their faces; because the tide having set them a little to the east of the other boat, they rowed up under shore, to come to the same place where the other had landed, and where the boat lay.

By this means, I say, we had a full view of them, and
the captain knew the persons and characters of all the
men in the boat, of whom he said that there were three
very honest fellows, who, he was sure, were led into this
conspiracy by the rest, being overpowered and frighted;
but that as for the boatswain, who, it seems, was the chief
officer among them, and all the rest, they were as outrageous as any of the ship's crew, and were no doubt made
desperate in their new enterprise; and terribly apprehensive he was that they would be too powerful for us.

I smiled at him, and told him that men in our circumstances were past the operation of fear; that seeing
almost every condition that could be was better than that
which we were supposed to be in, we ought to expect
that the consequence, whether death or life, would be
sure to be a deliverance. I asked him what he thought of
the circumstances of my life, and whether a deliverance
were not worth venturing for? 'And where, sir,' said I, 'is
your belief of my being preserved here on purpose to save
your life, which elevated you a little while ago? For my
part,' said I, 'there seems to be but one thing amiss in all
the prospect of it.' 'What's that?' says he. 'Why,' said I,
''tis that, as you say, there are three or four honest fellows
among them, which should be spared; had they been all
of the wicked part of the crew I should have thought
God's providence had singled them out to deliver them
into your hands; for depend upon it, every man of them

that comes ashore are our own, and shall die or live as they behave to us.'

As I spoke this with a raised voice and cheerful countenance, I found it greatly encouraged him; so we set vigorously to our business. We had, upon the first appearance of the boat's coming from the ship, considered of separating our prisoners, and had, indeed, secured them effectually.

Two of them, of whom the captain was less assured than ordinary, I sent with Friday and one of the three delivered men to my cave, where they were remote enough, and out of danger of being heard or discovered, or of finding their way out of the woods if they could have delivered themselves. Here they left them bound, but gave them provisions, and promised them, if they continued there quietly, to give them their liberty in a day or two; but that if they attempted their escape, they should be put to death without mercy. They promised faithfully to bear their confinement with patience, and were very thankful that they had such good usage as to have provisions and a light left them; for Friday gave them candles (such as we made ourselves) for their comfort; and they did not know but that he stood sentinel over them at the entrance.

The other prisoners had better usage. Two of them were kept pinioned, indeed, because the captain was not free to trust them; but the other two were taken into my

THE MUTINEERS

service, upon their captain's recommendation, and upon their solemnly engaging to live and die with us; so with them and the three honest men we were seven men well armed; and I made no doubt we should be able to deal well enough with the ten that were a-coming, considering that the captain had said there were three or four honest men among them also.

As soon as they got to the place where their other boat lay, they ran their boat into the beach, and came all on shore, hauling the boat up after them, which I was glad to see; for I was afraid they would rather have left the boat at an anchor some distance from the shore, with some hands in her to guard her, and so we should not be able to seize the boat.

Being on shore, the first thing they did they ran all to their other boat; and it was easy to see that they were under a great surprise to find her stripped, as above, of all that was in her, and a great hole in her bottom.

After they had mused a while upon this, they set up two or three great shouts, hallooing with all their might, to try if they could make their companions hear; but all was to no purpose. Then they came all close in a ring, and fired a volley of their small arms, which, indeed, we heard, and the echoes made the woods ring. But it was all one; those in the cave we were sure could not hear, and those in our keeping, though they heard it well enough, yet durst give no answer to them.

They were so astonished at the surprise of this, that, as they told us afterwards, they resolved to go all on board again, to their ship, and let them know there that the men were all murdered, and the longboat staved. Accordingly, they immediately launched their boat again, and gat all of them on board.

The captain was terribly amazed, and even confounded at this, believing they would go on board the ship again, and set sail, giving their comrades for lost, and so he should still lose the ship, which he was in hopes we should have recovered; but he was quickly as much frighted the other way.

They had not been long put off with the boat but we perceived them all coming on shore again; but with this new measure in their conduct, which it seems they consulted together upon, viz., to leave three men in the boat, and the rest to go on shore, and go up into the country to look for their fellows.

This was a great disappointment to us, for now we were at a loss what to do; for our seizing those seven men on shore would be to no advantage to us if we let the boat escape, because they would then row away to the ship, and then the rest of them would be sure to weigh and set sail, and so our recovering the ship would be lost. However, we had no remedy but to wait and see what the issue of things might present. The seven men came on shore, and the three who remained in the boat put her off to a good distance from the shore, and came to anchor to wait for them; so that it was impossible for us to come at them in the boat.

Those that came on shore kept close together, marching towards the top of the little hill under which my habitation lay; and we could see them plainly, though they could not perceive us. We could have been very glad they would have come nearer to us, so that we might have fired at them, or that they would have gone farther off, that we might have come abroad.

But when they were come to the brow of the hill, where they could see a great way into the valleys and woods which lay towards the north-east part, and where the island lay lowest, they shouted and hallooed till they were weary; and not caring, it seems, to venture far from the shore, nor far from one another, they sat down together under a tree, to consider of it. Had they thought fit to have gone to sleep there, as the other party of them had done, they had done the job for us; but they were too full of apprehensions of danger to venture to go to sleep, though they could not tell what the danger was they had to fear neither.

The captain made a very just proposal to me upon this consultation of theirs, viz., that perhaps they would all fire a volley again, to endeavour to make their fellows hear, and that we should all sally upon them, just at the juncture when their pieces were all discharged, and they would certainly yield, and we should have them without bloodshed. I liked the proposal, provided it was done while we were near enough to come up to them before they could load their pieces again.

But this event did not happen, and we lay still a long time, very irresolute what course to take. At length I told them there would be nothing to be done, in my opinion, till night; and then, if they did not return to the boat, perhaps we might find a way to get between them and the shore, and so might use some stratagem with them in the boat to get them on shore.

We waited a great while, though very impatient for

their removing; and were very uneasy when, after long consultations, we saw them start all up, and march down toward the sea. It seems they had such dreadful apprehensions upon them of the danger of the place, that they resolved to go on board the ship again, give their companions over for lost, and so go on with their intended voyage with the ship.

As soon as I perceived them go towards the shore, I imagined it to be, as it really was, that they had given over their search, and were for going back again; and the captain, as soon as I told him my thoughts, was ready to sink at the apprehensions of it; but I presently thought of a stratagem to fetch them back again, and which answered my end to a tittle.

CHAPTER 24

*Crusoe overcomes the sailors by a clever stratagem. He connives
with the Captain and convinces the men that the island is ruled by
a powerful governor. The Captain returns to his ship, regains
control and signals to Crusoe.*

I ORDERED Friday and the captain's mate to go over the
little creek westward, towards the place where the savages came on shore when Friday was rescued, and as soon
as they came to a little rising ground, at about half a mile
distance, I bade them halloo as loud as they could, and
wait till they found the seamen heard them; that as soon
as ever they heard the seamen answer them, they should
return it again; and then keeping out of sight, take a
round, always answering when the other hallooed, to draw
them as far into the island, and among the woods, as possible, and then wheel about again to me by such ways as I
directed them.

They were just going into the boat when Friday and
the mate hallooed; and they presently heard them, and
answering, ran along the shore westward, towards the
voice they heard, when they were presently stopped by
the creek, where the water being up, they could not get
over, and called for the boat to come up and set them
over, as, indeed, I expected.

When they had set themselves over, I observed that

the boat being gone up a good way into the creek, and, as it were, in a harbour within the land, they took one of the three men out of her to go along with them, and left only two in the boat, having fastened her to the stump of a little tree on the shore.

That was what I wished for; and immediately, leaving Friday and the captain's mate to their business, I took the rest with me, and crossing the creek out of their sight, we surprised the two men before they were aware; one of them lying on shore, and the other being in the boat. The fellow on shore was between sleeping and waking, and going to start up. The captain, who was foremost, ran in upon him, and knocked him down, and then called out to him in the boat to yield, or he was a dead man.

There needed very few arguments to persuade a single man to yield when he saw five men upon him, and his comrade knocked down; besides, this was, it seems, one of the three who were not so hearty in the mutiny as the rest of the crew, and therefore was easily persuaded not only to yield, but afterwards to join very sincerely with us.

In the meantime, Friday and the captain's mate so well managed their business with the rest, that they drew them, by hallooing and answering, from one hill to another, and from one wood to another, till they not only heartily tired them, but left them where they were very sure they could not reach back to the boat before it was dark; and, indeed, they were heartily tired themselves also by the time they came back to us.

We had nothing now to do but to watch for them in the dark, and to fall upon them, so as to make sure work with them.

It was several hours after Friday came back to me before they came back to their boat; and we could hear the foremost of them, long before they came quite up, calling to those behind to come along, and could also hear them answer and complain how lame and tired they were, and not able to come any faster; which was very welcome news to us.

At length they came up to the boat; but 'tis impossible to express their confusion when they found the boat fast aground in the creek, the tide ebbed out, and their two men gone. We could hear them call to one another in a most lamentable manner, telling one another they were gotten into an enchanted island; that either there were inhabitants in it, and they should all be murdered, or else there were devils and spirits in it, and they should be all carried away and devoured.

They hallooed again, and called their two comrades by their names a great many times; but no answer. After some time we could see them, by the little light there was, run about, wringing their hands like men in despair, and that sometimes they would go and sit down in the boat to rest themselves; then come ashore again, and walk about again, and so the same thing over again.

My men would fain have me give them leave to fall upon them at once in the dark; but I was willing to take them at some advantage, so to spare them, and kill as few of them as I could; and especially I was unwilling to hazard the killing any of our own men, knowing the other were very well armed. I resolved to wait, to see if they did not separate; and, therefore, to make sure of them, I drew my ambuscade nearer, and ordered Friday and the captain to creep upon their hands and feet, as close to the ground as they could, that they might not be discovered, and get as near them as they could possibly, before they offered to fire.

They had not been long in that posture but that the boatswain, who was the principal ringleader of the mutiny, and had now shown himself the most dejected and dispirited of all the rest, came walking towards them, with two more of their crew. The captain was so eager, as having this principal rogue so much in his power, that he could hardly have patience to let him come so near as to be sure of him, for they only heard his tongue before; but when they came nearer, the captain and Friday, starting up on their feet, let fly at them.

The boatswain was killed upon the spot; the next man was shot into the body, and fell just by him, though he did not die till an hour or two after; and the third ran for it.

At the noise of the fire I immediately advanced with

my whole army, which was now eight men, viz., myself, generalissimo; Friday, my lieutenant-general; the captain and his two men, and the three prisoners of war, whom we had trusted with arms.

We came upon them, indeed, in the dark, so that they could not see our number; and I made the man we had left in the boat, who was now one of us, call to them by name, to try if I could bring them to a parley, and so might perhaps reduce them to terms, which fell out just as we desired; for indeed it was easy to think, as their condition then was, they would be very willing to capitulate. So he calls out as loud as he could to one of them, 'Tom Smith! Tom Smith!' Tom Smith answered immediately, 'Who's that? Robinson?' For it seems he knew his voice. The other answered, 'Ay, ay; for God's sake, Tom Smith, throw down your arms and yield, or you are all dead men this moment.'

'Who must we yield to? Where are they?' says Smith again. 'Here they are,' says he; 'here's our captain, and fifty men with him, have been hunting you this two hours; the boatswain is killed, Will Frye is wounded, and I am a prisoner; and if you do not yield, you are all lost.'

'Will they give us quarter then,' says Tom Smith, 'and we will yield?' 'I'll go and ask, if you promise to yield,' says Robinson. So he asked the captain, and the captain then calls himself out, 'You, Smith, you know my voice, if you lay down your arms immediately, and submit, you shall have your lives, all but Will Atkins.'

Upon this Will Atkins cried out, 'For God's sake, captain, give me quarter; what have I done? They have been all as bad as I'; which, by the way, was not true neither; for it seems, this Will Atkins was the first man that laid hold of the captain when they first mutinied, and used him barbarously, in tying his hands, and giving him injurious language. However, the captain told him he must lay down his arms at discretion, and trust to the governor's mercy; by which he meant me, for they all called me governor.

In a word, they all laid down their arms, and begged their lives; and I sent the man that had parleyed with them and two more, who bound them all; and then my great army of fifty men, which, particularly with those three, were all but eight, came up and seized upon them all, and upon their boat; only that I kept myself and one more out of sight for reasons of state.

Our next step was to repair the boat, and think of seizing the ship; and as for the captain, now he had leisure to parley with them, he expostulated with them upon the villainy of their practices with him, and at length upon the farther wickedness of their design, and how certainly it must bring them to misery and distress in the end, and perhaps to the gallows.

They all appeared very penitent, and begged hard for their lives. As for that, he told them they were none of his prisoners, but the commander of the island; that they

thought they had set him on shore in a barren, uninhabited island; but it had pleased God to so direct them that
the island was inhabited, and that the governor was an
Englishman; that he might hang them all there, if he
pleased; but as he had given them all quarter, he supposed he would send them to England, to be dealt with
there as justice required, except Atkins, whom he was
commanded by the governor to advise to prepare for
death, for that he would be hanged in the morning.

Though this was all a fiction of his own, yet it had its
desired effect. Atkins fell upon his knees, to beg the captain to intercede with the governor for his life; and all the
rest begged of him, for God's sake, that they might not be
sent to England.

It now occurred to me that the time of our deliverance
was come, and that it would be a most easy thing to bring
these fellows in to be hearty in getting possession of the
ship; so I retired in the dark from them, that they might
not see what kind of a governor they had, and called the
captain to me. When I called, as at a good distance, one of
the men was ordered to speak again, and say to the captain, 'Captain, the commander calls for you.' And
presently the captain replied, 'Tell his excellency I am
just a-coming.' This more perfectly amused them, and
they all believed that the commander was just by with his
fifty men.

Upon the captain's coming to me, I told him my

project for seizing the ship, which he liked of wonderfully well, and resolved to put it in execution the next morning. But in order to execute it with more art, and secure of success, I told him we must divide the prisoners, and that he should go and take Atkins and two more of the worst of them, and send them pinioned to the cave where the others lay. This was committed to Friday and the two men who came on shore with the captain.

They conveyed them to the cave, as to a prison. And it was, indeed, a dismal place, especially to men in their condition. The others I ordered to my bower, as I called it, of which I have given a full description; and as it was fenced in, and they pinioned, the place was secure enough, considering they were upon their behaviour.

To these in the morning I sent the captain, who was to enter into a parley with them; in a word, to try them, and tell me whether he thought they might be trusted or no to go on board and surprise the ship. He talked to them of the injury done him, of the condition they were brought to; and that though the governor had given them quarter for their lives as to the present action, yet that if they were sent to England they would all be hanged in chains, to be sure; but that if they would join in so just an attempt as to recover the ship, he would have the governor's engagement for their pardon.

Any one may guess how readily such a proposal would be accepted by men in their condition. They fell down on their knees to the captain, and promised, with the deepest imprecations, that they would be faithful to him to the last drop, and that they should owe their lives to him, and would go with him all over the world; that they would own him for a father to them as long as they lived.

'Well,' says the captain, 'I must go and tell the governor what you say, and see what I can do to bring him to consent to it.' So he brought me an account of the temper he found them in, and that he verily believed they would be faithful.

However, that we might be very secure, I told him he should go back again and choose out five of them, and tell them they might see that he did not want men, that he would take out those five to be his assistants, and that the governor would keep the other two and the three that were sent prisoners to the castle, my cave, as hostages for the fidelity of those five; and that if they proved unfaithful in the execution, the five hostages should be hanged in chains alive upon the shore.

This looked severe, and convinced them that the governor was in earnest. However, they had no way left to them but to accept it; and it was now the business of the prisoners, as much as of the captain, to persuade the other five to do their duty.

Our strength was now thus ordered for the expedition. 1. The captain, his mate, and passenger. 2. Then the two prisoners of the first gang, to whom, having their characters from the captain, I had given their liberty, and trusted them with arms. 3. The other two whom I had kept till now in my bower, pinioned, but upon the captain's motion had now released. 4. These five released at last; so that they were twelve in all, besides five we kept prisoners in the cave for hostages.

I asked the captain if he was willing to venture with these hands on board the ship; for as for me and my man Friday, I did not think it was proper for us to stir, having seven men left behind, and it was employment enough for us to keep them asunder and supply them with victuals. As to the five in the cave, I resolved to keep them fast; but Friday went in twice a day to them, to supply them with necessaries, and I made the other two carry provisions to a certain distance, where Friday was to take it.

When I showed myself to the two hostages, it was with the captain, who told them I was the person the governor had ordered to look after them, and that it was the governor's pleasure they should not stir anywhere but by my direction; that if they did, they should be fetched into the castle, and be laid in irons; so that as we never suffered them to see me as governor, so I now appeared as another person, and spoke of the governor, the garrison, the castle, and the like, upon all occasions.

The captain now had no difficulty before him but to furnish his two boats, stop the breach of one, and man them. He made his passenger captain of one, with four other men; and himself, and his mate, and five more went in the other; and they contrived their business very well, for they came up to the ship about midnight. As soon as they came within call of the ship, he made Robinson hail them, and tell them they had brought off the men and the boat, but that it was a long time before they had found them, and the like, holding them in a chat till they came to the ship's side; when the captain and the mate entering first, with their arms, immediately knocked down the second mate and carpenter with the butt-end of their muskets, being very faithfully seconded by their men. They secured all the rest that were upon the main and quarter-decks, and began to fasten the hatches to keep them down who were below; when the other boat and their men entering at the fore-chains, secured the forecastle of the ship, and the scuttle which went down into the cook-room, making three men they found there prisoners.

When this was done, and all safe upon the deck, the captain ordered the mate, with three men, to break into the round-house, where the new rebel captain lay, and having taken the alarm was gotten up, and with two men and a boy had gotten firearms in their hands; and when the mate with a crow split open the door, the new captain and his men fired boldly among them, and wounded the mate with a musket ball, which broke his arm, and wounded two more of the men, but killed nobody.

The mate calling for help, rushed however into the round-house wounded as he was, and with his pistol shot the new captain through the head, the bullet entering at his mouth and came out again behind one of his ears, so that he never spoke a word; upon which the rest yielded, and the ship was taken effectually, without any more lives lost.

As soon as the ship was thus secured, the captain ordered seven guns to be fired, which was the signal agreed upon with me to give me notice of his success, which you may be sure I was very glad to hear, having sat watching upon the shore for it till near two of the clock in the morning.

DEATH OF THE REBEL CAPTAIN.

CHAPTER 25

After a day of great fatigue Crusoe sleeps sound. The Captain brings food, wine and clothes: 'My dear friend and deliverer, there's your ship, for she is all yours, and so are we and all that belong to her'. Impressively dressed as Governor, Crusoe offers the five criminal mutineers their freedom on the island, along with the expected Spaniards, in place of certain death in England. Crusoe shows them his defences, explains his plans of husbandry. Crusoe and Friday go aboard, Crusoe taking his goatskin cap, his umbrella and his parrot as relics. On 19th December Crusoe leaves the island.

HAVING THUS heard the signal plainly, I laid me down; and it having been a day of great fatigue to me, I slept very sound, till I was something surprised with the noise of a gun; and presently starting up, I heard a man call me by the name of 'Governor, Governor,' and presently I knew the captain's voice; when climbing up to the top of the hill, there he stood, and pointing to the ship, he embraced me in his arms. 'My dear friend and deliverer,' says he, 'there's your ship, for she is all yours, and so are we, and all that belong to her.' I cast my eyes to the ship, and there she rode within little more than half a mile of the shore; for they had weighed her anchor as soon as they were masters of her, and the weather being fair, had brought her to an anchor just against the mouth of the little creek, and the tide being up, the captain had brought the pinnace in near the place where I at first landed my rafts, and so landed just at my door.

I was at first ready to sink down with the surprise; for I saw my deliverance, indeed, visibly put into my hands, all things easy, and a large ship just ready to carry me away whither I pleased to go. At first, for some time, I was not able to answer him one word; but as he had taken me in his arms, I held fast by him, or I should have fallen to the ground.

He perceived the surprise, and immediately pulls a bottle out of his pocket, and gave me a dram of cordial, which he had brought on purpose for me. After I had drank it, I sat down upon the ground; and though it brought me to myself, yet it was a good while before I could speak a word to him.

All this while the poor man was in as great an ecstasy as I, only not under any surprise, as I was; and he said a thousand kind tender things to me, to compose me and bring me to myself. But such was the flood of joy in my breast, that it put all my spirits into confusion. At last it broke out into tears, and in a little while after I recovered my speech.

Then I took my turn, and embraced him as my deliverer, and we rejoiced together. I told him I looked upon him as a man sent from heaven to deliver me, and that the whole transaction seemed to be a chain of wonders; that such things as these were the testimonies we had of a secret hand of Providence governing the world, and an evidence that the eyes of an infinite Power could search into the remotest corner of the world, and send help to the miserable whenever He pleased.

I forgot not to lift up my heart in thankfulness to heaven; and what heart could forbear to bless Him, who had not only in a miraculous manner provided for one in such a wilderness, and in such a desolate condition, but from whom every deliverance must always be acknowledged to proceed?

When we had talked a while, the captain told me he had brought me some little refreshment, such as the ship afforded, and such as the wretches that had been so long his masters had not plundered him of. Upon this he called aloud to the boat, and bid his men bring the things ashore that were for the governor; and, indeed, it was a present as if I had been one, not that was to be carried away along with them, but as if I had been to dwell upon the island still, and they were to go without me.

First, he had brought me a case of bottles full of excellent cordial waters, six large bottles of Madeira wine (the bottles held two quarts apiece), two pounds of excellent good tobacco, twelve good pieces of ship's beef, and six pieces of pork, with a bag of peas, and about a hundredweight of biscuit.

He brought me also a box of sugar, a box of flour, a bag full of lemons, and two bottles of lime-juice, and abundance of other things; but besides these, and what was a thousand times more useful to me, he brought me six clean new shirts, six very good neck-cloths, two pair of gloves, one pair of shoes, a hat, and one pair of stockings, and a very good suit of clothes of his own, which had been worn but very little; in a word, he clothed me from head to foot.

It was a very kind and agreeable present, as any one may imagine, to one in my circumstances; but never was anything in the world of that kind so unpleasant, awkward, and uneasy, as it was to me to wear such clothes at their first putting on.

After these ceremonies passed, and after all his good things were brought into my little apartment, we began to consult what was to be done with the prisoners we had; for it was worth considering whether we might venture to take them away with us or no, especially two of them, whom we knew to be incorrigible and refractory to the last degree; and the captain said he knew they were such rogues, that there was no obliging them; and if he did carry them away, it must be in irons, as malefactors, to be delivered over to justice at the first English colony he could come at; and I found that the captain himself was very anxious about it.

Upon this I told him that, if he desired it, I durst undertake to bring the two men he spoke of to make it their own request that he should leave them upon the island. 'I should be very glad of that,' says the captain, 'with all my heart.'

'Well,' says I, 'I will send for them up, and talk with them for you.' So I caused Friday and the two hostages, for they were now discharged, their comrades having performed their promise; I say, I caused them to go to the cave and bring up the five men, pinioned as they were, to the bower, and keep them there till I came.

After some time I came thither, dressed in my new habit; and now I was called governor again. Being all met, and the captain with me, I caused the men to be brought before me, and I told them I had had a full account of their villainous behaviour to the captain, and how they had run away with the ship, and were preparing to commit farther robberies, but that Providence had ensnared them in their own ways, and that they were fallen into the pit which they had digged for others.

I let them know that by my direction the ship had been seized, that she lay now in the road, and they might see by and by, that their new captain had received the reward of his villainy, for that they might see him hanging at the yard-arm; that as to them, I wanted to know what they had to say why I should not execute them as pirates, taken in the fact, as by my commission they could not doubt I had authority to do.

One of them answered in the name of the rest that they had nothing to say but this, that when they were taken the captain promised them their lives, and they humbly implored my mercy. But I told them I knew not what mercy to show them; for as for myself, I had resolved to quit the island with all my men, and had taken passage with the captain to go for England. And as for the captain, he could not carry them to England other than as prisoners in irons, to be tried for mutiny, and running away with the ship; the consequence of which, they must needs know, would be the gallows; so that I could not tell what was best for them, unless they had a mind to take their fate in the island. If they desired that, I did not care, as I had liberty to leave it. I had some inclination to give them their lives, if they thought they could shift on shore.

They seemed very thankful for it, said they would rather venture to stay there than to be carried to England to be hanged; so I left it on that issue.

However, the captain seemed to make some difficulty of it, as if he durst not leave them there. Upon this I seemed a little angry with the captain, and told him that they were my prisoners, not his; and that seeing I had offered them so much favour, I would be as good as my word; and that if he did not think fit to consent to it, I would set them at liberty, as I found them; and if he did not like it, he might take them again if he could catch them.

Upon this they appeared very thankful, and I accordingly set them at liberty, and bade them retire into the woods to the place whence they came, and I would leave

them some firearms, some ammunition, and some directions how they should live very well, if they thought fit.

Upon this I prepared to go on board the ship, but told
the captain that I would stay that night to prepare my
things, and desired him to go on board in the meantime,
and keep all right in the ship, and send the boat on shore
the next day for me; ordering him, in the meantime, to
cause the new captain, who was killed, to be hanged at
the yard-arm, that these men might see him.

When the captain was gone, I sent for the men up to
me to my apartment, and entered seriously into discourse
with them of their circumstances. I told them I thought
they had made a right choice; that if the captain carried
them away, they would certainly be hanged. I showed
them the new captain hanging at the yard-arm of the
ship, and told them they had nothing less to expect.

When they had all declared their willingness to stay, I
then told them I would let them into the story of my living there, and put them into the way of making it easy to
them. Accordingly I gave them the whole history of the
place, and of my coming to it, showed them my fortifications, the way I made my bread, planted my corn, cured
my grapes; and in a word, all that was necessary to make
them easy. I told them the story also of the sixteen
Spaniards that were to be expected, for whom I left a letter, and made them promise to treat them in common
with themselves.

I left them my firearms, viz., five muskets, three fowl-ing-pieces, and three swords. I had above a barrel and half of powder left; for after the first year or two I used but little, and wasted none. I gave them a description of the way I managed the goats, and directions to milk and fat-ten them, and to make both butter and cheese.

In a word, I gave them every part of my own story, and I told them I would prevail with the captain to leave them two barrels of gunpowder more and some garden seeds, which I told them I would have been very glad of. Also I gave them the bag of peas which the captain had brought me to eat, and bade them to be sure to sow and increase them.

Having done all this, I left them the next day, and went on board the ship. We prepared immediately to sail, but did not weigh that night. The next morning early two of the five men came swimming to the ship's side, and mak-ing a most lamentable complaint of the other three, begged to be taken into the ship for God's sake, for they should be murdered, and begged the captain to take them on board, though he hanged them immediately.

Upon this the captain pretended to have no power without me; but after some difficulty, and after their solemn promises of amendment, they were taken on board, and were some time after soundly whipped and pickled, after which they proved very honest and quiet fellows.

Some time after this the boat was ordered on shore, the tide being up, with the things promised to the men, to which the captain, at my intercession, caused their chests and clothes to be added, which they took, and were very thankful for. I also encouraged them by telling them that if it lay in my way to send any vessel to take them in, I would not forget them.

When I took leave of this island, I carried on board, for relics, the great goat-skin cap I had made, my umbrella and my parrot; also I forgot not to take the money I formerly mentioned, which had lain by me so long useless that it was grown rusty or tarnished, and could hardly pass for silver till it had been a little rubbed and handled; as also the money I found in the wreck of the Spanish ship.

And thus I left the island, the 19th of December, as I found by the ship's account, in the year 1686, after I had been upon it eight and twenty years, two months, and nineteen days, being delivered from this second captivity the same day of the month that I first made my escape in the *barco-longo*, from among the Moors of Sallee.

In this vessel, after a long voyage, I arrived in England, the 11th of June, in the year 1687, having been thirty and five years absent.

EPILOGUE

Robinson Crusoe's return to his Island;
and what happened thereafter.

I VISITED my colony in the island and came to my old habitation on the 10th April 1695.

As soon as I saw the place I called for Friday and asked him if he knew where he was. He looked about a little, and presently clapping his hands, cried, 'O yes, O there, O yes, O there', pointing to our old habitation, and I had much ado to keep him from jumping into the sea, to swim ashore to the place.

As soon as Friday told me he saw people, I caused the English ancient to be spread, and fired three guns to give them notice that we were friends, and in about half of a quarter of an hour after, we perceived a smoke rise from the side of the creek, so I immediately ordered a boat out.

I ordered nobody to go on shore at first but myself, but there was no keeping Friday in the boat; for the affectionate creature had spied his father at a distance. He was no sooner on shore, but he flew away to his father like an arrow out of a bow. It would have made any man have shed tears in spite of the firmest resolution, to have seen the transports of this poor fellow's joy when he came to his father.

I saw my successors the Spaniards, had the whole story of their lives, and of the villains I left there. The history of their coming to, and conduct in the island, after my going away, is so very remarkable, and has so many incidents; a history, if it were entered into, as full of variety and wonderful accidents as my own.

Here I stayed about twenty days, left them supplies of all necessary things, and particularly of arms, powder, shot, clothes, tools, and two workmen, which I brought from England with me.

Besides this I shared the island into parts; and having settled all things with them, I left them there. But all these things I may perhaps give a farther account of hereafter.

*   *   *   *

*Robinson Crusoe did recount the full troubled history of the island
as he heard it from the inhabitants in* The Farther Adventures
of Robinson Crusoe. *He described also the many comforts he
obtained for the colony and told of the new people who were established there and all he knew of how they fared after his last departure from the island.*

*He told too how the death of Friday occurred. How, after leav-
ing the island, his ship was blown off course, and then becalmed,
and how, as they lay thus helpless, a great fleet of canoes all fully
loaded with warlike savages came against them, and how in spite of
their arrows Crusoe bade his men hold their fire; but how when
Friday stood out to speak with the savages he was shot at and
pierced by three arrows; and how Crusoe, in his rage at the loss of
the companion of his sorrows and solitudes, his Friday whom he so
loved and valued, ordered great and small guns to be fired which
effectively dispersed the one hundred and sixty canoes, causing
much havoc. And how he himself continued his roving life for ten
more long years, having many strange adventures by land and sea,
before at last he came home to England.*

GLOSSARY

*including words which have changed their meaning
since Defoe's time*

adventures, at all, regardless of risks, 25
affectionately, earnest, with great feelings, 313
amused, misled, 385
amusement, bewilderment, 231
ancient, ensign, 39, 371, 401
antic, grotesque, 295

barco-longo, 'a small, low, long, sharp-built vessel, without
  a deck . . . going with oars and sails'; the name given to
  the converted long-boat in which Crusoe and Xury
  made their escape, 399
beachy, shingly, 184
better-end = bitter end, the end of a cable left round the
  bitts when the rest is overboard, the bitts being the
  pair of posts to which the cable is fastened, 24
brandgoose, brant goose, 143
bulged, struck so as to damage the bilge, or broadest part
  of a ship's bottom, 79

calenture, fever or delirium attacking sailors in the tropics,
  34, 78

fusee, fuzee, fusil, light musket, 39, etc.
fustic, two kinds of wood yielding yellow dye, 323

grappling, grapnel, iron-crowned instrument thrown with
   a rope to seize object, i.e., grappling-iron, 201

half-pike, boarding pike, an iron spike fixed on a short
   ashen shaft, 35
height, 'came the height of', arrived off, or in the latitude
   of, 67

jealousy, suspicion, 118, 318

learn, to teach, 305

main, mainland, 232, 283
mere, used in the modern sense, 136, 234; and also in the
   senses of absolute, downright, regular, entire, sheer,
   166, etc.
mischieve, to do mischief to, 234
moidore, moydor, Portuguese gold coin, 279
motion, inward prompting, inclination, 30

Nicaragua wood, a red dye-wood, peach-wood, 323

original, origin, 311
other, the, the others, 284, 371

patron, *patroon*, an owner of slaves or captives
     (Mediterranean), 37 ff.
periagua, canoe made from a single tree trunk, 185, etc.
perspective, *perspective glass*, *prospective glass*, spy-glass, 56,
     236, 261, 287
physical, curative, remedial, 223
pickle, to rub (sailor's back) with salt or vinegar after
     flogging, 398
powder-chests, 'boards joined in form of a triangle, filled
     with gun-powder, pebble-stones, etc., set on fire when
     a ship is boarded by any enemy, which soon make all
     clear before them', 35
prudential (n.), prudent consideration, 248

rack = arrack, spirituous liquor distilled from the sap of
     the coco palm, or from rice and sugar, 80
royal = real, old Spanish silver coin, 277
runlet, cask for liquor, of varying capacity, 91, 120, 160

search (n.) = searce, a sieve or strainer, 180; (v.) to sift
     through a searce
signals, signs, evidence, 244
stuff, thin woollen cloth, 180
succades, sweetmeats, especially candied fruits, etc., 276

twist, fork of the legs, 41

uncured, uncared for, uncultivated, 59

waft, signal of distress, etc., made with a rolled or
knotted ensign, 56, 371
whelm, to turn (a hollow vessel) upside down, so as to
cover something, 181
wild-fire, priming made by wetting gunpowder, 254

The definitions of *barco-longo* and *powder-chests* are taken
from Nathaniel Bailey's *Universal Etymological
Dictionary*, 1721.

DANIEL DEFOE (1660–1731) was born in London and was educated at a dissenting school at a time when the Church of England was being re-established during the Restoration. Intended for the ministry, he started work and soon began employing his talents in producing political pamphlets. He became famous with the publication in 1701 of *The True-Born Englishman*, a verse-satire on the critics of King William III. He was a prolific journalist, interested in anything and everything, but always advocating moderation, the guiding principle of *The Review*, the periodical he founded in 1704.

Defoe was nearly sixty when he wrote *Robinson Crusoe*, a story based on the experience of Alexander Selkirk, who lived on the uninhabited island of Juan Fernandez from 1704 to 1709. The novel was an immediate success, perhaps because in its detail it is so convincing. As Charles Lamb wrote almost a century later, 'The narrator chains us down to an implicit belief in everything he says'.

WILLIAM JAMES LINTON (1812–1898) was born in London and spent over half his life there, working as a wood-engraver and a writer on Chartism. His wife, Eliza Lynn, was also a writer but when the marriage failed in 1867 he emigrated to the United States, where he set up a printing press in New Haven, Connecticut. In his book *The History of Wood Engraving in America* he expressed a firm belief in the power of the bold line drawn by an engraving tool, which he thought far superior to the effects of photo-engraving invented in the late 1870s.

KATHLEEN LINES (1902–1988) was born in Edmonton, Alberta, Canada, and was trained as a librarian at the renowned Boys and Girls House in Toronto – at that time the only professionally run children's library in the British Commonwealth. She spent most of her adult life in England, working as a selector and promoter of children's books, editing numerous anthologies of stories, and acting as consultant to a number of publishers, including Sir Francis Meynell, for whose series of Nonesuch Cygnets she prepared this edition of *Robinson Crusoe*.

CHARLES PERRAULT *Little Red Riding Hood and other Stories*
Illustrated by W. Heath Robinson

ANNA SEWELL *Black Beauty*
Illustrated by Lucy Kemp-Welch

ROBERT LOUIS STEVENSON *A Child's Garden of Verses*
Illustrated by Charles Robinson

Kidnapped
Illustrated by Rowland Hilder

Treasure Island
Illustrated by Mervyn Peake

JEAN WEBSTER *Daddy-Long-Legs*
Illustrated by the Author

OSCAR WILDE *The Happy Prince and other Tales*
Illustrated by Charles Robinson

JOHANN WYSS *The Swiss Family Robinson*
Illustrated by Louis Rhead